WASTELAND

THE PHOENIX CYCLE: BOOK TWO

by John G. Doyle

This book is dedicated to my wife, daughters, and one extremely dedicated BFF.

You all know who you are.

PROLOGUE

Jericho stepped over Klaus's body with ease, dropping the large handgun he'd used onto the dead man's chest.

"Looks like he won't be taking over the world today," he said, crouching beside where Chloe was sitting and leaning against the wall, holding the bleeding wound at her stomach.

Blood seeped through her laced fingers freely, and her face was paling rapidly. "He's locked the building down, Jericho," she said, her whisper of a voice barely heard above the blaring alarm. "There is an air duct two floors down that will take you to a—"

"Stop," he said, sitting next to her, leaning against the wall and putting his arm around her shoulders. "Not a chance, psycho-chick," he told her. "Have you really not realized that you're never going to get rid of me?"

"*One minute to self-destruct sequence,*" the computer voice announced over the loud alarm.

Chloe leaned her head against him, and he felt her ragged breathing. "You're stupid."

"Your face is stupid."

She chuckled weakly before saying, "Sorry you're about to die, then, I guess."

Then he felt her shudder and her breathing stopped suddenly.

"*Thirty seconds to self-destruct sequence.*"

"I'm sorry, too, Chloe," he said, kissing her forehead and standing. "What kind of an evil maniac doesn't rig his building to blow up if they happen to lose?" he asked the air before his earpiece crackled.

"Jericho, where are—waiting—" Piper's voice buzzed in his ear. "Have to—why—"

His heart sank. He wouldn't be coming back to her.

"Don't be a wimp," he said to himself. He'd known the risks beforehand and had gone on the suicidal mission to save humanity, anyway.

But just in case Piper could hear him through the static, he said, "I love you, Pipe. Don't let Beck push you around too much after this."

"Jericho, no!" she shouted, obviously hearing every word. "What happened? Why are you—I can't—"

Pulling his earpiece out, he tossed it into one of the many fires that were roaring in Klaus's rather large office.

"Ten seconds to self-destruct sequence."

"I know, alright?" he shouted at the ceiling. "I went to kindergarten and can actually count."

The countdown didn't slow. *"Ten, nine, eight..."*

Not knowing what else to do, he sat in Klaus's office chair and put his feet on the evil man's desk, lacing his fingers behind his head.

"Six..."

"Well, you saved the world, pal," he said to the air again. "Are you happy, now?"

"Four, three..."

He closed his eyes and sighed. After escaping death so many times in his short period as a time-traveler, the demise literally two seconds away seemed almost poetic.

"One, zero. Self-destruct sequence engaged."

Then the floor beneath him shuddered and fire was everywhere.

PART I

Life

CHAPTER 1
Jericho

Okay, number one, it was severely bright when I tried to open my aching eyes. Number two, I smelled hospital, and number three, I remembered what I was doing before everything went black, so I figured that I was more than likely in a morgue instead of a hospital. I was on some sort of hospital bed type thing, though, unless future morgues put bodies on mattresses.

I mean, I thought I was still in the future.

"Why is it so bright?" I tried to say, but my throat somehow wouldn't work.

I tried to say the same thing for about a minute or two and, after a lot of effort on my part, was finally able to get out a sort of gurgling sound before saying, "Sushi... tacos..."

"He's awake," I heard a female voice say from somewhere behind my head. I tried to turn and get a look at the owner, but realized, in horror, might I add, that my head seemed to be held in place by a vice.

Panicking, I tried to grab at the restraint and realized—yes, with more horror—that my wrists were bound.

"Let... me... go..." I managed, instantly out of breath from the sheer struggle of just three words, and I silently swore that if I got out of this alive, I would definitely go to the gym.

Then the owner of the voice appeared at my bedside.

She was maybe close to thirty, I was guessing, had jet

black hair and was slightly tanned.

"Name?" I got out, trying to narrow my eyes at her.

"Rest, Mr. Johnson," she said, typing at something in her hands. In a few seconds my eyes closed and I was out.

This happened more frequently over what I could only discern as weeks upon weeks. Me strapped to the bed, the no-named, plain woman in a lab coat appearing after I'd talked to myself for a while and sedating me, and on and on.

It was pretty much the worst month of my life. At least, I hoped it was only a month. It really could have been longer, I guess, because there wasn't exactly a clock or calendar on the only part of the wall I could actually see.

Then, the day of reckoning finally, finally arrived, and I said a complete sentence.

"What the Helheim? Why am I here, and what are you planning to do with me?"

After that day I was able to talk, shout, or scream. About two weeks post sentence, I was taken aback when the lights shut off in the room.

"Finally," I said. "I was wondering how long you idiots would make me sleep through miniature suns."

I wasn't worried about ticking anybody off, if you hadn't already deduced that on your own. I mean, sure, I was, in fact, strapped to a table and at their (whoever they were) complete mercy. But I figured that they wouldn't have been going through all the trouble of keeping me there, hooked up to a lot of machines with a nurse checking in on me every day, just to get annoyed at my wit and slit my throat or something.

Then one lone light appeared above me, and I closed my eyes. "And it's back. Thanks for the tease, guys."

"How are you feeling, Mr. Johnson?" said the only other person I'd seen in months as she materialized beside my bed, her face shrouded due to the bright light above her head.

"Am I really wearing nothing but a cloth around my nether regions, like it feels like I am?" I asked her.

Since it seemed a harmless question, she answered,

"Yes."

"Then, please, call me Jericho," I said sarcastically. "We're way past pleasantries."

But I needed to talk to someone, or I was going to lose it. I felt like I was trying to sneak up on a deer and that the least little bit of commotion would scare away my mystery nurse's seemingly talkative mood.

"So, are you, like, a mad scientist or something?"

"No," she replied. "I work for a scientist."

"Is he mad?"

"No."

"You sure? Because the last time I checked, I was strapped to a bed."

"It is merely for your own protection, Mr. Johnson, as your new bio-muscles are not fully compatible with your new synthetic ones."

Wait.

What. The. Helheim?

"Back up," I said, rolling my eyes around, mainly because that was the only thing I could actually move. "I could have sworn that you said I had synthetic muscles inside of me."

"You do. Only about 45% of your muscles were salvageable after the explosion, and even those weren't the easiest to save."

"So, you and, uh, whoever the mad scientist you work for pulled me out of rubble or something?"

"Exactly, yes," she said, still looking at the device in her hand before it vanished, the hologram puffing into a slight mist.

"Why?"

"I don't have clearance to tell you anything, Mr. Johnson," said the silhouette.

"Then why talk to me now? I've been here for two months, maybe."

She was silent.

"Why talk now?" I growled.

"You've been here longer than two months, Mr. Johnson," she said quietly.

"Okay, two months was undershooting it a little—"

"You've been here almost three years," she cut in, gasping softly as if she wasn't supposed to tell me that.

My breathing became rapid, and my vision blurred.

"What?" I asked as calmly as I could, my voice quavering.

"It's December of 2344. You've been here since February of 2342. We've been—"

I didn't hear the rest because by then I was screaming.

"Sedate him," I heard a male voice crackle over a speaker in the room. "Now."

I felt severely hot and began thrashing. I can't explain what was happening to me right then. Suffice it to say that it wasn't pretty. The bulbs in the bright fixtures above me suddenly shattered, dropping pieces of glass and phosphorous all over my almost naked body.

That's when I felt it the first time, a small tingling in my palms.

Then everything went black again.

CHAPTER 2

The next few days consisted of me waking up just long enough for Madam Truth Bomb to sedate me again and slip me back into unconsciousness. Not sure why they wanted me to stay out, but I'm sure they had their diabolical reasons.

When I finally woke one day and didn't get instantly zonked back out, I noticed that the light bulbs that had somehow exploded had been replaced. Hours passed as I lay there, and I was suddenly overcome with the sheer injustice of it all.

"I died for you people," I shouted. "I saved the world as all of you idiot scientists know it!"

Silence.

"What do you want with me?" I screamed.

More silence.

This was the worst.

I didn't know where I was. That was what I think was bothering me more than why I was even there in the first place. Was I still in Flagstaff? Had I been picked up by crazy future Nazis who were trying to break my mental willpower?

After what seemed like forever, I slipped back into the darkness. Actually, this was probably the first time I'd fallen asleep on my own since I could remember. The darkness was welcoming, let me tell you. It felt kind of warm, almost. Like an old friend.

Then I was standing in the room, completely

unshackled. I gasped and took a few steps backward, grabbing at my head and neck, which were now free from the vice, before glancing around the room. It looked pretty normal, really, for a future mad scientist lab, I mean.

There were chairs, a small table, a computer-looking thing in one corner, and even a patient strapped to a bed.

Wait.

I walked over to the bed and peered down at the poor schmuck in bonds. He looked terrible. His skin was almost completely white from either being indoors for a long period of time or from the fact that his skin might have been synthetic, I wasn't sure which. The only thing he wore was some type of white loincloth thing, so I got a good look at all his shimmering body parts.

I leaned over to examine his right arm, and I saw that the forearm seemed to be open, exposing wires mixed in with human veins. Yeesh. This dude was a mess. I glanced up at his face to give him a sympathetic grimace. Then I froze.

The Frankenstein dude was me.

I thought about screaming and running, but I decided that approach wouldn't help matters. I wasn't sure how I was standing there, in a loincloth of my own, looking down at my body tied down, but God knows I wasn't about to waste a chance to get out of that hellhole.

Without thinking about how or why, I instantly went to free my left wrist, except my hand went through the strap when I tried to grab at it. I straightened and frowned at my hands, noticing that I could see through them slightly. I tried touching them together, watching my hands phase through each other.

Okay, now felt like the right time to scream and run for it. The ghost version of Jericho was one step closer to freedom because, as was the case, Frankenstein Jericho was still strapped down and Ghost Jericho couldn't do a dang thing about it.

Then the eyes of Frankenstein Jericho shot open and he

screamed. I couldn't hear him at first, but after a few seconds, his primeval shriek reached my ears and I had to cover them against the noise.

Except my hands phased through my head.

Then I was lying on my back strapped to the accursed bed and screaming.

What had these people done to me?

CHAPTER 3

Two days passed before my mysterious nurse appeared again.

"Good to see you. Been a while," I said.

"How are you feeling, Mr. Johnson?" she asked, stopping beside my bed and peering down at me.

"Why do you always ask me that?" I shot at her. "You, like, put me back together and made me some freak of nature. Wouldn't you know how I was feeling without asking? Come to think of it, why come by in the first place?"

"Fine. I'll leave you," she said simply, turning on her heel and heading for the door.

As much as I hated it, if I went one more day without human interaction, I would have had it. "Wait. Please, come back."

I heard the door open, and I closed my eyes and almost wept. I didn't hear the door shut after that and stopped mid-sob. After a second, the door shut, and she walked back to the bed.

"I feel horrible," I told her once she came back into view. "I don't even care what you people want anymore. But can you please tell me that this Lysol-smelling hell is going to end soon?"

I just didn't care anymore. I'd been strapped to a table for three years, and I would've poured my heart out to the Devil himself if he'd shown up in my little room for a chat.

She looked at me for a few seconds, and I could tell she was deciding something. "It will end soon, Mr. Johnson."

"How soon?" I asked quietly, my throat tightening at the very idea of putting my real feet on the floor and touching my knees.

"Within the week. Dr. Cross is currently in Anchorage, Alaska, tying up a few loose ends. When he arrives, he will check your status and decide whether or not to test you out."

"Test me out?"

"I can't say anything else, Mr. Johnson," she said. "You're doing wonderful on paper, so I know he'll remove the bonds. Just please be patient."

"Lady," I muttered, "I've been tied to a bed for years. I'm all out of patience."

She didn't answer, leaving me without another word, but the small amount of knowledge she'd imparted was enough.

That's when I decided that I wasn't about to die in some hell of a hospital room at the whim of some crazy, mad scientist. I was going to find whoever had me tied down in despair, sorrow, and agony for the past three years, then find out who he was working for, fight my way to the freaking top, and make whoever was behind this pay dearly for thinking they could make me their little science project.

The mind games were over. Time for a little revenge.

CHAPTER 4

The infamous Dr. Cross arrived late the next day. He didn't come see me, but I knew he'd indeed shown up because the lab techs were all fluttering around acting nervous.

And a few had mentioned that he'd, you know, shown up.

It was super fun watching them buzz around while I stood in the middle of them with my arms crossed, completely invisible to all eyes.

Well, I mean, I would've had my arms crossed if I could actually touch my body. I'd been doing this for a few days now and had already deduced that being farther away from my body lengthened the ghostly episodes. Not sure why, exactly, but I wasn't complaining because it gave me a chance to look around the place that'd been holding me captive for years.

The longest ghost walk I'd done was almost an hour, which was when I discovered that the lab was underground and wasn't common knowledge to the general public of Flagstaff, which I'd also discovered was where I still was, if the chatter from the meager lab rats was anything to go by. If that doesn't scream mad scientist, I don't know what does.

I'd found out a few things while moving around the lab but the main thing was discovering my mystery nurse's name was Ritu. No one had nametags (probably an evil lab thing) or mentioned last names to one another so that was all I gleaned from phasing around.

Also, phasing isn't my favorite analogy of walking through walls, merely because the word has been used before, I'm certain. But if you think that's going to stop me from using it, then you, sir/ma'am, are gravely mistaken. I've discovered that, in life, sometimes it's easier to steal someone else's wording rather than make up your own. Occam's razor and all that.

I phased through a desk and the person sitting at it drumming his fingers in an annoying pattern then I made my way back to the hall that led to my room. I'd had enough for one day. There really wasn't much to the joint.

I strutted through my door feeling awesome, only to stop in my tracks at the sight of Ritu at my bedside, shaking Frankenstein Jericho's shoulder and glancing back to the door every now and then.

"Please wake up, Jericho," she was whispering fiercely.

What, not Mr. Johnson?

I closed my eyes, and in a split second I was able to feel the pressure of the air on my pale mortal frame once more and felt Ritu shaking my shoulder.

"What's up?" I asked groggily.

"Why wouldn't you wake up?" she asked. "Your vitals were fine."

"All this bondage wears on a guy."

"Dr. Cross is here," Ritu said, looking over her shoulder again.

"I know," I said simply.

She blinked at me for a few seconds before saying, "That's impossible."

"Tell that to the lab staff running around like lost orphans straightening microscopes and paperclip holders," I said confidently.

Frowning, Ritu asked, "What's a paperclip?"

"That's the most futuristic question I've ever been asked," I said dryly.

"How did you know he was here?" she asked, looking yet

again at the door.

Ritu, like everyone else around but me, had a Russian accent, which, incidentally, didn't instill trust right off the bat, let me tell you.

Call it racist, stereotypical, or just categorizing, but Russians sound inherently evil to me.

Too many movies, I'm thinking.

"Because I'm a ninja, duh."

"Listen," she said, ignoring my ninja japery. "Dr. Cross is pushing the testing forward quicker than I expected."

"Does that mean I'm going to get out of this bed?"

"Yes," Ritu said. "Jericho, please know that I was against the procedure from the start. I wanted Dr. Cross to let you die."

This was a new and unexpected unearthing of past events. "Why? I mean, I'm alive right now. Isn't that better than being a burnt corpse?"

"No," she said, locking eyes with me. "I feel that in a few days, you'll wish you wouldn't have been brought back to life."

"Why are you telling me this, anyway?"

"Because I feel guilty," she confessed. "Because I know what Cross is planning on doing with you. I can't explain it all, but I promise I'll get you out of here. I swear it."

She finished with her hand gripping my wrist. "I have to go. Don't mention me to Dr. Cross."

Then she left.

I didn't like thinking to myself much anymore, ever since I discovered I now possessed the uncanny ability to somehow leave my body, because I was afraid I'd turn into a sort of Jekyll/Hyde kind of thing.

But my thoughts were all I really had then. This Dr. Cross didn't exactly sound like the nicest guy in town. Any plans of his that included testing me or any other zombie-slave scenario weren't going to go well for him, though, that much I could say.

I remembered Chloe speaking of Cross before, about how he used to be her dad's colleague. He also was the one behind recreating Beck, Chloe's synthetic, crazy twin sibling.

I'm glad I had already decided this, before the door opened and the man himself walked in and I was looking at my re-maker, who thought he was about to have a nice little chat with his latest project.

Boy, was he wrong.

CHAPTER 5

"Jericho," he said, as if he'd just bumped into an old friend he hadn't seen for a while. "I'm glad to see you're doing well."

I was a little surprised by how young the guy was. I always thought you had to be over seventy, have crazy hair, and wear a white lab coat to qualify as a mad scientist. The man before me couldn't have been a day over thirty-five and had amazing, killer flaxen, brown hair that reached his shoulders.

And here I was, strapped to a bed with vampire skin, robot limbs, ghost-form, and, if I haven't already mentioned it, rocking a buzz-cut. When I say that I was a little ticked at the sight of Dr. Triathlon showing up looking like a toned, tan model wearing glasses and looking awesome in a lab coat, you can be assured that I was indeed ticked. Oh yeah, and he was also very American.

I remained silent.

"No doubt you have questions," he started, checking a holotab on his wrist.

He must've caught me looking and decided to enlighten me. "This connects all citizens of Flagstaff to the Holonet, a nasty business when you're trying to flee the country, but not a bad gadget to have if you're planning on actually obeying the laws of the land, I suppose." He held his right arm above me, and I could see the small floating screen, that seemed to be level with his forearm, x-raying me. The picture was backwards to me, but I still could see the sinews and metal in my—

"Geez, not my leg, too," I groaned.

"Afraid so, Jericho," Dr. Cross said. "You were quite a mess."

"Then why waste three years fixing me?"

Cross stopped his x-ray and turned his face toward me, cocking his head slightly to the side. "Who told you it's been three years?"

Uh oh.

I forgot that Ritu had told me to keep our secret conversations on the down low.

"I'm not stupid," was my reply.

"No, you most certainly aren't stupid," Cross said, smiling good-naturedly. "Your body seems strong enough. Let's see if you can walk."

Then he tapped a few buttons on his holotab, and I felt the vice holding my head in place disappear into the bed and my wrists and legs were loosed.

I was free.

In less than a second, I had the mad scientist supermodel pinned against the wall across the room, my robot forearm at his throat. "Three years!" I shouted into his face. "I was tied to a bed for three years, you maniac. You actually thought I'd sit up, shake your hand, and go take a shower?"

He coughed, struggling against me, which was frighteningly fruitless because I felt like I was pinning a five-year-old kid against the wall and not, in fact, a grown man.

"Weren't ready…" he wheezed.

"What was that, doc?" I spat, pushing harder with my arm and lifting him off the floor. "I'm afraid I can't hear you over the sound of your latest science project killing you." Then I dropped him, and he gasped, crumpling onto the white floor.

"Show's over, pal," I said, dusting my hands off. "I'm just going to go mug one of your lackeys for a change of clothes, and I'll be on my way."

"I couldn't... release you..." Cross gasped, grabbing at a desk to help himself to his feet.

"Why?"

"I said you weren't ready, Jericho. As much as I pride myself in my studies, I couldn't fix you in a day." He rubbed at the red mark I'd left on his neck. "Since killing doesn't seem hard for you, I suppose my tests involving touching your nose and writing your name aren't necessary anymore."

"The first right thing you've said yet," I told him, glancing around the room. "I've got to say, standing around in a diaper isn't making me feel menacing at the moment."

Dr. Cross laughed at that, surprising me, since I'd just, you know, almost killed him. "Chloe Sparks was right when she said that you were just full of those."

I stared at him for an explanation. When he finally got a rein on his chuckles and saw my stare, he said, "From your memoirs. I took the liberty of listening to the account you recorded on the first gauntlet."

I absentmindedly looked at my right forearm, the one I wore the gauntlet on. "Was my old arm still..."

"Yes," Cross confirmed. "It took a few days to get all the pieces out, actually."

Gross.

"Chloe's dead," I said, flexing my new hand and listening for the sound of gyrating gears.

"I know. We found her body not far from what was left of yours," he said, walking past me and through the doorway. "Come on. Let's get you some clothes."

"Then why not save both of us?" I asked, following him into the hallway and toward the elevator at the end of the hall.

"I'll explain everything in a minute."

Wait. Wasn't I supposed to be raining vengeance and mayhem on the heads of these ne'er-do-wells? Was it Cross's normalcy that was stopping me? I tried to imagine if him looking like Dr. Wiley from Megaman would've made me finish the job of offing him in my room as we passed a few women in lab coats, and they all gawked at me in my loincloth. They were still staring at us as the doors began closing.

"I think it's been a minute," I told Cross, glancing out the thick glass elevator and seeing the floors pass by with many other white coated individuals working on them.

"Taking away all the lies I could spin to keep my head attached to my shoulders, I just didn't have enough resources to save both of you," he said, not looking at me.

"What about Beck?" I asked him.

We reached the top floor, and the doors slid open. Stepping into the carpeted hall he said, "It's because of Beck that I didn't have the resources for both of you."

I followed him in silence, lost in thoughts about Chloe and her sarcastic robot sister—the latter without much fondness. We entered his office, and he showed me to a large, nice lavatory. We're talking walk-in shower, spa, spaceship toilet, and lots of other futuristic stuff I didn't recognize.

I don't know if you've ever had the opportunity to go three years without a shower. Let's hope you haven't ever died, been brought back to life, and strapped to a bed for almost one-thousand and ninety-five days. It's a kind of grimy feeling that I can't exactly describe.

Just know it's nasty.

The shower was amazing, by the way.

The only clothes laid out on the counter in the lavatory were a dark gray leather jumpsuit that looked like a male version of what Chloe used to wear, complete with the light-weight grey combat boots. The only addition to the outfit was a long black, form-fitting, hooded wool coat that reached a little below my knees.

I looked at myself in the full-length mirror once I'd put on the comfortable outfit, slipping on the matching thin, black gloves. It was odd to go from the basically-naked science project to the action-figure worthy man looking back at me in the mirror. I stood there a moment and pulled on the black hood before instantly pushing it back off my head and removing the gloves, too. It looked ridiculous to have them on inside a warm bathroom.

"Please tell me that all the kids are dressing like this nowadays," I said as I stepped out of the lavatory. Dr. Cross was on his holotab again, and he glanced up at me.

"I certainly hope not," he said, stepping out from behind his desk. "That's top-secret materials you're wearing, Jericho. Lots of bells and whistles."

I walked past him to the large window/wall that overlooked what I was guessing was Flagstaff. "Just what kind of gig are you running here, man? I already know about the mad scientist branch," I nodded to the shrouded city. "Tell me what they all think you do."

Cross removed his lab coat, dropping it over his desk chair, and leaned against his large desk, crossing his arms. "Generally, they all know what I do," he said. "Not to sound too high-and-mighty, but my research has saved this city countless times."

"So that gives you a pass, and they leave you to your own devices," I said.

"Mostly."

"Don't take this the wrong way, Cross, but you don't exactly seem like the scientist type," I told him, slipping my hands into the pockets of my long coat.

"The medical field will never lack for great minds in my time. I'm well known simply because I took risks no one else was willing to take, and I, as well as millions of people, have thrived from it."

"Risks like Beck?" I asked, turning to face him. "A little bird told me folks like Beck and I are illegal around these parts."

I was basically throwing all the knowledge Chloe had bestowed upon me back into his face. She'd told me that any tests or research that had to do with grafting synthetic parts to a human spinal column were illegalized by what little authorities were left.

"As you've stated, most people leave me alone," Cross

said, walking over to peer out the window himself. "And, as for Beck, you're not nearly as unstable as she is due to your being 28% synthetic to her 88%."

"Not to mention the brain cells you removed so her body wouldn't reject the grafting process on her spine." It was all there. One of the last conversations I'd had with Chloe about her obnoxious sister.

"Beck is my sister, Jericho, but that doesn't change the fact that she wasn't supposed to be like this. No one is," she'd told me on the catwalk in the Rebel base. *"That's the reason the cell grows back in the first place. The brain knows that the spine is being violated, and it tries to purge it."*

I explained the process to Cross, who watched me closely with a little fascination as I told him word for word what Chloe had told me—except I made it seem like I just knew that kind of robot talk to make him nervous.

"All true facts," Cross said once I'd finished my lecture. "Explained like a man who received a master's degree in teaching at the age of twenty-one." Sighing, he put his hands behind his back. "Beck has been a problem ever since she escaped into the world."

"Is she still around?"

"Very much so. She's a sort of figurehead for the Rebels now, as a matter of fact," he glanced at me. "You should also know that your Viking girlfriend is still alive. As far as we can tell by attacks on the city and from just hearsay, she aids Beck in her assaults and leads most of them."

Piper.

I couldn't think of her then. I almost began crying at the thought of her being alive, and for being stuck in a strange future away from her home because of me. So, I kept the subject on track. "Why'd you make Beck in the first place, if you knew she'd turn into what she is now?"

It was hard to read his facial features as he looked back over the city and said, "I did it for a grieving father who happened to be one of my closest friends."

Atrium Sparks. I'd forgotten about him. "How is Dr. Sparks doing these days?" I asked.

"Dead," Dr. Cross said, sighing. "Klaus had him killed minutes after you and Chloe left his lab, once he'd gotten information out of him."

I wasn't expecting that, and my heart sank.

"How's the city faring since the bombing?" I asked, changing the subject away from Chloe and her father.

"Surprisingly well," Cross said. "You may find this hard to believe, but Klaus wasn't exactly the most popular among the citizens of Flagstaff, and not because he wasn't the best company at social functions, if you know what I mean. All in all, it's a good thing he's dead."

"So, when do I get to go home?" I asked, knowing what the answer would be.

"To Chicago?" Dr. Cross said, walking back to his desk. "That may prove to be quite the obstacle since your only ticket home was basically destroyed in the explosion." Reaching in his top right desk drawer, he produced the gauntlet.

The gauntlet. My baby.

"It doesn't look destroyed to me," I said, approaching him and accepting it from his outstretched hand.

"It's still in one piece, but the element zero inside of it is depleted," he answered, looking annoyed. "Atrium was the genius on all things time-travel and was also very secretive about it. I've gone through his old files and notes several times, but there wasn't any mention of more element Z being found nor on how it worked. I suppose he decided that knowledge was best left in his brain."

I could tell Cross wasn't thrilled about the fact that all of Atrium's data was basically useless now that he was dead.

And, not to keep bringing the story back to, well, me, but I wasn't digging the no time-travel thing, either.

"Looks like I won't be eating sushi tacos anytime soon," I said, handing the dead glove back to him. "Let's talk about me being your science project."

CHAPTER 6

Once I was seated at his desk, Dr. Cross went back to the enormous window that also doubled as a touch-screen power point, which he decided to employ to aid in his argument of—

I'm not sure, really.

So, I just leaned back in his comfortable chair and listened to what he had to say.

"What makes our bodies work, Jericho?" he asked, swiping his hand across the large screen so multiple items popped up showing different parts of the human anatomy.

Shrugging, I said, "Heart, lungs, brain. I don't know. Take your pick."

"All three are needed, yes. But what makes the heart, lungs, and brain work?"

"Listen, if you've been preparing this for the last three years, thinking that I would actually participate in Mad Science 101 for extra credit, you're mistaken," I told him.

"Fair enough," Cross said, turning back to his presentation. "Blood was the answer—" he stopped when he saw my hand go up.

"Yes?"

"You've just discovered that blood makes our bodies work?"

"I thought you would have appreciated the summed-up version," he said.

"Then by all means, sum away, doc."

"I like to think of blood as fuel," he said, and the screen portrayed lots of science mumbo jumbo, no doubt backing up what he was saying. "In short, I have been able to create what you would call a supreme variety of the common blood."

I frowned at that. "Go on."

"Atrium explained Z-90 to you when you first met him, but he failed to mention that he and I made the discovery together, halving the stockpile. And while he was working on his time-travel theory here, I was in Anchorage studying various applications of the new element."

I frowned. No, the good Dr. Sparks had indeed left out that little tidbit. I had known that he and Cross had been science chums in the past, but that was it.

"I call it what it is. Z-90," Cross said as more pictures and graphs appeared on the screen. "We eat food, our bodies break the food down, and eventually the good parts are sectioned out to be used wherever our bodies think it needs it most. If a host has a full tank of Z-90, in the same liter amount as a normal person, over 50% of the blood count is composed of white cells, compared to the regular 1%."

"That's impossible," I said, shaking my head.

"So is time-travel, my friend," Cross said. "And yet here you are."

"How does having an awesome immune system benefit anyone, besides not having to get a flu shot every year?" I asked in a bored tone.

"I confess that the reason behind making over half the blood count white cells was at first to combat the other half filling the host, which is where Z-90 comes in." More graphs on the screen flashed. "Have you ever known anyone who had low blood sugar problems?"

"Dated one," I told him. "She ate me out of protein bar and home."

"The first test trials of Z-90 were a version of that, I suppose you could say," he told me. "All hosts transfused with it went into instant, irreversible comas, which put me back to the drawing board."

I narrowed my eyes at his back since he was facing his high-tech chalkboard and was full swing into his lecture. He seemed a little too cavalier when mentioning folks being placed into irreversible comas by his research.

"That's when I added the white blood cell count, which worked for a time."

"You mean no one died from it," I corrected.

Sighing, Cross said, "If that were only true."

"Geez, doc, how many people have died in the name of science around here?"

"Most were convicted criminals or deserters bound for incineration as it was, Jericho," he said, turning to me. "Z-90 could have changed the course of humanity, saving millions of people."

"And killing off the condemned in search of the greater good doesn't make you lose sleep?" I asked.

"Not in the least," he answered, and I could tell he meant it.

"Of course it doesn't," I said, leaning back in the desk chair. "You said Z-90 *could* have saved millions. What went wrong?"

Cross turned away from the window, and the entire context backing his argument vanished. I noticed that it had started snowing outside the thick glass. "After a few years of searching for a way to make a clean transfusion, I finally stumbled onto the reason none of the tests would take."

"Let me guess. God finally got tired of other people playing at his role in the universe and vaporized all of your research with a lightning bolt?" I asked sarcastically.

"I suppose future generations could see it that way, if they chose," he said, removing his glasses and rubbing at his eyes. He looked way older just then for some reason. "But it wasn't quite as lofty. In the end, it turned out that no one on the planet could be a perfect host because of the slight change in the atmosphere when nuclear war pushed us a few degrees from the sun. Not only did it bequeath the dawning of a new ice age, but it also unearthed new elements, Z-90 being among them."

Leaning against the desk and looking at the swirling flakes outside, he continued, "The change in pressure wasn't noticed by anyone on the planet because it wasn't enough to have us floating like astronauts or jumping hundreds of feet, but the effects were drastically different for our bodies. In short, anyone born after the earth shifted has grown with too much pressure on their bodies, and somehow it makes a complete transfusion impossible."

I took in everything he was telling me, and I finally saw where his entire monologue was heading.

"So, to have a good, complete host you would've had to get someone from before the nukes went off."

He nodded.

"I get it," I muttered, standing. "Is this the part where you ask me if I'll be your precious host, since I can't go home and everyone I cared about here is dead?"

Except for Piper. The Viking girl of my dreams was still alive and well.

"I'm afraid that you're already a host, Jericho."

Wait—what?

"You weren't exactly in the most talkative of moods when we pulled your burning remains from what was left of Klaus's building. After a year of doing everything I could, I had to infuse you with Z-90 to keep you alive."

Level-headed, Jericho. Be level-headed.

"Brilliant presentation, Dr. Cross," I told him in my calmest voice. "But if I may, you somehow didn't mention just what it is this Z-90 stuff of yours actually does, besides keeping me infinitely current on my shots."

Cross was watching me, and I think he saw that I was a little more than agitated and possibly might have been afraid that I would kill him. "That's just it, Jericho. I have my theories but I don't know much about what it does because no one housing it has lived more than two days. But you," his eyes were glassy then, and not because of his glasses. Cross had finally shown me his mad scientist stare. I'd seen Chloe's dad give me the same look when he was explaining element zero to me, and I'd also witnessed it countless times in movies. "You're the first and only host for Z-90 ever in existence. Beck was born after the event so the fact that she's even still alive is a wonder and she could never wield the power I believe you can. I know what my theories show on paper and what it's supposed to be able to do and what someone housing it has the potential to become, but that's as far as I've gotten. I honestly don't know what you're capable of, Jericho."

I had known something was different from the moment I first threw him against the wall in my room. I can't describe the feeling of just knowing that you could do something that's considered impossible, but that's the way I felt. I truly felt like I could jump twenty feet in the air and maybe even do two back flips before I landed.

Cross may not have known what I was capable of, but I sure did. I was thinking of my ghost-mode when Cross made his final plea. "I've had my best men and women in the field the past three years looking for more element zero to power the glove and keep my research up to date, and I'm going to keep them there until they find some, however long it takes," he said. "Until then, you can't go home, and I can't get another person willing to become a host for Z-90. All I ask is that you stay for a month or two. Just long enough for us to see what you can do, and then you can go looking for a way home yourself, if you choose. I won't stop you."

"You couldn't stop me now," I said.

"I know," Cross said sincerely. "That's why I'm simply asking. Whether you like it or not, fate has chosen you to be the first of a super-human race that could one day fix this god-forsaken planet."

He did make a good point. And here I thought that I was already a super-human for traveling through time.

"I'll stay on one condition." Cross looked at me hopefully. Pointing to the window I said, "We do the first test outside."

CHAPTER 7

"Try to keep your head down as much as possible, Jericho," Ritu told me through the… I'm not sure what, actually, because ever since Cross had given me my very own tab on the Holonet (not an easy thing to do, he had told me, because I wasn't a newborn infant), I didn't need an earpiece, and most incoming calls were directed to my mind somehow.

Checking the map on the holotab floating above my wrist, I saw that I was the only living thing within a mile radius that was dumb enough to step outside for a run through the snow-covered streets of Flagstaff. The four-inch-by-six-inch screen also let me know that winter was indeed upon us, by informing me that it was almost minus sixty degrees.

"Why should I?" I asked Ritu, glancing around at the abandoned skyscrapers riddled throughout the decaying city. "My tab is showing I'm the only idiot out for a leisurely stroll."

"You are currently using an older model of the holotab, as that was the only kind Cross could get you, to fly your account under the radar of prying eyes," Ritu informed me. "And you would need a military-grade holodock to have the infrared scanners primarily used for locating cloaked targets."

"Has anyone ever told you that you're kind of a know-it-all?" I asked her as I began trudging through the streets. The snow was about ankle deep for as far as I could see, which wasn't that far, actually, because of the snow that had begun falling yet again. "Does it ever not snow here?"

"It doesn't snow too much during the summer," Ritu answered.

"I've seen your so-called summer, Ritu. It's almost twenty below."

I could almost hear her shrug before she asked, "How does it feel now?"

I didn't exactly know how to answer that.

Mainly because I felt like I was walking through Palm Beach in the fall instead of the frozen planet I was on. "Is the Z-90 making me impervious to the cold?" I asked her, skirting around an old bus. "Because I'm not feeling cold."

I heard her tapping away at something before she said, "He had a few suspicions along those lines, considering what Z-90 does to a body's molecular structure. The suit you're wearing is more than likely the reason you're feeling so cozy."

It was odd to hear her use the word cozy because the expression didn't fit anything the future had to offer. "How's that?" I asked, punching the driver side window out of a nearby car with ease and peering inside.

"That suit is something Dr. Cross has been working on since before you arrived. He's been really secretive about it, but if I had to assume how it worked, I'd say that the material somehow uses cold air to power inner thermal tags placed here and there throughout the suit, to keep your body at a good ninety-eight degrees, even in the most freezing climates."

"That's just your assumed version?" I laughed.

"I suppose you could pull off your hood for a second and see if your ears fall off," Ritu said, and I knew she had to be smiling.

"Nice try, but my ears are my most fetching quality. Saving them from one element only to lose them to another would be more than I could handle."

"Speaking of more than you can handle," said the voice in my head. "Let's put you through some paces."

"Is Cross looking over your shoulder?" I asked.

"No, it's just us."

"The last time a girl told me that she turned out to be wrong, and I almost got shot by her father."

I saw a hurricane fence almost fifty yards ahead of me and instantly ran for it, the gap closing at an alarming rate due to my speed. Then I jumped clean over the almost twelve-foot-tall fence and landed in a crouch on top of a car. Slowly standing, I looked at my hands.

This was awesome.

"Do you just want me to do a couple willy-nilly tumbles in the snow, or do you scientists actually have a few tasks you'd like to see me do?"

"This is Dr. Cross," I heard the good doctor's voice buzz in. "I think the first things we need to see are all physical, since you're already outside."

"Cross," I said in a good-natured way, "are you feeding in live from that killer office of yours?"

"You know it," he said.

"And might I just say that it's great to hear an American voice for a change," I said. "All I wanted was to get a breath of fresh air, so I'm good. What do you guys want?"

"Let's see how fast you are," Ritu said, and since Cross didn't tell her to shut up, I decided to indulge her.

I began by leaping from car to car, landing with ease and not slipping, due to whatever Cross had made my boots out of, until I made it to a halfway cleared stretch of road. I rolled my neck once before bolting down the pavement. I could barely feel the wind on my face, and I didn't know if it was from being a superhero, from my suit, or just because I wasn't going that fast. In what seemed like a few seconds, I crossed about two city blocks before skidding to a halt and spraying snow. "How was that?" I asked, not even breathing hard.

"Your top speed was twenty-five miles per hour," Ritu told me.

"That was it?" I asked. "Usain Bolt's top was rumored to be a little over twenty-seven." Then I was off again, kicking snow up in my wake as I tore down the pavement as fast as I thought possible. I didn't stop at the four-way this time, but instead took a left turn and began car-hopping again, sometimes clearing four cars between jumps. When I came up to the last car before yet another good stretch of empty street, I put all I could into my last bounce, sailing sickeningly high into the air before landing hard in a roll and coming back up on my feet, using the momentum for a boost in my resumed sprint.

"Who's Usain Bolt?" Ritu asked.

"He's about to be dethroned as the fastest man alive," I said, smirking.

Any notions I may have felt before about not feeling alive were gone as I felt my speed pick up.

I could do anything, and somehow, I knew it.

"Jericho," Ritu said in my ear, "that's a dead end."

I saw the alleged dead end before she did on her city layout, and I had already laid out my next move for the crumbled forty-story building in my path.

"Is it?" I asked nonchalantly in mid-dash before leaping into the air and hitting the slanted remains of the building. Then I began climbing.

I started off at just a quick climb on the vertical surface of the building, using broken window frames, jutting iron work, or anything for a handhold. My grip was phenomenal, so I could make anything into a good place to grab. I felt like I was going too slow after a few seconds of climbing, so I started leaping up the sheer side of the old building and clearing almost a whole floor with each jump, powered primarily by a little push from my toes and strong pulls with my arms.

I hummed the old *Spider-Man* theme song as I traversed the wall.

On the last floor, I put all I could into my last leap, pulling into a ball and doing two spins before landing on the crumbling rooftop, snow flying everywhere from the force of my landing.

And I still wasn't breathing hard. I felt like I'd just

walked across a kitchen instead of running through and over a city like a madman.

"How was that?" I asked, putting my hands on my hips through habit because I think the old Jericho must've still been in me somewhere and felt that a run and climb like that should've been met with doubled-over gasps for air.

I heard Ritu stammering and struggling for words when Cross chimed in. "That was exceptional, Jericho. How do you feel?"

"I feel like I need to get higher," I said, eyeing the mammoth skyscraper beside the cracked apartment complex I was standing on. "Ritu, what was my fastest?"

"Almost fifty," I heard her say, still not believing it. "How were you even able to react fast enough physically at that speed?"

Shrugging, I said, "Not sure. I knew I was going fast and it felt that way, but I just knew what I could and needed to do."

It was still hard to believe even for me, the guy who'd just done it.

"No light-headedness?" Cross asked.

"None."

"Blurred vision?"

"Snow count?"

"I think you're ready for the next step, then," he said. "First, do you see the eighty-story building on your right?"

"Yeah."

"Climb it."

Smiling, I said, "I thought you'd never ask."

In about one minute, I'd scaled the said skyscraper and was standing on the ledge overlooking Flagstaff. "How was that?"

"Great," Cross said. "Now, can you tell me what you feel would be the best way to get down?"

I frowned at that, not exactly knowing where he was going with this. "I guess I could just jump. I mean, would the fall kill me?"

I heard him laugh at that before saying, "I'm going to say yes, I think it would kill you. But do you think it would?"

"You mean do I feel like it would," I corrected.

"Do you?"

I peered down. It really was a long way down, but I felt like I could keep going and do anything.

"I feel like I'd just make a crater and walk away without a scratch," I said finally. "But I think jumping wouldn't be the greatest idea. Am I supposed to be invulnerable?"

"I think testing whether or not you're indeed invulnerable by leaping off an eighty-story building isn't the best way to find out, but I appreciate your enthusiasm."

"Well, we know that I'm a parkour god now. So, when do we find out how good I am at hurting people?"

"Dr. Cross," Ritu said, "scanners are showing a category seven blizzard heading for the city. ETA is exactly ten minutes."

"Would you look at that," Cross chuckled. "Looks like you've now got a time limit to get back to my building."

"Fifty holos says he can't make it back in time," I heard a man say in the background of, I'm guessing, Ritu's link.

"You're on," she said confidently. "Come on, Jericho. I'll split it with you if you hurry."

I smiled, releasing my grip and sliding down the tower. Have I told you already that I felt awesome?

CHAPTER 8

"So, a holo is worth how much?" I asked Ritu for probably the hundredth time. I don't know if you've been following my exploits for a while, but you may or may not remember my being kind of bummed that the future didn't have credits.

Well, it turns out that they do, in a manner of speaking. From what I was given to understand by Ritu, there was still a little hard cash that was in circulation, but that hands-on money was used mainly by older, nostalgic people, for no apparent reason. And it was Russian currency, too, not even good old American dollars and cents.

We were in the room Cross had given me, which was nicer than any suite I'd ever stayed in back in my time.

"I've told you," she said, sighing and smiling at me. "One holo is worth about five U.S. dollars."

"And how do you give it to me?"

Ritu tapped away on her holotab, and in seconds mine lit up and told me my net account was plus twenty-five holos.

"Just like that?" I asked, touching the icon and looking at my account history, which was basically blank considering I'd only had one transaction ever done. It showed the deposit was from VOLVAKOV1899.

When she saw my questioning glance, she said, "It's your last name and a digit combination most of the time."

"Ritu Volvakov?"

She nodded. "Dr. Cross made yours JJ2012, I think."

"How quaint of him," I said, crossing the large, carpeted living room, which had a hologram fire going in the heater made to resemble a fireplace in one corner, to the large window that looked like the one in Cross's office. "Where is he, anyway?"

"More than likely he's poring over the data collected from your run through the city. That should be enough to last him a few days," she said, sitting on one of the black leather couches close to the fire. "How do you like your room?"

"Beats the Helheim out of the previous one."

She nodded but didn't say anything for a while.

Maybe it was the semi-awkward silence between us that caused Ritu to randomly ask, "You miss her a lot, don't you?"

I didn't have to wonder who she was talking about.

"Yes," I answered simply, keeping my eyes on the ceiling and my fingers laced behind my head.

"I listened to your recording on the glove," she told me, looking downtrodden. "I am sorry for all that's happened to you, Jericho."

"Don't sweat it," I said, leaning forward and placing my elbows on my knees. I looked at her and said, "So, what were you exactly saying yesterday about Cross being—"

Ritu's mouth dropped open and she began waving her arms in a "shut the heck up" fashion.

I shut the heck up.

Ritu typed out something on her holotab, and just before I could ask her why we were being all cloak and dagger, my own holotab flashed above my wrist.

Ritu: *We can't talk now. I can get our tabs on a secure line by tonight, but until then don't mention anything.*

To which I replied:

Jericho: *Wow. Instant messaging. I'm fifteen again. Thanks for the lovely stroll down memory lane, dear lol.*

I saw her screen blip and she read what I'd sent. I saw her smile to herself before she began typing her response.

Yeah, definitely fifteen again.

Ugh. Worst. Age. Ever.

We talked for a few more minutes about my snow day before I asked, "Hey, don't take this the wrong way, but why are you here?"

"I told Dr. Cross I'd get you settled in your room, make you feel comfortable, and also make sure you didn't try and escape," she told me.

I checked my holotab (man, that thing was really coming in handy) to see what time it was. "I'm going to hit the hay, I think."

I walked Ritu to the door, but before she opened it, Ritu turned suddenly and hugged me. "I'll contact you in an hour. Don't do anything foolish while you wait, please."

I hadn't been expecting the hug, but I think I played it off pretty well. After she pulled away, I informed her that Dr. Cross must have removed all the foolish brain cells while I was under, because I would never do anything foolish whilst I awaited her to contact me. "Good night, Ritu. Sleep well."

Then she closed the door behind her.

Crossing the room quickly, I entered the large bedroom and lay on the bed, closing my eyes and instantly entering ninja-ghost mode.

I left my body on the bed and headed for the door, deciding that I'd better take advantage of my ninja mode while it lasted. After I phased into the hallway and spent ten minutes sticking my head through every door, I ran across to see if there were any mad scientist shenanigans going on. I began to lose faith in my venture. Most of them were empty and looked like smaller hotel rooms and not, in fact, like future torture chambers.

I made it to the elevator and went to push a button, only to be reminded that I wasn't able to touch anything whilst in ninja mode.

That was also when I decided to start calling it super-sneak mode instead. I mean, calling it ghost mode didn't work because I wasn't dead and couldn't fly, which, to me, was a sure-fire sign that someone or something was a ghost. And ninja mode was out because, you know, I couldn't touch anything.

But sneaky? Oh, but it was sneaky, indeed.

Sighing, I glanced up at the elevator ceiling once before exiting, only to have Ritu phase through my body and hit a button. I stepped back inside quickly, and we started up. I was thankful and a little puzzled that I didn't fall through the floor of the elevator because that would've been awkward and quite frankly a little scary.

Ritu was humming a tune I didn't recognize as she watched the floor number increase. What was she still doing on my floor anyway? Had she just come back because my body wasn't picking up her secure-channel phone calls?

We stopped twelve floors higher, and Ritu exited with me close behind. This floor looked a lot like the lab below the building, as everything was white and probably smelled like a cleaning supply closet. Ritu walked past a few doors before stepping into one on her right, with me still on her heels.

This room looked basically like a normal room, I guess. No, really, there wasn't anything that grabbed my attention in the least. Ritu sat at a desk and hit a few things on her holotab. A screen projected in front of her and so did a keyboard. After typing away for a good two minutes, with me pacing behind her, the green holoscreen turned red and she spoke.

"This is Ritu," she said. "Put Beck on, please. We need to talk."

And that's how I found out that Ritu was a Rebel spy.

CHAPTER 9

As much as I would love to continue this tale and skip the rather loathsome chore of wasting the breath in my lungs to take time out of my busy schedule and spend that precious time explaining to you the heinous creature, the one known as Beck, I suppose I must.

Partly because she was, after all, Chloe's twin sister, but mostly because, if I had an agent overseeing this gig, he'd probably tell me that any second part to a story needs a minimal backdrop of the previous plot so that new readers/listeners of the said story won't be completely lost.

Well, if anyone rolling with me now had the privilege of rolling with me previously, welcome back. And, to any newcomers who missed out, just sit down, relax, and enjoy the ride.

And, considering there are people still here after everything we've been through, I guess it wouldn't hurt to give a little premise where it's needed.

Beck Sparks was the twin sister of Chloe Sparks, and that's pretty much where the familiarity stops. Yes, she does look identical to Chloe and, yes, she did fool me into thinking she was Chloe the first time I met her and, yes, she did kiss me while posing as her sister, just to mess with my mind.

And, yes, she is just that heartless.

No, really, she is, like, literally heartless, because when she was around eighteen, she was blown to smithereens, like yours truly, by her own sister in a firefight. Long, sad story later, Beck wasn't as salvageable as I was, which is, I guess, the most eloquent way of putting it. So, after a few weeks of Dr. Cross rebuilding her and, as I just found out a few days ago, using half of his stockpile of Z-90 on her, she made it out with a human brain and spinal column.

I had taken severe, sarcastic jabs at Beck basically being a complete robot when I found out that she'd played the part of Chloe just to get in my head, which wasn't the smartest move considering how unstable she was then.

Judging from the conversation I was able to witness between she and Ritu, not much had changed in the last few years.

"Ritu," I heard Beck say conversationally while I side-stepped to get a good look at the screen, "I must say you're looking ever so much paler than you did the last time we spoke."

I was standing right behind her, looking over her shoulder at Beck. Being in a comatose state for two and a half years must've done wonders for me because Beck looked a little more weathered than she had three years ago. I couldn't quite place anything drastically different until I saw that her long black tresses were gone, and she was rocking a buzz-cut.

"Dr. Cross is moving his plan forward much more quickly than I originally projected," Ritu told her, seeming unscathed by Beck's rudeness. "His test subject did extremely well in his first trial testing today, so he isn't going to be sticking around for long."

Test subject. Nothing like a good slap of reality every once in a while, I guess. Then my mouth dropped open when Beck asked, "Who is this test subject you keep going on about that's taking up all of Cross's time?"

I thought I'd missed something. Surely if Ritu was a planted Rebel spy, then she would've told Beck that Jericho Johnson still lived, right?

"I don't know who he is," Ritu told her. "But if he

continues to strengthen over the next week, Cross said that he might have to take him to Anchorage when he leaves."

Beck let out an aggravated sigh. "I'm dying, Ritu. Forgive me if I seem disinterested in Dr. Cross's travel plans. I contacted you so you could find out what's wrong with me and not, in fact, to tell me where the good doctor plans on—"

"He won't be back for a long time if he leaves again," Ritu said, interrupting her. "More so if he brings his new weapon with him."

Beck scoffed before going into a fit of coughs, but since I wasn't sure if she even had lungs, I was a little confused at the horrid sounds she made during the fit. When she'd finally regained her composure somewhat, she said, "So he's a weapon now?"

"I know what Cross is planning on using him for," Ritu said. "Weapon is the only plausible definition."

"Look, I don't know or care what Cross plans on doing with his new pet. All I care about now is not dying, and I need Cross for that. Not his latest project," Beck shot at her, leaning forward menacingly. "If I don't have him by the weekend, I'm coming right through the front door, and you're going to be the first white-coated coward I'm paying a visit to." Her voice rose during the threat and her glaring face vanished.

"Goodbye to you, too," Ritu muttered to herself before standing, half of her body phasing through me because I'd been standing close to the heated exchange. Ritu sighed, placing her hands on the now darkened glass desk and leaning forward, looking weary.

Then her holotab lit up.

"Did she believe you?" I heard Cross ask.

Nodding slightly, Ritu answered, "Yes."

"Good. Letting Beck make the first idiotic move is essential," he said. "All I need is for her to come here then Jericho will do the rest."

I just stood there, listening, waiting.

And seething.

"When will you activate him?" Ritu asked.

"After his training. If his brain hasn't recorded any of his abilities, then I won't be able to manually access them once he's under my control."

"Jericho doesn't suspect me," she told him. "As far as he's concerned, he and I are secretly in league against you."

"Can you keep up that ruse for at least another week?"

What the Helheim was wrong with these people? I mean, I knew they were evil a few seconds into their little chat, but the worst part was that they were talking about it like they were discussing picking up a cake for a lowkey office party. Calm, casual, friendly talk that included, but was not limited to, betrayal, murder, and mind control.

Which reminded me that I had a new, super-powerful body slumbering a few floors below me that I'd been just waiting for the chance to try out again.

"And I thought that you were educated," I said, even though I knew Ritu couldn't hear me. Then I closed my eyes and was back in my body again.

It was time to give Cross and his horde of scientists a test that they would never forget.

The first thing I did was put on my boots and hooded long coat, because I had a feeling that I was about to need warm clothes real soon. I'd just pulled on my last boot when I heard a knock on the door.

"Who is it?" I asked in a sing-song voice after I'd stopped in front of the door.

"Ritu."

I opened the door and smiled cheerfully at her. "Well, look who's back. Come on in, pal."

She gave me a semi-puzzled look while she walked past me. "You were awake?"

"I was indeed," I told her, closing the door. "I tried to sleep but the sound of your lying a few floors up was just too much."

Ritu froze before she entered the large living room, her

back to me. When she didn't say anything, I asked, "Say, *friend*, if a guy wanted to bust out of here—hypothetically, of course—how would he do it?"

Turning, Ritu looked at me with the classic "Who, me?" look.

To which I responded with a menacing "Oh, yes. You, dearest," smirk.

"Jericho—"

"Just don't," I said, and she backed away when she saw me walking toward her. "Here I thought that I had a magical confidant who was going to help me get my revenge. But you know what I realized after hearing your little two-way discussion upstairs?"

Ritu bumped against the large window, and I put my hands on the thick glass, my arms on either side of her. "I can do revenge just fine by myself."

Then I pulled back my right fist and smashed it into the window with all my strength, creating a large hole.

Ritu screamed and covered her head as large gusts of wind blew snow and shattered glass everywhere. Grabbing the front of her shirt and lab coat, I lifted her, dangling her out into the storm.

"Tell me how to get out. Now!" I shook her and she screamed again, kicking her feet wildly. Growling, I grabbed a piece of metal that was jutting out from my punch and leaned out further. "Tell me or you're dead," I roared over the gusts of wind.

"You need the passcodes for third floor," she shrieked, going limp as she closed her eyes against the freezing ice pelting her face unmercifully.

"Give them to me."

"I can't from here."

"Too bad," I loosened my fingers, and she grabbed at my forearm quickly.

"Wait! I can give them to you," Ritu screamed and began shuddering from what would have been sobs, only her tears froze instantly to her face. She held out her right arm, and her holotab appeared in the snow flurries. She hit a few icons, and my holotab lit up on my arm.

"Just wave your arm over … over the door … pad …" Ritu muttered, her eyes beginning to close.

"Thanks," I said, swinging back into my blustering suite. I headed for my room, dragging Ritu behind me, and not because I couldn't have carried her, but simply because I just didn't care about her getting a few scrapes. After I tossed her on the bed, I wrapped the heavy blankets around her.

"Peace out, Ritu," I told the unconscious woman. "I'll see you around."

Then I exited the room and headed for the elevator.

It was time to check out.

CHAPTER 10

I was about halfway down when I realized that I should've just jumped out of the hole I'd made in the window. I didn't know if I would've survived the fall but my half-cocked plan I was readily formulating might not pan out the way I wanted it to.

My short, peaceful elevator ride lasted only around ten floors before an alarm began blaring, letting everyone inside the enormous building know that I was escaping.

The third floor wasn't supposed to be an easy way out, I was thinking, but I just couldn't feel scared or even the least bit apprehensive about the coming onslaught.

Actually, I felt downright excited about it.

I began drumming my gloved fingers on my sides as I watched the floors tick down during my descent. Then I felt an odd twinge in my palms while I was drumming away. Frowning, I glanced at my gloves, flexing them into fists a few times and feeling a subtle vibration rush through my hands and slither up my arms and into my brain.

I knew what I could do. I hadn't tried it or even thought about it, but right then, without the least bit of practice or shocking revelations, I knew what I could do with my new hands.

I was still smiling when the elevator dinged on the third floor and the doors slowly opened. I stepped out into a shock-white hallway, which seemed to be filled with armored guards who also seemed to be pointing guns at me.

The hall was wide, as far as halls go, and the ten guards blocking my way were all taking a stance on the far side in front of the only door in sight.

I wasn't exactly sure how this place was set up, and I was beginning to think that Ritu had sent me on a wild goose chase just to get me captured.

"Evening, guys," I called to them as I started slowly walking toward the entourage of masked guards. No battle-armor. Good.

"Stand down," one of the guards shouted at me as I advanced toward them at a calm pace.

"Can't, bud," I told him, slipping my hands into my coat pockets. "I've kind of got somewhere I need to be right about now, so I'd really appreciate it if you and your group would kindly—" then I ran into a shimmering force field, staggering me a little from the small shock it administered upon contact.

"Really?" I said in frustration.

"Jericho, come in," I heard Ritu buzz in my head.

"Go for Jericho," I said, pacing in front of the light blue haze of a shield. "Please tell me you didn't lie to me."

"That's the only way to get outside. Taking the elevator to the bottom floor leads into the basement. You'll need the passcodes for all three to get out the door being blocked by guards. I gave them all to you, but now you'll need to get past the decontamination field."

"No kidding," I said dryly.

"That hall is strictly designed for cleansing anyone who has spent more than twelve hours outside," she said, and I heard key clicks. "You can deactivate it from the other side of the wall if you—"

Before she finished, I punched through the wall panel and ripped hard, pulling it free and exposing the gizmo powering the field. "You're slow," I said. "Now what? Just destroy this thing?"

"You could, but I would suggest using the field's energy

for yourself. I think you already know how to do that."

I glanced at the blue shield. She was right. I did know what I could do. I'm sorry if I never explain all the mental pictures and feelings that go along with what was happening to my body most of the time, but I'll explain it all later, I promise.

Removing my black gloves, I pocketed them and stepped close enough to the shield to put my palms onto it. I ground my boots on the floor to get a better footing, when the blue haze tried to repel me backwards. Gritting my teeth, I pushed hard, and suddenly all the struggle vanished and my right hand went through the shield.

The guards shuffled uneasily and cocked their assault rifles as they watched me look at my hand on the other side. I walked through the force field and saw that Ritu was right. There was another force field about ten feet away. Turning back, I placed my left hand back on the shield, took a deep breath, and then pulled my hand into a fist and the blue force field shuddered once before slowly being sucked into it.

I could feel it coming in, filling up my hand and overflowing into my forearm as the current climbed up my arm. I wasn't being shocked, burned, or hurt. The only feeling associated with charging up was, well, that I felt like I was being charged up.

After all the shield had vanished into my fist, I opened my hand and saw a faint blue light flicker out in my palm. "Sweet," I muttered to myself before turning back to the final shield. I didn't even touch this one. All I did was raise my right hand, and it just came into it, looking awesome as it went into my palm.

The same charged feeling happened, and whilst I was in Thor mode, Ritu buzzed in. "Don't get too much, Jericho."

"Why not?" I asked, but then I felt what she was talking about. Pure energy began seeping from my frame because I couldn't hold it all. By the time I finished pulling in the second force field, my arms were wreathed in lightning, crackling loudly, and I winced against the blue bolts. Not from pain. Just, you know, not being used to having visible electricity all over me.

Then the guard who had told me to stand down tried again, shouting at me and waving his gun a little.

"They've been told to take you alive," Ritu informed me.

"They aren't allowed to kill me?"

"No."

I flicked my eyes from my hands to the band of poor sods pointing guns at me.

"Sorry, guys," I told them, holding my arms up and pointing two finger-guns at them. "Nothing personal."

Then I fired.

The bolts that escaped my hands pushed me back several feet as the blue streaks hit the screaming troops. The stuff went everywhere, too, clawing up the walls and ceiling as the guards were blown in all directions. When the smoke cleared and the crackles finally died down, the last feeling I had was a slight tingling in my palms.

"What was that?" I asked as I stepped over the quivering guards.

"That was something Cross has been wanting to see for a long time."

"And that was?"

"The birth of a new species."

"Sounds good," I said, kicking the white door off its hinges. "Now, if you'll excuse me, I have a few more butts to kick before I can get out of here."

I entered the doorway and headed down the only flight of stairs, my boots making resounding echoes off the concrete walls. "You never told me whose side you're on," I said.

"You didn't ask before hanging me out of a window into a blizzard."

I shrugged as I continued down. "I've decided my new philosophy is to shoot first and search the corpse for chocolate chip cookies afterward. Might live longer doing that."

"Take the door on your right at the bottom of the stairs," Ritu said, ignoring my new philosophy. "It will lead to a short hallway and then to the lobby." She hesitated before saying, "There will be more guards, but there is also a possibility of several civilians."

"Great," I said, opening the door at the bottom of the stairs. "I could always use a few body-shields." When she didn't respond, I said, "I'm kidding, Ritu."

"You should be able to do the same thing you did to the decontamination shields to virtually anything else electrical in the lobby. Use that to your advantage," she said, and I heard more keyboard clicks. "These guards know you're coming and might not be as vigilant with orders now that they see how dangerous you are."

"I'm not bullet-proof, Ritu," I said, stopping in front of the door leading into the lobby. "I'm open to suggestions."

"If you can get a good feel of your energy level, you could possibly create a makeshift shield of your own."

"So just wing it."

"Pretty much."

I sighed, pushing open the door and entering the lobby. I saw a dozen guards waiting on me.

"Come on, guys," I said as they advanced toward me with their weapons cocked and ready. "I don't have to hurt—"

I stopped, wondering why I didn't have to hurt them. I mean, they were in my way, were they not? They were trying to keep me here as Cross's slave, right?

"Yeah," I said, starting my hands back up. "Never mind."

Then the lobby was filled with lightning.

CHAPTER 11

Blinding snow was everywhere as I tromped down the covered sidewalk through the mega blizzard that had gripped the city. It got deeper by the minute, and I was beginning to think that checking out of science camp during a snowstorm wasn't the best idea I'd ever had.

"Nice, JJ," I said to myself. "Great plan."

I guess it wasn't too bad considering I wasn't cold at all due to my suit, but the snow was becoming bothersome as I trudged through it. The other big problem was that I hadn't really thought about anything past escaping, so I wasn't sure where to go or who to go to.

Well, I suppose that wasn't exactly true. I knew who I wanted to go to. Considering the Rebels had been able to remain hidden from three different war factions for years on end, I was guessing that I couldn't just knock on a door and find them. I did, however, remember where I had surfaced three years ago, the day we had raided Klaus's facility.

It was a bit hazy, but, after almost an hour of snow travel, I was somehow able to remember enough destroyed buildings and ruptured landmarks to make it back to the general area. The location that I remembered and had rushed to had been a park years ago. The remains of a merry-go-round was what I remembered most, but since the snow was now waist deep, I was betting that finding the familiar item was out of the question.

Then I bumped into something buried in the snow right in front of me. I glanced around but still couldn't discern any kind of landmark to help me. The buildings were all considerably far away, so I was hoping that maybe I'd miraculously bumped into the merry-go-round.

I dipped my gloved hands into the soft snow, trying to touch what I'd bumped into, and in a few seconds, I found it, grabbing it with my right hand. It felt like some kind of metal pipe through my gloves, at any rate, and I sighed with relief at being lucky enough to stumble across just the thing I'd been searching for.

Then the pipe in my hands moved.

Shouting, I let go of whatever I'd grabbed and fell back into the snow, sweeping my arms and paddling through the whiteness, trying to get as much space between me and anything moving beneath the snow.

The area in front of me shuddered and snow blasted everywhere as the thing I had awoken leaped from the snow and soared through the air, landing about ten feet to my left.

"Oh, you've got to be kidding me!" I shouted in frustration into the wind, continuing my back-peddling.

It was an enormous spider.

For starters, it looked like a tarantula with shock-white hair. Not the best enemy to face off against in the middle of a blizzard.

Chloe had told me about ice-spiders before, stating that during the winter most of them stayed below ground in the abandoned tunnels riddling the city. She also told me that a baby ice-spider was almost four feet across, which didn't sound like a baby to me.

Apparently, the one I had walked into was somewhat of an adolescent because he wasn't the mammoth ten feet across that Chloe had said was the size of a full grown one, but it was bigger than four feet by a long shot.

"What're you doing up here?" I asked, sidestepping slowly as the ice-spider focused on me and began sidestepping too while keeping its eyes on me. It hissed suddenly and lashed out at me with one of its front legs, pounding snow into the air.

I pulled what little juice I had left into my hands and took aim, only to see that my target had vanished.

Or had it?

Squinting against the heavy snow, I tried to detect the white spider. After I'd searched for almost thirty seconds, I frowned, turning off my hands and guessing that maybe I'd scared it off or something.

I resumed sloshing through the snow that was getting deeper and began heading for a nearby building. My idea was that I could at least get inside and away from all the snow so I could get my bearings, since my magical landmark merry-go-round hadn't decided to show up for the second date.

I was almost to the crumbling building when the ice-spider I thought I'd scared off decided to try its hand at killing me.

All eight of them, actually.

When I heard the hiss, I swung around to face it, but it wasn't there. To say that I was impressed by the ice-spider's camouflage would be a gross understatement. I mean, that thing could blend in like a freaking ninja.

It wasn't until it latched onto my left leg with its enormous fangs from somewhere under the surface of the snow that I realized it had probably been there the whole time.

Actually, I was a little relieved to discover that my eyesight wasn't as bad as I was beginning to think, a notion that I was too busy to dwell on since I was being dragged through the snow by a man-eating giant spider.

After several obscenities being cut short by mouthfuls of snow, my arachnid captor pulled me into the building that I had been heading for.

"Great minds kill alike," I shouted at the thing as soon as we'd cleared the snow, and I punched it right between its eight eyes. The ice-spider made a sort of yelp/whine, dropping my leg and jumping away. We were in a poorly lighted area that looked like it used to be a sort of gift shop where someone had made a home, which burned and later became a school house, then a library, then a slaughterhouse, before finally becoming the rundown shop I was facing the ice-spider in.

Hmm. That has a nice ring to it.

I thought so then, too, and quickly had a vision of one day opening a ye old tavern on Svalbard and calling it the Ice-Spider Inn.

While the spider continued making a ridiculous noise and shaking its head slightly from my punch, I looked at my leg, grimacing because I just knew I was bleeding to death.

Only there wasn't a drop of blood. Oh, right. Robot leg.

"Metal doesn't taste good, does it—"

Then the thing tackled, and I landed on my back with it on top of me. It instantly went for my head with those enormous, awful fangs.

Here's a tip:

Normally, when two humans are fighting and one of them happens to be positively feral at best and tries to tear the other man's throat out with his teeth (yes, I've actually had that almost happen to me before), the best retaliation the almost-bitten can do against the biter is to grab the crazy man's neck and hope he's strong enough to keep him at bay.

Trying to incorporate this maneuver into fighting off a huge spider doesn't work that well, so don't try it the next time you're tackled by an ice spider.

Since it didn't have a neck or shoulders for me to get a good hold on, I grabbed the only other thing I could think of. The huge fangs I was just expounding about.

"Not. The. Face," I growled between clenched teeth. Then I felt it coming. It began like it always did, with a small hum in my palms. Although it was hard to tell because I was also trying to, you know, not get my handsome face crunched off by a spider.

"Time's up," I told the monster, pulling my hands together and switching both fangs to my left hand while slowly pushing the spider mouth up to expose the—

Huh. I guess spiders do sort of have a neck because that's what I punched through with a fistful of lightning.

My first feeling was of how awesome I felt for slaying a giant man-eating spider in real life, just like I'd been doing in role-playing games since I was nine.

The second feeling was the black blood running all over me, and then I screamed like a little girl and shoved the carcass off, struggling to my feet and attempting to wipe at the blood.

"Ew, ew, ew. Bleh. Gross," I muttered. My right arm and shoulder were really the nasty parts. The rest of my body lucked out on that particular ice-spider kill. "Totally just leveled up on that one."

I poked around the burnt-out building for a long time, going through all the floors thoroughly and scavenging, mainly because, you know, that's what you're supposed to do in a post-apocalyptic world. Most of the rooms still had lots of stuff in them, and I took my time sifting through it all because the snow was probably getting close to twenty feet deep. I was hoping that, whenever it stopped, I'd be able to walk on top of the packed snow and continue searching for the Rebels.

Only they were most likely all snug by a fire underground drinking hot cocoa and eating cinnamon rolls and therefore weren't going to be just walking the snowy streets for kicks.

Once I'd gone through all twelve floors of the rundown apartment building, I sighed, sitting on an overturned bed on the top floor. I'm not sure how long I sat there feeling sorry for myself before I realized that I was just sitting there feeling sorry for myself.

"What the Helheim, JJ?" I asked myself, standing quickly.

Underground. That's where I needed to get. I couldn't have been far from the park, and even if I couldn't find an entrance, then I was about to make one.

And with that thought in my mind, I exited the room

and headed back down the stairwell. I was probably on the fourth floor before I heard the troop of soldiers shouting orders to search the building and find me.

Geez, but I just couldn't catch a break.

CHAPTER 12

"He can't be far!" I heard an official-sounding woman yell at her cohorts. The only problem was that her voice sounded like it was coming through a radio.

Or, since I'd been in the future long enough to know, it was probably a chick rocking mechanized battle-armor. When I heard them start to move out, I confirmed that hypothesis, due to the sounds of very heavy footsteps coupled with whining gears and gyros clicking and whirring.

I glanced toward the nearest window of the fourth floor, only to see the last sliver of dim light be put out by the heavy snow. "Ah, man," I fast-walked down the hall to the other side of the floor and saw that the opposite window wasn't covered yet. I tried to just open it at first because I figured maybe, just maybe, that wouldn't make a lot of noise. But then I heard someone shout, "All units move to the fourth floor and engage target."

I growled in frustration and elbowed the window out before taking a step back and diving through it. Diving out of the fourth-story window normally won't get you the best escape of the year award because most people wouldn't be alive to claim it. Unless there's a mammoth freak blizzard outside and you fall literally two feet and land into soft snow.

I was relieved that the snow was compacted enough to not make struggling through it impossible, which wouldn't have been a problem, only I was trying to get away from killer robot men. I had gone about fifteen feet in the cold whiteness before I realized that this wasn't going to work.

I got to a crouching position, turned back to the building, pushed hard into the snow with my legs, leaped onto the side of the apartment building, and began scaling the side quickly. I heard some radio chatter, but it was too far away for me to understand what was said. I made it to the top easily, only to find that the roof was covered with snow (duh), and I glanced left and right as I held onto a shattered windowpane, looking for a way out of my current predicament.

Then I heard a shout and glanced down to see a helmet peering up at me from the fifth-floor window. "I see him!" he shouted, pulling his head back in.

Then everything slowed down, and I just knew what was happening. The snow flurries flew by slowly in my line of vision, and I knew that the guy who had spotted me was checking his rounds and in the process of leaning back out the window to pop off a shot at me.

I can't explain it. All I can say is what I've been saying.

I just knew.

The best part about just knowing what was happening and/or about to happen was that my reactions were almost automatic, and I'd be sailing into action and not know it until I was halfway there.

In this case, I didn't know, until after it was done, that I had released the wall and spun into a perfect freefall dive next to the building, my arms outstretched.

Just as the man in the suit dipped half of his body out the window to take his shot, I was there, my right arm hitting his chest and pulling him out of the window into the snow. We went deep into the whiteness when we landed, causing a crater, the walls of which collapsed onto us, and we were soon buried. I still had a good hold on the guy in the suit, who was by that time radioing his buddies for help, and I grabbed his throat as my hands began humming softly. I felt power from the suit flowing into my arm.

"He's shutting down my—" were the last words he was able to send before his suit was powerless.

The snow was everywhere now, and I could barely move or breathe when I let out my new charge, the blue-white blast issuing from my hands and instantly melting any snow within a good twenty-foot radius. Then I was falling before landing into the water I'd just made—which began freezing as I kicked under the semi-warm surface toward the first-floor window of the apartment building. It was almost all frozen by the time I made it, punching through the dingy window and falling into it. The last part to exit was my foot, and it got stuck in the now-solid wall of ice.

"What the—what?" I barked, turning my right hand toward my leg and letting off just enough juice to free my foot before landing in a wet heap on the ragged floor.

"I can't believe that worked," I murmured to myself as I lay there for a second before rolling onto my knees and climbing to my feet. I could feel my jumpsuit and long coat fighting off the frost that was trying to build up as I began sloshing along the hallway. Somehow, after what I'd just done, fighting the remaining guards on foot just didn't seem that bad anymore.

I heard heavy footsteps a floor above me, so I stopped, waiting for them to come down the stairs, where I had my right hand aimed at already.

Then one of them tore through the ceiling and landed behind me, planting a good kick to my back and sending me skidding almost down the hallway until I connected with the far wall below the window and next to the stairs.

Shaking my head, I got to my hands and knees.

"Target is down," I heard my surprise attacker say. "All units proceed to the first floor to…" his voice trailed off when he saw me climb to my feet and spit blood onto the icy floor.

Now I was just mad.

"All units—" he tried to say before I jumped the entire gap between us and planted my boots into his chest piece, knocking him off his feet and onto on his back, with me crouched on his dented armor.

He swung at me with his right arm, and I caught it easily, sending all the volts I had into his hand. After he stopped jerking, I stood and turned back to the troops coming down the stairs.

"Come on!" I shouted at them, opening my hands at my sides, palms turned slightly toward the oncoming troops and letting the visible, bluish-white sparks dance and lick all over my hands, the streaks climbing up my wrists on my coat sleeves.

There were three of them, and they had all stopped before attacking, watching me through their red-eyed masks, the same red veins pulsing up and down the black armor of their suits and meeting at the chest piece emblazoned with the scythe and hammer emblem. Their suits were a lot bigger than the Rogues I'd encountered my first time coming to the future.

"You're Rogues," I told them, taking a step forward. "Shouldn't you guys be raiding the Fascists or Bears and leaving random citizens to their own devices?"

"You just escaped from Dr. Cross's facility, didn't you?" one in the middle asked, taking me off guard because I didn't think these guys were exactly a local dispatch, and also because the speaker was a girl.

"Depends on who's asking."

The woman in the suit closed the gap between us, holding up the hands of her suit to show me she wasn't going to try anything. "We were scanning local line taps and overheard Cross sending out soldiers to retrieve someone who had escaped." She stopped about five feet in front of me, her suit making me over a foot shorter as I stared up at her and she down at me. "We figured anything worth risking lives in a category seven blizzard might be worth acquiring for ourselves."

I've described talking to someone who was in battle-armor before as it's not the best way to become acquainted, due to the fact that the person's voice sounds a little deeper and you also can't see their face. I was intrigued by her accent, though, which was certainly the thickest Australian I'd heard since Crocodile Dundee.

"I'm not acquirable at the moment, sweetheart," I told her coldly. "I'm just trying to get underground."

Turning her helmeted head slightly, she said, "You must be looking for Rebels. If you were searching for Rogues, then I'd say today is your lucky day."

"I don't want any trouble," I said.

"Tell that to your hands, mate," she said, pointing an armored finger at the hands in question.

Shutting them off, I felt the juice come back inside and stop somewhere in my chest.

"You dead, Jax?" the Rogue woman asked the person I was standing on.

"No," we heard a groan, and the suit powered back up, the lights flickering as he slowly got to his feet.

"Good." Then she asked, "What's your name, mate?"

"Jericho," I told her. "Jericho Johnson."

"Lovely name you've got there, mate," she said, hitting a button on the side of her helmet and raising the mask up, exposing her pale skin, red curls, and, no joke, deep red eyes to me.

"Name's Red," she told me, extending her suited hand. "And after seeing what you just did to some of my best men with those hands of yours, allow me to say that the pleasure is most certainly, and always will be, mine."

CHAPTER 13

Piper

December 25th, 2345, Flagstaff, AZ

"I'm not sure why Beck is making me do this," Piper started, before immediately pausing the recording.

It had been too long, in her opinion, to try and look back into the past and attempt to make sense of it. But since it was most likely because of Beck that Piper was even still alive to talk right then, she supposed she should oblige her.

Just this once.

Hitting the record button on her tab, she resumed, "My name is Piper and I'm—or at least I was—a Viking of Svalbard. I had seen nineteen winters when I left my home with Jericho Johnson to aid him in the quest to save his world. They tell me that I'm twenty-two now, although at times I feel ancient, and that I'm barely hanging on to my sanity in this place that the old gods seem to have forgotten."

She'd been stranded here in this frozen wasteland of the future for almost three years, swept away from everything normal in her life, and dropped into what seemed to be the remains of a war-torn world covered in snow and ice.

This day, the one Jericho had told her about a lifetime ago on a fishing trip, meant nothing to Piper or her kinsmen. She remembered him telling her that people from his time exchanged gifts and shared in food, drink, and song to celebrate the thing he called Christmas.

She hadn't listened too intently, because on that day

her thoughts kept being thrown into the wind whenever she considered his face and watched his wonderful mouth move as he spoke.

Piper sighed but didn't stop the recording. "I took him for granted then. Now he's gone."

She would've died a thousand deaths in the fires of Helheim to see him again. To hold his hand, touch his face, or kiss his lips. All the moments she was with him now seemed distant to her, and the notion of losing Jericho in her thoughts had been weighing on her a lot recently.

Sometimes she'd try to recall certain features about him only to discover, to her horror, that she couldn't. Somehow the idea of that, at times, felt worse than the day she actually lost him.

It was this place. It had to be. Where she came from, brave warriors like Jericho were honored after dying in battle and talked about for years to come.

Here no one talked about death or even contemplated it because death was everywhere. There was no laughter here, no joy, no mead halls bustling with life and tales of brave men and fallen heroes.

But here? Here there was nothing but frozen landscape and frozen hearts barely beating inside what was left of humanity. None of the many wars going on even seemed to make sense to Piper. Most wars were fought with the idea of finally obtaining peace and joy afterward—something worth fighting for.

War, here, was a different demon altogether. It seemed that the people of this time lived just to fight and fought just to live.

It seemed a very harsh and unforgiving cycle to her, and it didn't take a month of being there before she too became a slave to this snow-covered place, fighting to survive without any ray of hope in sight.

"I'll be back in a jiff, Pipe," Jericho had told her years ago, kissing her forehead and squeezing her shoulders. Then he turned to Beck and said, "Take care of her."

"It would be my pleasure—considering she seems to be the only person with any sense out here," Beck told him.

They had taken out most of Klaus's men with the chopper beforehand, and Beck and Piper were supposed to guard the entrance while Jericho and Chloe went into the tall building Klaus had escaped into.

"I want to go with you," Piper had insisted.

"And I want you to stay," he said, pulling her into a hug before releasing her and turning on his heel, the long coat he was wearing whirling around him when he did so. "Come on, Chloe. The world ain't saving itself."

It wasn't until after she watched the enormous building explode and collapse, almost burying Beck, her squad, and Piper in the rubble, that she realized his last hug had felt different than all his others. "No!" she'd screamed, crumbling to her knees, her hands reaching for the black smoke billowing into the white sky.

"We have to move," Beck's voice crackled in her ear, but she didn't hear her as she made a mad dash toward the falling building.

"Jericho!"

Beck, who, as she has told Piper on several occasions, wasn't your average girl, ran and tried to grab her. "Piper, he's gone. We have to get out of here."

Piper could barely hear her over the sound of metal on metal when the iron foundation shattered in front of them. Then she felt Beck grab her around the waist and sling her over her shoulder as she leaped and dashed through the icy streets to get them clear of the aftershock.

The next thing she knew, they were inside an abandoned building on the second floor, and Piper could still make out the dust kicking up into the air through the shattered window.

"Report," Beck said, touching her earpiece as she dropped Piper on the floor in a heap. "Robin? Gauge?" she tried. After no one answered her, she sighed, glancing out of the window toward the large fire engulfing the remains of the building Jericho had been in. "Looks like we're all that's left, pal."

Piper sobbed, lurching forward and trying to get to her feet. "Don't cry, Piper," Beck said, pulling her face into her stomach to try and shield it from the elements. "Your tears will freeze, and your face will get frostbite."

It was true. She could already feel the skin underneath her eyes burning.

But there was no stopping the crying then. Cursing, Beck removed her long coat and wrapped it completely around her head, and Piper felt her lift her shaking frame onto her shoulders again.

"Hang tight, Pipe. We'll be underground in a minute," Beck told her, and then she jumped out of the window, landing hard into a pile of snow built up at the door of the building.

Then she took Piper back to the Rebel base.

Days later, after she'd run out of tears, she knew then that he'd been saying goodbye with his final hug. Somehow, he must have known the great, invincible Jericho Johnson had finally reached the end of his journey.

Piper was thankful at first that he had not let her come, so that she could live, but her thankfulness toward living grew weaker each day.

Piper may still be breathing—but she truly died that day and knew nothing short of the gods sending Jericho back to her would ever make her truly feel alive. This wasn't a comforting thought, because she'd abandoned all prayers to the Norse gods over a year ago, after deciding that if they hadn't helped her yet, then they probably weren't about to start.

Not a word escaped her lips for almost a month after Jericho's death, and she ended up in the Rebel med-bay toward the end of it. Piper most likely would have died in there had not Beck stopped by for a talk one day.

"What's your deal, woman?" Beck asked her, leaning

against the bed she was in and looking her up and down. "I see all your limbs are still attached. So, why're you in bed?"

"Leave."

That was the first word she'd spoken in over a month.

"I'm not going to let a perfectly capable warrior die in bed from a broken heart," Beck had said. "Death will come to us all, Piper, but you have a lot more to do before you die."

"Such as?" Piper asked coldly.

"Jericho and my sister both died trying to save the world. I personally don't care about this world, so I didn't care about their mission and I still don't. But since they were, in a roundabout way, mind you, killed by the Reds—I got enough of those guys on my hands to last us both a lifetime, if you want to exact a little revenge by killing a few."

Beck watched her once she'd finished talking, and Piper thought about her offer. After a few minutes she sat up. "You people fight different than I."

"Weapons change, people change, goals change, but war," she shook her head slightly, "war never changes. I only had one mission with you, and that was enough to show me that you could take anything thrown, shot, or kicked at you, chew it up and spit it back out."

Piper swung her feet off the bed and glanced around the room so she didn't have to look at her. "I don't want to fight anyone. Sorry."

Beck was silent for a minute. Then, "Piper, I hate to bring up everything you might find painful, but you're stuck here and, since I'm about to throw you out of my med-bay because, you know, I need it for people who have actually lost a limb or two, I'm going to lay out your options: You can either commit suicide or actually use all those awesome battle-smarts I know you have in your brain, stay alive, and, who knows, maybe even take out a few pesky Reds along the way."

Piper told her to leave that day and the day after that when she tried yet again to get her to join her war. She ended up staying in her quarters most of the time, remembering the kiss she'd shared with Jericho in the same room.

Most days she ended up pacing the small room, trying not to think about Jericho's death, and being stuck in the frozen Helheim of a place.

Then everything changed.

"Piper, is it?" she heard a man's voice say one day, and she gave a start, whirling around to see who was at her door.

"Who are you?" she asked curtly to the black-haired man entering her quarters.

"Archimedes," he said. "Everyone calls me Arc due to Archimedes being a mouthful, though," he added with a quick smile.

He spoke like Jericho, his accent not at all thick like everyone else at the Rebel base. "What is it you want, Archimedes?"

"Please, ma'am, call me Arc," he said again, extending a hand to her, which she shook quickly before dropping it. Gods, his hands were cold. "I'm a traveler of sorts. I don't come this way often except to drop in on Beck from time to time and see how she's doing. Since she knows that I spend most of my days combing what's left of America looking for knowledge and remains of the past, Beck told me that I'd get a charge out of meeting you."

"She told you everything?" Piper asked.

Nodding, his smile widened. "I've read that your people hunted polar bears. Were you any good?"

She looked at him, not really knowing what to say to that. He was maybe a few years older than Jericho had been, his face unshaven, and his black hair reaching his shoulders. He seemed kind enough.

"I killed everything I set out to."

Laughing, he said, "I'm sure you did. Look, the only polar bears left are up around the Yukon—which isn't where they were years ago—and they're a lot bigger now. But has Beck at least taken you ice-spider hunting yet?"

The way he looked at her with hopeful eyes, hanging

on her every answer to his many questions, was strange, and Piper realized that Beck couldn't have told him everything. If she had, maybe this Arc would have left her alone.

"Listen, Archimedes—"

"Arc," he corrected.

"Fine. Listen, Arc, I'm not really up to entertaining you with stories about my past hunts. It was a pleasure," she turned away then, hoping he'd take the hint and leave.

"I've lost someone, too," Arc said suddenly, his voice quiet, and she froze.

"It never gets better," he said. "You can be sorry as long as you want and try to think what you could've done differently, but I've found the best way to cope is to do something you're good at. Since I'm only good at digging through ruined cities, that's what I do and have been doing for the last eight years."

Piper kept her eyes on the wall, her arms crossed tight. "And it worked? You forgot about the person you loved?"

Arc was silent for a few seconds before admitting, "No. You'll never forget. But I promise you'll be able to do something with the rest of your life, should you choose."

After mulling the idea over in her head, she made a decision. "I'll try it."

"Good," Arc said, and Piper could positively hear the smile on his face. "Now, what are you good at, Piper?"

She turned, took one last look at her room, then walked past him to the door.

"Killing things."

That same day, Arc took her topside for her first ice-spider hunt, which turned out to be quite a challenge—something she needed then. The weapons of the future were barbaric to her, and after a month of fumbling with rifles and pistols in spider hunts and Rebel raids alongside Beck, Arc decided Piper needed weapons she was more comfortable with.

"You two are insane," Beck said, leaning against a concrete pillar while she watched Arc and Piper work the makeshift forge they had thrown together in one of the work areas below the base. "A guy with a gun beats half a chick with a sword any day of the week."

"Says the liar," Piper said, this being something Jericho had said a lot and she'd adopted. Pulling the glowing sword out of the hot coals, she laid the blade on an iron desk and commenced to pounding on it with a hammer.

"It's not going to be your average sword, Beck," Arc tried to explain to the frowning woman. "The blade is made from the armor of a Raptor-6 I scrapped—"

"So, she'll die in style. What a consolation. Thanks, Arc, I feel ever so much better now."

"Lay off," he said with a smile. "Once we're done, it'll cut through any battle-armor out there, so I'd show some respect."

Beck snorted at that. "She still has to get close enough to use it—something that not a lot of assault-rifle-toting people are keen on."

Piper smiled to herself and kept pounding, stopping after a few swings to retie her blonde hair that had managed to work itself out of the braid she'd put in it and obstruct her line of sight.

"I'm way ahead of you," Arc told her, crossing the large basement to the only other table in the spacious room that was covered with a black tarp. Beck followed him, and when she was standing beside him, looking unimpressed, he pulled the tarp off, revealing the armor beneath it.

Beck was suddenly impressed.

"Where did you find this in such amazing condition?" she asked, getting on her knees immediately for a closer inspection of the snow-white battle-armor. "The Ghost armor hasn't been manufactured in close to a hundred years."

Shrugging, Arc said, "Found it in D.C. last year."

"Don't let his modesty fool you. He's crazy about that thing," Piper said, sliding the red blade into the barrel of oil on the left with a resounding hiss and leaning away from the tall flame.

"Understandable," Beck said. "Has he even told you what this thing can do?"

Piper shook her head while pulling the hot sword out of the oil and placing it on the iron table. "Anyone got a good whetstone?"

Beck stopped ogling the white battle-armor long enough to look at her like she'd just asked if she were a girl. "Really? A whet—oh, for the love of God," she stood. "I'll help, but don't think this is my stamp of approval, because sharpening your toothpick isn't."

"You do have a whetstone, then?" she asked again.

"Oh, Piper," Beck sighed when she picked up the red broadsword and turned it over in her hands, the extremely hot steel not bothering her synthetic hands. "You're so cute with your medieval talk." She headed for the stairs. "You kids behave while momma's gone."

When Piper pressed Arc about how she was going to sharpen her new sword, he explained that Beck would most likely use the laser-etch system that sharpens the blades on street mechs used to cut away ice. "She'll have to raise the settings some, but I'm sure she'll do a good job. She doesn't want you to die, obviously," he joked.

Winter had set in a few weeks after Arc had first shown up, and he had decided to wait out the thirty-foot snow drifts with the Rebels for the upcoming months. But just because he was waiting didn't mean he wasn't busy. Most all platoons that went topside over the course of that winter were accompanied by Arc, who could wield a rifle as good as any man. Piper was also part of the platoon, and that's when Arc had come up with the idea of making her weapons.

"So, what is so special about your suit?" Piper asked, crossing to him and looking down at it.

"It's yours now. It was made for lightweight pilots, anyway," he said, pointing to the chest piece. "Battle-armor has generally always been bulky from the beginning but was also very good at keeping men alive due to the thickness. It was never really an issue for years because both sides that happened to be fighting also happened to be using thick, heavy battle-armor. It wasn't until the Ghost was created that things started changing in the industry."

Piper laid a hand on the shock white armor. "Change how?" she asked, inspecting it.

"Ghosts were engineered to be light but just as strong as any armor out there. It took a while, but the men working on it finally succeeded and made the model you're touching now. They're capable of withstanding whatever the big armor can, and they're a lot faster, too. And check this out," he said, lifting the right arm of the armor and hitting a few buttons on the small screen occupying the wrist.

Then the white armor vanished. "These were used in recon more than anything."

"I've seen a Drago—uh," she attempted.

"Dragonov," Arc said, nodding. "Beck's father was without a doubt one of the greatest minds of the past century. His cloak design lasts longer than this older suit, but you can still get a good two minutes or so out of it—maybe enough time to hide if you need to."

"Or plan a good attack."

"Or that," he said, laughing. "Want to give it a try?"

"What, now?"

Still laughing, he shoved her softly. "No, yesterday. Of course now."

"Let's do this," Piper said, stealing yet another thing she'd heard Jericho say countless times.

Jericho.

There he was again.

It seemed no matter what she did or said, he was always there. But that's what she wanted or else she might forget him altogether.

That *is* what she wanted, was it not?

Piper was shaken from the thoughts of a dead love by the very much alive man who'd thrown himself into her life. "You okay?"

He must have seen her face. "I am, thanks."

"Piper," he said, shocking her when he took her hand in his. "I'm not trying to butt into your life in the least. I confess that if you weren't here, I would have left months ago, but I'm drawn to you because I know how you feel, and I wish someone had been there for me when I was going through it."

His hands weren't cold this time. Forging weapons has that effect.

"I understand," was all she said, and he let go of her hand and turned back to the Ghost.

"This isn't as user friendly as other armor, where putting it on yourself is concerned. Here," he punched more buttons and the chest, arms, legs, and helmet opened with a small hiss, on what looked like hinges. "It's a little snugger than the bigger ones, but it'll feel about like real armor, which is what I'm hoping for you."

Piper laid in the open suit, wriggling around a little and making a face. "It smells odd."

"You'll get used to that," Arc said while starting on her legs. "It works in a sort of auto-tumble fashion, and the legs and arms will close themselves if you push them in the right directions."

She felt the suit legs and feet close around her human ones. "How's that feel?"

"Fine," Piper said, holding up a leg and moving her armored foot around a little.

In less than another minute, Piper was swinging her steel-clad feet to the concrete floor and standing. She was shocked when she saw that Arc was still taller than she was. When she mentioned it, he laughed and said, "Yeah, you only get a couple of inches out of this thing. Sorry. But some of the most dangerous enemies are the ones we underestimate. Ready for the helmet?"

Piper took a deep breath and nodded before the mask lowered over her face. Since she came from what Beck had dubbed a medieval time, she wasn't ready to see Arc standing right in front of her with no distorted vision on her part. Reaching up, she saw her gauntleted hands when she felt the mask piece. It was a smooth, white surface without any mouth, eye holes or discernable face-like features.

Arc smiled at her. "Do you want me to explain how you can see and breathe?"

"Maybe later," Piper said, walking around and looking at her hands and feet while she did. After pacing around for a few moments, rolling her shoulders and neck and flexing her hands, she asked, "Now what?"

"You've seen other suits before," Arc said, leaning against the now empty table. "How about touching the ceiling for starters."

So that's when Arc began her battle-suit training.

In a little over an hour, Piper was confident with her new armor. In a little over a month, she was flawlessly executing missions as well as enemies. The only problem, or kink, as Arc called it, they ran into was that the first sword they made broke after a few missions. After going back to the drawing board, Arc was finally able to construct an unbreakable blade for her.

Except the final product turned out to be over six feet long and weighed close to three hundred pounds. "There's no way I can lift that thing," Piper said, shaking her head and crossing her arms as she looked down at the large weapon Arc had just unveiled.

"It'll be a cinch to use in the suit," he assured her.

"It's at least six inches wide at the base of the blade."

"I know it's big, Piper, but after all the folds I had to do with the Raptor-6 alloy, this is the best I could do. The sharpening job is of my own invention and, in theory, it shouldn't ever get dull."

"How?"

"Don't ask," he said with a small laugh. "Suffice it to say that it should actually sharpen itself the more it's used, as long as you're cutting through the same or different versions of the alloy. Theoretically, anyway."

"You mean other suits," she said.

"Exactly."

It looked wonderful, even though the enormous broadsword looked befitting a giant. The blade was a dark red and had been honed incredibly.

"Where will it be if I'm not using it on a mission?" she asked, sliding her hand along the wide blade.

Arc pointed to her white armor that was being held up by two iron hooks in the middle of the basement workshop so he could tinker with it. "I'll show you."

Piper crossed the room with him, and he pointed to the new gadget he'd attached to the back. "This is the granddaddy of all magnets," he said. "I fashioned it so the blade of the broadsword would stick to this when not in use. Demagnetizing it is as simple as the touch of a button."

"And you've tried it?"

Smiling, he said, "Not yet. Needed an extra hand to move the sword over here."

With a great deal of effort, the two of them somehow managed to drag the red broadsword to the suit and get it close enough to the magnet. Piper was shocked when they released it and the red blade instantly stuck to the eight-by-six-inch piece on the back of the suit. The edges of the magnet were raised a good inch to keep the blade in place at a diagonal slant, allowing for her to get at the handle easily with her right hand and help her not to drag the blade due to its length. They had a few seconds to exchange triumphant smiles before one of the chains holding the battle-armor broke and the suit and sword ended up in a tangled mess on the floor.

After a few weeks of testing and retesting, Arc said that her armor and weapons were ready for combat. "Merry Christmas, Piper," he'd said, smiling at her.

That was two years ago.

Piper had changed since the day she lost Jericho and, although she'd never be the same, that much is certain, nowadays her new life has started to make more sense, and Piper had begun to wonder if she had a purpose in this hellish future after all.

Jericho once told her that by every natural law they shouldn't have even met each other, let alone fall in love, because they were from two different times. But after close to three years now, she looked back at all she'd accomplished since she was stranded here, and now the Viking woman was beginning to think that this is truly where she belonged.

Piper didn't know what was in store for her on this frozen planet, but she did know that she had one day come to love the people that called themselves the Rebels. And as long as there was breath in her lungs and a beating heart in her chest, she would use up the last of both to protect and defend them.

Piper paused her recording, mulling over everything she'd just talked about for the last few minutes before knowing how to end it.

"I could keep going and mention how I am now second in command of the Rebels and about how I've somehow been able to forget my past long enough to love again—something that I never thought possible," she smiled suddenly. "But I think I've explained myself enough for now. Beck will just have to take what she gets, where this requested log is concerned. I have a date, anyway. This is Commander Piper of Ghost Squadron wishing you a merry Christmas."

Piper pushed back from the desk and stood, logging out of the private holonet while she did. She felt like she'd been sitting a long time and her legs felt stiff, although it was most likely from the cold. There really wasn't a place left anywhere that didn't at least have a cold draft, and the Rebel base was no exception.

"Nice touch with the Christmas bit," she heard from the door behind her.

"How long have you been there?" Piper asked accusingly, glancing at Arc leaning against the doorframe.

"Long enough," Arc said, crossing to her. "Has anyone ever told you how beautiful your smile is?"

Jericho did three years ago, Piper almost told him. "Not recently," she said, wrapping her arms around his neck and smirking at him. "Maybe you should."

"Your smile is beautiful," Arc said, smiling himself and kissing her forehead.

"Let's see if it's just as beautiful while we eat," Piper told him, pulling away and grabbing her white long coat from the desk chair she'd just been sitting at. "I'm starving."

Arc's smile faltered. "Actually, I came to inform you that Beck wants to see you."

Groaning, Piper let her head roll back, and she sighed at the ceiling. "I've finished her journal assignment. Beck can wait until after we get to spend a normal evening together. It's been weeks."

"I know, Pipe," he said, his face saying more than his words. "But I think you should go see her."

Piper frowned at him while she slipped into the white long coat that she and everyone in the battalion she commanded wore. "Is she worse?"

"I'm not sure."

Her normal evening suddenly forgotten, Piper headed for the door, stopping only for a quick kiss before she left.

"I'll see you later, love," Arc told her.

The Rebel base used to be a mech factory over fifty years ago, and it was just within the city limits of Flagstaff. Most of the bays used for mech creation were now being used for almost the same purpose. Piper walked across the long iron gangplank hanging from the ceiling and glanced down at the Rebel men working on the never-ending flow of broken-down machinery and weapons.

Shivering, Piper pulled her white hood over her blond hair. Reaching the end of the gangplank, she took the elevator to the floor that Beck's quarters were on.

Most leaders have better living areas than the men

and women they're leading. Even the Vikings did. But Beck's quarters were small and barely bigger than Piper's.

When Piper had asked Beck about it years ago, Beck had told her that she just didn't care and that a bed was a bed. But Piper knew now that the reason Beck didn't care was because she wasn't actually human.

Piper had known this from the start, but she was never more certain of the fact until the past few months. Beck had always been eccentric and downright hateful in her mannerisms—all of which were excused by everyone since she was physically able to rip a man's head from his shoulders if she wanted—but now things were different.

It had started with severe headaches almost two years ago, landing the Rebel leader in bed with most and sitting out missions with others. A year ago, Beck began blacking out. On the good occasions, she would simply faint. On the bad ones, she would do and say things for days, only to come back to herself having no recollection of what she had done.

In the past few months, Beck's health had declined drastically, and she had confined herself to her quarters, allowing no one in except Piper and Arc.

Beck didn't have to eat, drink, or do anything normal to stay alive, so the Rebel physicians were at a loss as to what exactly to do. The only thing Beck had to do that was human was sleep. Other than that, she was self-sustaining.

Or at least she had been, up until two months ago.

That's when her long black hair had begun to fall out in large clumps, resulting in Beck deciding to shave the rest off herself. "Now it's my idea," she told Piper when she first saw it.

These weren't comforting thoughts as Piper exited the elevator and knocked on Beck's door.

"It's open," Beck said from inside.

Piper pushed into the medium-sized room and found Beck sitting on the side of her bed, her hands gripping the sheets so hard her arms shook.

"What's happening?" Piper asked, quickly crossing the

room and dropping to her knees in front of the quivering woman, placing her hands on Beck's forearms.

"I'm dying," Beck said, her voice barely a whisper.

"No, you're not," Piper assured her with a smile. "You probably just passed out again."

Beck was already shaking her head, her eyes squeezed shut. "This was different. I saw my body on the bed, and I was standing beside it. I tried to touch my arm, but my hand went through it..."

Then Piper saw something she'd never seen before.

A tear rolled down Beck cheek when she opened her eyes. "I was dead. I know it."

"But you're alive now and talking to me."

"I don't understand it, but either way, I don't have much time left," Beck told her, suddenly grasping Piper's shoulders and looking her in the eyes. "Listen to me. Almost four months ago I was able to contact someone in Cross's facility. Some science loser named Ritu. She said that Cross was working on someone like me, only this someone was perfect and didn't have an expiration date."

She was talking fast, but Piper took in all of it. Dr. Cross had rebuilt Beck over seven years ago, after she'd been basically killed during a firefight in the streets when she was eighteen. Beck had become obsessed with somehow getting him to fix her, but attempts over the past few months had failed due to his building being a near fortress.

"Beck, you don't have an expiration date," Piper said while she still gripped Becks arms.

"Says the girl in the room who still has hair," Beck muttered. "Anyway, Ritu said that she'd contact me again once Cross was done with his little science project, and she'd know by then how to fix me."

Piper wanted to believe her. The idea of her friend, the person responsible for saving her life, somehow thriving again with her hair, strength, and attitude back was what she wanted to believe. But she also knew that Beck hadn't been mentally stable of late and had been prone to episodes bordering on schizophrenia.

Piper must not have been good at hiding her thoughts because Beck shook her head again. "I'm not crazy, Piper. Get me on the holonet and I'll prove it."

Before Piper could say anything else, her holotab lit up. "Commander Piper," a female voice chirped.

Beck was still looking at her when she answered the call, "Go ahead, Rone."

"S-20s, ma'am. Three of them just came across our borders. Looks like Bears," Rone said. "They're coming fast, too."

Piper stood. "Assemble the Ghosts, Rone."

"Aye, Commander."

Beck was staring hard at the floor when Piper closed her holotab. "I'm not crazy," she said quietly. "I don't know why my contact hasn't called me back yet, but I know I talked to her."

Piper squeezed her friend's hand. "I'll be back in a few hours, and we'll talk about it over chess. Deal?"

She was trying to lighten the mood, but Beck was more distant than usual. "Try to not die," she said, lying down on her bed and pulling the covers over herself. "Then we'll try and contact Ritu."

Piper headed for the door. Dying was the furthest thing from her mind. Before long she was suited and ready to go.

Piper rolled her neck once after the smooth face-piece of her helmet clamped down. In a few seconds, her visual display and HUD activated, and she could see perfectly while she glanced at the rest of her troops as they armored up.

The christening of the Ghost Squadron had taken place almost two years ago after Beck had insisted on Piper taking more responsibilities, besides following her around like a lost snow cat and bugging her for missions.

Originally, the Ghost Squadron was just a normal five-person team with Piper at the helm as commander. But after two years, the fame set by some of the most successful missions ever to be carried out had marshaled the white armored team to one of the highest ranks in the Rebel militia.

Sometimes Piper found it hard to believe that she now commanded the Rebels who had taught her not that long ago. There was even a special training program set in place and taught by Arc, just for men and women trying to get in the elite task force.

Since Piper had been the one controlling the outfit, her Viking ways had carried over into the future with her. The only reason, she felt, that a soldier needed to be replaced was if that soldier died, and since Ghost Squadron was, as aforementioned, an elite force, that didn't happen very often.

One, in fact, was the number of troops Piper had lost under her command.

And that had been recently.

"How do you like the suit, newbie?" Gustav, the squad sniper, asked the replacement.

"It's fine," Kavi, the new girl, said while she flexed her hands around.

Kavi was around eighteen and, as Arc had told Piper, one of the best the Ghost program had to offer to replace Wells, the scout that had been killed by the Bears on their last mission. Kavi's hair was cut short, reaching just below her chin, and was a light purple.

"Didn't get to pick my hair color, Commander," Kavi said during her interview when Piper had asked her about it. "My parents must have figured I was going to design clothes for a living."

Piper had laughed at that before welcoming the girl aboard the Ghost Squadron and issuing her a hooded white long coat and directing her to the Ghost barracks. Most of the people she'd met the last few years sporting a strange hair color had all told her the same thing—that they hadn't had a choice in the matter.

"You'd think whoever came up with that crazy idea could at least have thought of a way to change it again later in life," Piper had told Arc once Kavi had left with her duffel over her shoulder, heading for the small set of barracks assigned for Ghosts only.

"It's possible," Arc admitted with a shrug. "But a more severely inconvenient or bothersome process you'll never find. Most people just leave it because of that, but also because, since Flagstaff has never been at the forefront of fashion, finding a doctor with the knowledge to do it here is nigh impossible."

Kavi tapped away at the screen on her left wrist, and her helmet began closing, covering her bright hair. "There, now," Gustav told her. "Now you're not target practice."

"Leave off, Gustav," Baron, the largest man of the Ghosts, told the sniper as he checked his assault rifle. No one really knew how old Baron was, but he looked to be somewhere between thirty-five and forty, with tan skin and a shiny bald head.

Three of the five under Piper's command had been men until Kavi had replaced Wells. Now Baron and Gustav were outnumbered, something the other female Ghosts weren't allowing them to forget.

"About time we evened out the testosterone in this squad," Helena muttered to Rone while she clasped her white hooded cloak over her armor. Helena was the oldest of the Ghosts but just as capable. Rone had been the youngest until Kavi, and Piper was willing to bet that the black-haired girl was ready to pass the torch to someone younger, since being the youngest of any group always led to witticisms at every turn.

"Fall in," Piper said, and all murmurs and jests stopped as the men and women in white armor lined up. "For those of you who haven't met her, this is Kavi, our new scout."

Then she pointed to each of her troops and rattled off their part of the Ghost Squadron for Kavi. "Gustav is our range, Baron is our muscle, Helena is acting medical officer, Rone is explosives, and you're our new scout."

"And Commander Piper is all of those rolled into one," Helena said with a smile.

"Helheim, yes," Piper said, returning the smile. "Now who wants to go Bear hunting?"

This was what she always asked the Ghosts, and the simple question had escalated into an inside joke that was always met with chuckles. She asked this no matter which army they were hunting, since the term was used by her people on Svalbard and was meant to ask if someone wanted to go do something fun and maybe dangerous. Then they would all laugh and head for the elevator. Kavi didn't share in the laughter and frowned the whole way to the elevator that was about to take them topside.

"A warrior should always be able to laugh in the face of death, Kavi," Piper said after she hit the top-level button and the doors closed. "If you survive the day, then you'll know next time. We'll break into two-man teams," Piper said to her troops. "Each team will get an S-20. Gustav and Rone, Baron and Helena, and you're with me, Kavi."

Most accesses to the frozen surface were designed to be in a form of shelter, so that whoever felt big enough to venture forth from the Rebel base could have a few minutes to get their bearings before wading into the snow.

Piper stepped out of the elevator when the doors finally opened into what used to be the basement of a glamorous hotel. Rusted water heaters lined the walls of the large room, and wheeled baskets were cluttering up half of the room.

Five green blips appeared on the nav-map in the bottom right of her HUD, indicating her squad. Since she didn't see three red blips anywhere, the S-20s were most likely cloaked. Bigger mechs couldn't completely vanish from sight, but they could fool a targeting system.

"Fan out."

Gustav headed up the stairs on the left side of the basement with Rone on his heels. "Here's an idea," Gustav's voice crackled over the squadron's private channel. "How about we don't level a skyscraper this time?"

"Shut up," Rone said. "That wasn't my fault, and you

know it."

Piper took the opposite set of stairs with the rest of the Ghosts behind her. In a few short minutes, they had made it to what was left of the hotel lobby, fierce gusts of wind blowing through the shattered windows and kicking up snow all around them. Then everyone pulled their assault rifles and checked their rounds.

Except Piper.

"Kavi, with me," she said, demagnetizing the enormous red broadsword from her back.

Kavi couldn't help but stare, watching her commander stab the point of the red blade deep into the concrete floor with ease so she could pull on her hooded white cloak. Ghost Squadron had some of the best tech that the Rebels had to offer, and the cloaks had to be one of Piper's favorites.

The thick, wool-like material did nothing but blend the Ghosts all the better into the whiteness of the ever-present snow, but they also kept the squad off of enemy nav-maps. Devices to throw off targeting and locating had been around for centuries, Beck told her when she had presented her with the first white cloak. "But really for mechs and airstrikes. These are the first portable ones."

Piper pulled the broadsword out of the floor and headed for the street, with Kavi close behind, their armored feet tromping softly on the once, no doubt, beautiful floor.

The wind was worse out in the open while Piper and Kavi went a few blocks. Then Piper held up a hand to stop, crouching on the sidewalk close to the side of the building beside her. Heavy footsteps were just around the corner.

"Found mine first," Piper said in a sing-song voice, something she'd heard someone do long ago.

Jericho. It was Jericho who had said some things that way. She didn't want to forget. She couldn't.

Not yet.

Piper shook her head slightly to clear her mind before her attack. "We have visual," Helena's voice buzzed in.

"Ah, come on," Rone groaned. "Why am I always paired with the loser sniper?"

"Got ours," Gustav said dejectedly.

"Attack on my mark," Piper ordered, tightening her grip on the hilt of her giant sword.

"How do you want to do this?" Kavi asked, shifting the assault rifle uneasily in her armored hands.

"Ever go up against an S-20?"

"No, Commander," the girl admitted.

"Stay back, then," Piper told her. "Watch and learn."

"Commander—"

"That's an order, Kavi," then the S-20 rounded the corner not thirty feet away.

"Ghosts attack," Piper ordered, already sprinting toward her target, her broadsword whistling through the snowy air and connecting with the mammoth left leg of the mech, the red blade slicing through the armored ankle like butter as the white warrior kept up her momentum, spinning once to gain more power before severing off the other leg.

This all happened in almost two fractured seconds, and before the mech had time to respectfully fall onto its left side, Piper was in the air, tucked into a ball and spinning before landing on the dome of the S-20. Since it was in mid-fall, she landed on the leveling right side of the dome.

The unfortunate pilot never even saw who drove the large red blade straight through the eight-inch dome and into the side of his throat.

Piper rode the S-20 to the ground, pulling her broadsword quickly before flipping off the mech just as it hit the street, kicking up snow.

Kavi had watched the six-second attack with her mouth hanging open. She closed it quickly when her commander materialized from the blustering snow, her red sword in her right hand, the tip almost touching the ground as she walked toward her, the white cloak billowing on her left from the wind.

"They're pretty easy once you get the hang of it," Piper said. "Next time I'll let you have a go."

"That was… quick," Kavi said, standing.

"Think so?"

"Target neutralized," they heard Baron's voice say.

"A well-placed sticky grenade," Helena said. "You, Commander?"

"Red Falcon," Piper informed her before chuckling and asking, "What did you think I was going to use, one of your barbaric rifles?"

"Another one bites the flakes," Rone buzzed in.

But then, suddenly, another red blip appeared on their nav-map.

"You sure about that?" Kavi asked.

"Wait for it…" Rone said. Then there was an earth-shaking explosion causing Piper and Kavi to touch the building beside them for support.

Then the blip vanished.

"Told you," Rone muttered.

"Good job, Ghost Squadron," Piper said, heading back down the sidewalk with the befuddled Kavi behind her. "Let's pack up. I have a date to finish, anyway."

There was a tradition among the Ghosts following every successful mission. The celebration included, but was not limited to, a feast filled with laughter, battle-scar stories, and arm-wrestling.

The main course was mostly ice-spider legs that had been skinned and slow-roasted over a spit in the Ghost barracks, while the only thing to drink besides snowmelt, or smelt, as it was commonly known, was a concoction Baron had discovered years ago, officially called ice-spider wine.

"You won't find that stuff in any militia kitchen, love," Gustav assured Kavi while she peered curiously into the cup he'd given her. "Tell her how you make it, Baron."

Baron groaned as if he'd already explained it thousands of times—because he had—and said, "You know what's in it."

"Come on, big guy," Rone chimed in, propping her boots on the table of the small mess hall. "We want to hear it from the master."

Sighing, Baron gave up and explained the delicate process to Kavi, her eyes widening with each word. The first ingredient was the residual oil left over in the bottom of a pot after boiling spider skins in it. Then the oil was added to about a gallon of smelt and placed in a cellar to ferment.

But, like one would think, ice-spider wine didn't get its name exactly from the oil part of the recipe as much as the few drops of ice-spider venom added to the gallon container before letting it ferment.

"There's poison in this?" Kavi blurted after Baron had finished his meager seminar on the culinary arts.

The big man merely shrugged at her.

"Don't drink more than a cup a day," Piper said, heading for the door. "Their venom isn't exactly toxic, but it will give you hallucinations from Helheim if you're not careful."

Then she left the bewildered girl with her fellow troops.

Piper pulled on her white hood before sliding her hands in her coat pockets, her boots making soft clanging noises on the iron catwalk as she headed for her quarters. All mech and tech operations had ceased for the night, and Piper took in the silence, glancing down at the empty bays as she walked slowly, relishing the quiet.

Then her holotab lit up on her right wrist, and Arc's face hovered above it. "How was the Bear hunt?"

Smiling, Piper touched his face and entered the holochat. "Not too bad. Kavi did alright for her first time."

"You mean she didn't die."

"Yeah, that."

Arc laughed before asking, "What's your plan for the rest of the evening?"

"Well, I was hoping to share a quiet supper with this handsome geologist—except I don't know where he is."

"That sounds amazing, dear," he said, and Piper

frowned.

"But?"

"I have to pack. The drifts are lowering, and I need to hit the trail hard for Anchorage in the morning while there's still time."

Piper had known Arc was leaving soon, but she didn't know exactly when. This had happened more than once in almost three years, and Piper had thought that it would eventually get easier to be abruptly separated from someone she cared about without any warning.

At least with Arc, the separation was only by miles and not death.

"Will you come see me before you leave?" Piper asked.

"No," Arc said with a smile.

"Shut up," she laughed, signing out of the holochat.

It wasn't a strange thing for clansmen to leave their wives and children for months during the summer for hunting and fishing. But as harsh as Svalbard had been, the worst days there weren't even close to the good ones here.

When she made it back to her quarters, she removed her long coat, dropping it over the back of a chair before changing out of her black jumpsuit into her normal sleepwear, a lime-green American Eagle t-shirt and faded jeans.

She'd tried to throw the clothes away several times and even actually made it far enough to get the outfit, given to her by Jericho years ago, in the disposal bin, only to immediately dig the clothes back out. She even had the blue shoes he'd called Chucks, except the black and white laces had been removed and wrapped around the hilt of Red Falcon two years ago for better grip.

Climbing into bed, Piper pulled the thick covers up to her chin and peered at the ceiling.

The worst part about Arc leaving was that he made her forget. The only times she was able to not think was when she was fighting or with Arc. Even if they were too busy to talk some days, it was still fine because he was around.

But after he was gone and there wasn't anyone to fight, Piper would end up lying in bed like she was now, staring up at the ceiling. She didn't want to forget, telling herself this constantly, but she also didn't want to have the past in her mind all the time.

Then why keep mementos and sleep in them every night?

Those were always the first thoughts to creep in, and those alone were enough to make her question everything.

She would fall asleep eventually most nights, but even sleep sometimes brought dreams overflowing with the ghosts of days gone by. Most were of Jericho, and even Bjourn the Berserker, her chieftain, found his way into her dreams.

"Take care of her, Beck," Jericho would say, turning on his heel.

"Don't leave!" Piper would scream, except her love couldn't hear her over the sound of hundreds of blacksmiths beating on hundreds of red swords.

This night was no different, and Arc hadn't even left yet. She dozed for what felt like five minutes before she felt someone sit on the bed.

"Stay warm out there, Arc," Piper said quietly, her voice sounding like it needed more sleep.

"Arc's been gone for over an hour," Beck said, startling her.

Sitting up quickly, Piper asked, "He didn't stop by?"

"He stopped by but said you looked like you needed to sleep."

Piper squinted against the bright blue light when she switched on her holotab to see was time it was.

6:45 PM. The day after Christmas.

"How're you feeling?" Piper asked the synthetic woman while swinging her feet to the cold floor.

"Sorry for waking you," Beck said, ignoring the question about her health. Standing, she added, "But there's something you need to see."

Piper knew Beck well enough to know that, if it could

have waited a few hours, she wouldn't have come herself to get her.

In less than a minute, Piper had gotten into her boots and pulled her white long coat over her green shirt, following Beck out of her quarters.

It was a silent journey with nothing but footsteps echoing for ambiance and the quiet hum of the elevator as they ascended to Beck's quarters. Piper frowned when Beck passed the door to her room and went into the war room instead, not ten feet down the hall. Since the council consisted of Beck, Piper, and Arc, the room wasn't large.

"Sit down," Beck ordered, motioning to the steel table that was used for tactical planning.

"Ritu contacted me today," she said, pulling up her holotab. "She said Cross would be leaving for Anchorage this week sometime because his new test subject did extremely well on his or her first trial run."

Frowning, Piper said, "Arc just left for Anchorage."

"They won't cross paths, considering your precious geologist doesn't have air clearance and will be traveling on foot if that old snowmobile of his breaks down," Beck told her. "But I didn't wake you to talk about Cross."

Now Piper was really confused. "What, then?"

"Not thirty minutes after Ritu told me about Cross leaving, she contacted me again looking battered and said that the test subject had escaped. I sent out one of the drones to see if I could get a look at Cross's new toy."

Beck hit a few keys and Piper's holotab lit up. "Take a look for yourself."

Piper opened what she'd sent her, and the drone footage started. At first all she could see was snow, until a lone figure dressed in black with a hood appeared moving quickly along the side of the building. When the figure entered an old apartment building, the drone camera stopped suddenly.

"Here's an hour later," Beck said as she pulled the hologram slider along the bottom to skip forward.

Then Piper saw a five-man team enter the apartment building. Rogues, most likely, due to the mismatched battle-armor they all wore. The drone then flew around the other side of the complex when it heard a commotion coming from that side.

Piper wasn't shocked at first when she saw the hooded figure climbing the side of the building—until she noticed that whatever was climbing at the alarming rate wasn't wearing a suit of any kind that she could see. "How—?"

"Oh, but it gets better," Beck said, just as the man in black dropped from the top of the complex into a free-fall with his arms outstretched, snatching a Rogue who had just leaned out a window for a better shot on the way down, pulling the armored man deep into the snow. Piper frowned again when a bright blue flash exploded from the snow and ice, instantly melting a large radius.

"Was that an EMP grenade?"

"I thought it was," Beck muttered, while the drone hovered close to the building and peered through a shattered window. "Keep watching."

Piper saw the hooded man fall into a window soaked from the water he'd just made, and his foot seemed to get stuck in the refreezing liquid. In a few seconds, once he'd freed himself, one of the Rogues tore through the ceiling and kicked him across the gallery almost twenty feet away.

Piper was stunned when the man in black got to his feet and leapt the large gap between him and the armored assailant, taking the man to the floor before grabbing his helmet and—

"What was that?" Piper asked suddenly, sitting forward in her chair when she saw the same bright blue flashes. "That wasn't a grenade. That came from his hands."

"I know. I watched this already, remember?"

The remaining Rogues barreled down the stairs then, and the hooded man shouted something at them, holding up both his hands. Blue and white licks of electricity crackled in his hands, the streaks crawling up his arms to his shoulders.

Piper couldn't hear the exchange, but it ended with the man lowering his hands and one of the Rogues approaching him. The drone lowered a floor on the apartment building, zooming in on the hooded man talking to the armored Rogue.

Then the video paused.

Piper glanced at Beck after she stopped the vid and saw she was watching her. "What?"

"I just wanted to let you know that this next part shocked me a good bit, so just, I don't know, steel yourself," Beck told her.

Then she played the video.

Piper saw the Rogue's helmet open and recognized the female pilot instantly. "What's Red doing chasing after lost science projects?" she asked.

"That's not the wild part, Pipe."

Then the man in black removed his hood and shook hands with the suited red-haired woman.

Piper's heart stopped.

"You okay?" Beck asked.

She couldn't speak.

"Look, I don't know what's going on, but we just need to think about this and make a plan of action."

Piper wasn't listening while she stared at the man glancing around the burned-out gallery of the complex.

It was Jericho.

Beck and Piper sat silently at the table in the war room for a long time after watching the vid from the surveillance drone.

Then Beck broke the silence. "We know he's with the Rogues."

"And we don't know where the Rogues are," Piper countered, standing. "I'm going back to bed."

"Piper, wait," Beck tried. "Don't do anything stupid," were the last words Piper heard before she exited the room and climbed into the elevator. Once she was back in her room, she locked the door, removed her long coat, then began slowly pacing the small room, questions bubbling to the surface.

Jericho Johnson was alive.

But it couldn't be true, could it? Where had he been the last three years if it really was him? Why hadn't he tried to find her?

Jericho Johnson was alive.

Why was he so fast and able to climb up a vertical surface without a suit? Why was he wielding lightning like the god of thunder, and why did he go with the Rogues?

Jericho was alive.

She sat on the bed and drummed her fingers on the blankets before standing and resuming her pacing, her hands covering her mouth.

How could this have happened? She saw him die, had she not? She'd survived for three years without him, had she not? Why was he suddenly alive and back? Piper had spent years simultaneously trying and not trying to forget him because she knew he was gone and never coming back.

He was dead to her, and she had given what was left of her heart to someone else because she just knew he was gone.

But he wasn't gone.

Piper didn't know what the future held as she lay in her bed. Somehow, though, she found sleep easily that night, as no memories seemed to plague her and she knew, as her eyes slipped shut the last time before falling asleep, that her nights of tossing and turning were over.

She didn't know what the future held, but she did know one thing.

Jericho Johnson was alive.

CHAPTER 14
Jericho

In less than ten minutes, I had followed my newfound Rogue friends below the streets of Flagstaff. We entered through the basement of an old building right across the street from the apartment complex where I'd fought them.

It didn't take too long to fish out the guy I'd left frozen in the ice outside, but he wasn't in the best shape at first. Once his suit was back online, he got himself thawed out. The two men I had my run-in with broke off after a few minutes of walking, under Red's orders. She told them to go to east watch, whatever that was, and they left.

Since I wasn't sure if they were going to try and attack me on their own turf or something, I kept my guard up just in case.

"There isn't a merry-go-round outside close to an entrance, is there?" I heard myself ask Red while I followed her through the darkened tunnels. Powerful lights were mounted on the sides of their helmets, so at least we weren't stumbling around like blind beggars.

Laughing, Red said, "I don't think so. We have a sort of unspoken agreement with the Rebels, saying that we won't use each other's topside entrances."

"So, you guys leave each other alone?" I asked, stepping into a frozen puddle and slipping a little.

"More or less," she said. "There's the occasional

misunderstanding that results in both of our groups attacking the same supply lines, and those are never pretty."

"Call me crazy, but it sounds like you guys are fighting the same people. Why not unite?"

Red laughed again, and I have to say, it was really nice to listen to. Real deep and joyous laughter that was easy on the ears. "Tried that, mate, a few times, actually. Suffice it to say that the leader of our humble group doesn't see eye to eye with the Rebel one."

"You mean Beck," I said, and Red suddenly stopped, turning her bright beams on me.

"What do you know of Beck?"

I held up my hand, shielding my eyes from the brightness before saying, "I've met her once, about three years ago."

"Cranky, but that sheila's a handful," Red muttered. "How is it you came to meet her? I don't recall ever exactly meeting you during a raid."

"I'm not from around here," I said nonchalantly.

"I hear that, mate," she said, turning back around and resuming her trudge through the damp tunnel. "Not from here, my own self, but got here as quick as I could. Uncommon to popular belief, there actually are a few non-Russians left trying to make a name for themselves on this frozen planet."

"Where are you from?"

Red chuckled at that, "Where do you think, mate? Granted there ain't much left of the blessed Outback after the bombs went off, but she's still hanging in there. Lot less joeys and crocs nowadays, though. Few dingos left, but mind you they're a little bigger and meaner."

I listened intently, hanging on every semi-sarcastic word the thick-accented girl was saying.

"What about you, mate? Why'd you come to this wonderfully sadistic city?"

I didn't know what to say. I hadn't exactly been working on a story to spin to whoever might ask where I came from. I was probably too busy fighting for my life to think up a good one. "You really want to know?"

"Cranky, why does everyone always ask that?" Red laughed.

"So that's a yes?"

"Spit it out, Jericho. We got a long way to go as it is."

"I don't even know all your names," I said, and Red proceeded to introduce the rest of her squad, which was an older man and younger girl.

Devin was a cool guy, maybe in his late forties, with a graying beard and shaggy hair. He didn't talk much, unlike the last crewman, a young blue-haired girl around twenty who turned out to be Red's younger sister and was named (get this) Blu.

"I'm guessing you weren't born with blue hair," I joked to the talkative girl when Red introduced her and Devin to me before we started our journey through the tunnels.

"Sure was," Blu told me. "Our mother decided on my hair color." I could tell she wasn't embarrassed in the least by her blue hair, which, on closer inspection, was a deep blue that didn't look dyed at all and was most disconcerting, let me tell you.

And quite awesome.

"Dad got to pick my hair and eye color," Red informed me with a smile and wink from one of her blood red irises. "Blu got saddled with mom's crazy ideas."

"Shut up," Blu said with a glare aimed at her sister. "At least she gave me green eyes and didn't make them match, like dad did yours. Boring."

After we were all acquainted and, of course, after I had asked a ton of questions about how people could choose the hair and eye color of their unborn children, I launched into my story from the beginning, as I explained exactly how I came to be in Flagstaff.

And the answer to the hair and eye color questions was pretty simple. To them, anyway. It involved paying your doctor lots of holos and then they give you two pills and *poof* your kid has whatever color you picked.

Hopefully, whoever-you-are, you already know how I went from being a suave, time-traveling billionaire to a rebuilt, rebooted and reborn Jericho 2.0 with lighting mage capabilities, a buzz-cut, and super-sneak-mode.

And cool clothes, too.

Then I began my story, not really sure why I was telling it to them in the first place.

I talked for a long time, and that was with me summing up parts to save time and skipping almost all of my time strapped to Cross's table. Once I'd finished, we all walked in silence for a good five minutes. I was guessing that they were thinking about what I'd just told them and trying to decide whether or not to believe me.

I finally decided to break the silence myself. "How can I find Beck?"

"You mean your girlfriend, Piper," Red said with a smile before sighing. "Beck's base isn't that far from here. Granted, I'm not overly fond of the idea of knocking on her front door to drop you off."

"That breaks our distance rules and she'd kill us," Devin said in his scratchy Australian voice.

"Are all Rogues Australian?" I had to ask.

"Mostly," Blu said. "Immigrants."

We stopped when we came to a fork in the tunnel, and Red turned to me. "Here's the deal, mate. Either you can take the right tunnel by yourself and walk a half hour to the Rebels and hope that Beck doesn't have you sniped out before you get the chance to knock, or you can go left with us to our base and try to contact her first."

I glanced down both dark tunnels, neither of which looked too inviting.

I had to see Piper as soon as possible, even if it meant having to travel down a dark, damp tunnel alone.

But my feet weren't moving.

"Give me a minute," I said, walking away from them and slipping my hands into my coat pockets, looking at the fork in the tunnel hard.

Piper.

What was I even going to say to her? She thought I was dead. Showing up after almost three years would be insane. I just didn't know. What if she had moved on with someone else? Or what if she was married or had kids or something?

There, in the darkness of the underground of Flagstaff, in the year of our Lord, 2345, I made a decision that I would come to regret more than anything.

I wasn't ready to face her. Not by a long shot. Call me a coward, but I just couldn't make myself go to her. Not yet.

"I'm thinking your place," I told Red. "Lead the way."

We seemed to walk for a long time after that. After several twists and turns that, honestly, I wasn't paying attention to, we arrived at a dead end. Wait. Not a dead end. There was a door.

A voice crackled through the intercom beside the small iron door that seemed to be wedged into the face of a sheer wall of ice. "What's the password?"

"Open the bloody gate or I'll kill you," Red said good-naturedly, and in seconds the loud grating of metal on metal resounded around the icy hallway then the heavy door began slowing opening.

The way had become colder and icier the last half a mile of the trip, and when I asked why, Red explained.

"We're actually closer to the surface than you might think. Our base it set up in what used to be a dam of some kind on the outskirts of the city," she said. "I don't know if you've seen enough of the future to know, but ice doesn't exactly melt here."

Once the door was open, Red told me to stay behind her just in case someone decided to put a bullet in my unrecognized face. "We're a little wary of strangers here," Devin added from behind me.

I was expecting a long hall of ice, but was instead greeted by an enormous chamber that went on for as far as I could see and was housing an ungodly amount of people.

We're talking, like, a *lot* of folks. The walls of the chamber were rounded off close to the top and bottom and looked like someone had—

"Did you guys dig this place?" I asked in wonder.

"Most of it," Red said, glancing around as if she'd just finished it minutes ago and was giving it a final approval. "What you're looking at is the frozen remains of Lake Mary. We set up shop here about ten years ago after the Bears bombed our base within the city limits. Not a bad place, really. Somehow the large iron content in the frozen lake water throws off scanners, so we're basically invisible."

Wow. Lake freaking Mary. No wonder it felt like we'd walked for miles. Last time I checked in 2012, that lake was a good twelve miles from Flagstaff. "Who runs this gig?" I asked while still looking around like a nerd at Comic-Con. Pretty much the entire floor of the hollowed-out cavern was covered with the Rogue populace living in everything from tents and makeshift lean-tos. I even spotted a few igloos no doubt thrown up by the more industrious of the crowd.

"I did tell you that it was your lucky day, Jericho," Red told me. "I sort of run this 'gig,' as you call it."

"Sort of?"

Red's answer was a mere shrug.

We had an excellent view of the entire layout because the door we entered through was located on a ledge about halfway up the ice wall, and a sort of rigged elevator was about twenty feet or so to my left and seemed to be the only way to reach the floor.

"Do these people ever leave?" I asked, frowning and looking around the cavern for more exits. Did I mention I could see really far now? Because I could. Yet another blade on the awesome Swiss-hero-knife that was Jericho. Thank you, evil Dr. Cross.

"Not unless they want to die," Blu muttered as we headed for the elevator, which turned out to just be a large iron basket, really, and didn't exactly instill a safe feeling in anyone riding in it.

"What my irritating sister is trying to say is that none of these people have a reason to leave," Red explained as we all climbed into the rickety, rusted basket. Hitting a large green button, she added, "All of these people have been deactivated from the Holonet for various reasons, from trying to escape with a loved one to just trying to buck the system. Either way, they all end up here most of the time with nothing but a cold death awaiting them topside. Depending on how high up they were, some have to lose a hand or even a forearm to get rid of their tabs."

"Why?" I asked, trying not to gulp because I'd just remembered that I had a tab on the Holonet as well.

"The Holonet is just a cheap way to spy on what's left of the world," Red spat, and I could tell she had been on a soapbox more than once on the subject. "Thankfully, we've been able to catch a lot of them before they come here, so we can remove their holotabs. Otherwise we'd have all our enemies beating down the door."

My silence led all three sets of eyes to rest on me, and I tried not to fidget.

"So, uh, how long does it take to remove a tab?"

"It's kind of tedious," Blu said. "Sometimes it can take hours. Good thing you're not from our time or..." her voice trailed off.

Red was watching me now. Very, very closely.

"Cross put one on me a few days ago," I blurted. "He said it was an older model because anything new wouldn't be able to fly under the ra—"

Red grabbed my right arm in the tight grip of her battle-armor, the large iron hands clamping down hard. It didn't hurt because, well, I just didn't get hurt much anymore, but I could tell she wasn't messing around. "What kind of test subject gets a holotab?" she asked in a low voice.

"If Cross put an older one on him, then he'll be the only one that can track him," Blu said, placing one of her huge suit hands on her sister's shoulder. "We need to check it first."

"I have too many people here to wait on checking anything, Blu. Or have you forgotten that we're in the business of protecting the innocent nowadays?" Red shot at her.

I was glancing back and forth between them and wondering just exactly which one of them was on my side. After a few seconds, I finally decided that neither probably had my health and well-being on their minds. If this was such a big deal, then why had they just now thought to discuss it?

"Cross isn't interested in us, Red," Blu tried again.

"He may not be, but he sells weapons to the ones who *are* interested, all the time," she said, sliding up my coat sleeve.

"Red—"

"I'm sorry, Jericho," Red said simply to me.

"No," I struggled. "Wait, wait, wa—"

Then she ripped my arm off.

CHAPTER 15

We have to stop meeting like this.

I don't know if you remember from my previous tale of heroic exploits, but I have gone on record stating that I hate the number fifteen. My last chapter fifteen, I actually tried to skip, if you recall, but you guys wouldn't let me, so I ended up having to go all the way back and explain it to you.

Like I said, I *hate* the number fifteen.

It's true. I was fifteen when I first went to college and also when I was almost killed by a girl's shotgun-toting father.

A lot of other un-cool things happened at the age of fifteen, but I'm not going to waste my breath telling you about all of them because, as bad as they all were, I made it out of those scrapes with all of my limbs attached.

I screamed when Red ripped off my arm with ease, due to her powerful suit, and I crumbled to my knees onto the iron basket floor. Since I'd already lost my right arm before, there wasn't exactly a lot of blood or torn veins hanging out.

But it was the idea of it.

"What the Helheim?" I shouted at Red, who was now looking at my synthetic arm in her hands.

"You're..." she muttered, frowning at my arm.

It didn't hurt at first, but I was starting to feel a dull ache starting in my spine, of all places. "I'm sorry," I said between gritted teeth, as I cradled my leaking nub in my left arm. "What was I thinking not telling you that I'm short a few body parts since the explosion?"

Oh, yeah. I guess I'd decided not to tell them the Cross bits of my story.

Wires were poking out everywhere from my open wound, and every time I moved anything, a few sparks shot out from them.

"Why is it doing that?" Devin asked.

Blu got on her knees beside me (which didn't exactly help because of her battle-armor but, hey, she tried). "Cranky," she breathed. "Red, this isn't good. If there's an electrical reaction when he moves, then this is going all the way to his spine."

"It had to be done," Red told her.

Meanwhile, as the two sisters exchanged heated conversation about me, my head began spinning and I lurched into the side of the iron bucket.

"Try not to move," Blu told me quickly as she stood. "Power down," she said as the suit went to its knees again and the back opened.

"What're you doing?" Devin asked. "You can't undock here."

"Help me out," Blu said, all business as Red reached under her arms, lifting her out.

The pain had started subsiding when I found out that if all I did was breathe, the fire in my back wasn't blazing. "You know this is illegal, right?" Blu asked as she crouched down beside me.

"That's what I hear," I muttered. "Nice coat."

The inside of most suits was large enough for someone to keep on pretty much anything the pilot was wearing. Blu was rocking a white jumpsuit and a heavy hip-length coat with a fur-lined hood, which she pulled on, covering her blue locks.

"Thanks. Made it myself." She gently turned me over to get a good look at my arm.

"Well?" Red asked after Blu had checked out the lost-arm situation. We were nearly to the icy floor of the cavern when

Blu sat back on her haunches and sighed.

"It's not going to be an easy fix," she finally said. "It'll still take me about an hour, but it's going to look like Lucifer's hangnail afterward. Sorry, mate," she said, patting the top of my hood softly. "Because of my sister's rashness, I'm afraid you're going to lose a couple of hot points."

I felt drugged and sluggish for some reason, and I said, "That's fine. God knows I had plenty to spare. Maybe now some other guys can... have a chance to..."

Then I was out like a light.

You know what the best part of losing consciousness was? I don't have to explain what happened during the three hours I was out and in surgery.

For once I was glad I wasn't able to access super-sneak-mode and watch Blu fix me up. The next thing I remember was opening my eyes while lying on yet another table with the blue-haired girl standing beside me.

We seemed to be in a makeshift medical bay that was inside one of the many igloos I'd seen from the cliff top. It was kind of warm, really. For being inside a block of solid ice, I mean.

And I was back in my loincloth. Great.

"There he is," she said with a wide smile. "You got some good hardware in you, mate. Cross knows how to put his stuff together, that's for sure."

"I'm not his stuff, anymore."

"Could've fooled me. You're loaded to the gills, arsenal-wise, and that screams Dr. Cross more than anything." She whistled quietly before adding, "Remind me to fight on whatever side you're on, and even then you couldn't pay me enough holos to be in front of you."

"No kidding?" I asked, holding up my newly attached arm and flexing it around, inspecting it. "You do a pretty good patch job, Blu."

"Not too bad," she said. "Let's just say that I was able to save more of those hot points than I thought," she added with a wink.

"Speaking of hot points," I said, looking down at my pale frame. "Why am I almost naked?"

"We were just going to toss your jumpsuit because the right sleeve was gone, until we saw that it wasn't your average clothing," Blu said. "Red's trying to fix that now. She's not as fast as I am, mate."

"I'll say. She didn't take my clothes off," I muttered, glancing around the igloo.

"Can I ask you something?" Blu asked suddenly.

"Shoot."

"So, what all can you do, exactly?" she asked, glancing up and down my body like a kid might look through the glass of a reptile house at their favorite critter.

"I kind of checked out before I had a chance to learn all my new bells and whistles," I told her.

Blu pulled up a stool then and sat beside me, leaning her elbows on the table. Placing her chin on a fist, she looked me in the face for a few seconds, her liquid green eyes narrowing slightly like she was trying to read my mind or something.

"You looked like you knew what you were doing in the apartment building," she finally said.

I shrugged. "I know a few. I'm also pretty good at climbing up completely vertical surfaces with minimal handholds, like a ninja."

"So we saw," she said, her eyes still on me.

"How'd you learn to fix synthetic body parts so well? Don't take this the wrong way, but you're kind of young to be a nanotechnologist."

Without taking her gaze off me or moving her perched chin from her fist, she nonchalantly tapped a finger to her temple. "Imprints. You can learn anything so long as you've got the holos."

"Again, don't take this the wrong way, but the Rogue camp, although welcoming because I find it comfortably Viking-like, doesn't look like it's rolling in holos," I said, turning on my side and propping my head up with my new arm.

"It's not," Blu said. "Got imprinted back in Sydney by my rich parents. They had lots of plans that had to do with turning Red and me into a couple of perfect beings, or something like that."

"Why'd you come here if daddy and mommy were holonaires?"

Blu rolled her eyes around and pulled her cute lips to one side of her mouth in thought before saying, "Basically to get away from our parents. They were a couple of crazies. What about yours?"

"Never met mine. Got dropped off on an orphanage doorstep when I was a baby, they tell me."

"Really?"

"Yeah."

"And from such humble beginnings you ended up doing extremely well for yourself," Blu said, smiling at me.

"If being blown up, burnt to a crisp, and rebuilt by a mad scientist fall under the extremely-well-for-yourself category, then yeah, I guess I've done okay."

We both sat in silence for almost a minute, taking each other in. Not in a flirtatious way but in genuine curiosity. Then I broke the hardening ice. "So, where's a guy get some clothes around here?"

Blu stood and crossed the room to a few trunks against the ice wall. Squatting, she opened one and began rummaging through it. After a few seconds of apparently fruitless searching, the blue-haired girl snorted angrily and scooted to the next trunk. When she didn't find anything in this one, she got to her feet and slammed it shut hard, kicking it.

"Problems, dearest?" I inquired, sitting up and swinging my feet to the icy ground.

"Not exactly," Blu said, turning to me and crossing her arms. "It's just that I thought my ex-boyfriend, Sam, wouldn't have taken his clothes back so quickly. Those clothes would've been the best thing I ever got from that croc," she muttered in a sort of good-natured fashion, if the smirk on her lips was anything to go by.

"What, was Sam not into blues?"

"Look at me, mate," Blu said, sweeping her hand from her face to her feet. "Does it *look* like anyone cares what color my hair is?"

I couldn't help but smile at her ego. To be honest, it was good to finally meet someone like I used to be. Blu said it in a joking sort of way, but I could tell she was sort of serious, too.

"Just as well," she said, crossing back to me with the blanket she'd robbed from her cot. "He was a big bloke and his clothes probably wouldn't have fit your pale frame, anyway."

Accepting the blanket from her, I slung it around my shoulders and narrowed my eyes at her. "I used to look like the god Apollo, Blu. Next time you're tied to a bed for three years, I'll check on you to see how your tan's coming."

"Cry me a river, mate," Blu said as she tossed me a pair of boots. "And my tan is permanent, thanks to my parents."

Man, the future was just full of surprises. Being able to pick your baby's hair and eye color, not to mention its skin tone, sounds like something that people would've taken hook, line, and sinker where I come from.

Once I'd pulled on the boots that were too big, I followed Blu out of the igloo and into the Rogue mega-camp.

Whew.

Chapter fifteen is complete.

Since all that really happened was I had my right arm ripped clean off, I'd say that this particular chapter fifteen turned out pretty decent. Nothing too life threatening happened, making me start to feel more at ease with—

I was tackled by a big guy when I wasn't even ten paces out of the igloo, and the ogre slammed me up against it. I felt steel on my neck and almost sighed.

Really, fifteen? I was, like, literally a sentence away from ending this thing...

CHAPTER 16

"Who are you?" the man grunted out dangerously, and I felt the sharp machete bite into my neck.

"Listen, friend," I said in a low voice, grasping his large wrist in my newly-fitted right hand and slowly removing the blade from my throat as I shoved him back. "I don't think we've been properly introduced." I now had both his wrists and he couldn't pull away. "Name's Jericho. Who do I have the pleasure of punching?"

He was a big guy all around. Big framed, armed, necked, and handed—you name it and this dude had it in plus size. He wasn't exactly fat, I noticed, even though he was an easy three-fifty, but about twice my size in every way and about four inches taller than I was.

And he had a sort of small blonde afro going on, too, like he wasn't accustomed to a lot of hair maintenance or even looking in a mirror every once in a while. The scruff on his neck and chin wasn't blonde but sort of dark reddish, and what little was there was a wired, tangled mess.

"Sam," he said, and I saw a bead of sweat run down his cheek from trying to break out of my grasp.

"Oh, the ex," I said, releasing him, and he instantly stepped away, rubbing at his wrists and scowling at me. By this time, a sizable crowd had gathered to watch the exchange, and Sam turned his scowl on them, shouting, "What're you lot looking at, then?"

The crowd went back to their Rogue business, and the

large man turned back to me and said, "I was coming to get Blu and saw her come out of her quarters with a naked man wrapped in a blanket. What was I supposed to do?"

"I don't know," I said, adjusting the blanket around me. "Maybe not try and kill the naked dude? What kind of man attacks a guy who is only wearing boots and a blanket, anyway?"

Since I could feel the cold now, I was starting to think that the suit Cross had given me was the reason I was so resistant before.

"I'm sorry," Sam said, his head drooping a little. "Guess I lost my head for a second."

"Yeah, you've been known to do that," Blu said, appearing beside me. "Jericho is the new guy everyone's been talking about, Sam, and not my new boyfriend," then she glanced at me and smiled. "Not at the moment, anyway."

Ignoring his ex, Sam placed a hand on my shoulder and said, "I'm sorry, mate. Let's be friends until the day we die."

It was a strange way of asking someone to be a BFF, I must say, but, then again, strange was the new normal as far as I was concerned.

"I don't know about you, Sam, but I could use a friendship that lasted until the day I died." I didn't feel the need to tell him that I'd pretty much died already.

"I appreciate it," the big man said, extending a hand. "As Al Green would say—"

"Oh, for the love of all that's holy, stop with the Al Green quotations," Blu said, placing her hands on her hips. "You keep going on about that stupid music thing you found and yet no one cares."

That sounded a bit harsh. Mainly because I would've killed a hobo for the chance to hear some Al Green.

"Red needs you in the council," Sam told her. "That's all I had to say, you crazy—"

"Okay," I said in a sing-song voice, laying a hand on Sam's shoulder before he could carry out the insult directed toward his blue-haired ex. "Listen, pal, you're already a friend of mine because of the Al Green thing, which I will be asking about later, mind you, so there's no need for name-calling."

Sam nodded then pointed at Blu, narrowing his eyes. "Just be glad my friend is here, or you would've been burned."

"So, Blu, what about this council?" I asked. "I used to sit in on a few war councils back in the day. I'm sure they wouldn't notice the guy wrapped in a blanket if I tagged along."

I fell in step behind her, and my new homie, Sam, followed me. "I don't mind," Blu said. "Although I'm sure the main topic will be why Red decided to bring you back. And it's not really a council, considering there aren't many members on it."

We traversed the maze of tents and igloos for what seemed like forever because, well, I was still wrapped in nothing but a blanket, and it just seemed like it was taking longer than it should have. All the people we passed would stop whatever they were doing to stare at us while we went by, sometimes shooing their small children inside their respective places of abode, leaving the clothes they'd been washing or the meat they'd been roasting outside as they followed their children inside.

I'd finally decided that the Rogue parents just didn't want their kids marred by the near-naked man being escorted by. At least that's what I was hoping, anyway. This notion was shattered by Blu saying, "They're afraid of you."

"What?" I asked, truly not expecting that. "Why? I didn't do anything to them."

"Don't sweat it, Jerry," Sam said as he tromped behind me, glancing at the latest woman to tell her children to get inside. "Most of these people are runaways and castoffs. The castoffs aren't worried about someone noticing who they are, but the runaways sure are."

The huts and hovels began thinning when we neared the other side of the cavern, and while we passed the last few, I noticed something.

"Say, Blu?"

"Yes?"

"Why didn't I see one man in the camp?"

It was true. I saw lots of woman with their children, a few little boys littered here and there, but that was it.

"There aren't many men around," she told me, stopping in front of an iron door in the ice wall. "All males topside are tagged with a military grade holotab by the Reds when they turn twelve and are trained before they're sold to the Bears or Fascists."

"Yeah, that's a thing," Sam said when he saw my aghast expression. "I used to be a handler for one of the warehouses before I found my way here."

I wanted more information, but my escorts seemed to be done talking about the seemingly normal child trafficking of their time. I changed the subject.

"Well, however you got here, I'm just glad you did or else I might never have gotten the chance to hear Al Green again."

"Found it topside a few years back," he said, smiling.

"What kind of device is it on?"

"Red little thing," he said. "Says Zune on the back."

"I totally used to have a Zune," I said excitedly.

Frowning, Sam asked, "Really? Where'd you find yours?"

Before I had a chance to tell him I had ordered it from Amazon, I remembered that I hadn't exactly told him that I was from the past.

"He's from the year 2012, Sam," Blu said, like it wasn't a big deal.

Sam's eyes lit up. "I'd heard that crazy Sparks man had almost cracked his theory of time-travel back when I was in the program. He did it, then?"

"I'm half-living proof," I said. "If I survive this council, we'll talk about your Zune."

Nodding, we were silent for almost a minute.

Then, "Do you miss your time?" Sam asked.

"A little."

"Any regrets?"

I thought long and hard for a few seconds.

"Well, I did end up missing the Avengers and the election."

"It's time-travel, friend," Sam said with a smile. "If you ever get back one day, all that stuff will be waiting for you."

Our elevator ride ended with a shudder when we hit bottom. "I hope you're right, Sam."

"Hope? It's the past. What could go wrong?"

"You would be surprised."

CHAPTER 17

Stepping out of the raggedy elevator, I found myself in yet another ice-laden hall. "How far down did you guys dig?" I asked.

"Not far at all," Blu said. "These lower tunnels were dug out by ice-spiders years ago. It took almost a month to clear out the current residents when we moved in. The big cavern you just saw was only about a quarter of that size at first and housed lots of the white devils. Most of our digging took place in the main cavern. This tunnel leads to our command room, of sorts."

Sam chuckled at that. "More like out of sorts."

"Don't listen to him," Blu said while narrowing her eyes in his direction. "He believes in our goals, no matter what he says."

"It's not the goals I doubt, love. Our so-called leader is who I have my doubts aimed toward."

"He's the reason most of us are alive, Sam. Try and show a little respect."

"I said the Gazer's goals and motives aren't my issue, Blu," Sam said. "It's his whole universal peace jazz, coupled with the way he goes about things that I dislike."

Obviously, this was a bad subject between them, but I didn't exactly have another topic ready to delve into. "Red said she sort of ran things around here."

"Red answers directly to Stargazer, so I suppose you

could say she does—to Stargazer's standard, of course," Blu said as we traversed the white hall.

"Stargazer?" I asked.

"Here we go," Sam muttered to himself while shaking his head, as if I'd just asked the worst question imaginable.

"I wasn't around when Stargazer began leading the Rogues," Blu started. "He's a bit... eccentric, I guess you'd say, but he seems to care about the people, and that's good enough for most of us."

I couldn't help but notice that she glanced at Sam when she said the bit about most of them appreciating Stargazer. "Does this guy know I'm even here?"

"Red's in with him now, so I'd think so," Blu said. "Might be best if you and Sam wait outside the door while I find out what Stargazer wants."

Sam snorted at that. "What, he needs both the wonder twins on the case?"

Blu glared at him, and I was noticing that their relationship bore a striking resemblance to the one I had shared with Chloe before the both of us had died. The notion caused me to feel a slight twinge in my heart, and I wished that I wouldn't have brought her with me when I went after Klaus, which seemed like a lifetime ago.

Chloe had died in my arms that day, and recent events were causing me to revisit the unpleasant feeling of watching someone you care about die before your eyes. Thoughts on my past were never a good thing lately because eventually, they all led to Piper.

Sweet Piper.

Although my new Rogue companions had assured me that she wasn't far away, I was beginning to think that I'd never see her beautiful face and golden hair ever again.

We finally arrived at yet another iron door, and Blu entered while Sam and I waited outside as instructed, leaning against the ice walls at first and eventually sliding down and sitting on the ground.

"Red told me that you've run into a Dragonov or two," Sam suddenly said.

"I have," I told him. "Awesome to pilot but horrible to face off against."

"You ain't ever lied, mate. Most of the officers in the program were issued one, and we handlers were optional."

"You like it?"

"Never got one. Although they seem to be one-size-fits-all, the men behind the design apparently weren't thinking of us bigger blokes when they manufactured the things," he said. "Had to rig me up a piece on my own."

"What, like a bigger one?"

"Not really. Blu fixed it up for me," Sam stood, sliding his long dirty yellow coat off, and what I saw wasn't what I was expecting.

"What're you wearing?" I asked, looking his mechanized frame up and down.

"This is the exoskeleton of a Raptor-6," he said, flexing around, and I heard the whirring now. Funny, I hadn't heard it before. "Blu fitted my chest pretty easily, but she had to put some extensions on the arms and legs."

"So, the only thing you don't get out of it is the armor?"

"That, and she had to turn the power way down so I didn't break a hand with a small punch. I can run a lot faster and jump a lot higher, and it only weighs around forty pounds."

"Blu's really good at that stuff, isn't she?"

Sam nodded, reaching for his long coat. "Australia was the pioneer of imprinting when the stuff first hit the market. You can learn to do anything if you've got the holos for it. Blu hails from a long line of scientists who did have such funds and poured a lot of important jazz in her head. Blu said that her parents had it all figured out and that Red was going to be the general and she was supposed to be the next big thing in nanotechnology."

"She sure did a bang-up job on my arm," I said, holding

the arm up for him to see.

Shrugging, Sam said, "I don't know how important they were back home, but here Red's basically our general and Blu's our doctor of sorts. She also keeps all of our tech and mechs running."

"You guys have mechs?"

"A few," Sam said, sitting back down a few feet away. "Don't use them much topside, but it's nice to have the firepower if we ever did venture out in them."

After that we resumed sitting in silence, and I have to say that it was nice to have a new BFF who was just as satisfied with not talking as he was with talking. Years ago, I couldn't think of anyone I'd rather listen to than Jericho Johnson, but now things were different. Call me a buzz-kill, but for some reason, after the long months of being literally tied down with no one to talk to but myself, I was starting to not like the sound of my voice very much, choosing instead to hear and listen to what others had to say.

I didn't get to dwell too long on, well, dwelling on myself because the iron door opened, and Blu told me to come inside.

Standing, Sam and I exchanged fist-bumps. "I'll catch you later, Sam. Don't forget to charge that Zune for our Al Green fest."

"Way ahead of you, mate," he said, clapping me on the shoulder once before walking back down the hall. Blu stood aside, allowing me entrance to Stargazer's massive vestibule. I frowned while glancing around the large area littered with heavy cables, holocomputers, flood lights, and all sorts of unrecognizable science equipment.

"You said he was eccentric?" I asked, following Blu through the only path available in the tangled heap of the lab. Looking up, I saw that most of the cables and wires were leading to what I could only discern as some sort of mega-telescope. Made sense, I guess, Stargazer being what he was calling himself.

"Very," she confirmed. "Stargazer was a bit of a scientist/

astronomer/astrophysicist/you-name-it before my time. I could make Galileo himself cry with all the astrophysical imprints I have, and I still don't know what it is the man is trying to accomplish here."

Well, that was comforting. Just in that one sentence spoken by my blue-haired friend, I could deduce that I was probably about to meet yet another madman.

Don't know why I was surprised, because the future was positively infested with madmen at every turn. Hopefully, Stargazer wouldn't be bent on world domination, at least, because I'd had my share of that to last me the rest of my freak-of-nature life.

The corridor after the first cramped chamber led into a sort of force-field looking thing.

"This is the decontamination room."

Blu walked through the first light blue wall of haze and stood in the center of the ten by ten-foot space, holding up her arms while a beam came from the left side of the space and ran over her.

Then she stepped through the other side and turned to me. "Your turn, mate."

"Your accent is supposed to set my mind at ease?" I asked, stepping into the decontamination unit.

Laughing, Blu said, "Something like that. I've only heard one other person with an accent like yours. American, right?"

"Yay for someone remembering the stars and stripes," I muttered, closing my eyes as the beam passed over my frame.

Once we were both quite decontaminated and safely on the other side of the blue shields with all our limbs attached, I once again fell in step behind Blu. The next room was way different than the science explosion that greeted us at the beginning. It kind of reminded me of the boasting room in my mansion back in Chicago hundreds of years ago—except where there should have been furniture, there were ice sculptures.

Like, a lot of the damn things.

Blu led me through the freezing crowd of art while I

glanced left and right with a confused frown on my face. The oddness came from the variety. One of a small girl with what looked like an assault rifle, one of a bizarre wolf that towered over a smaller sculpture of a shirtless man, a woman robed almost Roman looking woman sitting on a rock, her clear, ice eyes aimed forward, and many other strange ice scenes unfolding before my eyes.

"Not the most common hobbies I've ever seen," I said, my gaze wavering on one of the statues. It was a man about my height with a checkered long-sleeved button up shirt and a flatcap. I'm not sure why of all the sculptures the one of the regular looking man with his hands in his pockets was the one that caught my eye.

Just as we were about to leave the sculptures, I saw one final piece that made me stop. Blu stopped, too, her boot touching the bottom of the stairs that led up to an iron pavilion as she looked back at where I was walking to the left and peering at...

What *was* this?

It was a detailed scene depicting two men locked in conflict. One of them was on his back, his hands held up in almost surrender, while the other man, who seemed to have gotten the upper hand but still on his knees, was lunging for the downed man, his right hand brandishing a rock. The scene was about half scale so whoever made it could flesh it out with barren landscape the men were fighting on and—

"What the—"

There were dinosaurs in the background of the piece, rushing around as the two men fought.

"So, like, what, it's a cavemen fight?" I muttered, frowning before blinking when I noticed the man on his back was the same man from the statue that had caught my eye a few moments before. His checkered shirt gave it away and this hypothesis was confirmed when I spied his flatcap on the ground next to the fight. "So, not cavemen?"

I was in the process of walking around the scene to get

a look at who was attacking the downed man but Blu touched my blanket-covered shoulder. "We need to go, mate."

"Guy's got a lot of time on his hands," I said as we exited the sculpture field and walked up a short flight of stairs hewn into the ice.

"Not as much as you'd think," Blu told me. Then we were standing on the pavilion that did have some furniture, and I got my first look at the mysterious man known as Stargazer.

Red was seated on my right at a desk, fanning through a holoscreen filled with something most likely important because she hadn't even noticed we were standing ten feet away yet. Stargazer was on the far side of the pavilion with his back to us, his wrinkled hands clasped behind his back.

He was balding, with a small rim of white hair, but he didn't exactly look frail to me in his white robes. Yes, you heard me right—the guy was wearing white robes.

Great. The head honcho of the Rogues looks like a bald Gandalf the White, and they wonder why they're living underground.

Then Gandalf spoke.

"You are late," he said, his accent hinting at British. Turning his head slightly, I saw half of the older man's weathered face, which had a short thick beard on it. "I thought you would have come to me years ago but, as the saying goes, better late than never."

"You were expecting me for that long?" I asked.

"My dear boy," Stargazer said, a strange smile forming on his face, "I've been expecting you for the last forty years."

CHAPTER 18

So, here's the thing.

Apparently, since I was the one and only time-traveling billionaire, maybe my future self had stopped in his travels long enough to acknowledge the man who looked like a young Gandalf forty years ago, and he must've lied to Stargazer and told him that he'd be right back when he jetted.

What a lying cad.

Wait—that's future me I'm talking about.

I mean, uh, what a great guy.

Millions of scenarios akin to that one bubbled up in my mind after Stargazer informed me that he had been waiting on me for a long time, and I was instantly trying to hash out how and why I would've met this strange man so long ago and what I'd said that made him think I was supposedly coming back.

Bah, that was confusing. Okay, let me try and lay out the questions I needed to ask in the order I needed to ask them.

First, where were we when we met?

Second, how did he even remember what I looked like for forty years?

Third, what had transpired in our meeting?

Fourth, had my hair grown back?

Fifth, was I a real boy?

And finally, sixth, what had I said that made him think I was coming back?

It took me almost a minute of awkward silence to

arrange all these questions in my head, and after the pause was over, I took a deep breath, readying myself for the onslaught of queries that I was about to release—

"Obviously, I can't tell you what transpired when we met years ago."

And, just like that, all my awesome, well thought-out questions went into the garbage.

Stargazer crossed the pavilion slowly, and I noticed he didn't seem to be focusing on anything.

"You're blind," I said, kind of thrown off. I mean, the dude called himself Stargazer which, to me, sounded like he, oh, I don't know, gazed at things.

Particularly stars.

"Quite," Stargazer said, finding the arm of a comfortable looking chair and easing down into it. The pavilion was set up like a study or small library with a coffee table and lamp. "Red, leave us. Blu, you stay."

Red stood without a word and crossed the pavilion to us, merely nodding once when she passed me. Out of her battle armor I noticed she was actually a little taller than I was and her red hair reached just passed her shoulders. Her tight jumpsuit looked like Blu's white one only it was—you guessed it—red.

"Please sit, Jericho," Stargazer said politely, waving a hand to the loveseat sitting opposite him on the other side of the oak coffee table.

Blu plopped down without hesitation and patted the spot beside her, giving me a wickedly adorable smile when she did.

"Behave, Blu," the old man that I had thought was blind said to her. "He's been through a lot, this young man, and the journey before him isn't an easy one, to be sure."

Sitting awkwardly beside Blu, I leaned forward, placing my elbows on my knees. "So, you *can* see?"

"Not for a long time now," Stargazer said, and he leaned back into his chair, letting out a sigh that made me realize just how old the guy actually was. "Blu ran some diagnostics on you while you slept off losing your arm. May I just say how honored I am to finally meet you, son."

"Why?" I asked.

Again, I saw the odd smile appear on the old man's lips. It was the kind of small smile that let you know that the smiler knew something you didn't.

I hate that kind.

"Do you even know what you are?" Stargazer asked simply, like he was asking his son if he'd taken out the trash.

"Cross's guinea pig."

The laugh surprised me when it escaped his lips. After a few seconds, he regained enough composure to say, "You are a good deal more than that, I am afraid. Blu, the layout, if you please."

Blu tapped at her holotab and a screen floated above the coffee table. It looked like a skeleton, mine, I was guessing, when she tapped some more and I saw the robot parts.

"You're lucky to be alive," Blu told me. "That's a lot of gyros for a breathing human to be packing."

"Quite," Stargazer said. "Red filled me in on your journey thus far and I must say, it was an intriguing tale."

"You say 'thus far' like it's not over," I told him. "But it is. As soon as I find a way out of this frozen hell, I'm grabbing Piper and we're out of here."

"Really?" The old man asked. "To what end?"

"I'm going back to Chicago after I drop Piper off at Svalbard." I don't know why I was talking to him like I had a plan set in stone, because I didn't. Deep down, though, I knew that Chicago was basically out of the question. Jericho Johnson suddenly becoming a cyborg would raise a lot of questions back in 2012, let me tell you. Questions that I wouldn't be able to answer without shattering the world as everyone knew it.

But maybe I could at least get Piper home. After that, I didn't care what happened to me.

"Surely an educated individual like yourself would know

that you don't belong in the past you once lived," Stargazer said, and I could've sworn he was looking right at me. "And as for your friend Piper, how do you know she wants to go home?"

"I know her," I said confidently. "She's always been about helping her kinsman and clan."

"Three years is a long time," Blu pointed out. "I've almost been killed by the leader of the Ghost Squadron several times myself."

I gave her a questioning look and she said, "Your girlfriend basically runs the Rebel topside ops, now."

"What about Beck?" I asked.

"We're not sure," Blu said. "She hasn't been seen topside in quite a while."

My mind went to Beck's clandestine exchange with Ritu. Her hair had fallen out and she looked like she had the flu from hell. While I was mulling over whether to let my new Rogue friends know about Beck's weakened state, Stargazer said, "What Blu says is true, Jericho. Piper hasn't just seen three long years of happiness and peace. She's been on the front lines of a war she doesn't understand, fighting for a cause she can't even grasp. You will come to learn, my friend, much sooner than you would care for, that war changes people whether they know fully what they are fighting for or not."

Everything he was saying made sense and I hated it. So, to change the subject, I said, "Enough about war and my travel plans. You were showing me something on the diagram thing?"

"Cross did an amazing job on you, I'll give him that," Blu said, fanning through a few more windows of up-close pics of my synthetic parts. "Although, as I said in my tent, you're a bloody weapon of mass destruction from where I'm sitting. And don't even get me started on whatever kind of blood he's got you running on."

"Z-90," Stargazer and I said together.

Blu flicked her bright green eyes from her holotab long enough to glance between us. "Okay," she said, shrugging once and turning back to her tab. "Everyone knows the secret but Blu. Super."

"All I know is what Cross told me," I said, before explaining everything Cross had said concerning Z-90 to them.

Once I'd finished, Stargazer was rubbing at his small white beard thoughtfully.

"Yes, fascinating," Blu said in a not-so-fascinated tone. "But what does the stuff do?"

Shrugging, I said, "You got me."

"Cross's experiments aren't the fascinating part, girl," Stargazer said in wonder. "I was hoping when I heard Red's account of you topside that you were the one. Now I know for certain," Stargazer smiled and a tear ran down his cheek as he extended a shaking hand toward me.

"Behold, Blu, the last hope of humanity has finally arrived."

CHAPTER 19

"Whoa, dude," I said quickly with my hands up. "I'm not here to save humanity."

"You are a perfect being now, Jericho, limited by almost nothing," Stargazer said.

"When are we supposed to meet again?" I asked. My tone was definitely that of a non-believer, that was for sure. "Because you say that you can't tell me about it. That's not helping me want to jump on board your crazy-train, pal."

That smile again. "I suppose the best way of explaining it is that we worked together."

"Worked together how?"

"I was a navigator of sorts," he said after a pause, like he was still dumbing down things to keep everything in the dark."

Which was getting old.

"So, you can't tell me any better details?" I asked, trying to not totally lose it.

Stargazer was silent for a moment, debating, I was guessing. "You have a destiny, Jericho," he finally said. "It is unavoidable but also fragile. All I can say is you are now of a new species that is also as old as time itself. The Paladins."

"Paladins?" I asked, testing the name out.

"Yes," he said. "You are not the first, but you are the first in eons."

Paladin, huh? I could think of worse names for an eons-old species. And guess who the lucky dog was who was now part of a super-human race named after his favorite class in Dungeons & Dragons?

This guy.

Blu was looking hard at the floor after Stargazer finished his meager story to us, and I recalled that she said she didn't know much about Stargazer. He took care of the Rogues, but his goals and motives were a mystery to a lot of them, it seemed. "What are trying to accomplish with us?"

Stargazer was silent for longer than normal this time before answering her. "I failed my mission years ago, dear. Helping these people is my way of atoning for that. All I want now is for the Rogues to prosper."

Blu simply nodded, but I could tell she was relieved about something. I, on the other hand, wasn't the least bit relieved about anything the old man sitting across from me was saying.

The worst part was that everything I needed to know that he wouldn't tell me was apparently told to him by future-Jericho, someone who was starting to cause me problems.

Irony upon irony.

"You are capable of virtually anything now, Jericho," Stargazer said to me. "Bending the elements around you is just a drop in the ocean that is your potential. You are the last yet the first, son."

"So, Cross's experiments, the resurrection or Z-90, has nothing to do with my current capabilities? How is that not a factor?"

"I didn't say it had nothing to do with it," the old man said, waving his hand in a non-interested fashion. "Cross isn't the creator of your species. That is important for you to know. The Z-90, though, is quite a powerful element and is part of your destiny. It will have effects that you aren't even aware of yet."

Then I thought of something.

"Beck has Z-90 inside her," I said suddenly. "Does that make her like me?"

"From the scans I got during combat, she's almost 90% synthetic," Blu said. "If that's the case, then she doesn't have much of the stuff."

"What is left of her vessel is tainted, thus restraining the full potential of the Z-90," Stargazer said.

"Restraining?" I asked, dumbfounded. "I've seen her lift cars and rip arms off of battle-suits like it was nothing."

Stargazer had gotten that same knowing smile again. "That is restrained. I'm surprised that Beck is still alive, to be sure, since most of Cross's test subjects died within days. Perhaps because she's mostly synthetic. Yet another uniqueness in her favor."

I was silent for a moment before saying, "I saw Beck on a holochat with someone in Cross's facility before I left. She looked pretty bad."

Blu, who had been frowning at her holotab again, glanced up at that. "What do you mean 'pretty bad'?"

"Her hair had fallen out and she looked sick. That was pretty much all I could see."

Blu glanced at Stargazer, who was rubbing at his chin again in thought. "She's 90% synthetic, you say? How long has she been like this?"

"Cross rebuilt her when she was eighteen, with methods that people tell me are illegal."

"You're illegal, too, mate," Blu threw in. "Your meager reading on tech is all attached to your spine."

"If what you say is true, then I'd say Beck doesn't have much time left," Stargazer said. "The white blood cells Cross added to his first trials are constantly fighting the Z-90 to keep it from destroying the nervous system. Eventually, one will win in this battle, and since Beck has so little actual human nerves left, the process has been spread out for years. Depending on which blood type is winning now will tell her odds. If the white cells are winning, then she needs more Z-90. If the Z-90 is winning, then she's as good as dead."

I didn't know what to say to that. I've already mentioned

that I had mixed feelings concerning Beck, but I didn't want her to die or anything. I mean, I couldn't fix her one way or another, right?

Right?

"Can I spare any Z-90 for her if she needs it?" I asked.

Stargazer was silent because he was, uh, you know, thinking about it, I guess. Blind people are hard to read sometimes. Then he said, "I honestly do not know."

"You didn't lose any type of unrecognizable fluid after Red removed your arm," Blu said, tapping away at her holotab again. "So, we can't use that little incident for verification."

"Too bad," I said. "Hate to think I just lost my arm to have my holotab removed. Is there anything specific I need to do to set me on this path you won't tell me about?"

Sighing, the old man stood slowly, wincing as he finally got to his feet. "Walk with us, Jericho. Red will be along with your repaired clothes shortly."

I followed them down the stairs while clutching the blanket around me. The next room looked like the old man's bedroom because, well, it had a bed, for starters, and it just looked a lot homier than the rest of his lab. Blu helped him to the bed and eased him down onto it before laying him down softly.

Once she'd pulled the covers around him, she asked almost affectionately, "Anything else, grey hairs?"

"Find your sister, and the two of you can begin diagnostics and tests on Jericho, if he chooses."

"Of course," Blu said, patting his shoulder once before leaving the room, her deep blue hair bouncing while she walked.

I went to follow her, but Stargazer said, "A word, Paladin."

I sheepishly crossed to the bed and waited for him to say whatever he had on his mind. He seemed out of breath, and after a few seconds of getting his breathing under control, he said, "I'm dying."

What was I supposed to say to that? I'm sorry? How much longer do you have? Do you have an advanced directive in place?

Since I couldn't think of anything to say, I remained silent.

"The Rogues are good people, Jericho, and they are the only reason I have lived this long."

"What is their endgame, here?" I couldn't help but ask. "I mean, they're not officially in the three-way war going on topside. All they're doing is hiding from everyone because they're weak and raiding the occasional supply line for resources so they can keep hiding."

"You are inquiring about the purpose of all this?" he asked, sweeping his hand around feebly. "Is not self-preservation the first human reaction to everything?"

I shrugged—an act, might I add, that is completely wasted on blind people. "I guess I'm saying that it all just seems pointless to me. If you guys joined the Rebels—"

"Who do not listen to reason. We attempted that in the past, and they quickly declined us."

"Why?"

"The Rebels are barely hanging on themselves. What good would a camp full of dead weight do them?" Stargazer said. "The only thing I have been able to give these people is hope, Jericho. Hope that the next day won't be the hell they've come to know as daily life, that things will get better. For all of us."

"Sounds like a pretty big dream," I said quietly.

"I thought so, too," he said, smiling slightly. "Until you showed up."

I was silent again, not really knowing where the old man was going with this.

"The Rogues will need a leader after I'm gone," he started.

Ah. So that's where he was going.

"I hate to bust your bubble, pal, but I'm not exactly

leader material."

"On the contrary," Stargazer said. "Your entire being is leader material, son. You have the capability of rallying these downtrodden people to any cause you care to throw your lot in. Wherever you go, they will follow you. Whatever you say, they will take to heart. All I offered was hope. But you, Jericho, you have the ability to offer them something so much greater."

"Like what?" I heard myself ask.

"An actual future, for starters," he said, his voice growing distant. "You will lead them into a better tomorrow."

It sounded good, I'll give him that. The whole saving-the-helpless gig, I mean.

"My death is nothing," Stargazer said. "But the death of this planet is. If this war doesn't end soon, I fear that our world is doomed."

He surprised me by grabbing my hand. "You can save it, Jericho."

"I've already saved the world," I tried.

"You cast your feeble, human efforts into the fire, stopping a madman from altering his and your reality, and you died. Fate is a harsh mistress, Jericho, but she is not without her sudden acts of kindness. Had you not been caught in the explosion, you would not be standing here now with the capability of saving humanity from themselves? You are a Paladin, Jericho."

When I didn't say anything, he finally said, "Stay with us for one week and allow Blu and Red to put your new body to the test. Then give me your answer."

I told him I'd stay for a week and left his room with everything I'd just learned whirling around in my head.

There were a lot of things I didn't know, but I was sure of one thing. I wasn't about to become the silver bullet for the Rogues.

CHAPTER 20

"You ready?" I heard Blu's voice ask in my head, once again making me regret letting her fit me with a new holotab that was, as she put it, off the grid. Instead of answering, I made a face that told all just how Jericho was feeling about the voice in his head, which I'm thinking she saw because she said, "It's really the best form of communication, Jericho. Now, if you're quite done making faces, let's do this thing."

"Says the blue-haired girl safely tucked away in a lab," I muttered, rolling my neck around and swiveling my torso a few times.

"You know I can hear everything you say, right?"

"Oh, I was counting on it," I replied, glancing at my surroundings. At first I thought Red and Blu were taking me topside for a few tests, but the elevator stopped about midway in our ascent and we stepped out onto the level where Blu said she worked primarily. "When I'm not reattaching someone's arm, that is."

"Shut up," Red told her, stopping beside me. She was rocking her battle-armor, which had me thinking that the tests I was about to do weren't going to involve a treadmill or urine culture. I had gotten back my awesome duds from Red, good as new, mostly, and I felt great in my hooded long coat. I had to hand it to Cross. He sure knew how to make cool clothes for a mad scientist.

The room we were standing in was about the size of a

football field, with a ceiling of ice almost twenty feet above us. Our testing stuff looked like a pile of assorted items from a junkyard.

"We're going to be testing your strength capabilities first," Blu said, and I glanced at her, safe and sound, behind ballistic glass on the other side of the massive testing area. "Red will lead, and we'll see if you can pull off everything she can in her Raptor-6."

"Don't worry, mate," Red said, winking at me before her face mask clinked down and the eyepieces lit up. "I'll go easy on you this time," she said, her voice deeper coming out of the helmet.

"Try and lift something that an average person couldn't lift normally," Blu told us, and Red made her way to what looked like the remains of a piano.

"God knows we aren't ever going to lack for junk around here," Red said, lifting the piano easily over her head once before placing it back down.

"Alright, Jericho, now you. Try and take it easy—"

I lifted the piano over my head with one arm.

Epic.

On the almighty list of heaviness, the piano, to me, always fell somewhere in the top ten between elephants and rhinos. Don't know if you've tried to lift a good-sized piano over your head lately but, if not, why don't you go give it a try? That way you'll be able to hone-in on my new level of strength.

"That was unexpected," Blu said. "Okay, let me adjust my material."

"Adjust this," I said, grabbing the piano with both hands, spinning once, and throwing it about twenty yards.

"Nice," Red said, nodding her helmet.

Blu wasn't saying anything, but I could see her blinking at the spectacle through the thick glass, with her mouth slightly open. Then she said, "Try the car."

I strutted to the rusted remains of a nearby car and, with two hands this time, lifted the hunk of twisted metal over my head. I noticed it was a little harder for me to lift than the piano.

But I knew I could lift more.

"Red, drop another car on top, will you?"

"Sure thing," she said, and in seconds I felt the weight of another car crunch on top.

"Stressed?" Blu asked.

"Feeling it," I admitted. "But I might still be able to hold more."

"How about not," Blu said. "I get it. You're strong. Let's move on to other tests."

I laughed at that. "Ah, come on, Blu."

"No lie," she chuckled. "I'm going to file this test under 'don't-make-Jericho-mad.' How about a little go against Red's suit? Just physically this time. Can't have you cooking my sister with your, uh, lightning whatever stuff."

I turned to Red and she took a stance in her suit, holding up massive clenched fists. "Are you smiling?" I asked her.

"You'll never know," she said before launching toward me at an insane speed, closing the gap between us in a split second and attacking me with a right jab, which I stopped with my left hand, clamping onto the fist.

Red tried her left next, and I stopped the enormous pressure delivered by the Raptor-6 easily with my right.

I guess I was too involved in how strong I was to be paying attention to my opponent—something Red exploited big time when she drove the right knee of her suit into my chest hard, sending me skidding all the way to the thick glass Blu was behind.

And it wasn't your average kick-boxing kind of knee attack, either. The crazy Aussie had engaged some sort of blast from her right foot to add more power to her sneaky move, resulting in me spinning and skidding over thirty yards from the force.

When I got to my feet, I heard Blu lighting into her sister about how she could've killed me with her uncalled-for maneuver. "You okay?" Blu asked, peering at me through the glass I was leaning my hand against.

"I'm good," I told her, turning back to Red. "And I thought we were on our second date until that love-tap. That was some serious third or fourth date stuff you just pulled there, pal."

"I always take the initiative in most of my relationships, Jericho. Next time just move faster, mate."

"You said it first," I said, pushing off the glass and rushing her. Red tried to time a haymaker on me, which I dodged with a sideways somersault, spinning over her head. She swung a blind fist behind her in an attempt to hit me mid-landing, but she was too late so her arm passed over me as I landed in a crouch.

Red, who was a lot faster in her Raptor-6 than I originally thought, spun around and tried to stomp me while I crouched and—

And then I don't what came over me.

I've already mentioned something about just knowing that I could do certain things, but some of the real crazy stuff just came naturally to me and, at times, automatically, like my hands flying behind my head and stopping the thousand-pound stomp.

I heard Blu gasp before I pushed upward with my arms and legs, sending the massive suit sailing into the air and pinwheeling behind me.

But I wasn't done yet.

I kicked off hard, tucking into a ball and spinning backward after Red, making it to her in the middle of her hang time and delivering an earth-shattering kick with both barrels into the stomach of her suit.

The double kick that sent me into a perfect Superman dive sent the flailing Red into a fast, straight line to the floor, giving her a taste of her own skidding medicine as she tumbled over the hard floor and into Blu's blast glass.

Red groaned and slowly got her suit into a sitting

position while I landed in a roll. "Cranky," she muttered before coughing once. "What just happened?"

Rolling onto my feet, I turned to where she was slumping against the wall. "I just took you on our fourth date."

In spite of having her butt positively handed to her on a platter, Red laughed softly, letting her helmet clunk back against the glass in exhaustion while her face mask opened. "I think we should start seeing other people. But don't worry, mate, it's me, not you."

"What do you know," Blu said. "This can be filed under 'don't-make-Jericho-mad,' too. Hey, guess who's not going to be spending the night doing paperwork?" I stopped in front of the glass just in time to see Blu smile, hook two thumbs at herself, and say, "This girl."

"Guess who's going to be spending the night in the infirmary?" Red muttered, climbing to her feet.

"Walk it off, Red," Blu told her sister while flipping through her holotab. "We're on the clock here."

"You okay?" I asked Red.

Red took a deep breath before nodding. "My pride is the only thing wounded."

Red got out of her armor after that, and Blu ended up coming out to at least see if she was actually hurt. She wasn't, and Blu told her she could split if she needed to, since the rest of my lineup wasn't going to involve her anymore.

Red decided to stay, stating that she'd come this far and wanted to see what else I could do, although I noticed she took up residence with her sister behind the thick glass for the remainder of the Jerichathlon.

Smart girl, that Red.

"Let's get a look at those bells and whistles of yours that I've been drooling over for the last twenty-four hours," Blu said, and her sister gave her a sideways glance, raising an eyebrow. Blu just shrugged. "What? I'm a fool for hardware, okay?"

"What kind of bells and whistles did you have in mind?"

I asked, walking toward the center of the testing area.

"Duh, lightning," Blu told me. "I can monitor you while you do it and gauge a lot of my analysis off that."

"So, what, just hit the junk heap?"

"Try aiming for the piano you tossed," Red told me.

I could feel the slight hum in my palms; the tingling had started just at the mention of it. This was a relief to me since all my previous lightning mage stunts had been in the middle of battle, and I'd been wondering how easy it was to turn on and off.

I snapped my right fingers, and visible blue flecks buzzed into sight.

"I think I love you," Blu said, sighing dreamily.

"I know," I told her with a smile, holding up both my hands and leveling them at the remains of the smashed piano with my left hand extended farther than my right, almost in a fighting stance. Then the brilliant streaks erupted from my hands and tore through the air into the trashed piano, exploding it and sending off-white keys and rotten wood everywhere.

"Care for a spot of target practice, future husband-of-mine?" Blu's voice sounded over a loudspeaker in the testing area, and I saw thin shields appear in front of me all down the length of the spacious room, projecting from the floor and ceiling in random patterns. "Try and sharp shoot a few, love."

I put my left hand behind my back while holding up my right, sniping out the thin green holotargets with a slim jolt from my index finger. Somehow, I didn't actually have to aim, almost like the lightning itself was finding any target I had in mind. After a minute or so of this, Blu buzzed back in. "Enough of that weak stuff. Bring out the big guns and try and take out as many targets as you can in one shot."

"Go easy on me," I told them. "I've only done this once before."

Actually, the move I was about to try was one I attempted years ago whilst trying to save Chloe Sparks from murderous Vikings. That time I'd tried it with the two gauntlets of time, and I had to worry about overheating, my dismemberment if it went south and, honestly, it didn't work out the way I'd hoped. But now was different.

I cupped my hands together, sending electricity into my palms, my hands instantly flying apart almost a foot from the force of the voltage. Back on Svalbard, I had to grit my teeth and push with all my strength to keep the compressed ball of lightning from going everywhere as my human body tried feebly to wield a force it didn't understand. But now I didn't have to push in the least as I continued to flow volts into the buzzing, blue/white basketball-sized storm in my hands, the pure energy not fighting against me because it was now part of me. I slowly began pushing my hands together, compressing the lightning ball. I closed my hands, the air around me shimmering while my long coat billowed behind me from the breeze that had begun swirling around. When it was the size of a baseball, I held it in one hand, squeezing it one last time and bringing it down to the size of a golf ball.

"Check this out," I said, rearing back and throwing it like I was skipping a stone. The small buzzing ball bounced a few times before rolling to a stop among the green shields about thirty yards from me.

Then I snapped my fingers and my lightning ball exploded, bright jolts flying virtually everywhere. All the shields vanished, while my personal bomb hit the ceiling, floor, and far walls on both sides. The aftershock slid the entire pile of junk metal a good twenty feet or so while I, who was standing nearby, just got my coattail blown around.

All was quiet after the last faint buzzes and shocking sounds died away and the smoke cleared. Then Blu spoke.

"Seriously, I bet Stargazer could marry us right now," she said quickly. "And don't worry, mate, none of our kids will be born blue-haired, I promise."

"No way," I said, laughing. "You only want me for my body."

"So?"

"So, that's not the best basis for a relationship, Blu."

"Minor details..."

"Slow down," Red told her sister. "Are there any more tests you want to put him through?"

"Oh, I could think of a few," Blu said knowingly, a small, wicked smile appearing on her face.

"Could you possibly be serious for a change?" Red asked the blue-haired girl.

"I am serious. Seriously in love."

"Technically, if you only want my body, then love isn't the word I'd use," I said, pulling off my hood. "But the thought is appreciated."

"Anytime, dearest," Blu said, tapping on her holotab. "Actually, I've got enough readings and data to last me a few days. And here I thought I wasn't going to be up all night doing paperwork. Thanks for nothing."

I shrugged a shoulder. "Sorry to be a burden. Why not just sift through your data tomorrow?"

Blu looked at me like I had just grown a hand out of my stomach. "And lose eight precious hours that I could've used trying to figure out what makes my future husband tick? I think not."

When we climbed into the elevator and began our descent to the Rogue camp, Blu became serious for the first time since I had met her and said, while shaking her head at what I was guessing were energy readings or something of that nature on her holotab, "If any of these stats are even half of what they look like..." her voice trailed off for a few seconds before she locked her emerald eyes on me and said, "I don't know how you took Stargazer's reaction to you, but whatever he thinks you are, I can already confirm you're about a thousand times more."

"Is that good or bad?" I asked, a little taken aback by Blu's sudden graveness.

"In the right hands, Stargazer is correct; this can save the world. Or at least stop the war that's tearing it apart."

The next question hung in the air like a thick fog until I finally broke down and asked it.

"And in the wrong hands?"

Blu looked away from me. "What do you think?"

CHAPTER 21

Oh, my love, oh, my darling...

I closed my eyes as I heard the first melodious words of Al Green.

Then I cried.

Thankfully, I had foreseen my breaking down and had just borrowed Sam's Zune, informing him that I'd get it back to him tomorrow. The big man had simply nodded knowingly, almost as if he knew why I wanted to jam Green alone, and he'd left me.

...and time goes by so slowly, and time can do so much, are you still mine?

I exited the igloo I'd been set-up in. It was located on the outskirts of the camp, which was good because I didn't want people—okay, mostly women—to see the all-powerful Paladin, that they had already been whispering about in wonder all day, cry because he heard a song that reminded him of his home.

The one he'd most likely never see again.

I walked away from the meager lights of the camp and headed for the ragged elevator that I was riding in when I'd lost my right arm, climbing in and hitting the red button.

Then the gravity of my situation, and how much I hated it, came back to me in full force. It was my fault, really. All of it. Chloe and her father were both killed, and Piper, the Viking woman of my dreams, was stranded in the future while I died right along with Chloe in a monster explosion.

...lonely rivers flow to the sea, to the sea...

But instead of staying dead like any normal person who'd finally run out of cement on the road of life and paid his dues with his life like a good little soldier dying to save the world, I was brought back as something considered to be bottled salvation to a frozen wasteland.

The only person I was interested in saving at that moment was Piper. I didn't know how yet, but I wouldn't rest until I got her back to Svalbard. She'd left with me on a hellish date across time and space that lasted over three years and was, by far, the worst date in history or in the future. The least I could do was drop her back off at her home when I got the chance.

...time goes by so slowly, and time can do so much, are you still mine?

I stepped off on the frozen ground after the elevator stopped, walking about twenty foot before stopping. I didn't know where I was going, or why, so I ended up just walking around the embankment that looked over the entire flickering camp, with my hands stuck deep in the pockets of my black long coat. Eventually I sat down, crossing my arms over my knees and looking out over the Rogue camp.

...I need your love, I need your love...

It just wasn't fair. I wasn't ambitious three years ago. I didn't have crazy, life-altering plans for my time-traveling. All I wanted was a real-life history lesson. But I had to save the world, right?

Right?

...time can do so much...

"Amen to that," I muttered to myself.

I realized then, like, right then, that I needed some sort of a plan, so I laid out what was on my agenda for the rest of my unforeseeable future.

The first thing still on my list was finding Dr. Cross and making him pay, so the next list was all the things I needed to obtain so that I could make that happen.

First, I needed to learn more about the Paladin stuff that Stargazer had been yammering about and also try to persuade him to find another candidate for leading the Rogues after he was dead.

Second, I needed to find Piper. No matter what.

Then I could find Cross, make him pay, and find out how the progress on time-travel was looking. Look at me killing two birds with one stone like a champ.

...speed your love to me, speed your love to me...

I lay back with my hands behind my hood and my ankles crossed, peering up at the dark ceiling of the cavern as the last few lines of *Unchained Melody* played out. A notion took hold of me then, and the revelation that I was living out every twelve-year-old's fantastic dream of starting a new life in a brave new world with chosen-one status struck me.

No ties to my former life, not really a plan for my future —nothing but my heroic need to save the helpless and defeat the wicked.

Except I wasn't exactly down for saving the helpless, although the few people I knew who were leaning toward the wicked side of things were on my hit list.

Who knows? Maybe by taking out the few wicked people that had ticked me off, I actually would aid the helpless in a roundabout way.

Circle of life and all that.

I don't know how long it took me to listen to the entire Al Green album twice on the Zune, but I didn't budge an inch until I did. Man, I needed that. Sitting up, I checked my holotab and realized I'd been up there for almost two hours. When I climbed back into the shaky elevator and started my descent, I noticed that all the lights in the camp had been shut off and the fires extinguished.

"Where are you, handsome?" Blu's voice asked, and my holotab lit up. Holding my right arm up, I hit the swirling icon and Blu's face appeared above my forearm. "There he is," she said with a smile. "The man of the hour. You look like death with that black hood on, by the way. Kind of hot."

"What's up, Blu?"

"Sam and I came to your igloo with some ice-spider wine to celebrate your super-humanity. You going to be back soon?"

"Ask him how he liked the Green," Sam's voice chimed in, and Blu turned her face away from the screen to scowl at him. "Ask him yourself. You know I hate Al Green."

Then another icon appeared beside the floating holoscreen Blu was on. Frowning, I poked it and Sam's smiling face appeared next to hers. "A lovely night for the Green, eh, mate?"

"Helheim, yes," I told him, returning the smile. "I'll be there in a few minutes. Save me some of the—did you say spider wine?"

"Ice-spider wine," Blu corrected while Sam nodded. "A recipe from the Rebels, they tell me. It'll knock your gears out if you're not careful."

"I'm on my way," I said, closing out of the holochat before leaning on the rusted railing, pulling my hood off and looking at the large camp. It really was a lot of folks, to be sure, and mostly women with small children.

Fish in a barrel, really, if an enemy found the location of the Rogues. Nothing but a meager thirty or forty men, and even some of them were older and not suited for combat.

Fish in a damn barrel with nothing but the hope that the raging war topside wouldn't stumble onto their hidey hole.

It seemed so pointless.

"*Is not self-preservation the first human reaction to everything?*" Stargazer's words echoed in my mind as I took in the enormous barrel of defenseless fish before me.

I pushed the thoughts from my mind. I couldn't help these people like the old man thought I could. My own personal agenda that included, but was not limited to, sweet revenge/retribution/whatever-I-wanted, didn't involve saving thousands of women and their kids.

I was different now, whether I liked it or not. Had I been

bestowed with super-human powers three years ago, I would have accepted Stargazer's offer and become the Rogue leader on the spot.

My entire outlook on life was different now, and it made me feel cold, calculated, and downright menacing at times, but that's how I felt. Paladins may have the power to save the world, but that doesn't mean that they're going to want to.

Cheers went up from Blu and Sam when I entered my igloo. They were sitting at the table, and Blu had her ankles crossed and propped up on it, looking awesome in her white jumpsuit, which complimented her long blue hair. Sam was in his off-yellow long coat, and I noticed that he must not have been wearing his makeshift exo-suit underneath it because he looked a tad slimmer than usual.

"What happened to being up all night doing paperwork?" I said to Blu while I removed my long coat.

She shrugged. "I finished quicker than I thought. Do you know that you're a bloody weapon of mass destruction?"

Sitting at the table, I said, "You've said that before but, no, I wasn't aware of that. Where's this ice-spider wine of yours?"

I noticed they each had a small cup that was only half-filled. "You guys really didn't have to go easy on the stuff to save me some," I said to them.

Sam opened his mouth to speak, but Blu cut him off. "Of course we did. Here," she said, leaning forward, grabbing the jug and pouring me a tall glass of the black liquid. "We wanted you to have some."

"Thanks," I told her, taking the glass and turning it up, chugging the entire thing. I gave a satisfying "ah" when it was empty and plunked the glass back down. "Not too bad."

It tasted like sour raspberry tea, actually, but better than snowmelt. Then I noticed that Sam was looking at Blu with his mouth dropped open and his eyes bugged out.

"Something wrong, Sam?" I asked him as Blu refilled my glass. He was still blinking at her when I downed the next glassful.

"Are you trying to kill him?" Sam finally managed to get out.

"Relax, mate," Blu told him in a calm tone. "My theories are never wrong."

"What're you two going on about?" I asked.

"Ice-spider wine is toxic in large amounts. Most people can only take half a cupful a day," Blu casually said. "But the Z-90 in your body is impervious to any infection. You can't get poisoned, sick, or even drunk."

"No kidding," I mumbled, staring into my glass and frowning.

"And you're not hallucinating?" Sam asked, truly perplexed. When I just shook my head, the big man put his cup down, pushing it away. "Well, there goes my record."

Blu turned her cup up and finished hers, shuddering as she swallowed then exhaling a short breath. "Whew, that stuff's hard." She went to pour herself some more, but Sam stopped her.

"You've already had too much, Blu. Ease off."

"Says the ex," she countered, pulling her arm away and pouring her cup, but then her head hit the table with a resounding thump and she was out.

"Told you, you bloody blue-haired sheila," Sam muttered, shaking his head.

"That stuff really is potent," I said, poking Blu's shoulder. "How long will she be like this?"

"Wait for it," Sam said with his arms crossed and his eyes closed.

I waited a few seconds and was about to ask what I was supposed to be waiting for when Blu shot back up with a small snort and shrieked, "Lightning man!"

She cut her widened eyes at us before narrowing them in suspicion, "What're you two doing here, anyway? You should be asleep."

Sam motioned to the jug of ice-spider wine, raising an

eyebrow at her. "Oh," she said, laying a hand on her forehead. "Why'd you bloody let me drink so much?"

It was an odd thing to bear witness to because she hadn't even drunk a full cup before passing out. "He tried to stop you," I told her, refilling my glass. Figures that the same stuff that could knock someone out with a sniff was like grape juice to me.

I couldn't help but think that I could win any drinking contest in the world if I were back in 2012, and I immediately regretted thinking about home. Trying to take my mind off Chicago, I asked, "What's the plan for tomorrow?"

"You'll be hooked up to a machine tonight so I can monitor you while you sleep. I stumbled onto something in the data from today's testing, and I think you may be able to do something impossible during REM sleep. But since you can do it, I guess it's not impossible anymore, is it?"

"Blu, you're rambling," Sam said.

"Your face is rambling," Blu said in a raised voice, pointing a finger at him. "So help me, I will sic my unicorn mate on you," she gestured to something next to her that Sam and I couldn't see.

Yeah, she was soused.

"I think you need to hit the hay, Blu," I told her, standing. "Hook me up, and Sam will take you to your hut."

In a few minutes I was on my cot with Blu's wires and pads on my temples and forehead. "G'night, mate," Sam told me, nodding to me and exiting the igloo with Blu thrown over his shoulder.

"You're a bloody mess," I heard him say.

"Don't judge me," Blu said, and the sound of their voices faded away.

I sighed, closing my eyes. I had an idea what Blu had picked up in her data, and I was wondering when and where I could do it. So, super-sneak mode only worked during rapid eye-movement sleep, huh?

Time to put that to the test.

CHAPTER 22

The Rogue camp was a kind of depressing place when it was empty. I mean, don't get me wrong, it wasn't exactly Disneyland when there were people milling around the tents, huts, and igloos in the first place, but it seemed even more glum when it was lifeless.

I trudged through the camp in super-sneak mode, worming my way slowly around the shacks and smoldering ashes of put-out fires. I wasn't sure where I was going, but I figured that the longer I stayed in SS mode the better, uh, reading, I guess, Blu would get on her device, or something like that.

I had been walking around the camp in random directions for almost a half hour when I turned a corner and ran into someone, starting as the girl, who was out for a midnight stroll, phased through me. I turned, watching her walk away quickly before falling in step behind her. You might say I was snooping.

And I would say to shut up and mind your own business —except I was, you know, following some random chick through the darkness all stalker-style.

She stopped at a tent that had a flickering light behind the canvas and stepped inside. Since I wasn't exactly feeling private, I walked through the side of the tent. There were three others inside, a woman who looked to be in her forties, who also looked like she wasn't feeling the best, and two other small girls between the ages of maybe five to ten.

The girl I'd been following was probably around sixteen, I figured, as I watched her get on her knees beside the mat the older woman was on. "This is all Sasha could spare, mother," she said, reaching into her overcoat and pulling out a small wrapped bundle. "I've already eaten, so you and the girls can share this."

"You lie like your father," the girl's mother said, her voice barely audible and weak sounding. "We can all share it, Kat."

Shaking her head, Kat handed the bundle to her mother. "Sasha said that the next chance of a food raid is over two weeks away, and we're already running out. I'll get in the lines earlier tomorrow."

The two younger girls fell on the bundle like a little pack of wolf cubs, while their mother slowly pulled a chunk off the meager loaf of bread.

Bread. They were starving, and all they had to eat was bread.

I had realized two days after I'd awoken strapped to a table that I didn't seem to be getting hungry. I confirmed weeks later, when I wasn't dying of hunger, that I probably didn't run off food anymore, which had its perks. I could think of one person in the Rogue camp who wasn't about to die of starvation, at any rate.

"I saw the Paladin man today," the youngest of the girls said after she'd swallowed her small portion of bread. She was sitting crossed-legged next to the candle and holding her fingerless gloved hands close to it.

"When?" Kat asked.

"Where?" the middle sibling asked, suddenly forgetting about her food.

"On my way from lessons. He was with Commander Red and Miss Blu."

Interested, I sat, watching the small girl, waiting to hear her account of me.

"What was he like, Dana?" Kat asked, sitting beside her

sister quickly.

"Couldn't tell until he pulled off his hood. He looked nice," Dana said, nodding as if agreeing with herself.

"But how did you know it was the Paladin? It could have been anyone," the apparently skeptical and so far nameless middle child shot at her, starting back on her bread while Dana just shrugged.

"Do you think the rumors about him are true?" Kat said, glancing at her mother. "They say he can shoot lightning out of his hands and read minds."

I smiled. I just adore rumors. I don't know where someone got reading minds, but it was a nice touch, I must admit.

"Stargazer said that when the Paladin came, we'd be safe," the mother said. "That's all I care about."

Well, at least I now knew the hope Stargazer had been telling some of them. Apparently, it was me.

"But how will he make us safe?" Kat muttered. "I want things to get better like everyone else, but he's just one man."

"Paladin," Dana corrected her. "They're better than plain old men. I bet he could take on seventy-frillion Bears at once," she said, nodding again.

Kat stood, crossing her arms and walking toward the tent door. "Let's hope that the Bears never find us," she said, then she stopped short, wincing and grabbing at her stomach. Her family didn't see this, which she was probably thankful for.

But I saw it.

Judging by her eyes and figure, I was thinking it had been probably more than three days since this girl had eaten.

"I can't help you people," I said aloud. Not that they could hear me. "I'm not salvation in a spray can, like you guys think."

"It's warm in here," Kat said. "I'm going to sit outside for a while." Then she left.

"It's not your problem, Jericho," I said to myself. "You're just passing through on your way to revenge."

I phased through the door and frowned when I saw Kat walking away. Apparently, she wasn't just sitting. I wasn't following her this time. She just happened to be going the same way I was.

Kat ducked among the tents and huts all the way to the camp outskirts. After leaving the camp and walking a good distance away, she stopped when we made it to the wall. Frowning, I glanced around, not really sure why she'd walked all the way out here.

Then, after checking to make sure she hadn't been followed, the girl leaned against the wall, slid down to a sitting position, and began crying, her face buried into her arms. She'd left the family she was fighting and starving for to make sure they wouldn't see her this way.

Placing my hands on my hips, I began pacing, really abusing my being invisible. Not able to contain it anymore, I shouted, to no one in particular, "I'm not a hero, people! I'm not here to save anyone. How many times do I have to tell you that? As far as I'm concerned, your problems don't happen for over three hundred years."

After my rant, I glanced back at the sobbing girl.

Ah, crap.

I closed my eyes, and in seconds I reopened them in my body. I heard Blu's monitor whirring beside me. I checked my holotab and saw that it was around 5:00 a.m. I sat up and removed the gear from my face.

"Call Red," I said and my holotab lit up and an icon appeared. In a few moments, that I could only discern as her having to wake up and groggily accept my holochat, Red's face appeared.

"Jericho, what's wrong?" she asked in a quiet, sleepy voice.

"Morning, sunshine," I told her, smiling. "How about you grab a small team of troops and accompany me topside for a spot of hunting?"

Red sat up slowly in her bed and must have rubbed her

eyes because the camera swept around the room a few times. Her face reappeared and she yawned before saying, "What're you planning on hunting at this hour?"

I grabbed my coat and exited the igloo.

"Bears."

CHAPTER 23

"We've never hit a convoy this big before," Red's cautious words buzzed in my ear while I crouched on the ledge of the crumbling four-story building I was examining our catch from. It really was a big procession. Two very large and very armored vehicles the size of train engines hovered slowly down the cracked street below me. Red and her three-man team were set up on the opposite building across the snowy street.

"Why not?" I asked. "I'll bet these things are packing some major calorie intake."

On the elevator ride to the surface, Red had given me a short rundown on how a normal raid worked. Generally, they listened for chatter until they heard about a small food convoy that they thought meager enough to overtake. The problem wasn't stopping them, she said, because all they had to do was launch an EMP anchor into their target, thus crippling it. The real problem came from the troops who came out of it with assault rifles blazing.

"I've already told you why not," Red said. "Each one of these transports has fifteen to twenty soldiers accompanying them."

"And?"

I heard her sigh before asking me, "So, what's your brilliant plan here, Paladin?"

I stood, rolling my neck around. "I'll take out the convoys. You guys just snipe anything that tries to make a run for it."

"You're insane," Red said.

"You may not believe this, but you're not the first girl to ever tell me that," I countered, smiling in spite of the oncoming bout. Of which, might I add, I was thoroughly looking forward to. "Ready?"

"Let us know when you want us to hit them with an EMP anchor."

"Save your anchors, Red," I told her. "I brought my own."

Then I jumped off the ledge headfirst.

I aimed for the first convoy, flipping once halfway and landing on the front of the armored hovercraft in a crouch, denting it slightly. I focused my juice and slapped my hands on the cold steel. Instantly, I felt the power from the craft flow into my hands and up my arms to my shoulders, head, chest, and into my legs, blue electricity jolting off my entire frame.

The tram shuddered once before dropping onto the street, completely powerless. The hatch opened almost immediately, and a masked trooper popped out, wielding an assault rifle. I wasn't able to make it to him, even if I'd tried. The first round of bullets evaporated almost three feet from my body, and after wasting a ridiculous amount of ammo, the man stopped firing long enough to gawk at the invincible lightning familiar in front of him.

"Morning," I said simply, blasting him with a small bolt, rushing forward and grabbing the lifeless man and flinging him into the snow. Then I turned both hands on the open hatch, blasting into the transport, filling it to the brim with volt after volt.

"First tram down," I said. "Scan it to see if I missed one," then I ran the length of the transport and jumped the wide gap between the convoys, landing on my last target. I'm thinking that the second armored craft had more warning because the first thing that greeted me upon landing on it was about ten soldiers, five of which were wearing large, wicked black power armor that I'd never seen before.

Unlike a lot of people I'd had the pleasure of butting heads with lately, the Bears before me didn't waste their breath telling me to stand down. Instead, all ten of them fired their weapons at once.

Let me go ahead and let you guys know that, of all the awesome items in my new Paladin arsenal, finesse didn't happen to be one of them at the time.

Bullets came in violent torrents when I landed, and I turned up my power output, increasing the distance of my shield and keeping me baby-blanket safe against the horde of lead aimed in my direction. I walked toward them, my shield getting closer to them and causing the troops to panic, cease their fire, and turn to get away from me.

When they broke fire, I turned both barrels on them, throwing my hands up and unleashing a massive wave of voltage toward the fleeing Bears, catching all of them in the blue whips of lightning. The soldiers in power armor were thrown a few yards, knocking them off their feet and exploding the black armor in clouds of fire and smoke, while the men not wearing suits were flung farther away, skidding down the snow-covered street out of sight.

"How do we do this, Red?" I asked, walking to the open hatch and peering inside. "Do we just take all we can carry or commandeer these things?"

"We've never had the chance to commandeer one," Red confessed. "I still can't believe it."

"Be astounded later, lady," I told her, waving my arms at the building she and her troops were on. "Get down here and help me take these things back to camp. We're on the clock here."

It felt good quoting Blu's comment from a few days ago. Red leaped from the roof of the building in her armor, engaging the blasts on her feet close to the ground and cushioning her fall. I noticed she still left a crater in the pavement, though. "Whatever you say, Paladin."

"Please, no titles," I said, closing my eyes and holding my

hands up modestly.

In less than five minutes, I had juiced back up the first tram and both food-laden transports were on their way back to the Rogue camp while I stood in the street, watching them hover away.

"You coming?" Red's voice said in my ear.

"In a bit," I answered. "You guys head on back and I'll meet you later."

"Thank you, Jericho," Red said sincerely. "Please come back so I can convince you to stay. We need you."

"Red—"

"Just think about it, please," she said. "I know you're in high demand, but you could save so many lives if you stayed."

I began walking, stuffing my hands into the pockets of my long coat. "I'll think about it."

I'd catch up with them later. Right now there was something I wanted to try again.

Then I was scaling the side of the nearest building at breakneck speed, finding handholds that would be impossible for a normal person to use, leaping when I could, while I made my way to the roof of the building.

I felt amazing, like there wasn't anything I couldn't do, and I wanted to push my limits, experiment impossible, gravity-defying things and just keep going no matter what. The thought of going back to the camp was coupled with the feeling of caging a dragon. Well, maybe not that dramatic, but nothing compared to the feeling I had while climbing, running, jumping, and wielding fistfuls of lightning against enemies. That's when I felt complete, I'd realized. That's when I felt like I was truly moving forward.

I reached the rooftop and bolted across it as fast as I could, pumping my legs and kicking up snow behind me. When I reached the opposite side, I jumped hard, clearing the street and landing in a roll on the opposite building.

I kept going, not wanting to stop, while I pushed myself to the max, hurtling two more streets before I saw something familiar. It was the building I'd climbed during my first test with Cross.

"Come on," I said through gritted teeth. I was unstoppable. I could do anything.

I felt it then, the power. It was building up inside of me while I watched the upcoming skyscraper, my next conquest, loom before me. Wanting to go faster, I channeled the flow into my legs and feet. I couldn't help but glance down when I felt my lower half charge up, and I saw that my running legs were now overflowing with the same blue jolts that appeared on my arms during combat.

Then I was flying through the air toward the skyscraper.

My feet dug hard into the side of the mammoth building, and before I knew what came over me, I was bolting straight up the side of it.

Literally.

Sparks flew every time I sank a foot into the concrete while I loped up the skyscraper, the wind blowing my hood off.

Laughing, I hit the brakes over halfway up, grabbing the top of a window to slow myself down, my legs flying up. Whooping loudly, I let my feet drop down and I swung them into the glass, breaking through. I hit the abandoned floor running, immediately leaping a few cubicles and crossing the darkened, dusty floor.

When I saw the opposite glass window coming, I shot off a bolt from my right hand and blew it out seconds before I jumped, grabbing the shuddering iron frame and swinging out then up, connecting my feet once again with the concrete side of the building, and then I was off again.

I made it soon, holding onto the point of the tower right at the tip-top of the thing, my feet propped on the thin pole that swayed in the wind, while I took in Flagstaff from over a hundred stories in the air. The city had changed a lot, I noticed. Mainly because Flagstaff now resembled New York in a way, due to all the mammoth buildings. Most were old and not used, but they were still there.

"Now can you tell me what you feel would be the best way to get down?" Cross's words echoed in my mind.

I remembered telling him that I felt like I could jump and walk away from the landing, but he'd discouraged me from attempting it. Probably because he'd sunk over three years in me and didn't want his project to die too quickly.

Now I was back, and I still felt like I could jump. I recalled how it felt when I'd jumped from four stories earlier. It had felt like I'd jumped four feet instead. Did that mean this would feel like I jumped over a hundred feet?

My long coat blew around in the brisk wind while I mulled over whether or not I was going to jump. Then I made a decision.

"Well," I said, "no one can ever say that I chickened out twice, I guess."

Those were my last words before I jumped, pushing off the pole and assuming a dive position, tearing through the air toward the street with my hands tucked at my sides.

I guess I was about halfway down when I realized that I might have taken my Paladin status a bit too far this time. I didn't panic, but I sure wasn't feeling the same confidence I had been feeling before I jumped.

Nice going, Jericho. Next time, after you're dead, how about you *not* jump off a skyscraper?

Then I felt the power coming back to the surface, dripping from my frame and engulfing me in it. When the energy had surfaced on its own last time, it had been before I got riddled with bullets. Maybe it worked like a defense mechanism?

The quickly approaching street was coming fast, and I tucked into a ball and flipped once, my boots hitting mega hard and shattering the concrete and sinking me into the street almost two feet.

I stood slowly from my crouch, peering in wonder at the crater I'd just made and noticing I didn't even feel stiff. "It's official," I said to myself, looking at my hands. "I really am awesome."

I used to boast this not too long ago when it wasn't true, and I just thought it was. Now that I knew for sure, I wasn't feeling puffed up about it at all and merely just shocked.

I know. Funny how that works.

I felt like I'd just gotten something out of my system. I'm not sure what, but I did feel like I could go back underground now, at least.

I started back to the Rogue camp with my answer to Red's question in my mind.

I would be sticking around for a little while.

CHAPTER 24

I was almost to the camp when my holotab lit up and I saw Blu was hailing me. Sighing, because I figured she wasn't too happy about being left out of my raid, I tapped the spinning icon.

"You are the worst future husband ever," were the first words she said.

"Good morning to you, too," I said, smiling at her.

"We've been together for two days and you're already cheating on me with my sister," Blu said, scowling.

"Red didn't have an ice-spider hangover."

"I wasn't hung over," Blu said defensively. "And, even if I had been, I still could've run diagnostics on you while you were cooking Bear meat."

"You can come the next time," I said. "How about you forgive your future husband and eat some of the bacon he brought home."

Huffing, Blu turned her face away, "Like I have the will power to stay mad at you in the first place. Besides, my dear, back-stabbing red-haired sister already ran the proper readings on you during the course of your affair topside. I also looked over the readings on your REM graph from last night, and after glancing at the data, I think we seriously need to talk sometime after you get through all of your awaiting fans."

I frowned while I pushed open the iron door to the camp. "What?"

"Apparently, your grabbing an almost six-month supply of food and medical supplies in one shot has the camp in a joyous uproar."

"Ah, shucks," I said while I trudged down the short hall that led to the rusted elevator.

"Shucks, indeed," Blu said. "I knew from the start that you were lightning in a bottle, but now everyone else does."

Blu signed off, and I walked out onto the short cliff that overlooked the camp that seemed to be in the middle of a riot.

"There he is!" I heard someone from over two hundred feet down shout when I stepped into sight, and a loud cheer went up through the thousands of Rogues. Red had driven the two trams right to the middle of the encampment, and a soup line of sorts had already been set up close to the convoy where rations were being handed out.

My holotab beeped.

"Get down here, mate," Red said, all smiles. "You're a regular bloody war hero from where I'm standing."

When I was rich, I'd given millions to just about every charity organization that came calling, but this was different.

I wouldn't have traded the feeling brought on by the sound of true, sincere thankfulness for anything in the world. The sound was wonderful, and while I listened, taking in the smiling thousands, something clicked in my brain.

This is what I was born to do. Anything great I'd done or thought I'd done in the past was meaningless now in light of what I was doing then. And what I was going to do.

"The Rogues will need a leader after I'm gone," Stargazer had said to me.

I didn't know what I'd do, exactly, to help them if I took the reins. I mean, I was over three hundred years out of the loop on how the world was supposed to work now, but after seeing my share of what the year of our Lord, 2345, had to offer, maybe that wasn't such a bad thing.

"You coming?" Red asked me.

Without answering, I took a few steps back before

taking a running leap off the cliff, and a chorus of gasps and shouts resounded through the crowd while I tore toward them, landing hard. The ground buckled a little beneath me, cracking.

All was quiet at first, and once I stood, the cheers resumed.

I walked toward the mass of people, who parted, making a path for me all the way to the trams, nodding or saluting while saying, "Paladin."

Some reached out and squeezed my shoulders, smiling at me, while some even dipped their heads in a small bow. I shook my head at some of the first bowers and tried to let them know not to overdo a good thing, but it didn't help much. Before long almost all the other Rogues had picked up on what the person next to them was doing, and they were all bowing.

I'm going to argue that, although it resembled a bow in more ways than one, I believe that it was a long nod. Yeah, that sounds better. At least it wasn't a full-blown bow, because that would've been a tad bizarre.

"Paladin."

"Thank you, Paladin."

"Paladin, sir."

The name echoed throughout the Rogues as I walked toward the trams, and the people parted like the Red Sea all the way for me. I finally made it to the rear armored tram, but just before I went to climb on it, a little girl rushed to my side, wrapping her small arms around my synthetic leg.

"Love you," she said.

Not wanting to break down in front of, well, everyone, I gingerly patted the straight black hair of the toddler. "Love you, too, kiddo," I said, and she released me, stepping back and smiling while waving a mitten-clad hand.

"Bye," she chortled while skipping away. She looked familiar. Then it hit me.

It was Dana, the youngest girl of the family I'd sort of spied on.

Once I was standing on the tram, I turned to address the Rogues. I wanted to say something inspiring, you know. Something that would make them all lay a hand on the person next to them and scream "Huzzah!"

"Who's hungry?" I shouted and the cheers roared.

I never was very good at inspirational speeches.

"Enjoy," I told them, walking across the tram to Red, who was out of her battle-armor, standing with her hands on her hips and a smile on her face.

"Paladin," she said simply, nodding to me.

"Commander Red," I said back to her, returning the nod. "Your sister has informed me that I have cheated on her with you."

"I never wanted that to happen," Red told me, her smile broadening.

"I know. We need to stop this now because, obviously, I'm meant for your sister."

"Understood," she said. "I had a good time, though. You were great up there."

"Flattery will get you nowhere with me, Red," I said, shaking my head once before glancing back at the mob lining up for food. "So, what happens now?"

Shrugging, Red stepped closer to me so I could hear her over the crowd. "That depends on you, Jericho. I know what Stargazer asked you to do, and I can guarantee you my utmost support if you choose to accept his offer."

"Why?" I couldn't help but ask her. We must've looked odd just then, standing on the tram while leaning toward each other so we could exchange words. "You know I don't know anything about this place or what the Rogues are even fighting for."

"You're perfect for the job, mate," Red assured me, laying a hand on my shoulder at first, then surprising me by pulling me into a hug. "I don't know what you planned on doing if you left," she said into my ear. "But I know what you can and will do if you stay. You're just what these people have been waiting on for years now. You're a godsend, Jericho. A real godsend."

Then she pulled away, lifting my left hand into the air and cheering "Paladin!" and the entire camp joined in.

"Paladin! Paladin! Paladin!"

CHAPTER 25
Stargazer

Godsend: An unexpected thing or event that is particularly welcome and timely, as if sent by God.

Stargazer groaned softly as he eased down into his armchair, cursing his old body. The day had been a joyous one, to be sure, but it had left its mark in his fatigue.

Blu had burst in early that morning, shouting about how Jericho had left her for her sister and went topside without her for God-knows-what reason.

Stargazer had comforted the girl, telling her that the Paladin probably just needed some fresh air and would be back soon enough for today's testing. Blu wasn't exactly comforted, but she had snorted a reply before leaving.

Blu may not have known Jericho's reasons for going topside, but Stargazer had.

He knew that, fight as he may, Jericho could not escape the destiny that fate had dealt him. No matter how much he may not have wanted to stay and aid the Rogues in their survival, Stargazer knew Jericho wouldn't be able to say no to it.

It was in him now, whether he liked it or not, that special something that drives a person to achieve impossible goals in the name of the just, righteous, and honorable.

"It was good to see you again, old friend," Stargazer said to the air around him, his eyes closed, and his head tilted back slightly. "Good luck on your Crusade, Jericho."

Then he heard it, the faint yet discernible cheers of the Rogue camp. Smiling, the old man whispered the chant along with his people, "Paladin, Paladin…"

Stargazer opened his white eyes. "Don't lose sight of your path, Paladin. You will stop this wretched war that's tearing this world apart."

No. He couldn't fail. Not if he stayed the course. Straying from his destiny was the only thing that could stop him from saving the earth. But that could not happen. It must not. Jericho Johnson now had the means to save the world, Stargazer knew, yet the journey was still wrought with danger, fear, and retaliation. The only thing that could stop Jericho was another Paladin—an impossibility because Jericho was the only one.

"Give them tomorrow," Stargazer said. "Stay the course, save these people, and stop the war. Goodbye, Paladin, perhaps we will meet again one day."

Then he ended the recording. He just couldn't talk anymore. He'd been recording the message intended for Jericho for almost an hour, and he was depleting drastically. "I wish I had more time," he said to himself.

It was true. Stargazer hadn't told Jericho everything he knew about being a Paladin. If only he had more strength…

The meager recording would have to do. Though it didn't tell Jericho all the details about his journey, it did, however, lay out a few aspects that would aid him in coming to full grips with his new powers.

Stargazer wished he could have answered Jericho's question truthfully. Telling him about their meeting years ago would have jeopardized everything, so Stargazer had held his tongue and lied to the only hope humanity had left.

Because he and Jericho weren't common acquaintances. Stargazer had known the Paladin for a very long, long time.

Sighing, the old man wiped at his eyes, laughing at himself because of the tears he found yet again. "Emotional," he mumbled to himself.

"I need the Rogues," Jericho had told him ages ago, putting a hand on Stargazer's much younger shoulder and smiling at him. *"Make it happen, bro."*

Stargazer had completed his final mission, it seemed. The first of the reborn super-race was about to take his place as the Rogue leader, just as Jericho had told him so many years prior. Stargazer couldn't think of a more perfect ending to his life.

"My Partisan days are over," he whispered. "He's yours now, Sybil. Guide him well."

He was tired. So tired. He tried to make it to his bed but ended up collapsing midway onto the cold floor of the pavilion.

He wasn't in pain, nor was he afraid when he felt the cold begin to take hold of him.

Then a poem appeared in his mind.

Out of the night that covers me,
Black as the Pit from pole to pole,
I thank whatever gods may be
for my unconquerable soul.

Stargazer smiled.

In the fell clutch of circumstance
I have not winced nor cried aloud.
Under the bludgeonings of chance
my head is bloody, but unbowed.

"Jericho Johnson," he murmured. If he would've been able to, he would've shaken his head and chuckled. Stargazer had not chosen to be a Partisan and aid the Paladin in his Crusade, but he had done his best. The rest would have to be up to Sybil, the next Partisan in line to aid the Paladin.

Beyond this place of wrath and tears
Looms but the Horror of the shade,
and yet the menace of the years
Finds, and shall find, me unafraid.

Stargazer gasped softly as he felt the icy hand of what he could only discern as death creeping up his spine, yet he still wasn't afraid. Stargazer closed his milky eyes for the last time and greeted death like an old friend. The last thing he heard were the chants and cheers of the Rogues.

"Paladin! Paladin!"

Later, when Blu found his body, she discovered that he had died with a smile on his face.

It matters not how strait the gate,
How charged with punishments the scroll.
I am the master of my fate:
I am the captain of my soul.
  —Invictus, William Ernest Henley

CHAPTER 26
Jericho

Over the next few weeks, following my rise to command and Stargazer's death, a lot changed in the Rogue camp.

The first being that no one went hungry.

But every one of them still mourned the loss of Stargazer, and I didn't blame them. I was missing him myself, considering he was the only person that could even halfway tell me what I was supposed to do.

Red and Blu had gotten me up to speed on everything the Rogue camp was going through, and it was pretty rough stuff, let me tell you. Apparently, the Reds weren't exactly keen on folks not doing what they told them, and the public executions of said disobedient folks were employed on a regular basis to ensure that they were doing everything in their power to keep the underlings in line. Every member of the Rogue camp was considered either deserters or criminals of war and were to be executed, mostly on sight, but saving a few for an example to any other workers with funny ideas about escaping.

And here I was, now leading the escapees and aiding them in their attempt to take out the Man.

I spent a lot of time poring over the recorded message from Stargazer, hoping that in the fifty-five-minute excerpt he'd left me, I'd find more answers as to what, exactly, he wanted me to do. I ventured topside every other week to rob a supply line or two with a strike team consisting of Red, Blu, and Sam. I was relieved that I never crossed paths with any of Cross's men topside, but I was also surprised. And here I thought I was his special science project. According to Ritu, on the day of my departure, Cross was in Anchorage, Alaska, at his mega lab. Good riddance, I guess.

"Best team ever," Sam said to his fellow squad mates after the first day of raids. "All we have to do is watch while Jerry calls lightning bolts of judgment on the Bears."

Only we weren't just hitting Bears. We'd also run into a Fascist tram on one occasion and, from where I was fighting, they seemed to be weaker than the Bears in more than a few ways. This led me to ask Red on the elevator ride down, "Who exactly is winning the fray up there, anyway?"

"Not sure," she answered. "We see more Bears than any of them, so I'd say they're winning in this region. The Rebels are basically like us, except with firepower."

"So, they run and hide, too," I said, pulling off my hood and leaning against the elevator wall.

"More or less," Blu said, once again flipping through her holotab.

"I'm going to try and meet with Beck," I dropped casually, and all eyes were on me.

"Why?" Blu asked.

"I'm going to ask about a union."

"We've already tried that," Sam said. "Didn't end well, mate. Beck's a bat-crazy sheila if you didn't know."

"I do know, Sam, but I have to try. Plus, you guys don't have a history with Beck. She'll listen to me."

Or at least I hoped she would.

It had only been close to a month, and I could already see that the path I was taking the Rogues on was a dead end. I could give them food, clothes, medicine, and even make them smile. But nothing short of stopping the fighting in Flagstaff was going to actually save anyone. All I would be doing was prolonging the inevitable.

To end the Rogue oppression, I would need the Rebels. Or Beck, to be more specific. Loathe as I was to ask for her help,

I felt that we super-humans needed to stick together.

And, from what I gathered while sifting through all the data Blu made me read to catch up on the year of our Lord, 2345, the Rebels had way more intel than the Rogues could ever hope to get. I'm guessing it was because they were actually a viable faction in the war and the Rogues were just hiding from it.

At least the Rebels weren't trying to kill the Rogues and chose to just ignore them, something that they weren't going to be able to do for very much longer.

Blu and I parted ways from Sam and her sister after we left the elevator. "You need to go over the maps again," Red informed me before she walked away.

"And don't forget about the battle-suit shipment tomorrow," Sam told me. "We sure could us a bloody upgrade around here. Might even train a few sheilas while we're at it if we had enough of them."

"The Paladin can worry about your petty requests after I'm done with him tonight," Blu said to them smugly, linking her arm through mine and pulling me down the icy hall. "He's going to have such a good time that he won't even remember your names tomorrow," she added while giving me a dazzling smile.

"Don't mind me, Jerry," Sam said as we walked away. "I'm just the ex, mate."

"Yeah, you are," Blu called over her shoulder.

"Make sure my face is on next week's milk carton," I said, receiving a hard elbow jab in my synthetic ribs from Blu.

"Croc," she mumbled, still smiling.

"Just so you know," I said as we slowly trudged down the hall with our arms linked, "if your parents hadn't made you look like a perfect blue-haired, tanned super-model, I would have burned you with a scathing retort."

"Yeah, well, they did," Blu said, leaning into me while we walked.

"How goes your research?"

Blu shook her head. "Nope. You're not getting it for free, mister."

"Oh, come on."

"No. You're going to have to try a little harder to get on my good side," she said with a wink.

"I'm already on your good side."

Blu narrowed her eyes at me, chewed on her lower lip, then blurted, "Okay, fine." We stopped in front of her lab door. She punched in the key code on her holotab, and the iron door slid open. "I've finally isolated what I believe is the key to your REM walks. If my theory is correct, then you might be able to achieve a successful projection while you're awake."

I stopped walking long enough to gawk at her. Blu turned to face me with a hand on her hip and a smirk on her face. "Now that I've got your attention, Paladin, what am I to do with it?"

"Enough," I said, all business while I headed for the center of the testing arena, pulling off my long coat and dropping it on a sterilized table when I passed it. "Less banter, more scientific magic."

Pouting, Blu entered her command center, and her voice beeped on my holotab. "You know, most girls don't like it when a guy rushes them."

Laughing, I said, "You've been rushing me since day one."

"Touché."

"Now, how do I do this?" I asked, rubbing my hands together eagerly. "Focus? Think happy thoughts? Gather chi?"

"No, no and no," she said. "It's actually a lot harder than all those, and since I'm not a Paladin, I'm not going to be able to help you that much."

Frowning, I put my hands on my hips and asked, "Why are you here, again?"

"Hey, cut me a break," Blu said. "The Z-90 is literally pushing thousands of Tera joules of raw radiant and thermal energy, Jericho. It's taking me a while to sift through all my data."

"Tera joules?"

"Indeed. Here's a fun fact: the first atomic bomb ever tested produced sixty-three Tera joules. You do that when you put on your bloody boots."

"No kidding?"

Now my level of bodacity was tallied in joules. Awesome.

Nodding while she typed away on a holocomputer, she said, "Yep. You're like a bloody compressed hyper nova, mate. It's amazing to study, but a real croc when trying to find the on switch to something."

"How close to it are you?" I asked, sitting on the gurney that I assumed was for me. "And I thought I wasn't supposed to sleep."

Blu exited the lab and walked to me carrying a small case. "You're not. I'm taking a shot in the dark here."

Placing the small black case beside me, Blu opened it and I saw the curious contents.

"I thought you were being metaphoric about shots," I said, peering at the row of syringes in the box.

Pulling one out, she held it up and tapped it, swirling the vial of neon blue liquid. At least, I thought it was liquid. "Ever heard of a lucid dream, love?" she asked, moving the case and easing me back onto the gurney.

"Sure," I told her. "A dream in which the dreamer is conscious that they are dreaming and can have fun with it while it lasts."

Laughing, Blu said, "That's the best way of putting it, yes. As far as scientists are concerned, though, it's when someone has a higher amount of beta-one frequencies during REM sleep, thus making more activity in the sleeper's parietal lobes and enabling consciousness during the dream."

"How does that help us here?"

Sighing, she said, "It doesn't, actually. The strange thing about your brain is that there wasn't any parietal lobe activity during your REM sleep. Like, zero beta waves. I would be shocked if you were a normal person, but since you're actually somehow able to leave your body during that time, I think it's safe to say you're plenty lucid while you're doing whatever it is."

She held up the syringe for me to see again, placing a hand on my chest. "This is an alternate version of a drug used to induce someone into a perfect lucid dream that lasts an hour. I say alternate because I made this myself and it does the exact opposite."

"But won't me, uh, not being lucid make my super-sneak mode not work or something?"

"I told you this was a shot in the dark, love," Blue said with a small shrug. "Realistically, yes, it should. But let's be honest, you're not exactly normal, mate. What I'm hoping it'll do is make it where you can access SS mode while you're awake."

"But—"

"No buts. Let's do this," Blu said suddenly, sliding the long needle into the side of my neck.

Then everything went black.

CHAPTER 27

I was standing beside Blu in a few seconds, fully immersed into super-sneak mode.

Only I could still feel her hand on my chest.

"This is so weird," I stated to myself—only, the Jericho on the gurney moved his mouth and the words came out.

"How's that?" Blu asked.

"Weird," I said again and, again, the words came from my body.

What the—?

I could feel everything I should feel while in my body, but it was like my mind was elsewhere, and I just knew, like I just knew everything else that I could do now, that if I opened my eyes, I would exit super-sneak mode.

So, I opened my eyes and, sure enough, I was blinking up at Blu.

Then I saw that my projection was still standing beside her. Screaming in shock, I rolled sideways, hit the icy floor, and monkey crawled away.

"Jericho, what're you bloody doing?" Blu asked quickly.

Standing slowly, I watched the blue, hazy form of myself standing beside her, and it seemed frozen.

"You don't see me there?" I asked, pointing.

Frowning, Blu glanced beside her. "Should I?"

I walked to the projection, stopping when I was beside it, and looked it up and down. "Do I really look like that?" I asked, frowning. "At least my hair is growing back," I said, poking at the hair of the projection.

Except I felt it on my real head. Not cool.

"Get me out, Blu," I said quickly, and my breathing became rapid. "I'm not loving this."

Something wasn't right.

Blu phased through the projection to get to me, putting her arms around me. "It'll only last a few more minutes, Jericho. Just hang in there."

"You don't understand," I told her. "It's like I'm in two places at once and it's—"

I closed my eyes while I was in mid-talk, and I was in my SS form again watching my body collapse into Blu, pulling her down with it.

"Jericho!" she shrieked. "Tell me what's happening?"

"I'm not sure," I said, watching the mouth of my lifeless body say the words.

I'd had enough. This was inexplicably, without a doubt, *not* cool.

Blu tried to pull my body up and ended up tripping on her own feet in the process. Without thinking, I reached out to help her, my hands phasing through her arms when I realized that I couldn't touch her. Then, for the second time in too short a period, everything, once again, went black.

Then I opened my eyes in my body. I knew it was my body, and I was out of SS mode because I opened my eyes and I couldn't feel my dismembered mind running loose when I did.

Whew. What a nightmare. I actually couldn't think of a worse feeling, to tell you the truth. I guess you could compare it to—

My body was on the ground in front of me, and I was on my knees. Instinctively, I held up my hands and inspected them.

They were dainty, girlish, and lightly tanned.

God, no.

I felt sick when I reached for my head, feeling the long

thick tresses on top of it, pulling a strand into my line of sight and seeing my horrifying confirmation.

It was blue.

I also felt severely weak. Like I'd just been run over by a truck and thrown off a cliff.

"Blu?" I asked quietly, instantly covering my mouth because it wasn't my voice that came out but the one that belonged to the owner of the body I had accidentally commandeered.

"Yes?" I heard in my head in a singsong voice.

"Good God, Blu, what did you do to me?" I almost shouted, my voice very female and Australian.

"Me?" she asked in my head. "I'm not the one who took over someone's mind without asking."

"I'm so sorry," I blurted while getting, with much effort, to my feet. "I just touched you."

"Easy on the hardware," Blu's voice echoed in my mind. Then I heard her laugh and ask, "So, how's it feel to be a girl, mate?"

"Stop," I growled.

"Fine. Geez," I heard her say before chuckling and adding, "Try not to get *my* knickers in a—"

"Make it stop," I said, leaning against a nearby table and feeling sick.

"I can't. For lack of a better description, I'm locked in my own subconscious. I can't take back the reins until you leave my body."

Retching, I vomited beside the gurney. Sorry. I just couldn't take all the weirdness anymore.

"Nice," Blu's voice murmured. "I should make you go brush my teeth before you give me back my body."

"Blu!" I screamed, feeling ridiculous because my voice was hers. "Stop with the jokes, I'm begging you. Just tell me how to get out of this mess."

"Okay, okay," Blu said. "Check in the case for the vial with red fluid in it."

I struggled to the open case across the table, having to lean on it for support with each step. "Why am I so weak? I can barely walk."

"Really?"

"Yeah," I said feebly, grabbing the needle-filled case and finding one with red liquid in it.

"Odd side-effect," Blu's voice muttered in my head. "Maybe it's because you're used to your super-human body and a normal one feels mega weak to you."

"Whatever," I gasped out. "I got the red one. Now what?"

"Inject your dormant body with it."

"Why?" I couldn't help but ask when I headed for my body, losing balance and falling to the floor, crawling the rest of the way.

"This should turn it off," Blu told me.

"Let's hope," I said before injecting the syringe into the neck of my downed body.

After a few seconds, I opened the mouth of the body I was occupying to say that I didn't think it was working before I felt myself being pulled from Blu's frame.

I'm not going to waste time explaining what it feels like having your entire being ripped from a body, but I will say that, if you haven't had the pleasure of the feeling, you aren't missing out.

Whenever my SS mode was fully out, I was able to open my eyes, and I was breathing blessed air into my precious, patchworked body. I sat up quickly, just in time to see Blu retching on her hands and knees beside me.

"Blu," I said, pulling her to me, and she laid her head on my chest and took in deep breaths.

"Well, that was unexpected," she said weakly.

"Tell me about it," I said, standing and lifting her into my arms, carrying her to the gurney and laying her on it.

Blu had her eyes closed for what seemed like a long time while she lay there with me standing beside the bed watching her.

"What was that, Blu?" I asked her in my calmest voice.

She had a hand covering her eyes for a moment. "It was the worst feeling in the world," Blu said. "The only weapon I have is my brain, and I couldn't even use it. It felt like I couldn't breathe, but then I didn't need to. It was just all messed up."

"You didn't know what would happen," I said, taking her free hand in mine.

"Yeah, well, I should have. I shouldn't have just jumped into an untested situation like that. Sorry, mate."

"Not as sorry as I am," I told her and I meant it, pushing some of her hair out of her face.

"How much of my mind were you able to see?" Blu asked, finally looking at me.

I felt something flip in my mind and my eyes unfocused on her face, my left one twitching slightly.

Everything. That's how much I'd seen.

Every memory, thought, desire, dream, and even daydream Blu had ever had was laid out in my mind like a popup book as well as the feelings associated with every single one of them. It was literally like I'd lived her life and gone through everything.

But the scary part was that it wasn't just the things she remembered, either. Visions of looking through her eyes when she crawled for the first time blurred in my brain along with her first steps, first sippy cup, and first loose tooth. Before I realized it, I had flipped through Blu's entire life like a magazine.

I was shaken from it all by Blu's voice. "How much did you see?" she repeated, and I could tell she was frightened by the very idea of my seeing her secret thoughts.

So, I thought I'd take one for the team.

"Didn't see a thing," I lied, and she let out the breath she'd been holding. Her shoulders sagged with relief.

I held my hand out to her. "I'm in the mood for a little ice-spider hunting," I said. "Let's go kill a few before it gets dark."

Swinging her feet to the floor, Blu said, "Sounds good. That's actually the only pastime I've found that calms my nerves, for some reason."

I nodded while we headed for the lab exit. "Cool," was all I said.

But I knew what her calming pastime was, just like I knew every other minor detail about Blu—like how she really felt about me, and it made me want to die.

I had to do something because she was head-over-freaking-heels for me, for some reason, and was disguising her feelings with loads of playful flirting and jokes. Piper was starting to show up in my thoughts on a daily basis now, and I couldn't shake the thought of seeing her again.

The hunt was a good one, and after a few hours, I parted ways with Blu that night and headed for the quarters that had once been Stargazer's before the Rogues put me up in it.

I dropped my hooded long coat on a chair and headed for the holocomputer first thing, plopping into the hover chair at the desk. "Play Stargazer's message," I said, and the computer lit up quickly. In seconds the recording was playing.

I sat and listened to the whole thing like I'd done dozens of times before. Besides the strange monologue at the end talking about my capabilities, most of the message was a lot of science talk for Blu's benefit, I was thinking, because it wasn't like I could understand it, right?

But that night I understood everything the old man had said, thanks to Blu's memories. All the nanotechnology, astrology and even, oddly, cello imprints her parents had saddled her with in Australia, exactly seventeen years, two months, and eight days ago at exactly 5:18 pm with thirty-seven seconds left until 5:19 pm, were now in my mind for use.

That was also the night I swore to myself never to do that again to anyone. Fate had dealt me Blu's entire life in a freak accident because I hadn't been careful. So that night I retired SS mode. I couldn't help when it did its own thing in my sleep, but at least I couldn't take over other bodies during the

REM walks.

Every night I closed my eyes for sleep since I had woken up strapped to a table months ago, I had thought of Piper, the Viking warrior woman of my dreams and love of my life.

That night all I could think about was Blu and that I'd lied to her.

CHAPTER 28

The next day I informed Blu, Red, and Sam that they were to accompany me to the Rebel base for a lovely chat. When they all vehemently told me they'd rather be eaten alive by snow-cats, I told them that I wasn't asking, so they had to go whether they liked it or not.

Actually, I asked what snow-cats were before I told them to put on their church pants for our Rebel meet.

And, from what I gathered, snow-cats are snow leopards the size of polar bears. And if you're wondering about the size of polar bears nowadays, like I was, which is why I asked, then I can inform you that they're still around and are now about the size of a wooly mammoth.

I checked on those, too. Apparently, they're still extinct, so, you know, kind of a bummer.

It felt weird being the most powerful of my squad while we traversed the frozen tunnels, because they were all rocking battle-armor and towering over me while I was in my jumpsuit and long coat. Sam just looked like a really big guy because his armor was covered by his signature dingy, yellow coat over his exosuit, while the girls' suits were both the rusty red Raptor-6.

We had traveled about an hour before Red decided to drop the bomb that they didn't exactly know where the Rebels were located.

"Well, we know the general area," Blu added after I looked at her sister like she was a lunatic. "We just never had a reason to show up uninvited."

"I'll say," Sam grumbled. "That white suited sheila's a real croc to go up against. Almost lost a leg to her."

"Who?" I asked.

"He's talking about your girlfriend," Red said while she led us through the darkened tunnels.

Nodding, Sam said, "She totes around a massive sword and is a little trigger happy with it, if you know what I mean. Gets a real rush out of severing limbs, I always thought."

"I thought you guys didn't fight them," I said, trying not to think about all the Rogues Piper might have put down in three years.

"It's more of an understanding than a truce," Red told me, taking a right into a tunnel burrowed through the ice, unlike the paved walkway we'd just been on. "We agree to stay out of each other's way. There's a reason we came to that understanding, mate."

"I still don't know why you're so dead set on this union thing," Blu muttered, and I couldn't help but recall our incident in the lab yesterday. Whatever she may have said, I knew why Blu didn't want me to meet with the Rebels.

Piper.

"I know," Sam threw in. "You're a damn lightning nuke thing. We don't need the Rebels now that you're here, mate."

"Guys, I don't know if any of you have thought about it, but how do you think we, the group of women and children, are going to free Flagstaff from not only the Reds but also the Bears and Fascists who make daily pit stops here?"

No one said anything.

"The Rebels have more of a grip than we do, whether you like to think it or not. Being a warring faction means they're not plagued by the thought of where their next meal is going to come from. I know I'm a powerhouse, and I mean that in the least conceited way possible, but we need to stick with what we know. The Rebels were just like the Rogues not three years ago. I know because I was there."

My companions were still silent. The only sound besides my voice was our echoing footsteps resounding down the abandoned tunnel.

"If anyone thinks the Bears, Fascists, or Reds will know how we feel and be more hospitable than the Rebels, speak up now."

"We don't just need soldiers," Blu said, her face turned away from me.

"You're right there, Blu," I told her. "We need an unholy amount of them."

"Firepower isn't everything," Sam said.

I stopped walking, causing all of them to stop and look at me. "What do you want the Rogues to accomplish?"

Sam frowned. "What you mean, Jerry?"

"I mean, I'm here now, placed in command by you guys," I said, pointing at them. "I don't know what any of you want from me, but if it's to save the Rogues, I'm telling you that we need to do just that."

Nothing.

"Listen," I told them, trying to sound a little less agitated. "This is the part where you guys ask me where I get off telling you what to do, and I get it. But the only way to save the Rogues is to take Flagstaff from the Reds."

Blu's eyes widened, and Red's mouth dropped open while Sam grinned from ear to ear. "Yeah," he said, fist pumping the air.

"Jericho—" Red started to say.

"You know it's true," I told her, crossing my arms. "What, did you guys think I was going to sprout mighty wings and carry the Rogues away on a mass exodus?"

"There are tens of thousands of them," Blu said bluntly. "It's impossible."

Shrugging, I walked past them. "Nah," I said. "Just got to hit them where it hurts."

Red fell in step behind me. "And just where is that open, unarmored sweet spot, Jericho?" she asked, sarcasm evident.

"I'm so glad you asked, Red," I answered, my own sarcasm on display. "Sadly, I don't know where it is," then I glanced at them over my shoulder, smiling. "But I know a bat-crazy sheila who sure does."

There wasn't much talking after that, and I was wondering whether or not to maybe apologize for being so gruff. Instead, I decided to try and change the subject that was still hanging in the air.

"So, how're we going to find the Rebels if we don't know where they are?"

"Don't worry, mate," Sam said, nodding his knowing nod with his eyes closed. "They'll find us in a few minutes, I'd say."

There wasn't a movie/tv show/novel/comic book/whatever-story-you-care-to-think-of where someone said that sentence while carousing through dark underground tunnels and it didn't end badly.

I'd like to tell you guys that my tale is completely different, fresh and original from anything you've ever heard, seen, or read. I really would love to not have to tell you that, as soon as the words left Sam's mouth, red dots began appearing all over me and my troops.

"Well, what do you know," Blu said under her breath in an uninterested tone, raising her armored hands into the air. "That took a lot longer than I thought."

"Rogues, halt!" an amplified voice blared, and more laser dots crawled over us. "State your name and business here."

With my hands held high, I walked a few more steps forward, and a bright light shined on me.

"My name is Jericho Johnson," I called to them. "And tell Beck not to worry. We'll wipe our feet."

In less than two minutes, word of my arrival must have gone up the chain of command and reached Beck's synthetic ears because the targets literally painted on us vanished after that, and we were escorted through the large rusted gate into the Rebel base.

"Business?" a battle-armored guard asked me roughly,

brandishing his assault rifle like, I don't know, he actually thought that would make me talk or something.

I shook my head. "Nope. Get Beck."

"I don't think you heard me," he said dangerously, his accent thick Russian. I hadn't heard one of those in a while, come to think of it. "State your business here. Now," he finished with the cocking of his gun.

In a nanosecond, I had wrenched the weapon from his hands and punched him square in the chest of his black suit, sending him skidding on the ice floor into his two buddies, and they all three ended up on the ground in a tangled heap of battle-armor.

"No, I don't think you heard me, bro," I told him, keeping my tone good-natured and snapping his rifle in half like a twig, dropping the pieces on the ground. "I said go get Beck."

My team had already pulled their weapons at the first sign of my attacking, but I held up a hand. "Easy, guys."

"Easy?" Red said. "You hit the bloke first."

"Yeah, well, I hate repeating myself," I said, crossing to the guards I'd just gotten a perfect strike on and pulling the man up by his right arm. "Now that we've established our male dominance, how about you take me to your leader, Rebel?"

"Well," I heard a woman say to my right, and I turned to see the Rebel leader herself standing at the top of a flight of stairs with a smirk on her face. "Jericho Johnson. Looks like someone's been learning the proper way of playing house."

"What, this?" I asked, releasing the guard I was trying to help up and letting him fall back onto his downed comrades. "Nothing you haven't seen before, Beck."

"I'm sure," she said, glancing at my team while descending the steps slowly, her synthetic hips swaying slightly. And though she moved in an almost liquid manner, I knew the amount of power she was packing. "You've certainly been busy making new friends. For a dead person, I mean."

I walked toward her while taking in her appearance. She didn't look sick like she had in the holochat I'd witnessed a few months ago, but she looked about the same. Buzz cut and all.

I met her halfway up the steps, and she stopped in front of me, accepting the hand I held out and squeezing the ever-loving Helheim out of it.

So I squeezed back.

Her never-changing, bright blue, catlike eyes brightened when she felt the pressure I was applying, and her smile broadened. "Not too shabby. Tell me, love, are they mass producing you yet? If so, I'll take four."

"Not yet," I informed her. "They seem to have run into a hiccup of sorts at the dashing good looks part of the assembly line, but God knows they're trying."

Releasing my hand, Beck once again turned her attention to the Rogues with me. "Red," she said politely, nodding to her.

"Beck," Red said, returning the nod.

"I believe I told you the next time we met I would kill you," Beck said, cocking her head slightly. "Ring any bells?"

"A few," Red replied simply, and I could tell she was having trouble not attacking the female synthetic right then and there. "I'm only here because of Jericho."

"Ah, yes, Jericho," Beck said dramatically. "Don't tell me they have you calling the shots?"

"Let's talk," I told her.

"How about you convince me that you're worth my time first," Beck shot at me.

Good old Beck. I tried to play nice, but she had to go and be herself right at the front door.

"I get that, Beck," I said, nodding understandably. "I mean, I know if I was going to die in a few months, I'd make sure that all of my conversations were meaningful."

Her smirk faltered. Bingo.

"So tell me, how does knowing that make me want to talk to you, again?"

I pulled off my hood. "Because I can fix you."

Beck narrowed her eyes at me for a few seconds before

turning around and heading back up the steps. "Come on," she said. "And you can bring your feral Rogue friends with you if you like. Just don't expect them to get a warm welcome."

CHAPTER 29

"Piper's topside, in case you were tired of looking like an idiot swinging you head left and right trying to see her," Beck told me after we'd been walking through the Rebel base for almost five minutes and I was, uh, so *not* doing what she was, you know, talking about...

Geez, fine, I looked like a freaking bobble head for the last five minutes, and she just let me do it, knowing why.

"How is she?" I asked, conscious of my teammates listening intently to my and Beck's conversation.

"She's good," Beck said, and we climbed into a large elevator. "Indispensable, really. Piper's really made a difference around here, ever since you supposedly died and left her stranded."

This had to be the most uncomfortable conversation ever in the history of the universe. I was sure of it.

"I did die," I told her, trying not to sound like a defensive twelve-year-old.

"Bites, doesn't it?" she said with a small laugh. "So, where has the boy wonder been for the past three years?"

"Brain dead for over two and half of those, they tell me, and strapped to a table for the rest."

"Where?"

"In the lab of a good doctor by the name of Cross. He came highly recommended, you see," I said bitterly.

Nodding, Beck said, "Yes, I was in the middle of trying to

abduct that maniacal genius not soon after you escaped him. Thanks for that, by the way. If you'd have stayed put like you were supposed to, I could have grabbed him. But you just had to run away and make him leave for Anchorage, didn't you?"

Wait a minute.

"How'd you know when I escaped?" I asked her quietly.

Shrugging, she said, "Wasn't that hard. I had a contact in Cross's facility who kept yammering on and on about the doc's new project. I didn't know it was you, though, until you ran out in a blizzard while I was droning the place. We got footage of you attacking these guys," Beck said, hooking her thumb at Red. "Then, after you almost killed a few of them, they decided to take you home. How special."

I was staring hard at the elevator floor. "Did, uh, Piper—"

"Yeah, she saw it," Beck told me, leaning against the wall nonchalantly. "I have to say, Jericho, that Piper was expecting you a lot sooner."

"It's only been, like, a month—"

"Really?" Beck said and I noticed a little venom creep into her voice. "The last time I checked, it's been over three years."

"What part of brain dead did you not understand?" I shot at her.

"She's stuck here because of you!" Beck suddenly shouted, causing everyone in the elevator to either jump in surprise or stare at her with their mouths agape.

Okay, I was the only one staring at her with a mouth agape. Not because I was shocked by her unexpected outburst, but more so because I just didn't know what to say.

"Piper saw you on that vid and almost had a heart attack," Beck said, her voice still ferocious. "You should've seen the blonde sap all in tears because the love of her life had just magically come back from the dead. She just knew that you only went with the Rogues so they could send you to her. But did you show up later that day, or two or three days later because, obviously, you'd gotten lost on your quest to find your love, right? I mean, why else wouldn't you have made Piper your top priority?"

"Enough," I growled at her. "I'm not taking advice from a —"

I couldn't say it. The same verbal stabs I'd used on her years ago stuck in my mouth because I was almost just like her now.

"From a what, Jericho?" Beck asked, holding a hand to her ear like she hadn't heard what I just didn't say.

"I said enough, Beck."

She looked just like her now-dead sister when she glared. Then she scoffed and turned away, crossing her arms. "Not that it matters anyway, since Piper's been with Archimedes for over a year."

I knew what she was doing, and I wasn't digging it one bit. Not only was she trying to make me feel bad for something I had no control over, Beck was throwing out random names like it would make me ask her who she was talking about.

The elevator finally stopped, and Beck exited first, with me close behind. Then, somehow against my will, my mouth opened and I asked, "Archimedes?"

Shrugging, Beck said, "Don't know much about what he does, actually. He normally just shows up here to wait out winters before resuming his endless pilfering of abandoned cities. Until you dumped Piper here, that is. Now he's a regular. Few years older than you, I'd say," she said before glancing at the buzz cut I was rocking. "He's got great hair, too. Bit of a history nut. You'd like him."

"I haven't met too many people I like nowadays," I told her while entering the doorway into what looked like a small war room.

"Nor I," Beck told me, plopping into one of the chairs at the holotable and crossing her ankles on top of it. "Piper is the only person I think I've ever given a flip about. Without her, my cause here would've fizzled out years ago. All it took to get her into action was making her forget about you long enough to kill something. Then it was all downhill from there."

Red and Blu both powered down their suits and climbed out of them, taking seats next to me at the holotable. When Beck noticed Sam standing awkwardly and keeping an eye on the door, she said, "Nervous, big guy?"

"I don't like the idea of not being able to see the ghost," he admitted to her.

"She'll be back in a few hours," Beck told him, flicking her eyes at me. "Archimedes left a month ago heading for Anchorage, so don't get any funny ideas about rekindling a romance that died in an exploding, collapsing building."

I'd had enough.

"Since it's none of your business, I guess I won't waste breath telling you that I'll do whatever I want," I told her, leaning back in the chair. "All I want for Piper is to get her home."

"She *is* home, idiot," Beck said then, and the same venom from the elevator crept into her voice. "And if you can time-travel again, why are we even having this conversation?"

Dropping my eyes to the table, I admitted, "I can't yet. But I know who can."

"Let me guess," she said. "Cross?"

"He has my gauntlet," I told her. "All he needs is element zero to make it work, and he said he had men scouring the globe for the stuff."

Beck had started smiling while I was talking, and I glared at her. "Something funny?"

"Actually, yes," Beck said. "Because I happen to have some element zero in my quarters."

I stared at her for a few seconds, narrowing my eyes before saying, "Please tell me you're not lying."

"I raided my father's lab after Klaus was killed, and I found element zero," she said. "Much good it does you since the gauntlet is in Anchorage."

"I needed to kill someone there, anyway," I said casually. "I'll pick it up when I'm done."

"Jericho, it would take almost a month to get to Alaska," Blu said quickly. "All unchecked air traffic is shot down on sight throughout most of the route by the Bears, so you'd have to go on foot."

Beck's eyes locked on Blu, and she stared at her like she'd just noticed the blue-haired girl sitting next to me. "Love the hair," she told her sarcastically.

"At least I have hair," Blu said, glaring at her.

Before Beck had time to retaliate with a no-doubt scathing comment, I jumped in and said, "Why don't we get down to the reason I'm here."

"Yes, let's," Beck said, waving to the door. "Tell your underlings to wait outside and we'll talk."

Then Blu was on her feet like a lightning bolt, delivering a hard punch square to Beck's left cheekbone.

Beck didn't even blink. Cocking her head (which hadn't moved at all) to the side and looking at blue-haired girl, she simply asked, "Really?"

I could see that Blu's knuckles were already bruising and bloodied. It was like punching a concrete wall. I stood, placing my hands on her elbows and pulling her back away from the smiling synthetic woman. "Easy, Blu," I told her. "We're not here to fight."

"Good thing, too," Beck muttered, and Blu lunged at her, swiping hard, and she would've hit her again if I hadn't held her back in time.

"Croc," Blu spat.

"Charmed," Beck said, smirking at the shaking girl.

"Wait outside, guys," I told my squad, and they all protested at once. After I calmed them down, they left the room, but they weren't happy about it.

"Call if you need us, Paladin," Red said, glancing at Beck one last time, closing the iron door behind her.

I sighed heavily before turning back to Beck, who was still laid back in her chair without a care in the world. "Paladin?" she asked.

Sitting back down, I said, "That's what they're calling what I am now."

"Is it?"

"Yeah," I said, placing my elbows on the table and lacing my fingers. We watched each other for what seemed like a long time before Beck said, "You said you knew how to fix me?"

Then I launched into my past few months. I skimmed through anything that didn't have to do with being a Paladin and explained the Z-90 issue in as much detail as I could, combining what I knew from Cross and Stargazer, and I must say it was very educational.

Beck even told me so.

"How very educational, Jericho," she said. "And who is able to tell me if I need any of your blood or not?"

"The girl who just punched you can," I told her. "But I think it's time we got to my terms."

"You're in no such position," Beck said, narrowing her eyes at me.

"Dying woman says what?"

"What?"

"Exactly," I said.

To my annoyance, Beck simply snorted, ignoring my total pwnage and waving a hand for me to spill what I wanted.

"A union between the Rebels and Rogues,"

Beck shook her head. "Not interested. Next, please."

"I wasn't asking," I said, leaning back in my chair. "We know things you don't, and you know things we don't. It's a win either way."

"Unlike your camp of whining women, I have actual soldiers that can fight back if the need arises," Beck said. "And trust me, the need arises quite frequently."

She was right, I knew. My only card left to play was one I really did not want to throw out.

Groveling.

"I can't save them without your help," I tried.

"Not my problem. You should've thought of that before

you signed up with them."

"They'll die."

"What will I get out of this union?" Beck asked gruffly.

"Your life, for starters," I told her. "And me. I could level this base if I wanted to, Beck. Tell me you don't need that kind of firepower."

"Vain much?" she asked with a small scowl.

"It's true," I said, holding up my right hand and turning on the juice, my palm instantly filling with blue sparks. "I could black out this whole city."

"So why don't you?"

Shaking my head, I looked at the lightning in my fist. "Haven't had a good reason to yet."

"What is your plan exactly?" she asked me. "So long as the Reds hold Flagstaff, then neither of our sides has a good chance of winning."

"I know," I said. "That's why I'm going for them first. I don't know enough about this place to do it alone, and you couldn't without my help."

"You're over-selling yourself, Jericho,"

"I'm not," I said confidently. "Not to sound like a Sith lord, but you and I together on the battlefield, we'd be unstoppable. It wouldn't take us long to route this place and take over."

"Sounds a little too good to be true," Beck said quietly. "The Reds have the city in an ice-spider's grip."

"Then we'll cut off all their legs, and when they don't have one to stand on, we kick them out," I told her. I don't know where all my confidence was coming from, but it felt good talking about my cause. Even if the person I was talking about it with didn't care.

"You know," Beck said, watching my hand, "I could just kill you and drain your blood for myself."

"Try it," I told her menacingly. "You couldn't do it in your prime, so I'm not that worried about you when your batteries are almost dead."

Beck was silent for a good while, watching me and thinking, at least I hope she was, about my terms.

"Your blue-haired girl had better get to it, then," Beck said finally, standing. "Because if I'm going to die anyway, you and your Rogues won't be far behind."

I tried not to sigh with relief when I stood. "You won't regret this," I said.

"Oh, I doubt that," she muttered. "I'm already regretting it."

Then her holotab lit up.

"I swear, Beck, I don't even know why the Fascists try anymore," a woman's voice buzzed, and my heart stopped.

It was Piper.

"Self-preservation, Piper," Beck said. She hit the icon above her wrist and Piper's face appeared. Since I was behind the screen, Piper couldn't see me. "We've talked about this before."

"Yeah, well, they're not very good at it," Piper told her with a small laugh. "Kavi got in a jam again, and I messed up my right suit leg saving her sorry hide. I'll see you in about an hour after I get it fixed."

I could see her face through the hologram, and she looked just as beautiful as I remembered. Beck was watching me while Piper was talking, and the Viking girl must have noticed.

"Who's there with you?"

"An old friend," Beck said, never taking her eyes off me. "Fix your suit later, commander. I have a surprise waiting for you in your quarters presently. Beck out."

Piper tried to ask another question, but Beck exited the holochat before she got two words out. "Now then," she said to me. "You kids be good while momma's at the doctor."

"I don't know how to get to her room," I said, lying for some reason.

"I think you do, lover boy," Beck said, heading for the door. "Just know that she's different now, Jericho."

Then she left me.

CHAPTER 30

Nothing but hazy memories greeted me on my way to Piper's quarters. The iron catwalk, men working on mechs below, Beck kissing me, me kissing Piper, and my maddening desire to spend a whole night recording my journey on the glove. It seemed like a long time ago, yet almost like it had been just a few days, too.

So much had changed, though, and at least I knew it, I guess. I hadn't seen Piper in over three years, and to top it off, Beck had informed me that she saw me escape Cross's building close to two months ago and expected me to show up a few days later.

How was I supposed to know that? I couldn't have just left the Rogues, could I? I was certain Piper was safe and didn't need my saving, so I'd stayed and literally saved thousands of helpless people.

So why did I feel sick when I thought of facing Piper?

I shoved all maddening thoughts from my mind when I entered the room where Piper and I had shared our one and only moment together. The day I'd finally kissed Piper in the same room I was entering was basically the only time we had a lull in the almost-dying department that lasted long enough for us to share a few kisses.

Well, maybe more than a few.

I walked around the room at a slow pace, my hands behind my back while I glanced around the living space like a tourist at a museum. The bed looked more comfortable than I remembered, but that was probably because it was an actual bed and not the gutted couch that used to be there.

I stopped in front of the dresser when I noticed the shoes on top of it.

Blue Converse. Chuck Taylor's.

The strings seemed to be missing from the sneakers I'd given Piper when we were in 2012 chasing Klaus, but they looked in pretty good shape. You know, for an almost four-hundred-year-old pair of shoes. Reaching out, I ran a hand over the bright blue material, my fingers grazing the white logo sporting the signature. I remembered her confessing to me fully how she felt in Chicago while we rode in the taxi taking us to our possible deaths. I also recalled the clothes she'd been wearing with the Chucks, and though I tried not to, I opened the top drawer out of curiosity and found the faded jeans and lime green American Eagle t-shirt.

To tell you the truth, I couldn't believe she still had them. I mean, aside from the clothes probably being super-comfy, they really didn't fit the frozen, war-torn future. Closing the drawer, I sat on the edge of the bed and looked around the room again. She'd been here for over three years.

The thought was still baffling. I looked almost the same as I did three years ago, and I wasn't even sure about adding them to my age because I was unconscious for most of them. That would make Piper close to twenty-two and me, uh, well, twenty-two also, I guess, if I wasn't adding the comatose years.

Although I had been doing a good job keeping my idiot brain in check and hadn't thought any unsettling thoughts for a good three minutes, I ended up letting my guard down enough for all my doubts to spill out all at once.

What was I supposed to even say to her?

"Hey, Pipe, how have you been?"

"What's up, girl? Been a while, huh?"

I closed my eyes and sighed. There was nothing clever to say or ask. Nothing but the cold hard truth of me not being there for her and, when I could've been, still deciding not to be. Then there was some guy named—what was it—Archibald? Achilles?

I heard the sound of boots on the catwalk coming my way, and my heart began beating like crazy. I felt like I was short of breath. *It's just Piper*, I told myself, trying to slow my breathing. *You and her are just old chums.*

I stood, not being able to remain still while the steps drew closer.

It was Piper. She was alive and almost to the room, and I was about to lay eyes on her for the first time since I had kissed her forehead goodbye in the streets of Flagstaff.

It's just Piper. You and her are just old chums.

Then she walked through the doorway.

I felt foolish standing beside her bed, my hands shoved into the pockets of my long coat, because I just couldn't think of anywhere else to put them.

I stopped breathing.

Just old... chums...

She. Was. Gorgeous.

It had never occurred to me when I was loping beside her on a horse through the snowy forests of Svalbard that she was just a girl barely nineteen who was still mistaken for a fifteen-year-old at times.

But seeing her then, wearing a white jumpsuit and fiddling on her holotab, and remembering what she'd looked like years ago, it was like a reality check in the form of a ton of bricks cascading down the mountainside of horror onto my unaware noggin.

The only way I was able to tell it was her, actually, was by her long, white-blonde hair, which was in a ponytail when she entered, but a few feet in, she pulled it loose with her left hand and it spilled onto her shoulders and all the way down her back. Her face was familiar, too, I guess, but was now aged into perfection in every way. I caught a glimpse of her eyes.

God, those eyes...

She didn't notice me standing there at first because of whatever she was doing on her holotab while I was staring at her with big hearts practically bouncing in and out of my eye sockets. It was only after she'd stopped in the center of the room, finished up on her tab, and closed it out that she saw me.

"Piper," I said, my tone odd because, well, I felt odd.

"Jericho?" she said quietly, her brow furrowed in slight confusion. I merely nodded. Piper covered her mouth with her hands, her eyes locked on me, and I saw the tears brimming.

"It's me, Pipe," I told her, pulling my hands out of my pockets and easing toward her while feeling like I was sneaking up on the last deer on the planet.

Piper closed her eyes for a few seconds, during which she regained her composure and removed her hands from her mouth. "What happened to you?" she asked simply, her eyes still shut like she wasn't going to like my answer.

"Dr. Cross fished my corpse out of the rubble of Klaus's building after the explosion," I said. "After he finished rebuilding me years later, I escaped."

Hmm. It seemed a tad drab when I summed up my God-awful existence in Cross's care in a short sentence.

"I saw you escape," Piper said, and she opened her reddening eyes, turning them on me. She didn't say anything else. She didn't need to.

"I couldn't come find you right off the bat," I started to say.

"Why not?" she cut in. "The Rogues know my whereabouts as well as anyone."

"Piper—"

"Two months, I've waited," Piper said, shaking her head slightly, and I saw a tear slip down her cheek. "You didn't think that after three years of me believing you to be dead, I wouldn't want to see you?"

Remember a chapter ago when I told you the elevator ride with Beck was the most uncomfortable conversation I'd ever had?

I was wrong, there, whoever-you-are.

This was, without a doubt, the most awful moment of my entire life. I would've gladly strapped myself back onto Cross's table for all my remaining days if I thought it would've maybe fixed the situation even a little bit.

Not being able to look at her, I glanced at the wall. "I didn't know you knew I was alive," I said, wincing a little. It was hard and untasteful, but it was the truth. I had seriously thought things would pan out okay because Piper didn't know I was alive and kicking when I decided to help the Rogues.

"What difference does that make?" Piper snapped, and all signs of weepy joy/sadness/surprise were out the window. She was now cold as ice.

I looked at her, almost not believing my ears. I mean, I had steeled my mind for her vehemence and ferocity, hadn't I? So why was her reacting the way I thought she'd react throwing me for a loop?

When I didn't answer, Piper growled in frustration and stomped past me, sitting on her bed and removing her boots. Once she'd ripped the last one off and flung it across the room into the wall, Piper stood and faced away from me with her arms crossed.

The truth was all I had left. I hadn't planned on lying to her or anything, but I also hadn't planned on explaining every detail from when I first woke up to standing in her room.

Taking a deep breath, I said, "Have you seen the Rogue camp lately?"

"Of course I haven't," was her curt reply, and she may or may not have rolled her eyes. I wasn't sure because I couldn't see her face.

"It's basically nothing but women and children," I said. "They were starving when I arrived, so I helped them get food."

Piper turned her face slightly and asked. "Are you like Beck?"

"Why do you ask?"

"Because of what you were doing in the surveillance

footage. Normal people can't do the things I saw you do, but Beck can," she turned around to face me, her arms still crossed.

I paused for a second, trying to think of the best way of putting my answer, finally deciding on, "Yes and no," I told her. "Since she's more machine than me, I'm about ten times stronger than she is, and I got a few more bells and—"

"I loved you," she said suddenly, and my words stuck in my throat. The angry expression that she was doing a bang-up job of keeping on her face melted away then, and she looked like the girl I remembered. "I didn't want to live after you died. If not for Beck, I wouldn't have."

"I'm sorry, Piper," I told her, glancing away yet again, shaking my head and closing my eyes. "I didn't mean for any of this to happen, I swear."

"I know you didn't," I heard her say, her voice cracking.

About time, too. I didn't want to be the only person about to sob uncontrollably. Then something wonderful happened.

Piper hugged me.

I almost gasped, it was so unexpected, but I ended up wrapping my arms around her and returning the tight hug.

Hugs are powerful things, if you haven't aged enough to stop playing Xbox for a while to get a good, nice hug and therefore don't know yet how powerful they are, I mean.

Kissing is great, don't get me wrong. But unless you're, well, a bit of a word-I'm-not-going-to-use-in-case-there-are-children-present, you don't just run around kissing everybody you meet. Hugs are sort of the same, I guess, because most people don't randomly hug strangers, either.

But the thing with hugs is that, if they're genuine, you can always sense the feeling that the person hugging you is trying to express.

A nice "Well done, son" hug from a proud father. Or an "I don't want to leave your side" one. Even the "Yes! Team blue is unstoppable!" bro-hugs. And there's also the dreaded "I haven't seen you since Easter Sunday, you naughty nephew!" kind that

I hate.

Piper's hug was none of those, in case you were wondering. It said something of a different nature that I hated, yet understood.

"I'm so sorry, Piper, really," I said, my voice muffled by her hair while we hugged.

"It wasn't your fault. I just didn't know what to do after you were gone. It took me over a year to even accept that you were dead."

"So who is he?" I asked suddenly.

And that, ladies and gentlemen, was when I decided to address the hug. I guess I could've eased into it better, what with my being the resurrected ex and all, here stirring up crazy emotions.

Piper pulled out of the hug and faced away from me again. She was quiet for about a minute. Then, "You were dead," she said weakly, lifting one shoulder slightly in a small shrug. "I didn't have anyone after you were gone."

I could see it all so clearly now. Boy meets girl because of time-travel, girl falls for boy, boy leaves and returns to her a few minutes later, girl leaves with boy to save the world, boy leaves girl so he actually can save the world, boy dies trying, girl almost dies because boy died, girl feels helpless and alone, new boy shows up to comfort the sad, and of course beautiful, girl.

Then girl forgets about the dead first boy and falls for the very-much alive second boy.

Who apparently has great hair.

Not sure why I mentioned that...

"Does he love you?"

She nodded, her back still to me.

"And you?"

Turning to face me, she said, "Yes, I do," the words seemed confident enough, but the tears had returned to her eyes.

"I'm happy for you, Pipe," I said. "God knows you never

deserved to be stuck here," then I turned toward he door.

"Wait," she blurted quickly, taking a few steps in my direction. "What about you?"

I froze.

"Do you still love me?"

How was I supposed to answer that? Either answer was bad, so why'd she even ask? Saying yes would just make her feel bad and quite possibly throw a monkey-wrench into a relationship some mystery guy had been cultivating with her for over two years; whereas, saying no sounded worse because it would seem like I didn't ever love her in the first place.

Worst. Day. Ever. In my life and quite possibly the upcoming lives of all human males on the planet.

And that was when I decided that the truth had run its course, and it was time for me to tell the biggest lie of the century.

Shrugging, I smiled halfheartedly at her. "Three years is a long time, Piper, especially in this frozen hell of a place. Just you being alive is all I care about."

I thought it was well put. Not enough push to make her want to kill herself over some dude I didn't even know, and just enough to make her feel loved by a friend.

See how awesome I am?

I stepped out of her room so she could change before we went to find Beck, and not two seconds after the door closed, my knees weakened and I sank to the catwalk, wrapping my hands around my head and squeezing as hard as I could, gritting my teeth and slamming a fist into the thick iron grating below my feet. Then I sprang up and went to the concrete wall where the catwalk ended behind Piper's door, and I laid my forehead against the cold stone.

I pounded my head against it softly a few times, my eyes squeezed shut. Then I rammed my head into the wall, shattering the concrete. Chunks of it fell onto my boots and slipped through the catwalk, and I opened my eyes, watching the rocks fall.

"Don't feel bad," I muttered. "People can slip through cracks, too, it seems."

Piper came out about a minute later and found me leaning on the railing with my arms crossed. "Took you long enough," I joked to her, plastering on the best smile I could muster.

Then we walked down the catwalk in awkward silence side-by-side, and my mind wandered to the checklist I had made while being strapped to a table months ago.

The list consisted of two things left in my life actually worth living for.

And I had just lost one of them.

Now, it seemed, there wasn't anything left holding me back from the second, and now *only*, item left on my list.

Revenge.

CHAPTER 31

Beck wasn't the best patient a doctor could ask for.

Maybe it was her dazzling personality.

"Fix me or die," Beck told Blu from the operating table, although Blu didn't seem exactly scared for her life.

"Unless I kill you first accidentally because you won't be still like I instructed and also because I'm not familiar with your mechanics at all," Blu said calmly. "Or I could cut the wrong wire on purpose and make you go into synthetic cardiac arrest."

"Whatever you're going to do, just do it fast," I said from my own operating table not three feet away, scowling at my body. "Did we have to be restrained?"

"You'll see why in a minute," she promised.

It was weird to be back in the med bay where years ago I had stayed up all night and recorded my exploits on the gauntlet. Piper had left to fix her armor and check on some member of her squadron while Beck and I were in surgery.

Or, at least, I hoped it wasn't going to entail surgery.

Blu was standing in between our tables in the tangled mess of wires and IV tubes that she claimed wasn't disorganized. My right arm was attached to most of them, it seemed to me. Blu had wanted us to get into a couple of green hospital gowns, but we both told her no in about fifty hateful ways. I ended up just taking off my shirt before lying on the oddly warm operating table, and Beck unzipped the top of her black jumpsuit, slipped her arms out, and tied the sleeves around her waist before she lay back in her tank top.

I couldn't help but notice all the exposed gears, gyros, wires, and even a few blinking lights showing through the cuts and slashes I spied in more than a few places on her exposed arms and neck. Her left arm was rocking a long gash on the tricep, which reached from her elbow to her shoulder and was showing off the more robotics than the other cuts. I noticed the skin ended on the front of her torso, stopping a few inches beneath her throat and, even though her figure was feminine, I could tell that she was missing a *lot* of skin. "Looks like someone's been learning the proper way of playing house," I said, turning my face back toward the ceiling.

"Try not to stare. It's quite rude, you know," Beck said, smiling and glancing at her arms before putting them at her sides so Blu could strap her down. I noticed that Blu tightened hers down harder than mine. "Wanted to fix them, but the only guy who could've done that died over a year ago."

"Alright," Blu said after finishing up with Beck's bonds. "Here's the rundown. Beck needs almost half a pint of Z-90 to get back to being her charming, super-human self. Only problem is that I'm not sure what will happen if I take that much from Jericho. It should be about the same as taking that much from a normal person, like with mild dizziness and so forth, but I can't be sure." Glancing at me, she asked, "You sure about this?"

Closing my eyes, I said, "Let's do this."

Nodding, Blu turned to Beck, holding up the set of needles attached to the tubes. "You know where I have to put these, right?"

"Yeah, yeah," Beck mumbled, squeezing her own eyes shut. "Try not to enjoy it too much."

I cracked open my right eye just in time to see Blu smile almost sadistically and say, "No promises."

Then she slid two of the needles straight into the side of Beck's head, square in the left temple. Beck winced and her back arched a little against the heavy straps.

"Uncomfortable?" Blu asked, sounding like a waiter asking if someone needed another basket of chips. It was wrong of her, really, because I found out later that Beck wasn't able to speak while it was going on.

The last IV Blu had had went in the neck just below the left jawline, and I almost gasped when I saw that she had to wiggle the needle around to find a good vein while Beck's body semi-thrashed on the table.

"Uh, Blu?" I said when I saw some type of fluid leak out of Beck's left eye.

"Wait for it," Blu said, finding the right spot for the last needle, and I saw Beck's body slump back to the table. After running her holotab over the top half of Beck's body, she said, "She's stable for now."

Turning back to the holocomputer amongst the wires and tubes, Blu hit a few keys, and I saw the Z-90 pull into the tube running out of my arm.

It was like normal blood, but it glowed a vibrant, almost florescent red.

So, I guess it didn't look like normal blood.

"You okay?" Blu asked quickly. "Tell me to stop anytime."

"What, like a safe word?" I joked.

"Jericho—"

"I'm good," I told her. I actually was feeling fine and not the least bit dizzy or dying, and after about thirty seconds, Blu stopped the flow and we were done.

"That wasn't so bad," I muttered while she pulled out my IVs.

"You sure you're fine?" Blu asked again, putting fingers to my neck and feeling my pulse.

"Seriously, I'm okay," I said, smiling reassuringly at her.

"Please don't die, Jericho," I heard her say—only her mouth hadn't moved.

This had happened a few times since our incident a few days ago, and I found that if I didn't focus too much on her, I wouldn't pick up any of her thoughts.

Reaching my right hand up, I covered hers on my neck and gave it a slight squeeze. "Has anyone ever told you how good you are at playing doctor?"

Since I knew what made her tick now, the smile I was expecting bloomed, and she pulled her hand away. "Croc."

Pulling off the wires taped to my chest, I sat up, swinging my feet off the table. Beck was still unconscious after Blu removed the IVs, and I gave her a questioning glance from where I was sitting on my table.

"She'll be fine," Blu assured me. "The easiest way of putting it is, she needs to reboot," she said, turning back to me.

"Really? How long before she's—"

"Long enough," Blu said, stepping forward quickly and kissing me, grabbing my head in her hands.

I was surprised. Like, extremely so. Mainly because if she'd been planning on doing that, I should've picked up on those thoughts big time.

After a good ten seconds, Blu pulled back and locked eyes with me. "Please don't go to Anchorage," she said, rubbing the back of my head softly.

"I have to," I told her, and she sighed, touching her forehead to mine and squeezing her eyes shut.

"Why?"

It was a hard question to answer, I discovered. I mean, I did know why, I suppose, but I also knew that explaining my motives behind the frigid road trip from Helheim to anyone else would make me sound, for lack of better wording, unpleasant.

So I decided that I shouldn't sugarcoat it.

"I'm going to get my gauntlet back from Cross then kill him," I said simply, like I was telling her that I was going to pick up a Snickers bar on my way home from work.

"Then you'll leave for good?"

"I don't know," I answered truthfully. "I need to give Piper the option, though."

"But Beck's agreed to the union," Blu said quickly, her hands still framing my face. "What about all your talk of revolution, freeing the oppressed, and sending the Reds packing?"

"They'll be here when I get back," I told her, placing my hands over hers. "We'll move the Rogues to the Rebel base while I'm gone."

"My head hurts," Beck said suddenly. Blu didn't release me, and I didn't feel the need for us to pull apart like a couple of busted adolescents. Beck groaned slightly before ripping her arms clean out of the thick restraints. Sitting up, she went to work on her legs. "Hope you had fun stabbing my head with needles," she muttered, freeing her legs and swinging them off the table. She rolled her neck around a few times and rubbed at the punctures on the side of her head.

"I'm going with you," Blu said to me, crossing her arms.

"Sorry, Blu," I said. "This is a Paladin-only vacation."

"You'd be dead in less than two days, anyway," Beck said.

"You can't go," I told her, hating to agree with Beck even though she was probably right. "You're needed here a lot more than you would be with me."

"Is that so?" Blu asked, cocking her head slightly. "So you know how to reconnect foreign stimuli to the spinal column in the event of a severance?"

I just shrugged, glancing at Beck who scowled and said, "You'd freeze to death in a hundred yards."

"You need me, whether you like it or not," Blu said finally. "I'm going. Period."

I won't lose you, was what she was thinking. *I need you, Jericho, just like the rest of the world.*

This was bad. Blu was awesome, don't get me wrong, and also appealing in about every way possible. But, even at the risk of sounding lame since, well, just look at my damn life, I wasn't sure about my relationship status, not only with Blu but with the rest of humanity as well. Every day I was reminded of how different I was from humans, and it was disconcerting.

See? I totally just called other people humans like some Skynet freakshow.

Whatever. The point was that I didn't feel like I had the time to develop healthy interaction with anyone or anything because when presented with the thought of having to save the world, even though I hadn't for sure decided to even save the popsicle planet, the people around me felt kind of small.

But Blu's kiss had gone a lot deeper than just a normal kiss. That much was certain. Although I knew how awesome it felt, there was no way I was going to act on any Blu-related feelings. Partly because I didn't feel two months was enough time to proclaim undying love to someone after having a semi-broken heart and partly because I needed to sort out my Piper issues first before I jumped at the first girl with willing lips.

And blue hair. Man, it looked wickedly awesome.

"When would you be leaving me in despair?" Beck said, not looking the least bit in despair while flexing her hands around, watching them. "And, just so you know, I feel fantastic."

"ASAP," I said, reaching for my shirt. "And I'm glad you're feeling better."

Blu checked her holotab and flipped through a lot of scientific gibberish. "I'm sending you my final diagnosis."

"No need," Beck said, slipping back into the top half of her jumpsuit. "I'm past trust issues now. Just tell me and I'll most likely believe you."

Blu was a little taken aback by Beck's sudden bout of random niceness. "Uh, okay," she said, taking a deep breath. "I didn't fix you, if that's what you're thinking."

Beck and I froze in the middle of putting our clothes back on. "What do you mean?" I asked.

Blu went back to her holotab. "Everything about you is working as it should, which is good," she said, "but this doesn't solve the main problem. In another two or three years, the same thing is going to happen, and a simple dose of super blood might not be able to reverse the process then."

Beck was silent for a few seconds, staring hard at the floor. Then her liquid green eyes flicked to me. "Looks like you just got another volunteer for your suicide mission, Jericho," she said. "I need five minutes with Cross before you rip his head off."

"Fine. Five minutes only, though."

"Great," she said while zipping her jumpsuit up. "Piper can take the reins while we're gone."

I tried to not act relieved that the ex-Viking warrior chick of my dreams would not be joining us on our voyage.

That's all I needed. A long, freezing cross-country trek filled with thousands of miles of awkward.

Yeah, I was glad Piper wouldn't be going.

PART II

Road Trip

CHAPTER 32

Jericho

"I'm going," Piper said, dropping into a chair opposite me in the war room. It didn't sound like an argument.

"No," Beck told her from the chair next to me. She'd been giving me the rundown on the way things worked outside of Flagstaff, pulling an updated map of what was left of North America. "And who told you?" Beck asked her, frowning.

"Kind of a hard secret to keep, considering you were at death's door yesterday," Piper told her, crossing her arms. "And now you're leaving for Anchorage. May I ask why?"

"Ask the Paladin," Beck told her in an uninterested tone, typing away on the green holokeyboard. "He's the one with all the ambitions."

"Paladin?" Piper asked, flicking her eyes to me.

"Long story," I told her. "Summed up version is that I need Cross and so does Beck."

"You're fools," Piper told us harshly. "Beck, you know the trip to Anchorage is near impossible to make on foot."

Scowling, Beck said, "Archimedes does it all the time, and it's not like I haven't made the trip myself before."

"Archimedes," I said, like I'd just remembered the name of an actor I had been trying to recall for hours. "I thought it was Achilles or Artemis."

The look I received from Piper let me know just how funny she thought that was. Shrugging, I said, "Sorry. Never met the guy."

"Anyway," Beck said. "Enough about your ex-Viking. Here's the route."

Piper looked away from us after Beck's comment, and I noticed big time, watching her. I would've gotten away with it, too, had Beck not seen me and snapped her fingers right in front of my face. "Hey, I said enough about Piper. You died so she moved on. Get over it."

Then Piper pushed away from the table hard and stomped toward the door.

Years ago I would've most likely called Beck down for her harsh mannerisms, but since all she was saying was true, I just looked at the map. "That was a little uncalled for, Beck."

"You better write all the human girls off right now, JJ, because you and I are destined for each other," Beck said, her smile broadening while she leaned her shoulder against mine. "Can't you see us, sweetie-pie? Ruling the world with an iron fist, the little Paladins crawling around the foot of our thrones made out of the bones of our enemies?"

"I have more hair than you do," I said. "Something tells me I'll never be able to look past that."

Rubbing at the peach-fuzz on her head, Beck said, "Yes, you prefer hair of a more primary color, I saw. Blu said my hair would grow back in the next few years, but I've grown attached to this look."

When I didn't say anything, Beck gave me a side glance. "We haven't even left yet, and you're annoyed with me?"

"You wouldn't have been my first choice for a traveling companion, no," I told her. "Now, how do we do this?"

Beck hit a few keys, and Arizona lit up red on the map. "The main thing to remember is stick to the west coast. The only exception is we'll skip California altogether and cross through Nevada." Every time she mentioned a state, it lit up on the map. "We'll hit the coast in Oregon then head up to Washington."

I watched the states light up, and I raised my hand. Sighing, Beck said, "What is it?"

"Why the west coast?" I asked. "I mean, straight north through Utah, Idaho, and Montana seems like it'd be easier."

"The westernmost coastline has been considered the badlands ever since 2037, which was the year when the American government decided they were wasting precious time trying to fix the impossible, so the West Wastes isn't exactly being fought over by the Bears and Fascists," Beck said. "Mind you, there are still other dangers in the Wastes. Most of the abandoned cities are the homes of unfriendly clans of both raiders, deserters, and maybe even a few cannibals. We can skirt around most of them, but we'll for sure have to stop in Seattle to get more supplies because after that," the U.S. ended on the map and Canada started, "we hit the real badlands."

I frowned at the map. "British Columbia?"

"If that's what you want to call it," Beck said, and the map zoomed in. "You can forget all of the national parks and beautiful landscape of your time and just gird your loins for nuclear fallout. British Columbia was where the nuke that crippled North America hit, and it is home to some of the most grotesque abominations known to what's left of man."

I peered at the holomap, and pictures of destruction flashed up for me to see, floating above the map. "Check this out," Beck said, reaching for a picture on her right and pulling it out of the stream to my waiting hands.

Have I mentioned that I love future technology?

I looked at the small tab for a few seconds before realizing what she wanted to show me. "There's no snow," I said, not really believing it. "How?"

The picture depicted an enormous city curled up in the horrifying embrace of mother apocalypse, complete with collapsed buildings, streets cluttered with destroyed cars, buses, and whatnot. Although mother apocalypse has a bad habit of giving her kids bad nose jobs, I still recognized the trashed city.

"Vancouver," I said. "Looks like a real fixer-upper."

"Quite," Beck confirmed. "There's lots of theories about

why it's only seventy degrees there all year, but no one really knows because the city's populace keeps any curious scientists from stopping by to investigate."

"Maybe it's from the radiation?" I proposed, shrugging and tossing the picture back into the holostream.

"Could be. Considering what the inhabitants look like, I wouldn't be surprised."

I nodded before a strong thought came to me. Well, it really just walked up and slapped my brain all hard and rough like. "Does Archimedes go this way?"

"That he does," Beck muttered. "Though he's got a rigged up cycle-hovercraft thing he's been riding for years now. The thing is, Arc is so known to most of the armies, he can come and go as he pleases."

Frowning, I asked, "How's that?"

Beck just shrugged. "Maybe geologists are granted an infinite number of get-out-of-death-free cards at the beginning of wars. I don't even know what he's looking for, to be honest, and since he hasn't exactly been vocal about it, I never asked."

Call me the paranoid ex-boyfriend if you want, but something wasn't right. "Why is he going to Anchorage again?"

Beck glanced at me with narrowed eyes. "Don't tell me you're the paranoid ex now."

"Just tell me why," I said, trying not to groan. "I mean, how many other major things could Anchorage have that would attract him there at least once a year? That's not a little weird to you?"

"Anchorage is one of the four operational and surviving cities left standing," Beck said, like it wasn't a big deal to have only four whole functioning cities left in North America. "It's not weird that he makes the trek a lot because Anchorage is home to the great minds trying to make the world a better place. We call it the School for that reason, actually."

"Chloe told me there were only three cities left," I said,

looking at the map again.

"Sounds like her. She was a Red to the bone and therefore wouldn't mention the only other city that rivals, or, to some people, surpasses the Reds tech and mechs," she said, smirking and shaking her head. "That's why she, along with almost the entire population of Flagstaff, left out Dallas, TX."

"What is the specialty of these places?"

"Anchorage is the School, New York is the food market of sorts, Flagstaff is home to lovable warmongers living off death, and Dallas is doing that better," Beck said. "Education, food, and weapons. What more could you ask for in a country?"

"Welcome to the new American dream," I muttered.

Flagstaff, Anchorage, New York City, and Dallas being the last cities was kind of depressing.

Could've been worse, though. I mean, Detroit could've still been around. That'd be the assassins, for sure.

And if you happen to be from Detroit, don't be too hard on yourself. Since murder is the only crime a state, by law, has to report to the FBI, maybe the city was just packed with a lot of serial killers and not a conglomeration of assorted law-breakers.

Wow, why am I defending a city that no longer exists? Whatever.

Keep your chin up, people from Detroit, and if you happen to live there around nuclear holocaust o'clock, you might want to think about moving to one of the four previously mentioned cities.

And learn to let go, for God's sake. It's only Michigan, after all.

"What about the Yukon?" I asked, pointing.

"Hmm," Beck mused quietly. "Not much to it, really. Lots of open, snow-covered spaces. I guess the snow-cats could be a problem to the humans traveling with us. Also, Archimedes swears he saw a wolf in the Yukon once. Probably not true, though."

I'd already heard about snow-cats, but I asked her about

them anyway. "Snow-cats are pretty common along the whole route," Beck said, and a red line appeared that trailed from Flagstaff to Anchorage, lighting our path and coursing with color. "They're biggish but nothing a toddler in a battle-suit couldn't tear apart. The cats are in greater numbers in the Yukon, though, and have been known to attack in large packs."

Frowning while nodding, I took all of that in before asking about why she didn't believe Archimedes about the wolf. "Wolves aren't as common as snow-cats?"

"Because they've been extinct for over a century," Beck said. "Plus, we're not talking about the wolves you remember. These are much bigger."

"How big we talking?" I asked.

"They were bigger than snow-cats and a lot meaner, too. A lone wolf could've easily taken out a squad of twenty armed and armored soldiers in a matter of minutes," Beck said, tapping at her red keys. "Here's what they looked like," she said, and a picture floated to me.

My mouth dropped open a little, and I squinted at the wolf in the hologram to make sure my eyes weren't playing tricks on me. The build was about the same as the wolves I was accustomed to, but it was massive and didn't have a wolf's signature bushy fur.

Or any fur, for that matter.

"That is skin you're looking at, and normal weapons couldn't penetrate it," Beck said after I'd blinked at the grotesque picture for a few seconds. "A tank or mech might've been able to. They could bite straight through just about anything, too, armored cars included. Some even say they could breathe fire, but that's not a fact."

"Yay," I mumbled. "Any other crazy-big animals I need to know about before we set out?"

The question was sarcastic and quite frankly rhetorical as well, but Beck answered anyway. "I didn't mention Roc in Portland because I still don't believe in that myth."

"Roc?" I asked, finding Portland, Oregon, on the map.

"Mammoth-sized bird of prey that adopted the city as a nest. Eats anything that enters, Arc says. Some stories say it's a ferruginous hawk and others say it's a sort of sea eagle. Roc is what Arc calls the thing."

Roc. There the famed geologist goes again, stealing my thunder. Not satisfied that he took my girl, he also gets to name possibly real enormous birds after legendary enormous birds.

What a croc.

"Arc says he skirts about seventy miles west of Portland on the shoreline because of the bird, but he also admitted to me that he's only seen signs of its prey, which didn't exactly make me a believer. But I suppose we shouldn't risk it," Beck said, and the red line moved a few centimeters to the east.

We discussed the trip for another hour, hashing out items we would need to take with us as well as pit stops along the way that would accommodate our human travel companions.

Human. There it was again. The word meant more to me now than it ever did, since I'd lost the right to call myself such. I once met a man during my trip to the Crusades who said humanity was a choice and not something a man or beast is born with.

Although I didn't really understand what the old man had been getting at then, I now grasped at the words like a drowning man, hoping they would become shackles of sanity for my clouded mind.

I know. Dramatic, right?

It took three days of prepping, but the witching hour arrived and we were finally ready to go.

"Take care of the place while I'm gone," Beck said to a big guy that I learned later was part of Piper's infamous Ghost Squadron. "We'll get back when we get back."

"I wouldn't keep the light on," Red said, stepping into the elevator, against my better judgment. Red wasn't the only other person who'd insisted—okay, demanded—that she be part of our trip. Sam had also told me that he was going, whether I liked it or not.

"You realize that if things get bad out there, Beck and I are going to be saving your skins constantly, right?" I asked all four of our human companions when we'd gathered them up to try and talk them out of going.

"Jerry," Sam said, laying a big hand on my shoulder, "like I'd want to die doing anything else."

I wasn't exactly sure how to respond to that, and after stuttering and fumbling around a second, Red said, "The Rebels don't need you like we do, Jericho. I can't stay here while you go risk your life."

Piper was staring hard at the elevator wall, and I saw her jaw tighten at Red's words. The Australian girl could've kissed me right there and probably not have drilled as deep into the awkward thickness as what she'd just said.

It was like Piper wanted to explode at times and scream about, well, I'm not sure. She looked on the verge a couple of times, but I also knew after our little chat in her quarters that she had moved on.

Beck was watching the levels climb on the keypad. "Don't be dramatic, Red," she said. "I need him, too. Maybe not like your blue-haired sibling, though."

Thinking that Blu was going to attack Beck again, I looked at her but saw that she was smiling. "I do," Blu said. "No way was I going to let my future husband leave me."

Just wow. Let's recap here, shall we?

I was starting a cross-country trip with an estranged ex-girlfriend, a girl who almost wanted to have my synthetic super-babies, a crazy psycho-chick who just loved pointing out the first two things, and a big guy who just wanted to go so he could possibly go out in a blaze of glory at my side.

Sounds like a trip for the ages, does it not?

Then the elevator stopped, and in less than five minutes, the six of us were standing on the streets of Flagstaff next to our ride, which was a lightweight armored vehicle I'd swiped from the Bears a few weeks back. It wasn't roomy like some of the other transports, but this one was faster, Blu said when I had told her we'd kill each other in less than an hour that close quartered. After she explained that the smaller white rig, the one she called a MK-Waltz, was also able to cloak against radar, I said that maybe we'd survive being packed in like sardines if it meant we wouldn't be blown to smithereens by Bear missiles.

The MK-Waltz, to my utter delight, looked like something straight out of an armored car videogame, complete with a mounted machine gun, pulse-cannon, and wicked wheels that looked like they could shred through anything.

Only it was white. Not bucking the system or being picky, but the MK-Waltz looked like more of a granite or charcoal kind of ride. And it wasn't really small compared to 2012 cars, but in 2345 it was almost puny. I had said that if four people riding in it were wearing battle-armor then, yeah, we were in for a packed trip, but Red showed me the diagram on her tab and said that the cabin of the MK-Waltz was warm enough for them to not be in armor, showing me where the suits would be held somewhere in the back.

All in all, it wasn't that cramped once we all climbed in and got situated.

Except the whole state of Texas wouldn't have had enough room for me, as far as Piper was concerned.

"How far are we going today?" I asked from the copilot seat next to Red, who was the designated driver at the moment.

"Las Vegas," she said, flipping a few switches and the powerful engine roared to life. Everything the driver needed, save the pedals, was a complete, soft blue hologram, even the steering wheel, which Red grabbed in her left hand while shifting the holostick into gear with her right, and we were off. "It's around four hours away," Red said. "It'll be dark when we get there, so we'll hole up in Sin City for the night."

I nodded, not really listening while I glanced out of my thick passenger window. I heard bickering in the back and instantly shouted, "Don't make me come back there."

"But Beck started it," Blu said, and I knew she was smiling because, well, there wasn't much she could do anymore without me knowing.

"I will turn this armored car right around," I said, and everyone got a chuckle out of that.

After all passengers fell silent and turned to their own thoughts, I reclined my seat and pulled my hood over my eyes. "Wake me up if anyone needs their butt saved," I said to Red, crossing my arms and settling into the semi-comfy chair.

In five minutes we pulled out of Flagstaff and started our journey to Nevada.

Vegas, baby.

CHAPTER 33

The four-hour trip to Vegas was pretty uneventful, but I guess that's what I get for sleeping the whole way. My comrades actually didn't try to wake me up until we hit the Strip. You know, only the best place in Sin City to uh, sin, I guess.

But after my first official glance out of my window, I saw that there wasn't going to be any sinning going on in what was left of the once great city. I wasn't surprised by the abandoned cars and buses or the gutted, falling down buildings.

What was surprising was the first sign of life we saw when passing by the Stratosphere, the giant hotel/casino that had one of the tallest towers in the city.

"Does anyone else see the lights on in the tower?" I asked my travel companions, pointing to the mammoth tower and the two lit up rooms on the top floor. The flickering let me know it was probably a fire and not actual electricity. The Stratosphere was a big joint, if you didn't already know, and it seemed like mother apocalypse hadn't exacted too much discipline on the place. Most of it looked to be old, of course, but intact or at least not completely collapsed. And the signature super-tall tower was still standing.

And possibly housing feral raiders.

"There's a building with literally almost twenty-five-hundred rooms next door, and they decide to stay in the Top of the World restaurant," I said. "How very awkward of them."

"Raiders, most likely," Sam said like it wasn't a big deal. "This place bustles a few months out of the year with raider activity during the summer, so they're most likely here for the rally."

"Rally?" I muttered, frowning when both the lights went out in the rooms. "Looks like whoever is up there spotted us."

"It's not really a rally, per se," Red said while getting out of the driver's seat and stretching. "Most tribes are actually pretty friendly with one another but still have a bad habit of killing each other. They meet here under a white flag and exchange resources, since they hunt in different territories and steal different things that the other tribes might need."

"Sounds like a peachy ordeal," I said, standing. "But how many people can they really raid throughout the year?"

"You would be surprised," Beck said, and I noticed her cock a wicked looking handgun before holstering it on her hip. "It's way too early for the raider meet, though, so Jericho and I are going to take a look while you humans stay here."

"Not a chance," Blu said.

"Agreed," Piper weighed in.

"We don't know who or what's up there, geniuses," Beck told them. "We'll fly up there, take a look, kill a few people, and be back in a few minutes."

Everyone started protesting at once, and I heard Blu's mind going overtime on degrading names directed toward a certain synthetic woman. I was too busy frowning in thought about Beck mentioning that we were going to just fly up to the top of the tallest free-standing observation tower in the United States and second tallest in the western hemisphere.

Beck watched them bicker with her arms crossed and a small smirk on her face before cutting them off by saying, "Oh, I'm sorry, you all thought it was up for discussion. Because it wasn't. Come on, Jericho, let's go kill stuff."

I followed her out into the cold while giving everyone else a shrug, pulling my hood on. "Sorry, guys," I said. "Super-human duty calls."

Blu followed us. "This is not a dictatorship, Beck," she almost shouted, wrapping her arms around herself and trying to glare and shiver at us simultaneously.

"Get back inside, idiot," Beck growled at her. "It's twenty below out here."

"Not until you... you..." she hadn't been outside for a full fifteen seconds and she was already having trouble speaking.

Meanwhile, Beck and I felt like we were on Laguna Beach in bathing suits soaking up rays whilst sipping on something coconut-flavored with an umbrella in the glass.

When it looked like Blu was about to crumble to the pavement, I grabbed her, throwing her over my shoulder and stepping back into the MK-Waltz.

"Give us a second," I told Beck, who was standing with her hands on her hips while tapping a boot in the snow.

"Make it quick."

I laid Blu onto one of the cots in the back of the small compartment, trudged back to the hatch, and pulled it closed. Turning around, I said, "I tried to tell you people before we left this would happen, and you still came."

"You can't tell us what to do," Piper said almost menacingly.

"The Ghost is right," Sam added.

"I'm not like you," I said loudly. "I could go outside butt-naked if I wanted, and none of you can stay thirty seconds without freezing to death."

"That's what suits are for. I'm going," Piper said, starting for the back.

I stepped in her path. "You're not," I growled. "You're going to sit here while Beck and I check things out."

Piper's hands were clenched at her sides and her jaw was tight. "Get out of my way."

"Nope."

How could it have come to this? The once love-of-my-life was now ready to slug me because I was in her way.

Everything was quiet in the cabin while Piper and I had

our toe-to-toe moment. "Face it," I finally said. "Beck and I are way stronger than any of you, even in suits. I'm not saying that you'll all have to stay in the car the whole trip, but you're all sitting this one out whether you like it or not."

After a few more seconds of glaring, Piper turned on her heel and stomped back to the front of the cabin. "Be safe, Jerry," Sam said half-heartedly, flopping back into his seat in a very dejected fashion.

"For God's sake," I muttered, heading for the side hatch. "We'll be right back."

I was pretty mad when I exited the MK-Waltz, slamming the door hard. I glanced around when I didn't see Beck waiting for me and frowned, looking around the dark place.

Sighing, I started walking toward the Stratosphere. Of course Beck hadn't waited. Why did I think she would have, and why was I surprised by her ticking me off?

Just as well, really. I suppose it was better for everyone traveling with me to get on my last nerve so I wouldn't be playing favorites with the select few who—

Something grabbed me from behind, and I was hauled into the air at a sickening pace, the roar of wind blowing in my ears while the white vehicle shrank quickly and my boots dangled in the air. I instantly grabbed at the hands that were under my arms and clasped on my chest, thinking to free myself, when I heard Beck say into my ear, "Easy, Jericho. I haven't dropped anyone in a long time."

"How?" was the only word that came to me, and I glanced left and right at the large flapping wings.

"Arc gave me these over a year ago," she said, again in my ear to be heard over the wind, and I recognized the make and design after a few seconds.

"They look like the wings on a Dragonov," I shouted over the wind. Then I heard Beck's voice tab in my head. "Why're you screaming?"

"Shut up," I told her.

I couldn't help but feel a little squeamish when I couldn't

even discern where our ride had been on the ground, and the tower looked small. "So what's the plan?" I asked, trying to hide the fact that I was ready to be back on the ground.

Laughing, Beck said, "Fly through a window with guns blazing was mine, unless you had a better one."

"Maybe we should see who it is before we kill them," I said. "I would hate to be killed and not at least know who did it. Know what I mean?"

"Sounds good," she said, stopping our ascent and flapping in place. "You ready for this?"

"No," I answered truthfully.

Her answer to that was to beat her wings hard once to flip us then shutting them off, letting us fall into a diving position.

"Uh, Beck?" I asked nervously when we had plummeted too close to the ground.

I saw her wings materialize out of the corner of my eye, and I felt our pitch rise. In seconds we were gliding straight for the tower. The light had been turned back on, and I could make out what looked like a silhouette.

"You go through this window," Beck said. "I'll hit them from the other side."

I was feeling a lot more confident now that we were almost done flying. "Let's do it."

When we were almost there, Beck released me, and I held up my fists, smashing through the thick glass and hitting the floor hard, sliding all the way across the Restaurant on Top of the World and into what I was thinking was the kitchen.

What can I say? I did already tell you guys that finesse wasn't my strong suit at the time.

I rolled onto my back just in time to see Beck crash through the window I happened to be under, and she darted above me into the main dining area. Kicking onto my feet, I ran after her, and no sooner had I entered, I saw the raiders we were attacking.

Only it wasn't raiders.

It was a little girl.

"Really?" Beck groaned, turning off her wings and landing on top of a table with finesse, I noticed with annoyance. "All of that awesome theatrics for nothing."

"Oh, I don't know," I said, crossing the large room to her. "I'll bet kids nowadays love being attacked by bald winged demons of the night."

"Don't come any closer," shouted the girl, who I realized couldn't have been older than six or seven, brandishing an assault rifle that she could barely lift.

"Easy there, kid," I told her calmly, holding up my hands. "We're not going to hurt you."

"Yeah, right," she said in a small but fierce voice, fiddling with the large rifle in her arms. "This is my house, and you both have to leave."

I glanced around the broken-down restaurant and saw the few mattresses strewn on one side and the empty cans of beans and other discarded food. "How long have you been living here alone?"

"Forever, idiot," she said harshly. "Now leave before I shoot you both to death."

Beck was still standing on the table with her arms crossed, watching the child with an uninterested expression on her face. "Hear that, Jericho?" she said. "The kid says she's going to shoot us to death."

I could tell the girl was starting to get nervous because of our lack of, uh, nervousness, I guess, so I tried to calm things down. "Look, kid, we came up her because we saw the lights and thought it was raiders," I told her, and she narrowed her eyes at me. "We're just passing through and looking for a place to stay for the night."

She watched me closely for a few more seconds before asking, "And you'll leave tomorrow?"

"Promise," I said.

Lowering her weapon, she said, "There's a bazillion rooms in the big part of this place. You can't stay in my tower."

"So, you're a miniature raider, huh?" Beck said, glancing at me before asking. "Got any parents coming back for you?"

The girl looked at the floor. "No, don't think so."

Beck nodded once before walking toward the shattered window. "We'll be going, now," she said. "Wouldn't want to impose on your raider hospitality any further."

Then she noticed I was hanging back and turned, giving me a questioning look while I gave her a wincing look that said what I was thinking.

"A word outside, Jericho," she said, and I followed her, stepping through the broken window onto the blustery balcony.

"No," Beck said quickly.

"You heard her yourself," I said, just as quickly, might I add. "God knows how long she's been alone here, and she doesn't even have anyone coming back for her."

"Is this going to be a regular thing with you?" Beck asked coldly. "To pick up every sad face we run into along the road?"

"She's like five years old."

"I wouldn't care if she were five days old," Beck said. "I'd still leave her here."

I stared at her in disbelief, which she noticed and smirked. "What? Is my lack of humanity off-putting to you, Jericho?"

I didn't have an answer for that, and I glanced out into the blacked-out city.

"When are you going to come to grips with the fact that we are nothing like the rest of the world anymore?" Beck asked. "I don't know why we're the way we are, but I'm not about to waste my time trying to save every single weak human I come in contact with."

That, in fact, I did have an answer for.

"I am," I said simply, turning back to her. It was the feeling, again. The same thing I felt when I was in the position to help the Rogues. I couldn't shake it, and no matter how much I had tried to tell myself everything Beck was feeding me right then, I couldn't make myself do anything but.

"You can't save everyone, Jericho," Beck said, and she almost sounded like she felt sorry for me for some reason.

I glanced back through the hole at the small girl with the assault rifle slung across her back while she brushed the hair of a small ragdoll in her hands.

I couldn't help but laugh a little and shake my head. Beck looked, too, chuckling and saying, "Okay, even I got to admit that's pretty awesome."

"I know I can't save everyone," I said suddenly. "But I think starting with an abandoned little girl is a good start."

Sighing, Beck finally said, "How do you know she'll even come with us? She seems pretty stubborn to me."

"Look who's talking," I said, stepping into the restaurant.

"You guys are dressed funny," the little girl said, looking me up and down. I decided not to point out what she was wearing, which was a large man's jacket that almost touched the floor and a beanie hat with long ears.

"What's your name, kid?" I asked her, leaning against a table.

"Don't have one," she informed me, tucking her doll away into one of the enormous pockets of the oversized coat. "Names aren't good for people these days because it's easier to forget them after they're dead."

"Where'd you learn that?"

She shrugged. "An old lady told me that once."

Wow. Talk about tough love.

"Well, what do you call yourself?" I tried again, not really wanting to delve into the whole people-dying discussion.

"Hmm," she murmured, narrowing her eyes and placing a small gloved hand to her chin thoughtfully. "Never thought about it much." After almost half a minute of thinking, she finally shrugged and said, "I got nothing. I guess you can call me whatever you want."

"No kidding?" I said, placing my own hand to my chin in thought. After I'd thought for half a minute myself, Beck sighed loudly and said, "Are you serious right now?"

I glared at her. "Well, I don't want to saddle her with a horrible name, Beck," I said. "This is a big responsibility for me."

"She has a doll," Beck said, waving her hand at the girl in annoyance. "So just call her Doll and get it over with."

"Yeah, right," I said, shaking my head like I knew the secret to the world and she didn't. "Like I'd call a raider girl—"

"Doll's good," the little girl chimed in, nodding. "I like that name."

"No, you don't," I told her, once again glaring at Beck. "Doll is a name for a little whiny girl." I put my hands on my knees and leaned down so that I was at eye level with her. "You're not a little whiny girl, are you?"

Scowling, because she obviously didn't like the very mention of the whining status, she put her little hands on her hips and said, "I'm not whiny."

"You sure?" I said, straightening and lifting one shoulder into a shrug. "I mean, you *did* say that you liked the name Doll, and all."

"I'm not!" she screamed, stamping her small boot hard and, as if in emphasis, reached into her coat pocket, produced her doll, and threw it across the restaurant. "You're mean," she said to Beck.

"Yeah, Beck," I said quickly, shaking my head at her. "Just what were you thinking trying to trick her into that name?"

Rolling her eyes, Beck turned and headed for the balcony. "Whatever you decide to call it, just hurry."

After she left, I immediately plunged into the lists of names I had.

"Razor?"

"No."

"Power-Girl?"

"Nope."

"Vegas Baby?" I said.

She shook her head.

"Little Widow?"

She just stared at me.

"What do you want, kid? I'm not damn babynames.com here, you know," I said.

"Those names suck," she said.

"Watch your mouth."

"Stink. I meant stink," she corrected then sighed. "How many more do you have?"

I counted in my head before answering. "Like, eleven."

"If I pick the next one, will you shut up?"

Wow. And here I always thought I was good with kids.

"That seems fair," I told her.

"Hit me," she said.

"Sloan?"

Her expression changed. "What's that mean?"

"Uh," I thought about explaining the whole background but decided to sum up since I was losing her by the second. "It's a version of an old Irish surname."

She nodded slightly. "I don't know what that is, but I like it."

"Really? Because after that was Sakura—"

"You talk too much," the newly named Sloan said, walking past me. "We better leave now before I change my mind about going."

I nodded but then frowned in confusion. Had I even gotten around to asking her if she wanted to go?

"I'm keeping my gun, though, so you can't take it," Sloan said before scowling at the shattered window. "We can't stay up here now that you broke my house. We'll have to stay in the big place downstairs."

She headed for the exit to the stairs across the room, and I glanced back in time to see Beck extend her wings and leap from the windswept balcony. "I'll get the others," she beeped in on my holotab. "Make sure your new pet doesn't have a trap waiting for us."

"I heard that," Sloan said while I followed her through

the exit and into the stairwell.

"Tell Sam to bring some Al Green with him," I said, peering down at the girl with the assault rifle slung across her back. "Something tells me this is going to be a long night."

CHAPTER 34

"Dibs on sharing a room with the best-looking guy here," Blu said when we entered first floor hallway.

"Ah, Blu," Sam said with a smile. "You don't have to flatter me like that."

Beck and I looked small again because everyone was wearing their battle-armor and the floor shook with each step. It took about three seconds down the stairs for Sloan to calmly imply that she was "Snug as a bug" in the heated restaurant but didn't know how she was going to keep warm after she left. So I had to improvise.

"You sure you're not going to freeze and die?" Sloan inquired from her perch atop Sam's shoulders, while pulling the hood of my long coat down further over her little head. "I saw that happen to a guy once."

"I'm sure," I told her. "The cold doesn't really bother me."

"Are you a vampire?"

Everyone got a chuckle out of that. *He can bite me anytime,* I heard Blu think.

"We'll split two rooms," Beck said all business-like. "That way each room will have a super-human to save them should danger arise."

Blu rolled her eyes at that, and Piper looked agitated, which was starting to be a regular look for her.

"No one fight over who gets to sleep in my room, please," Sam threw out, holding up his hands. "It would only embarrass everyone."

We ended up staying on the top floor after Sloan had insisted it was safer because we'd have a chance to get ready during a raid. Smart kid, really. Blu rigged some kind of contraption on the ceiling of each adjoining suite, and after she tapped out a few commands on her holotab, the small red boxes blinked a few times before a blue haze extended from them, reaching past the walls, floor, and ceiling.

Then she climbed out of her suit and stretched in the now perfectly warmed room. She caught me staring at the device, and she smiled. "A little something I came up with a few months ago. They'll last about seventy-two hours before they need to be charged, and the range is about sixty feet of toasty comfort."

Everyone was *oohing* and *aahing* over Blu's invention, and even Piper stopped looking mad long enough to say, "You are a genius, Blu."

Blu was loving the attention and was all smiles while she sat on one of the old couches in the room. Once everyone had exited their battle suits and gotten about as comfortable as they could get, Sam produced a large iron kettle and started breaking apart an armchair to start a fire. "Nothing like a little ice-spider meat on a cold night, eh, Jerry?"

I nodded, but my mind was elsewhere.

Primarily in the land of women.

Red was too bent on following me to the grave like a good soldier, I didn't trust Beck even a little bit, Piper hated me for something that I had no control over, Blu was obsessed with me but was too scared I would reject her if she mentioned it.

Clearly there were too many women on my trip. If they'd have all been guys, then I wouldn't have had a problem in the drama department.

Only they were all a lot easier on the eyes than a camp full of grizzled men swapping war stories and fart jokes.

I don't know who I was kidding. The only one that I

really didn't want there was Piper because she was a total ice cube. Every time we made eye contact, she would immediately avert or drop her gaze like she couldn't stand the sight of me, and I was thankful then that she and Beck were in the opposite room.

After an hour of too much thinking, I closed my eyes. I wasn't exactly sleepy but in severe need of alone time.

And I knew just the place to go.

I hadn't actually tried to access super-sneak mode ever since I'd accidentally taking over Blu's body, but that didn't stop it from happening almost every time I slept. I learned that all I had to do was simply touch my dormant body now and I would enter it without a hitch, sometimes without even waking up during the transition. It was a relief to know that I could end it, but it also scared me because now I didn't know if touching someone was all I needed to do to take over other bodies—something I wasn't in a hurry to do again.

Maybe if I didn't hear Blu's thoughts all the time I wouldn't have been as worried about accidentally body-snatching someone else. But the worst part was not hearing her thoughts so much as knowing literally every thought she'd had in her entire life, which was what I was having trouble coming to grips with more than anything.

But I needed to get away, and I was willing to risk it just to have a little peace and quiet. I also had an idea that I wouldn't hear Blu's thoughts in SS mode, and I was eager to test that theory. Since I never heard her thoughts while she slept, I hoped it would work the same for me. I was able to tune out a lot of her mind just by not paying attention, but it would be nice to not have to work at it.

In ten minutes, I was standing beside my slumbering body. I put a hand to my ear, like that would help me hear thoughts, and listened. Nothing. I watched Blu messing with her holotab while she lounged on the ragged couch, her legs crossed daintily. She suddenly frowned and slowly glanced at my sleeping body before flicking narrowed eyes around the room, a sly smile appearing on her face before she said to the air, "I know what you're doing, mate."

"Huh?" Sam mumbled through a mouthful of spider meat, glancing at her. "Who're you talking to, then?"

After looking at the exact spot I was invisibly standing in, Blu said, "No one," and went back to her holotab, though I noticed that her small knowing smile stayed.

I walked through the wall and into the room occupied by Beck and Sloan, who were having a heated debate on the best use of a grenade, and apparently Sloan was making more sense, if the scowl on Beck's face was anything to go by. "Shut up, kid. You're six," was the last bit of the conversation I heard while I made my way through another couple of walls.

Like I said, my mind was elsewhere. It clearly wasn't residing in its usual spot, because I almost walked out of the building completely, shouting into the whiteness and pinwheeling my arms like an idiot before getting my overstepped foot back inside the wall. I still wasn't sure why I didn't just go through the floor in SS mode, but I suppose I also didn't care enough to find out because, let's face it, it would've blown to go through literally everything I touched.

And a little scary, too, because I had this whole envisioned scenario of winding up at the center of the earth on one of my ghost walks, which was a tad unsettling. I guess I wouldn't have died if I'd walked out into thin air and sort of floated to the ground, but I wasn't ready to test that theory just yet.

I doubled back a room or two before going to the hallway and heading for the stairs. I still wasn't sure where I was going, but it didn't matter. I went down a flight of stairs before exiting to the hall and walked the long length of the hall to the last suite. I phased through the door, hoping to find some peace and quiet.

But I found Piper instead, standing on the outside balcony in her white armor.

"How far are you from Anchorage?" she asked her

holotab. The smooth surface of her bodacious looking mask was raised, and I could hear her pretty clearly, even though her back was turned.

"A few days, I guess," I heard, thinking it was the infamous new boyfriend, what's-his-face.

Poseidon? Hercules? Bah, whatever.

"Just please be careful, Arc. Don't take any unnecessary risks."

Archimedes. That was the guy's name.

"I won't, love. I'm just glad you don't have to make this trip. I know you're a force to be reckoned with, but some of the things I've seen on this trip alone…"

I frowned. So, she was lying to the new boyfriend about her whereabouts. Stranger things have happened, I'm sure, but why would Piper not want him to know that she was on her way basically on his heels?

"So, how's Beck doing?" Archimedes asked.

"About the same. I hope she takes a turn for the better soon."

More lies. Beck was doing stupendous after a transfusion from yours truly, so the reasoning behind Piper's untruthfulness was still heavy in the frigid air.

I made my way through the empty room and walked out onto the balcony so I could hear better.

What? Listen, if she'd have been talking about how much she loved the guy and being all googly-eyed and mushy, I would've left in an instant. But since I knew she was lying like a rug, I wasn't feeling like privacy was at the top of my list right then.

Don't know how, really, but I didn't care at that point.

"Things will look up in a few months, sweetie," Arc told her, sounding odd but mainly because it was 2345. Surely the term sweetie had been retired by now. "I'll be back by then and you won't have to deal with Beck's… eccentricities by yourself."

Eccentric. Definitely not how I would've described Beck.

"I miss you," Piper said suddenly. "Things are different

when you're gone but… but they're worse this time."

"Worse how?"

"Yeah, Pipe," I said aloud, not that anyone could actually hear me. "Please feel free to lie about how the long-lost dead love of your life hasn't returned."

I guess I was kind of mad, to be honest. I got that it wasn't exactly my business whether or not Piper decided to lie to or withhold information from anyone, but for some reason, the idea of her not even mentioning me to the new boyfriend of nearly two years was just downright aggravating.

After a few seconds of silence, Piper just shrugged and said, "I don't know. I just miss you more this time, I guess."

"Why?" the new guy with a weird name asked. Man, he wasn't dense, I'll give him that. He clearly knew something was up, but for his own reasons, somehow felt like he couldn't pry.

"I prefer to be with you, that's all," Piper said, glancing away from the holoscreen.

"Do you remember what I told you about losing someone you care about?" Archimedes asked her, and she nodded slowly, still looking away.

"You said you never forget, but you learn to live with it."

"I'm not going anywhere, Piper," he said. "I never asked about who you lost, for a reason, and I always stopped Beck if she tried to tell me. I know I said you'll never forget, but I didn't say you couldn't try to. Grief is the most natural part of human nature, no matter what time you're from, but you need to focus your attention elsewhere."

Well, I guess Piper had told him she was a Viking after all and didn't lie all the time.

And why the Helheim didn't he want to know about me, anyway? I understand the whole not-wanting-to-know-about-the-ex part, but if the mentioned ex was dead, then you better believe I wouldn't mind talking about him.

I mean, it's not like I would risk losing someone to a dead person, and it seemed Arc wasn't going to have that problem, either.

I'd heard enough.

I turned and started across the suite, wishing I would have just eaten spider meat with Sam and listened to Al Green instead of going on my stupid ghost walk.

"I don't want to forget."

I stopped.

"Whether you asked or not, whether you love me or not, it doesn't matter. All I know is that I won't forget, and I'm not going to try to."

I walked back to the balcony slowly. To some, this would've been just what an ex was waiting to hear. But guess who wasn't buying it?

This guy.

I guess she didn't know I was eavesdropping basically three feet away, but it wasn't helping anything that she was all "mourning ex" until the dead person she supposedly didn't want to forget was in her face, and then she changed her tune from sad to mad. The worst part was that I didn't know why. Sure, there was Archimedes putting her in an uncomfortable place, but she could at least act civil.

"Piper," Arc said quietly "he's gone and he's not coming back."

She was crying now, and after a frozen tear or two she said, "I have to go. The squad is about to move out."

Lula-lies-a-lot strikes again.

"Please be careful," he told her. "I love you."

"You, too," she said, exiting the holochat.

While I watched her try to stop crying, it hit me that I couldn't imagine what she was going through. I was inconvenienced for three years, too, but at least I was in a vegetative state for the most part. I wished I knew everything that had gone on while I was gone, and I mean every detail. Then maybe I would've known exactly what to say and do to fix the mess I'd left behind.

She was my dream girl, and I'd known it since the

first day I met her. Beautiful, loving, great teeth, dangerous—everything I ever wanted in a woman.

It was so different now that I was back in the land of the living, and I hated it.

"I wish I could take it all back," I said aloud, watching her shake her head and squeeze her eyes shut tight as one last tear slipped down her cheek and froze.

Then I had an idea.

A wild, horrifyingly wonderful idea that was questionably moral on a few levels and just plain wrong on the rest. And while I stood there on the windswept balcony of a once-great hotel in what was left of a once-great city, I knew how I could know everything I needed to know about Piper.

All I had to do was touch her.

She wasn't but three feet away, her white armored arms folded.

I moved in front of her and slowly raised my right hand. This was it. In a few seconds the means to fix my relationship with Piper would be mine. I might even be able to help Beck, too, from Piper's memories. At least that's what I told myself when I started having second thoughts.

"Forgive me," I said, my voice a whisper while I extended my hand, my fingers almost brushing her cheek, but my hand stopped.

"Come on," I growled, my eyes squeezed shut. "Stop being a pansy and just do it already."

But I couldn't.

My eyes flew open and I stepped backward quickly. "What am I doing?" I asked, truly perplexed, like I'd just awoken from a sleepwalk with a bloody machete in the hands that I was now looking at like they weren't mine while I walked back slowly.

Just how selfish was I that I would literally try and steal every memory someone had just because I was uncomfortable being around—

I walked off the balcony, falling into the snow-filled

night sky toward the ground.

"I'm sorry," was all I could think to scream, and before I knew it, I was back in my body—standing in the suite with my arms outstretched and my heart beating like crazy while Sam, Blu, and Sloan all stared at me.

"Sorry for what?" Sloan asked, cocking her head.

"What?" I asked.

"You just screamed you were sorry, like a crazy person," the little girl informed me. "Scared me, too."

"Jerry's an important bloke, ankle-biter," Sam told her. "Important blokes, them like Paladins, have lots of plaguing dreams, I'd imagine."

Frowning, Sloan said, "I'm important and I don't dream like that."

Blu was silent and I felt her eyes on me while I looked anywhere but at her with my hands on my hips. She was the only person who had any inclination about what I had been doing.

Did he go see her? I heard her think. *Let it go, Blu, it's none of your business.*

"It was just a dream," I said, falling back into the dilapidated armchair.

"About what?" Sloan asked, crossing the room and standing beside my chair, peering at me with narrowed eyes. "You're not one of them crazies from the outer wastes, are you?"

"No," I said, sighing and leaning back. "It was about my old home."

After a few minutes, the little girl finally left me, and I instantly closed my eyes. I still hadn't gotten to be alone, not really, and after the Piper incident, I needed it more than ever.

I walked away from my body and into the hallway, ready to leap out of the window this time.

Beck was standing in my path with her arms folded, but I didn't slow down, altering my course slightly to pass her without touching. That was all I needed, knowing everything in Beck's mind and hearing her thoughts would've been hell on earth.

"There he is, ladies and gents," the synthetic woman said theatrically. "The great Paladin himself."

I didn't even acknowledge her because, well, I didn't see a point since she couldn't even see—

Hold the damn phone.

I stopped walking and blinked at her before saying, "Beck?"

She had been smiling until I addressed her. "How can you see me?"

"I was going to ask you that," I said, noticing she was a tad transparent now that I was closer. "No one has ever been able to see me when I do this."

"Me either," Beck said, approaching me. "It's been like a bad dream for years. It wasn't until you gave me some of your blood that I discovered I wasn't dreaming. It's handy, but I just wish I could touch things."

"Touching things isn't all it's cracked up to be," I muttered.

"Why not?" she asked, glancing at her hands and smirking slightly. "You could be the ultimate assassin."

Killing. That really was where her mind immediately went first most of the time.

"Blu tried an experiment involving my ghost walk a while back, and it didn't turn out so good," I explained. "I was about to go for a walk in the city. You want to come?"

I'm still not quite sure why I invited Beck to join me. I mean, I actually couldn't think of anyone I didn't want to be around more than the sarcastic and slightly maniacal Beck Sparks.

But we left together, anyway.

CHAPTER 3,550,146

(Actually, it's 35. Just wanted to keep you on your toes)

While we walked through the snow-covered streets of Sin City, Beck asked what went wrong with Blu's experiment, and I told her the whole story. After I was done and after Beck had gotten her fill of jokes about me being in a girl body, she said, "I've tried to touch people before, and I just went through them. Maybe it was the serum that made it happen."

"I'm not about to try it on someone to find out," I said, shaking my head slightly.

"So you hear *everything* she thinks?"

I nodded and Beck whistled. "I could think of a few people I'd like to do that to, but your little blue-haired girlfriend wouldn't make the list."

We walked and talked for close to an hour, her asking me lots of questions and me strangely answering them. We ended up sitting on a park bench at one point and phased through it, landing on the ground.

"So, why'd you go into SS mode?" I asked her, leaning back into the snow.

Beck shrugged before lying next to me. "I just needed to get away for a while. I can only take so many doses of Piper's newfound mood swings."

"Glad to know I still have a way with the ladies," I said dryly.

Beck chuckled at that before getting serious and saying,

"She's been through a lot, that girl."

We lay in silence for a few minutes before Beck sat straight up and said, "We should try and touch each other in ghost mode and see what happens."

I instantly rolled away and stood. "Yeah, that's a big no," I told her quickly.

"Oh, come on," Beck said with a smile. "We're the super-humans on this outing, are we not? Think of how unstoppable we'd be in combat if we could communicate telepathically?"

I thought about that before saying, "What if something goes wrong? What if I get stuck in your body or you get in mine and—"

"Keep it because mine is slowly dying?" Beck said, cocking her head to the side.

"I, uh, wasn't going to say that," I said, narrowing my eyes at her. "But you're not exactly selling me on the idea by mentioning it."

Laughing, Beck got to her feet. "Don't worry, Jericho, I've been a girl for too long to change up now. And I'm also afraid you'd be in the back of my mind for the rest of my life."

I thought a little more about trying out Beck's idea, but I ended up just shaking my head and telling her no again. Not only was the thought of her hijacking my body now whirling in my mind, but I was not liking my new powers as much anymore.

To put it plainly, without the drama, I guess you could say that I wanted to be a real boy again. Trust me, all you aspiring super-humans out there, the pressure will kill you.

"Let's head back," I said and started walking.

"Why don't we just jump back to our bodies?" Beck asked before standing and following me.

"Not ready yet," I told her. Any minute that I could spend not hearing Blu's thoughts or bearing Piper's disdain was precious to me now.

Heck, I didn't even mind Beck being with me.

"Why do you want to kill Cross, again?" Beck's query cut

through my thoughts.

"Why *wouldn't* I want to kill Cross?" I countered.

"Because he kind of saved your life," Beck said, glancing sideways at me. "Mine, too, actually."

"If he would've saved either of us out of the goodness of his heart instead of as his guinea pigs, I might want to kill him less. But he didn't," I said. "Not to mention I overheard his plan to make me his puppet with a chip in my brain. Not cool, Beck."

"But think about it," Beck said, and she stopped walking. "What if this is all part of something bigger than us, Cross, my father..."

I turned toward her. "What do you mean?"

"By every natural law, you and I should both be dead, but we're not, thanks to technology my father and Cross cooked up."

Sighing, I started walking again. "Please don't tell me you, of all people, are buying stock in destiny now. Stargazer had better ideas than Cross, anyway."

"Who?"

"Used to be the leader of the Rogues," I said. "He died not too long ago."

"And left you in charge?"

"Something like that."

"Well, whoever was responsible, it's still a little too coincidental for my taste," Beck said. "I would much rather prefer to see things coming from a long way off."

I just shrugged. I had already tried to hash out all the bizarre things that had happened to me along the way and didn't want to think about it anymore. Stargazer seemed to think I was this sort of long-lost hero that was fated to save the planet and that all the events that happened to bring me to the place I was in was by some greater design.

And yes, there was a time when I almost started believing it myself.

But after seeing that my new powers were starting to feel like a curse rather than a gift, I realized that I wasn't some mystical savior sent by destiny to unthaw the planet, promote world peace, and stop warring factions with lightning bolts of justice. It took me a few months, not going to lie, but I finally found my true self.

I was just a guy who needed a ride home.

We walked a few more blocks before we saw the four new armored cars parked near our MK-Waltz.

Then we heard gun fire.

"Bodies," I said quickly and closed my eyes, instantly opening them again in the suite and jumping out of my chair. When I didn't see anyone else in the large room, I ran to the adjoining suite and almost collided with Beck.

"They're not in there, either," Beck confirmed, rolling her shoulders once. "Too bad we can't talk to each other with our brains, or else I'd have time to explain my plan to you in mid-flight."

Then she jumped headfirst through the suite window and flapped her holowings once, instantly vanishing.

And yeah, now, I guess, I was starting to see how the telepathic thing might've came in handy right about then.

I had about ten seconds to make a decision, and I hated the final outcome already. Somehow, after my almost taking over Piper's mind for my own personal gain, the Paladin gig was sounding less appetizing by the minute. I knew that, long before I came on the scene, my friends were hardened soldiers of fortune, if you will, that had seen many battles and always managed to not die.

But no matter how much I wanted to just sit back in my chair and wait for Red to pull her men through another victory, something deep down inside of me wouldn't let me.

An old man had once told me in a recording that I was different now, that my entire being was one of pure justice, righteousness, and good, these being the sole reasons why I wasn't able to stand by and watch my fellow men be kicked and abused in every way and do nothing.

It's a great story, really.

Except now I had the proof to show that I hadn't changed. No matter how many people I saved the past few months or how many starving children I fed or how many people may have been sent a glimmer of hope through my arrival, I knew that it would only be a matter of time before I relapsed, as it were, and became the old self-centered Jericho Johnson we all know and love, who has no problem using people just because he can.

Bah. Stupid drama is all this crap is.

I don't even know why I'm telling you this. I know that you're only here for the action scenes, anyway.

Well, it just so happens that you're in luck, whoever-you-are, because I finally made the decision to be a Paladin for five more minutes that day so I could let off some steam on poor raiders who were just trying to make a dollar by robbing us and mutilating our corpses.

"Once more unto the breach," I muttered, closing my fists and letting white flecks of voltage flow around them. Then I jumped out the window.

CHAPTER 36

"Jericho, where are you?" Red's voice buzzed in my head, and my holotab lit up. "We tried to wake you and Beck, but neither of you would budge and Blu said just to leave—"

"I'm here, now," I cut her off, landing on the sidewalk hard. "What do we have?"

"Four raider convoys spilling over with the bleeding devils," she said, and I heard and saw an explosion that sounded close to her. "Sam and I are trying to hold the front entrance while Blu and Piper laid fire on them from the second floor."

"Good plan," I said, walking leisurely down the snowy sidewalk, my hands in my pockets, toward the massive amount of raiders using their vehicles for cover. "Save your bullets, Red. I got this."

They were a ragged group, I'll tell you that much. I suppose men (and even a few women, I saw) that raided innocent people for a living weren't exactly much for looking trim and neat. Most of them were wearing heavy hooded coats and masks against the weather. I saw a few battle suits, but they were severely rusted and looked to be hundreds of years old.

I was about twenty yards or so away when some of them first noticed me and screamed my location to their buddies whilst leveling their guns toward me. "How many people are in the building, stranger?" a man shouted, but I kept walking.

I guess raiders weren't exactly keen on diplomacy, because that was all the warning I got before over sixty assault rifles opened fire in my direction. Not that it did them much good because I'd had my static shield up since I landed. The bullets that hit direct evaporated instantly while the ones that hit the sides of my bubble of protection ricocheted off into the night.

Incidentally, ricochet is a really fun word to say. Go on, say it. I'll wait.

Satisfying, isn't it?

It amazes me every time when a lot of people fire at an impregnable force, don't put a dent in it, yet still fire a constant stream of lead for way too long before they decide to stop shooting long enough to glance at a comrade and say, "What the heck?"

I waited for all of them to reach this conclusion and stop firing. Then they all stared at me in disbelief. A few even raised their masks to make sure their nano-optics weren't playing tricks on them.

"Yeah," I said to my audience, letting the juice flow more than I normally do, and the white volts flooded my entire frame, engulfing me in lightning before I slowly lifted off the pavement, floating almost twenty feet above them. "I get that a lot."

I opened my hands at my sides, and all the raider vehicles instantly shut down. A barely visible stream of energy pulled out of the now dormant rigs and into my palms. "It's a devil!" one of them yelled, dropping his gun and hauling butt back through his companions and into the night.

Coward? Maybe. Alive? Yes.

I tired of the theatrics quickly and raised both hands. "No hard feelings, guy," I told the scrambling men and women. "Next time know who you're trying to kill."

Life is a great thing. The feeling of breathing in air and knowing that you're surviving the craziness of the world on a wing and a prayer, just flying by the seat of your pants, is probably the most invigorated a human is going to feel in his/ her lifetime, whether they know it or not.

The ability to take life is also an invigorating feeling, whether people know it or not. And not just the getting into a fist fight with a guy your size and barely making it out alive kind of taking life, either. I'm talking about the ability to completely vaporize over sixty people in a nanosecond without breaking a sweat or losing sleep about it.

What can I say? I was having a bad day already, and some folks decided they needed to shoot at me.

Just before I let off both barrels, I stopped long enough to think about what I was doing. Did I really need to kill *all* of them?

Then the idiots all starting firing weapons at me again. Yeah, all of them would do.

The energy began whirling in my hands, like eager pit-bulls jerking at chains to get at a limping fawn. I leveled down my hands, thinking that if I hit their cars, the explosion would get the ones I might miss, but who was I kidding?

I wasn't going to miss. Not even one of them.

"Jericho," I heard Blu's voice buzz in my ear, but since I had white lightning flicking all over my body, I couldn't hear her. Whatever. I'd talk to her after the wind blew away piles of ashes.

The whirling energy quickened in my hands, and I held my right hand back, ready for the throw.

"Sloan—" Blu's voice crackled.

I was in mid-pitch when I heard the name and swung hard left, sending the ball way off course and into the snow-filled sky. I pulled back most of my juice and sank back to the pavement. "Where's Sloan?" I asked quickly.

"Oh, thank God," Blu breathed, almost gasping for air. "Sloan was downstairs when the raiders arrived, we think. She's not with us, and Beck said she thinks she saw her with the raiders."

"Like, *with them* with them?" I asked.

"No," Blu said. "She's being held toward the back... poor ankle-biter's been roughed up some, too. I guess they were trying to get information out of her."

You can't help her, I heard a voice say in my head, and it was so crazy audible that I glanced to my right to see if someone was there. *You're good at helping yourself and that's it.*

Man, I really needed some actual sleep.

But, since no one else could hear my thoughts, I answered my own subconscious. *She's got my coat.*

Keeping my shields up, I walked slowly toward the raiders. "Who's in charge?" I asked.

"I am," a man to my right said proudly, sticking his chest out before I shot a bolt straight through it, sending the tall man's corpse flying back into one of the raider vehicles.

"Now everyone knows the score," I told them sharply, lighting up my hand again. "Now, who's second-in-command?"

No one said a word until a woman came from the back. Her hair was jet black, and she looked to be in her thirties. She was also very, very dirty. Like, she probably never had a bath since the day she was born, and I even had doubts about that. "I am," she said.

"Congratulations on your rapid promotion, lady," I told her.

"Get the girl," she barked roughly to her men.

In seconds, Sloan was dragged to the front of the line. After the dirty lady had placed the barrel of her gun on the child's head, she glanced at me and said, "Stop your light show and let us leave, or I'll blow the kid's head off."

"Look, lady," I said, nodding toward Sloan, noticing her lip was bleeding and her left eye was blackened. "We just met the kid, so I don't care about her. But she's wearing my coat, and if you get kindergartener brains all over my favorite duds, so help me God, you and your pathetic followers will be dust."

"If you don't care about her, why did you stop attacking?" Madam dirt asked, her eyes narrowing.

"Like I said, she's got my long coat," I still didn't know how my plan was going to pan out, and when the raiders removed my precious coat and tossed it my way, I officially ran out of ideas.

"There's your coat, stranger," she said. "So kill us and be done with it."

Placing my hands on my hips, I sighed and glanced toward the sky. "Well, that's all I've got, Beck. Your turn."

"On it," Beck's voice buzzed in my ear, and in a split second she tore through the night sky, snatched Sloan, and disappeared into the darkness.

"That'll work," I said, lighting my body up yet again and wasting no time sending two concentrated bolts into the raiders. The explosion sent most of them sailing and a few, as I promised, were turned to dust.

After the air cleared, I was almost disappointed that I didn't get all of them. Not because of the fact that the world was only short about forty maniacal raiders instead of sixty-five, but because I felt like I missed.

Madam dirt ended up surviving the bout, and I sent her and her remaining men packing in one of the vehicles that still worked. She didn't look too happy about it when she climbed into her rig, but she was smart enough to know that vowing verbal revenge would've probably made me go ahead and kill her and what was left of the raiders, just so I didn't have to bother with them anymore.

Good call, really.

Sloan loved the flying rescue and talked of nothing else while Blu checked her out and dabbed at her cuts and bruises. Since the fighting hadn't lasted long on the human part, no one else was hurt, which was lucky, considering how many guns were aimed at them.

But, of course, the only time Sin City would decide to yield a little luck was after the apocalypse had closed virtually everywhere luck was needed.

The fact that none of our companions were able to rouse

Beck and I was brought up later that night, and both of us had our own way of telling them what happened. I explained in a nice tone that it was something personal and confidential that I might one day tell them.

Beck, ever the charmer, told them all in a not-so-nice tone that it was none of their damn business.

We left Las Vegas the next morning with our new team mascot in tow. Sloan said she'd left the city only once before, but she'd been too little to remember and was thoroughly looking forward to the long voyage ahead.

That made one of us.

The next three or four days were long ones, let me tell you, and lots of driving was involved. We stayed in Nevada the next day until we reached Reno, where Red hung a left and entered the last little piece of California, stating that this section shouldn't be too dangerous.

We ended up making it to the coast of Oregon that day and made camp on the frozen beach.

Like, I mean it was literally frozen. All the ocean for as far as the eye could see was a dark gray block of ice. I'm not sure how that affected the rest of the planet, but considering it was an ice cube, too, I wasn't exactly worried about a high number of seal deaths this year.

Later that night, while our ragamuffin crew got snugged into the now thawed area created by Blu's magnificent homemade device and after Sam had once again started charring spider meat, Beck pulled up a map on her holotab, linked the few people she thought important enough to discuss travel plans with, and started doing just that.

"We're about three hundred and fifty miles from Portland, give or take," Beck said to Red, Piper and me. The important people, you see. "Staying on the coastline will still bring us within at least seventy miles of the city, so I suggest going another forty onto the Pacific. Unless, of course, anyone wants to actually go to Portland and check out the enormous, legendary bird story?"

Beck glanced at us hopefully, waiting for one or all of us to tell her that of course we wanted to check out the Roc issue. None of us did, though, and she looked downtrodden. So downtrodden, in fact, that I said, "There isn't a huge bird of prey in Portland, Beck. I don't see a reason to go forty miles out to sea over something so bogus."

Beck narrowed her eyes at me and finally caught on to what I was saying. "You're right. We'll just stay on the coastline."

"How long before Seattle?" Piper asked. "Arc is almost there, and he said he always stops there a few days to get ready for Columbia."

"Thinking about surprising the boyfriend, are you, Pipe?" Beck said, making the ever-present awkwardness that much thicker.

Piper just shrugged, but I noticed that she smiled for the first time since we'd reconnected. Since I didn't want to seem like I hated the idea, which I did, and since I could operate a holotab like anyone else, I decided to answer for her.

"We're close to five hundred miles from Seattle. Depending on whether we all get eaten by a giant bird in Portland or not, I don't see why we couldn't get there in a little over a day, maybe."

"Should be fine if the weather isn't too bad," Red said. We were able to drive the Waltz-MK at close to one hundred miles per hour most of the time, so the trip wasn't taking as long as it could have.

After everyone had eaten and agreed on the course we should take, we all settled into our rolls for the night. Most of us could sleep easily.

I couldn't, though. I thought about going into SS mode but decided against it. Being still at odds with the changes I was undergoing was the main reason Las Vegas was the last time I left my body as a projection. Another reason was that I didn't want to.

Ever again.

I thought it was just a choice with no ramifications. One that was similar to picking out which shoes to wear.

But my mental decision to not use my new powers anymore, be it ghost walking or lightning bolts, was more substantial than I could've ever imagined. My reasoning was good. I just wasn't ready to have the amount of power that I was now packing, plain and simple.

The thought was good. The timing, however, wasn't.

Like, at all.

CHAPTER 37

I guess now would be a good time to explain that all travel arrangements were being created in the year 2345 and not in 2012, which is the last year I remember, if you hadn't already caught on by now. That being said, I would like to state that the good old USA isn't as traversable as it used to be, let's say. So figure in going around raiders, possible man-eating giant birds, there being a total lack of highway I-5, and the fact that every square inch of the world was covered in deep snow, then maybe you'll understand.

Also, I'm not expecting anyone from 2012 to actually hear this and, to be honest, I'm not sure anyone will hear it. I do this because I feel like I'm going to go bat-crazy if I don't talk to someone, and you're it, whoever-you-are.

When I was in college getting my master's in the great studies of history, I took a required creative writing course, and in it the teacher addressed something called author intrusion.

Basically, what it means is, when an author breaks the main storyline to address the reader/listener personally, thus wavering, however slight or major, the reader/listener's interest in the actual story.

These incidents are frowned upon because authors are supposed to paint vivid pictures for people and not talk about grabbing a coffee sometime.

I know if I ever get back to 2012 and decide to have

any of this stuff actually published, I'd get caught with author intrusion a *lot*. But, since I don't plan on anyone besides you, my dear, unnamed friend, hearing this story, I'm not worried about New York working me over in an edit.

I mentioned earlier that you may or may not have heard my first account. I'm treating this volume of my life like you have because, even though I don't know who, where, or when you are, I feel connected to you, nonetheless.

So, when I refer to you as "whoever-you-are," please don't take it as a non-descriptive term that I use to make myself feel sane. Wear it like a badge of honor, and one day, should our paths ever cross, I'll buy you a coffee.

Or a Lamborghini.

It's a coin flip, really.

CHAPTER 38

"Are we there yet?" Sam groaned from his unrolled cot where he'd been stretched out for hours on the floor of the Waltz. "My bum's been asleep so long I don't think it'll wake up ever again."

"We're passing Portland, more or less," Beck said. She was driving while Red napped in the passenger seat. "Still a little over seventy miles away, but we'll be in Seattle in about three hours if the Roc doesn't attack us."

Blu and I were playing chess against each other on our holotabs when Beck casually mentioned this for the fiftieth time.

Blu: *Why does she always say that like she wants it to happen?* The message appeared beside the holochessboard.

Jericho: *Go easy on her. The poor thing just needs a little excitement in her life, is all.*

By the way, it was way wrong of me to play chess with Blu, considering I could hear what she was thinking. After I won the first game with ease and I saw her flabbergasted expression, I let her win every game afterward. Not that I was worried she was a sore loser or anything, but the girl was a certified genius. I laughed the first game off as fluke because I really wasn't ready to tell her that I heard her thoughts.

Piper was leaned back on the bench across from us with her hands behind her head, her eyes on the ceiling, and for once I was starting to not notice her presence long enough to enjoy Blu's when she suddenly spoke.

"Did you lie about the big cod on our fishing trip?"

What the—?

I didn't know what to say. Yes, I had lied about the massive Icelandic cod I said I'd caught during the month-long fishing trip on the isle of Svalbard with her. But it seemed like she hadn't addressed me in forever.

"Random much?" I said.

Piper turned her head sideways and looked at me. "You did, didn't you?"

"No. And why didn't you ask me about that when we were actually on the trip?"

Piper let one side of her mouth lift into a smile (that's right, a real smile) and said, "I had other things on my mind other than the authenticity of your big fish tales, Jericho."

"Ooh, burn," Sam said with a chuckle from his cot. "She didn't believe you from the get-go, mate."

Blu was still frowning at our holochess game, but I knew it wasn't because she was pondering a move. Her mind was going light speed on why the heck Piper was suddenly talking to me about old times.

"Hey," I said, leaning forward, "I totally speared the mammoth cod. What did you think I did? Buy it from someone?"

Piper was still smiling, but it was aimed at the top of the car now. "Don't know. Sounds like something you'd do."

The truth about the huge cod was less about me spearing it from afar like a ninja-warrior and more about my time-traveling to Svalbard in 2011 and buying it off a modern fisherman by the docks. All I did was stab my spear in the already dead fish when I got back and found Piper whilst toting my new catch like I'd owned the beast without a hitch.

I'd only done it to impress Piper. Because, you know, I really liked her.

"Whatever. I have a great spear arm and you know it," I told her.

Turning on her side, Piper propped her head on a hand and looked at me. "Do you remember Hazel?"

Hazel. He'd been the sort of town bully of Piper's village. "Yeah. What about him?"

"Do you know his father tried to buy me for him from my mother for six sheep?"

I couldn't stop the laugh that escaped out of my mouth. "No way."

Nodding, Piper said, "My mother literally attacked him."

Six sheep. Sounds a bit steep, Blu thought, and that sounded as good a thing to say as anything.

"Six sheep sounds a bit steep, don't you think?" I asked smugly, and Piper laughed, something else that Blu wasn't digging too much.

Sam, who for some reason seemed to also be in the conversation, said, "If it were an auction, I'd start my bid off at maybe two lambs, them that was of the weak and lame sort, you see."

"Shut it, Rogue," Piper told him, but she was still smiling. "I find the start-off being sheep offensive. If the man would've offered a couple of yaks, then my mother probably would've agreed."

We all got a good laugh out of that, and Blu even plastered on a fake smile. "You kids better keep it down back there," Beck said from the driver's seat, "or else momma's coming with a vengeance."

It was strange to see Piper in an almost good mood, but I wasn't about to pass up the chance of seeing her smile. It was most likely because she was hours away from being reunited with what's-his-name, but I didn't care.

I mean, it wasn't as if I was trying to win her back from the guy—which was why I didn't understand her cold behavior toward me.

But while we all talked, joked, and laughed the remaining few hours to Seattle, the thought of stealing Piper away wasn't sounding too bad. Maybe it was because all I'd gotten from her since I saw her again was harsh disdain, and I couldn't remember all the things that had made me fall for her in the first place.

Even though she didn't show the full personality that I had gotten addicted to in the past, Piper did show me enough to kick in some major withdrawals. So powerful were the stirring emotions that had been dormant for so long that, during the course of the remaining trip to Seattle, I don't recall hearing Blu's thoughts.

They were probably there, don't get me wrong, but I wasn't listening.

CHAPTER 39

I have only been to Seattle two times in my past life, and if I could compile a few words to describe it, I think the list would be short and definitely have the word "morbid" in it.

I could only think of one word to describe 2345 Seattle, though.

Wet.

The ever-present snow had disappeared almost half an hour away from the city and was replaced by sleet, which didn't freeze when it landed, so when we finally made it to Seattle, the Waltz was treading through almost two feet of cold water.

"Something tells me the suicide rate is still high here," I muttered, peering through the top porthole, located above the windshield, at the few buildings that were left standing—which wasn't many. Even the Space Needle, the first thing most people think of when Seattle is mentioned, was missing from the skyline. "So what kind of folks live here?"

"Traders, mostly," Red told me from behind the steering wheel, guiding the Waltz onto a collapsed bridge. "There'll be a roadblock ahead where we'll be forced to show we're not cannibalistic raiders, and then we can go in."

"Beck and Sloan will have to stay in the car, then," Sam said, getting into his exosuit while the little girl stuck her tongue out at him.

Blu, who had been quiet for almost two hours, spoke up

while she was getting into her battle-armor. "Be on the lookout for Synners."

Beck waved that off. "Synners haven't been this far west in years."

Whilst Blu was assuring Beck that her intel was wrong and that the "Syns," as she called them, had been branching out from their usual treks over the last decade, I was frowning in confusion about why sinners would be something we needed to watch out for.

I mean, I'm no saint myself, but I also hadn't exactly stumbled upon a whole lot of devout people in 2345.

Piper, who was now in her white armor, saw my expression and said, "Synthetic hunters."

"Hunters?" I repeated. "Like Bladerunners?"

"No," Beck said in an unimpressed tone. Clearly she still wasn't buying the Synner scare. "They hunt humans with synthetic parts."

Then it all came back to me about how Beck and I were illegal things that some people didn't even count among the human race. "Why?" I asked. "I mean, what is so wrong about someone getting a robo-leg if they lost the real one?"

"Politics, Jerry," Sam said, and I could tell he hated the very word. "I've been trying for years to forget the terrible things what was done to synthetics below the warehouse in Flagstaff. Syns shoot to kill, and their weapons aren't like anything we normal blokes fight with."

"How many could there really be to have a whole group of people dedicated to hunting them?"

"You mean hunting us, love," Beck said. "And the Syns aren't involved in politics, Sam. They're more of a crazy organized group of self-proclaimed zealots with a mission to cleanse the earth from our whirring motherboard hearts whilst getting paid for it. Their philosophy isn't that far from mine, really."

"What philosophy is that?" Sam asked, pulling on his dingy yellow long coat.

"If you don't agree with something, kill it."

We drove over the collapsed rubble of the bridge for a few minutes at a slow pace before we saw the first signs of the scheduled roadblock.

I may never be able to go through an airport in 2012 again in my life. But if ever do, I will kiss all the TSA people full in the face, give them sincere hugs, and then tell them how much I appreciate what they did for our country.

That's how bad the "roadblock" was. The number of guns and soldiers was uncountable at first glance, and all the glances following, while I looked on with an open-mouthed stare at the soup line of mother apocalypse.

"Amazing, isn't it?" Red said quietly. "Most of these guys are mercenaries who take a cut out of the city sales in exchange for bullets and bloodshed."

"Safe to say Seattle doesn't get much trouble," I said, still in awe at the display of firepower. Then I glanced at the lineup of combat suits and asked, "So, how will we know the Synners from the mercs?"

Blu took a deep breath in preparation for a long-winded explanatory subject on the looks of synthetic hunters, but Piper cut her off.

"They look like that," she said, pointing a white-armored finger ahead of us.

And there, at the very front of the line, waving through an armored car that had just been checked, was my first sighting of a Syn.

Or Synners, since there was a ton of them.

Their battle-armor was white like Piper's and about the same size, but not bulky like most armor. The general make and model of the suits were different, but the helmets were something to behold. Mainly because they weren't helmets but looked like cowls that covered their heads while a small, barely discernable shield flickered in front of their faces, blocking the wind and rain.

"This is bad, guys," Red said. "The only reason they're

here is because they're looking for someone in particular. Syns don't just stay at the gates of cities hoping to nab a catch."

"Cargo hold," Piper said.

"They have scanners specifically designed to find smuggled synthetics, so I'm pretty sure that won't work," Blu said. "They can't be in here when we get to the gate."

"Good idea," Beck said, standing. "Time to fly, Jericho."

"Drones," Red said. "And lots of them."

Beck growled in frustration and kicked the wall of the Waltz. "What are we supposed to do, then? You're all the geniuses of the outfit, so figure it out."

Blu was chewing at her lip, the motion that told me her brain was in light speed. Sam tried mentioning another suggestion but was hissed and scowled at by Blu at the first noise.

All of us watched her in silence, waiting for the brilliant blue-haired girl with her eyes squeezed shut to save us all with her vast intellect and—

"Nope. I got nothing," Blu said, opening her eyes. "All I can think of is stuffing you two in the engine compartment and hoping the heat throws off their scanners."

I shot a questioning glance at Red, as if she could back her sister's meager plan. Shrugging, Red said, "Better than nothing, I guess."

It didn't sound that bad until Sam and Blu escorted us to the back of the Waltz and showed us our hidey hole.

"No freaking way," I said, shaking my head when Sam lifted the floor panel and exposed the engine compartment.

"Stop whining," Beck said, squatting down and sticking her head in for a quick look. "We'll fit."

"Yeah, if we plaster together like a couple of newlyweds," I said, scowling at her. "Forget it. I'll take my chances with the drones."

Then Blu shocked me by grabbing the sleeve of my dark gray jumpsuit and almost shouting, "This isn't a joke, Jericho. The Synners are a force to be reckoned with, and even if you get away, we won't. Now get in the stupid shaft!"

She was visibly angry, but I knew better because I heard what she was thinking about, how she was afraid the Syns would kill me and she'd die without me, or something along those lines.

"Fine," I said, stepping into the cramped space and lying down next to Beck, who winked at Blu.

Without another word, Blu turned and walked away.

"Sorry, Jerry," Sam said with a slight grimace. "The panel won't latch on the side all the way with the both of you on your backs."

"Sam, if we don't get out of this alive, please remember me as I was," I said, turning on my side and scooting closer to Beck, who was on her side facing me with a smirk on her face.

Then the panel slammed shut above us, and I was instantly aware that I was going to die of claustrophobia. Not only was the panel touching our shoulders, but the iron grate we were on top of was mega uncomfortable and a large crankshaft was spinning inches below us. Beck's face was also inches from mine, which was worse than the crankshaft. Just when I was about to tell her to stop smiling at me in the glow of the smelly engine compartment, my holotab lit up on my right arm, which I was on top of and therefore could only see the light and not the message.

After a few seconds Beck asked, "You going to get that?"

"No," I said.

"Could be something important from Blu."

"Don't care."

Sighing, Beck said. "Just check it. If there's trouble up top, we need to know to be ready."

That did make sense, and my arm *was* uncomfortable on the grate.

Leaning as far as I could away from her, I pulled my arm from beneath me, slipped it under her neck, and held it up behind her head so I could see. Then, to make it more awkward, I had to put my left arm around her also, just so I could touch the swirling new message icon and see what Blu had to—

It wasn't from Blu.

Beck: *Thanks for the hug. I needed that.*

I instantly tried to pull away but found that I was somehow stuck in the position I was in, unable to move my right arm.

"Why do you have to aggravate me every second?" I whispered furiously into her face.

"Because you're cute when you're angry," Beck told me, slipping her right arm around me. "There. Now we're both hugging people we don't like."

At the time, I could've thought of billions of women I'd rather be smashed against in a tiny cubbyhole, including the smelly raider from Vegas. When I say that I wasn't a happy camper, I am putting it mildly, so I don't go on a rant about it and have another bout of author-intrusion.

Wouldn't want that, now would we?

Then, since being stuck below plastered against the single most annoying robot-woman living wasn't bad enough, I also stumbled on the fact that being severely stressed about something could make me accidentally slip into SS mode.

Which is what happened, and before I had a chance to be horrified, my being melded with Beck's and I was in her head.

CHAPTER 40

"But it's mine!" I shouted, glaring at my twin sister and stamping my small foot. "Dad gave you the last one, Chloe."

Chloe, my older sister by a few seconds, shook her head, causing her dark hair to sway, which made me inwardly smile. My hair was a lot prettier than my sister's, and I loved to tell her that all the time.

My hair is my favorite part of me because it's shinier than Chloe's.

"No," Chloe said, still shaking her head and swaying her lame hair. "We traded trips fair and square, Beck. I get to go again tomorrow because I did your essay for you."

Oh. I'd forgotten about the accursed essay that father had demanded of both of us. Chloe had done mine in exchange for the next outing with dad. How could I have forgotten that so quickly?

I gasped for air and opened my eyes quickly. "Stop it," I growled, the images of Beck's life flashing before my eyes in rapid procession, blinding me of everything else while the chapters of her life completed themselves. Then, the worst part of Beck's memories collided, and I saw the day she died. I felt everything. Not one speck of emotion or feeling was left out.

And I died for the second time.

"I said stop," I tried again, gritting my teeth against the blackness that now enveloped me because, like I said, I'd just died with Beck, killed in a firefight on the streets of Flagstaff *by my own wretched, perfect sister who father always loved more than me because I was always the black sheep and never lived up to his standards—*

"Stop!" I shouted at the top of my lungs and felt Beck's hands cover my mouth. *Or were they Cross's hands as he rebuilt my mutilated corpse after my father had brought my body to him?*

"Stop what?" I heard Beck ask, but her voice seemed far away and then I was back in, a few years after Beck's resurrection.

"Stop what?" Devlin asked me, pulling me close. "Baby, I can't help you if I don't know what's wrong."

"Just get away from me!" I shouted, pulling away from him and running out the door. I needed to go topside and run. That always cleared my head.

My mind wouldn't stop racing with what I'd witnessed earlier that day, even after I'd run for almost an hour, leaping between buildings. Finally, I landed in the street, furious with myself for being such an idiot and slammed my fist into a burned-out car, denting the side in.

"Idiot..." I said between gritted teeth while I pummeled the car door in and moved to the next one.

Devlin Tygas, leader of the Rebels and love of my life. The man who'd swept me away from my pathetic existence as my father's lab rat after Cross's success in reviving me, gave me purpose in the rebellion and in the world, in general.

And he was a traitor.

I screamed, kicking the beaten car hard and sending it skidding into the sidewalk then flipping it over when it hit the curb.

He didn't know I saw or heard the exchange he'd had with the Bear leaders. He had sold the location of one of our squadrons days ago, and we hadn't received contact from them since.

And for what? Thousands of holos and a spot in the Bear's Reich.

I'd tried to get alone and figure out what I was supposed to do, when Devlin had found me, smiling like nothing was wrong and trying to kiss me with his traitorous lips.

Then I left for a run.

I stood in the center of the snowy street and glanced at the darkening sky. A storm was coming.

As I watched the clouds roll in and the snow increase, I knew what I had to do. My father, Chloe, Devlin—no one was ever going to hurt me again.

I was going to make sure of that.

"Jericho, what's happening?" I heard Beck's voice, and it sounded closer. Her hand was still over my mouth, so I think I shook my head. I can't be sure because I lapsed back into Beck's memories.

"Please..." Devlin said from where he was lying on the blood-stained concrete of the overpass. It had only taken one punch.

"Please what, Dev?" I asked him quickly, dragging him up by his tunic collar. "Send your body back to the Bears for safekeeping?"

He tried to say something else, but I snapped his neck before he could. "Goodbye, love," I said, giving him one last kiss on top of his head before flinging his lifeless corpse off the bridge and into the streets.

Later that day I returned to the Rebel base, told everyone of Devlin's treason, and took control, whether anyone liked it or not. They couldn't stop me. No one could stop me.

I went to my quarters because I felt tired and climbed into the bed that was now lacking a person, due to my killing him. I had thought there would've been tears, but none came. I thought there would've been mourning, but that never came, either.

I lay on the bed and watched the ceiling with my hands behind my head. "They want robot," I whispered. "I'll give them robot."

Years from now people will say that the day I died in the streets of Flagstaff was the day I truly died, but they will be wrong.

Beck Sparks died the same day as Devlin Tygas.

The last few memories finally subsided after a quick flash of our first meeting and what had happened during my three-year nap. After the lights had dimmed, I heard the hum of the engine and realized where I was.

Beck's arms were wrapped around me, and I noticed she'd been talking. "Please stop shaking. I don't know what's happening to you, but we're going to be fine."

"I'm fine," I said, my throat dry.

"Jericho," Beck's relieved gasp was a strange sound to hear. "You've been out for over fifteen minutes. What happened?"

I now knew everything about Beck Sparks from birth until present, and instantly my image of her had changed. I didn't see the tough, inhuman, cyborg-woman I'd been seeing for so long, but now saw the way she was inside and out. No matter what she said or what anyone else tried to tell me, I knew different.

And apparently I couldn't contain it, because a tear slipped out of my eye and I asked, "Why're you so scared?"

"I'm sorry?" Beck asked. "Are you crying—?"

"There's nothing wrong with you," I said, letting it all spill out. "People get hurt all the time by parents, sisters, and traitor boyfriends. But you're the only one out of all of them that is still here alive and fighting for what you believe in."

Beck was shocked into silence, which was a first for her.

"No one's out to get you, Beck," I said, trying to stop the crying. I'm sorry but it was too real. All of it. "Everything bad that's happened to you is in the past, so just let it go."

The grate we were lying on shuddered once before lowering a foot closer to the engine, and I heard the gears shift.

"I guess we made it through the roadblock without incident," Beck said quietly. For a second, I thought she was going to ignore everything I'd just said in the darkness before she finally said, "You saw everything?"

I nodded. We were still holding each other for some reason, our foreheads touching.

"And now that you've seen it, what do you think of me?" she said it in a way that sounded almost sarcastic, but it didn't matter. I knew what she needed to hear.

And it was the truth.

"I think you're amazing. I took a two-year nap and went through a bizarre breakup and I'm a mess. You've been to hell and back more than once and you're still going strong."

"Some would say it's because—"

"You're not human, right? Don't give me that crap. You're more human than a lot of people left in this god-forsaken world, believe me," I said, starting to feel a little more in control of my idiotic emotions long enough to add, "and not many women can pull off a buzz-cut, which you rock like a boss."

"Think so?"

"Yeah." Residual memories tried to climb up in my mind then, and I had to focus hard to suppress them, sending Beck's life back into the blackness of my subconscious.

I felt that the connection now made between Beck and I would one day help the both of us somehow, but the notion of hearing the thoughts of two people at the same time was making me sick.

"Well," she said. "Not many men can redeem themselves from crying the first time they climb in a dark closet with a girl."

I chuckled but listened for her mind's eye to see what she really thought about me hijacking her memories.

But I didn't hear anything. I tried again, this time concentrating. When I didn't hear anything the second time, I was a little confused. Blu's mind had been going bajillions of miles an hour the past few minutes and, although I was keeping them at bay, a little trick I'd learned recently, I still didn't understand why I couldn't hear Beck's.

We lay in silence for the next five minutes, all the while Beck's inner thoughts didn't make a peep, until the engine panel opened above us and Sam said, "Alright, lovebirds, honeymoon's over."

His smile faltered when he saw we were holding each other with our foreheads touching, and he said, "Cranky, mate,

I was just joking…"

"How'd it go?" I asked, sitting up and ignoring his comments.

Sam shrugged. "Decently. Blu was a heinous croc to the Synners and caused an awful fuss about being searched, but when the blokes in white didn't pick you two up, they waved us through."

Beck climbed up after me and asked, "What's our allotted time in the city?"

"Twenty-four hours," Red called from behind the wheel. "They've been having a lot of raiders trying to storm the gates recently, so the permits have been shortened for any non-merchants visiting Seattle."

"Just as well," Piper said, and I noticed she attached her large red broadsword to the back of her armor. "This place doesn't feel right."

"Isn't your boyfriend here?" Beck asked, holstering her handgun on her right thigh.

"No," Piper admitted. "He rode on just before we got here."

Beck was still rattled from getting her memories peeked at, and I could tell she wanted to comment about why Piper didn't want to stick around, but Blu spoke up first. "She's not wrong. The Synners aren't just at the gates. They're crawling all over the whole bleeding city, and we still don't know why."

"Bollucks," Sam said and immediately received glares from Red and Blu. The big man winced and looked down at Sloan, the six-year-old girl who was narrowing her eyes in thought about the new word usage. "Uh, I meant what unfathomable rubbish, Blu."

"Why?"

"How many blokes like Jerry do you think are roaming North America right about now? Cross somehow knew we left Flagstaff and let his underlings know to keep a look out."

Blu shook her head. "Sam, it's literally impossible on a mountain of different levels for Cross to know that."

"Can we please discuss this later?" Red said. "We need to gear up, get out, and get lost ASAP."

Gear up, get out, and get lost. Sounded like a good plan to me.

Only, I had heard what Blu had been thinking when she mentioned the Synners.

I checked him, she'd thought. *Cross couldn't be tracking him without me knowing. It's impossible. Just impossible. It has to be. There's only one way to turn off a bug planted that deep in someone's brain and that's to kill them.*

I won't lose him.

CHAPTER 41

The next few hours spent buying and haggling in the sodden streets of Seattle were a blur for me, partly because we were in a hurry but mostly because my new cache of unwanted memories kept trying to creep up in my brain.

The city was in pretty good shape considering, well, the apocalypse, and also because there was a minimum of six inches of freezing water everywhere you walked. It wasn't bad for everyone in suits, but Beck and I had bootfuls of the stuff. Piper had stayed back at the car with Sloan, so at least I got my hooded long coat back. The sidewalks had been cleared of all old cars and buses, and vendors were set up as far as the eye could see in almost every direction, selling wares that ranged anywhere from weapons, custom weapons, weapon repair, battle-armor, custom/modified battle-armor and repair, then food.

If you wanted to call it food, I mean. Some canned food was available, but nothing was, as Sam put it, fresh.

"What's this, then?" he asked a weasel-faced female vendor sharply, snatching up what she was calling a tomato, even though it was blackish and looked to be in the shape of a smashed carroty-looking thing. "You call this fresh vegetables, you lout?"

"Begging you're pardon, sir," she said in thick German. "But the tram due from New York two weeks ago was taken by the raiders, sir."

This was the story all over, it seemed. While we trudged through the flooded streets, we found out that any good produce or canned foods had already been sold when news of the lost tram had hit, long before we got there. Anything that was left was—

"Idiotically expensive!" Sam said angrily, glaring at yet another price-gouging food merchant who'd just told him the price of the canned beans he had left.

"Just pay the man," Red said exasperatedly with a sigh. "We've the holos, Sam, so let's just take what we can."

Grumbling about how the now-smiling vendor was stealing from them, Sam shook hands with the man, which I found out later transferred holos between their tabs, then Sam lifted the large wooden crate onto his shoulders with a small grunt.

I offered to take the crate off of Sam's hands because, you know, I was way stronger than him, but Blu shook her head. "Can't, handsome. You need to look normal and weak around these people."

Just as well, really, since the Beck incident had made me make up my mind that the super-power gig just wasn't working for me anymore. I had a chance, but now I was done. I knew how to suppress Blu's thoughts and even the super strength and agility for the most part, so I'd actually been feeling normal the last few days, anyway. I didn't feel the way I had when I'd taken over Blu's body and could barely walk, but I'd also been injected with crazy-juice at the time so that might have been partly to blame.

Weeks ago, when I'd taken my run through Flagstaff, I had just begun to know what I was capable of, so I just did anything and pulled it off. Now, since I'd been trying to stop being, well, me, the urges to run like a madman turned into Thor and also to save the world, in general, had sort of worn off.

The Rogues now had the Rebels, so technically I'd helped tons of people, right?

Hard to explain, really. All I knew was that I was feeling halfway normal lately, and I was loving it. Except, of course, for the whole copy and paste shenanigan with Beck. But other than that, yeah, I was on a normal roll.

We made a long loop through the city, buying food and fuel cells. Red even bought a massive rifle for her battle-armor that the seller assured her fired .95 caliber rounds. For those of you who aren't familiar with bullet size and power, the rounds were about the size of a smaller Maglite.

When we finally got back to the Waltz, which had been parked on the third floor of a rundown stacked parking lot that was sectioned away from the long-term vendors and reserved for people just passing through, we stowed our goods and thankfully climbed into the dry, warm cabin of the white armored car.

"Anything happen while we were out?" Red instantly asked Piper while powering down her suit. "Cranky, but it's cold and wet out there."

"Says the girl snug in her suit," Beck muttered, frowning at her soaked boots in annoyance.

"Uneventful," Piper said from where she was lounging comfortably on her cot, her head propped on a hand while she watched us enter. With her almost white-blonde hair and emerald eyes, she looked positively catlike while she lay there. It also could have been because of the white color of her jumpsuit, too. I moved my gaze before I started remembering just how drastic and amazing her transformation from the cute eighteen-year-old girl to the wickedly hot woman in her mid-twenties had been.

"Did you get the stuff?" Sloan asked Sam seriously, lifting an eyebrow up at him expectantly.

"It wasn't easy," Sam told her, producing a package from his yellow long coat. "But I landed you a few grams."

I was more than a little flustered until I saw the girl pull what looked to be some form of chocolate out of the bag and gleefully attack it.

"What's the plan, Red?" Beck asked, sitting next to me on one of the benches along the right inner wall.

"Well, we only have about nineteen hours left before we're thrown out," Red said, sitting across from us close to where Piper was on the floor. "Since the two of you are the super-humans, I'm guessing you don't need a few hours of R&R before we head into British Columbia."

I just shrugged and Beck shook her head.

"I'd like to stay," Piper said, and I was a little surprised, since she'd found out that Archimedes had moved on the day before we got there. "Anchorage isn't going anywhere."

Everyone unanimously agreed and climbed into their respective corners to either sleep or dry off. I wasn't tired, and I wasn't about to try and sleep again. Bad things happened when I slept, so I thought it was just better for everyone if I didn't get a few hours of the stuff.

Piper and Sloan were curled up on her cot snoozing while Sam, Red, and even Beck slept in the back. Blu and I ended up in the only other place available that was halfway comfortable and took the main cockpit, reclining in the driver and passenger seats next to each other.

Blu had her eyes closed for maybe an hour, and the only reason I knew she wasn't asleep was because I could still hear her thoughts. Most of them were about me and how she didn't want to bother me or say anything because she might talk too much, or how she really just wanted to straddle me and make out for hours.

The last thought was funny in a way, but before I started hearing Blu's mind, I'd thought any attraction she had toward me was strictly physical. Not because I'm super-hot (which I am, obviously), but because I was a new species that any scientist would go bonkers over, who also happened to be easy on the eyes.

I'm really just messing around, actually. Any hotness I may or may not have had prior to, you know, dying and all, was completely gone as far as I was concerned. Truthfully, I was never actually model material or anything, but just not ugly and kind of normal looking. But I was also a billionaire at one point. A massive amount of cash has a way of making a plain guy look like the god Apollo.

Now, though, I wasn't rich, my hair had just started growing back, and I was still deathly pale. The only thing halfway cool about me now was my new powers, and I hated and wished I didn't have them.

So I guess you could say I was now a total loser with nothing going for me but being able to kill lots of people really fast if I wanted.

I enjoyed Blu's company, though, because I still felt strangely connected to her after the incident, and also because we hadn't been alone in weeks. It was a tad unsettling because by my hearing her thoughts, I knew that she was about a quarter-inch from being madly in love with me. The unsettling part was mainly that I wasn't sure why she felt that way toward me. I thought the world of her, don't get me wrong. I mean, she fixed my arm, helped me develop the powers that I now hated, and was completely gorgeous.

And she had blue hair. How freaking awesome is that?

The month I'd spent with the Rogues, with Blu, Red, Sam, and even the few weeks with Stargazer had been some of the best ones I'd had, not just since I'd came back from the dead, but in a *long* time.

Then Piper came back in my life and things had been uncomfortable ever since. I already had decided I wasn't ready to commit to Blu or anyone until I figured out myself first, but now that Piper was back, I'd removed the pins holding every picture of anything that looked like happiness and let them drift to the floor.

And yes, the picture of Blu's beautiful face had also been unpinned.

I couldn't put my finger on what was making me question everything now, but all I wanted was to get to Anchorage, kill Dr. Cross, fix the gauntlet and—

And that's as far as I'd gotten with my plan.

Blu's thoughts turned a little dark and hopeless, so I decided to take her mind off of her plaguing notions. "Why doesn't Seattle count as a functioning city?" I asked. "Beck mentioned the big four and that was it."

Thankful that I'd finally spoken, Blu explained it to me. "There are still cities across the continent that people live in, but very few and none near as booming as this wet place. The only reason it's thriving, though, is because they're selling supplies to people on their way to an actually functioning city."

"Good old Anchorage," I said. "Ever been there?"

Like I said, I was just trying to make conversation to take her mind off things. I already knew everything about her.

"Just once," Blu told me, and I instantly saw the journey from Australia with her cruel uncle after her parents had died when she and Red were eight. They landed in Anchorage, and after three years they had both escaped their abusive uncle and hitched a ride with a tram bound for Flagstaff, which they weren't at for two days before Stargazer found them and put them in with the Rogues, who weren't called Rogues then but just runaways.

I must have been thinking about this part of her life too hard because Blu asked, "What's wrong?"

I guess I'd been frowning in concentration or something. "Nothing," I said, smiling at her reassuringly. "Kind of spacey right now, I think."

Blu nodded and smiled back, turning sideways and facing me. She looked like she wanted to say something but didn't want to. Then alarms started going off in my mind because I knew what she was thinking.

And it looked like the jig was up.

Blu opened her mouth to speak, but I said, "It's been different since the experiment, hasn't it?" I pulled my hands from behind my head, sat my seat up, and turned to face her, our knees almost touching.

"What?"

"You've noticed how different things are between us since I accidentally took over your body and you want to ask if I've noticed, but you've been afraid to because you aren't sure if the feeling will be reciprocated."

Her dark blue eyebrows were furrowed while she stared at me a few seconds before saying, "You haven't felt different about me since it happened?"

I wasn't sure how to answer this. I did feel different, obviously, but I heard every thought she had and knew literally *everything* about her since day one. That could've been the main reason for the connection I felt, right?

Or had I felt a connection before and just didn't want to admit it because I liked her so much, and my future was so unpredictable, that I didn't want her to get hurt?

"I have, Blu," I finally said.

"Me, too," she said, sighing and looking out the rain-splattered windshield of the Waltz. "I can't explain it, but sometimes it feels like a lot more than just a crush."

I heard her thoughts, so I always knew what I could or couldn't say. And I mean *always*.

"Ah, Blu, are you in love with me?" I asked with a smile, nudging her knee with mine.

"Shut up," Blu told me, smiling back and returning the knee nudge. "You know I adore you and want to have your babies."

"Only if the first girl can have yellow hair so we can name her—wait for it—Yellow," I said, throwing my arms out theatrically. "That way I'd have the real red, blue, and yellow version in my life."

I was having fun, not going to lie, while Blu and I laughed as quietly as we could so not to rouse our sleeping comrades. Then I noticed we were holding hands once the humor had subsided. Funny, I hadn't remembered doing that.

I looked up from our clasped hands and met her green-eyed gaze, which was locked on me. Her smile had faltered, and she looked like she was contemplating something in her mind.

Which I heard. Every detail. Gosh, but she was beautiful
—

No. I couldn't let anything else happen. The pin was out, Jericho, remember? You took it out to protect her and her phenomenal good looks from getting heartbroken.

Or something. Bah, I just couldn't.

"Blu—" I said before she pounced, straddling and kissing me faster than a ... a ...

I'm sorry. Just thinking about that made me forget my witty description of how fast Blu could lay one on a guy.

I tried to stop for lots of reasons, ranging anywhere from not wanting Blu to get heartbroken to just not wanting anyone else in the Waltz to awaken and catch us snogging in the front seat like a couple of hormonal teenagers.

It took me a good twenty seconds to realize that I wasn't supposed to be running my hands through her silky, long blue hair and regained some of my mental faculties.

I broke away long enough for us to stare at each other with about six inches between our faces while we both tried to catch our breath. I knew what to say to stop everything and not sound like a complete jerk.

But I ended up saying, "You're really good at that."

"I know," she said, and we were back at it.

I deserved a little happiness, didn't I? I mean, I'd been going for years now trying to save the world, and I was just tired and needed, I don't know, comfort. Yes, lots and lots of the stuff because—

Gah! No. I pulled away again.

"What's wrong, Jericho?" Blu asked, her hands on my shoulders.

"We—I mean, I can't," I said.

"Why?"

"I just can't focus on anything else but Anchorage right now," I told her, deciding the truth didn't sound as bad as I thought it was going to. "I think you're amazing, I do. I just can't give you anything you want until after I've sorted through my crazy issues. Does any of that make sense?" I watched her hopefully but mainly for show because, you know, I could hear what she was really thinking.

Smiling wickedly, she said, "Not being able to give me what I want until later isn't entirely true."

"Blu, I'm serious."

"So, you *are* saying that after Anchorage you'll think about it?" Blu asked, letting one hand slide down from my shoulder to my chest.

"I don't think I'll be able to stop thinking about it," I answered truthfully.

"Good," she said and went to dismount me only to stop and glance back to me. "How about one more kiss? You never know when you're going to get another one."

She was joking on the outside, but I knew inside she was dead serious. So I took her up on it.

I mean, honestly, what could it hurt? We'd already done it, so what the Helheim, right?

We were about ten seconds into the final kiss of the night when we got interrupted by everyone in the Waltz catching us.

And I mean every last one of the bleeding people who were supposed to be asleep.

Red scolded her sister about making me lose focus, Beck just shook her head and told me that if I didn't shape up she wouldn't marry me later, while Sam and Sloan both gave me a thumbs up, accompanied by toothy grins.

Piper didn't say much about being the first one to spot Blu and me making out, but it didn't take Sherlock Holmes to see she wasn't thrilled about it.

Geez, but would this trip never end?

"Try to limit the amount of physical contact near Vancouver," Beck told me. "The radiation might fuse the two of you together, lover boy."

CHAPTER 42

The next day we drove for almost two hours before we started seeing the first signs of British Columbia. Canada had never been my favorite place in the world. I hadn't been there very many times, and I never had that great of a time when I did. So I decided to spend most of my trips in the past instead of in Canada.

"I still can't believe it," I muttered, shaking my head when I saw the first pieces of landscape that were snow-free. "Not a speck of the stuff."

"And it'll be in the seventies outside in another hour or so," Red said, making a right and pulling us onto a shattered highway. "I'm going to skirt around Vancouver, but not too far because the locals there don't have long range scanners, anyway."

"Speaking of which," Sam said, tromping from the back suddenly. "We're being followed."

"By who?" Beck asked, like she couldn't think of anyone dumb enough to follow us.

"Can't tell by the vehicle, but my guess is Synners. Feral abominations don't roll in rigs that advanced," he said, holding out his holotab for Red and me to see the oversized armored car he'd picked up.

"How far are they behind?" Piper asked.

"Maybe two miles by now. I only pinged them because they got sloppy and came too close," Sam said.

Beck stood, patting my shoulder. "Jericho and I will go pay them a visit."

"Not a good idea," Blu said, shaking her head. "If even one of them gets in a good shot with their shackles, you won't be able to use any of your synthetic parts. Jericho will lose a lot of body usage, but you'd be completely paralyzed."

Beck seemed unimpressed. "It's going to take a lot more than super-shackles to take me and Jericho out."

"Blu's right," Red said in a no-nonsense manner. "They're far enough behind where we might still lose them if we do some fancy footwork."

As if in answer to what she just said, an alarm started beeping loudly on the holocontrols. Blu clambered up between us and checked it out, confusion evident on her face. "They... firing on us."

"What the Helheim?" I said, looking into the rearview mirror like I could see them. "Not cool, dudes."

"Who's shooting at us?" Sloan said, rousing from her slumber. "And why? What'd we do to them?"

"Missiles locked," Blu said. "Now would be a good time for some of that fancy footwork you mentioned, sis."

"Cranky," Red said, pulling the wheel hard to the left and sending everyone who wasn't strapped in, which was basically everyone, flying across the cabin. "Hang on to something, mates."

"*Now* you tell us that?" Beck shouted, shoving Sam off of her roughly.

Then we were tearing across the blackened landscape, flying over hills and swerving through small ravines. An explosion to our right shuddered the Waltz and lifted the right tires off the ground.

"That was bloody close, Red," Blu shouted at her sister.

"I know, I know."

"Where are we going?" I asked, watching the last red blip try to land on our map marker.

"Vancouver," Red said, swerving hard to the left and

escaping another blast. This one was way closer, and Sloan screamed and fell into Sam. "And would everyone buckle up? That's what the harnesses are for, idiots."

"Two more inbound," Blu said quickly.

"I thought you said this thing could cloak," I said to her.

Blu shook her head. "Not if they already can see us. It just masks our—"

Another explosion sent the Waltz peeling into a spin, and everyone inside screamed like we were on a ride from hell. Red finally righted us and sped off again. "Come on, baby, just a little further."

"How is this going to help us?" I asked when I saw the city rise in front of us. "And what about the abominations you've all been mentioning?"

"Our distance is already suicidal," Beck said from behind me, and I felt her hands gripping my chair. "If we can make it to the riverbed, the Synners should break off their attack."

"Should?"

Red shrugged and switched to the last gear, barreling us toward the cliff leading to the river. "Whoever isn't buckled in is about to be hating life."

Blu crawled quickly into the back and found an empty seat. "This isn't going to end well," Sam decided to throw out. "I can feel it."

"Shut up, Sam," Red shouted and then we were airborne. I don't know if Red thought there was going to be a steep ravine leading to the riverbed, or what, but we were greeted by a sheer cliff and no incline to catch us on the way down.

Thankfully, the drop wasn't but about forty feet or so and, yes, I do understand that a forty-foot fall in any 2012 vehicle would result in eminent death. All I can say is that armored cars in the future can take a beating and keep the inhabitants therein baby-blanket safe.

Unless there's heat-sinking missiles involved. Yeah, those will do some damage.

The landing jarred everyone except Red, who must have

been the only one of us smart enough to brace for impact. Switching gears, she put it to the floor and aimed us toward the broken mega city.

"They've stopped," Blu said from the back. "They know we're done for anyway if we keep this course."

"Bleeding Synners," Sam said. "If we all get eaten by cannibalistic mutants, I'm holding them solely responsible."

Piper, who hadn't been saying much since the start of the chase, said, "Just how close do you plan on getting?"

"Double-edged sword," Red said, taking a hard right and we sped down the dried riverbed. "They're still watching us, so they'll know if we skirt around for too long."

"What's that mean then, Red?" Sam asked incredulously. "You're not actually planning on going inside that hellhole, are you?"

"No, just painfully close."

I don't know if you've ever been to Vancouver or not, so let me try and explain how the city is set up. Most of the normal-sized houses and building are located around the island that the big, beautiful city part sits on. We'd been driving through the rundown spread-out city for a little while before the Synners started shooting at us. The main piece of city, complete with tall buildings and main attractions, is on the island part surrounded by the Fraser River, which had been gone for years, I'm thinking, because that's what we were driving through at the moment.

"We're not going to lose them if we don't get out of sight," said Blu, fanning through her holotab and resuming her post on her knees between Red and me.

"I know," Red said, looking aggravated. "I can't do anything else, Blu."

"Yeah, she can't, Blu," Sam said quickly, nodding. "You heard her yourself. We can't go into Vancouver."

Blu looked over her shoulder. "Stop being a baby, Sam. If, in fact, there is rotten zombie-like beings within the city, how hard could they be to kill? We've got two Paladins aboard, don't forget."

Zombies, she said?

I always wanted to kill a zombie. Like, with a melee weapon of some kind. Either a baseball bat or samurai sword.

Samurai sword. Most definitely.

But I wasn't too crazy about killing the walking dead at that time because, even though Beck and I would have a blast crushing spongy melon heads, the rest of our crew could possibly die or worse, get infected or something. That's a thing, right?

No, better to avoid Vancouver altogether. That way no one would have a chance to kill or be killed by anything.

Looking back and taking into account all the amazing future technology in our wrists, available to literally everyone aboard, I can honestly say that our falling into a trap was really, really stupid.

I mean, if it'd been a death ray blasted down on us by a damn satellite or something, I wouldn't complain. But since we actually drove the Waltz headfirst into a manmade pit that had been covered up with rusty tin, I have to say it again for emphasis—

We were so, so stupid.

CHAPTER 43

The drop down the shaft was long, scary, and scream filled. We must've fallen for almost fifteen seconds, with the Waltz scraping off the walls and sending bright sparks shooting into the darkness. Red screamed for everyone to hold onto something, and I saw the upcoming pile of cars we were about to land on.

The Waltz hit hard, crushing the old burned-out car underneath. Blu was still beside me, unbuckled and bloodied on her forehead. "Blu," I said quickly, pulling her in front of me and holding her to my chest while her feet dangled lifeless into the dashboard. "Wake up, babe," I said again, patting at her face.

Something wasn't right. And no, it didn't have to do with everyone hanging by our seatbelts while the Waltz teetered on its nose in a pile of rusty cars.

It had to do with the fact that I was having trouble holding Blu's body. It wasn't my grip, because I had a good one, and it wasn't because she was lifeless and therefore dead weight.

I just didn't have the strength to hold her.

"Something's wrong," I said.

"Damn right something's bloody wrong," Red said, squinting through the cracked glass in front of us. "Why haven't we fallen over yet?"

"No, that's not—"

"It can't be the cars holding us up," Piper said.

Then the Waltz shuddered once and dropped another gut lurching foot. It took Red about two seconds to realize what was happening.

"Sam, move!" Red shouted. Without question, the big man slapped the button on his harness and fell, catching himself with both hands on the back of the front seats and flinging himself hard to the left just as the huge, blackened iron spike finished sliding through the front of the car and into the cabin, grazing my left arm as it climbed higher into the Waltz, wrenching metal while it did.

I heard Sloan scream. "Is she alright?" Red called.

Piper answered after a few seconds. "Yes. Just scared, I think."

"That makes two of us," I said, losing the grip that I thought was good. It wasn't a far drop to the windshield, but it was cracked up horribly and there was a big chance of her breaking through if I let her go. Or when I let her go, rather. "I can't hold Blu."

I couldn't see Red because of the spike. "What do you mean you can't?"

"Pretty open and shut, Red," I said between my gritted teeth. "Beck, can you get to me?"

"I could rip the back of your chair off, but your harness is connected to that," Beck said. "I'll try and go over the top."

The Waltz groaned when it shifted due to Beck's movement, and I felt her hand touch my head. "I'm going to reach over you. Can you swing her up?"

"I don't think so," I answered truthfully, and I felt, for the first time since I could remember, a bead of sweat trickle into my eye.

"What's wrong with you?" she asked, kneeling onto the back of my chair, which put more pressure on me.

"Let's chat later, genius," I gasped out. "Just grab her!"

Beck stretched out and snatched Blu's right arm just as I lost her, my arms burning from the strain. I panted with my head almost touching my chest. "This is bad," Beck said, and I glanced up to find her face inches from mine and upside down. "The only reason Vancouver wasn't even a far-stretched option was because you could shock the crap out of everyone."

"I know," I said, panting. "Let's just get out of here."

Then we all heard it. A deep yet shrill screech that resounded around us. Since the Waltz had died, we couldn't see our surroundings at all. The echo from the scream made it sound like we were in some kind of cavern, and it kept going for a sickening amount of time.

Sloan was the first to speak after the unearthly noise had finally died. "I'm scared. Tell the lady with wings to get us out of here," she said with a sniff.

Hey, why hadn't I thought of that?

"No can do," Beck said. "The shaft is probably too tight. I could probably climb out if—"

Another scream echoed around us and Sloan whimpered. This one was worse than the first one because it sounded not only closer but more discernable.

It almost sounded like a word.

The cry went off again but with more voices added to it.

"*Visitors!*" We heard. "*Food!*"

"I don't want to be eaten," Sloan said. "Get us out of here!"

I heard Red click her harness and land on her side of the windshield. "Piper, get to the suits," she ordered. "Beck, if you can't wake Blu up in ten seconds, put her somewhere and gird your loins, sheila, because it's time to earn those wings of yours."

This was bad.

You know how I said before that I was starting to feel normal and was loving it? Well, normal is great until it's time to go super-hero on feral abominations to save your comrades and can't.

"Sam, are you in your exosuit?" Red asked, and I heard her cock an assault rifle.

"I've got my breeches on, don't I?" Sam huffed.

"Keep Sloan safe," Red told him. Then, "Cranky, there are hordes of them."

I slapped the button on my harness and landed hard on the same glass that I didn't want to drop Blu on, breaking through and barely grasping at some lose wires that had become exposed during the whole spike intrusion.

It was somewhere between trying to climb back into the Waltz and trying not to care about the broken glass cutting through my suit that I saw the first one come into my line of vision. The cavern wasn't dark like before because it seemed someone had switched on the lights or something, since I could see all around us while the trappers poured in through the three tunnels set up on the separate walls.

And they had weapons. Lots of them.

"Red, what's the plan here?" I asked quickly, scrambling like crazy in an effort to get back inside the stupid car.

She didn't answer.

Sloan was still crying, and Sam said, "We can't win this one, Red." This didn't make Sloan stop weeping at all.

"I—I don't know what to do," Red said, and I could tell she sounded scared. "What's your status, Jericho?"

I finally managed to haul myself inside, leaning my back against the huge spike and panting from the exertion. "I can barely move," I said.

"No lightning?"

Lightning. I had forgotten somehow. I looked down at my hands and tried to summon my mage abilities to the surface, focusing all my will power into the effort and hoping that would be enough.

I felt a small hum.

"I think I got a little juice," I said quickly.

"Light the crocs up," Red shouted, although I could barely hear her over the sound of the gathering mob below me. They formed a circle around the pile of cars and peered up at us, their rifles and pistols aimed high.

I couldn't see all of them but, for the most part, the horrifying things under me were smiling with what was left of their rotten features. "Welcome, strangers!" one of them, who seemed to be missing half of his face, called up to me. Like, half of his face was just gone. Not with messed up skin, or anything, but actually some of his jaw and skull were completely missing. "Why don't you all come down nice and easy so we can talk about dinner arrangements?" he asked, smiling broadly with the half of a mouth he had.

"Blimey," a man close to half-face said, and he sounded like he didn't have a throat from the gurgling. He was terribly hard to understand. The accent wasn't helping, either. "I 'ope there's better lookin' fleshies in that bucket what can fight. Joshua's not going to like the look o' this lot for the arena, 'e ain't."

"Forget the arena," half-face said, and his abnormally long tongue shot out of his mouth, licking the air and what was left of his mouth. "This weak fleshy is mine."

"Come on," I said to myself, gritting my teeth and watching my quivering hands.

Nothing. Everything—my strength, speed, lightning— was gone. "I can't help," I said to Red, closing my eyes. I was useless, and my friends were all going to probably die because of it.

No. I may not have been rocking my Paladin status, but I sure as Helheim wasn't about to just sit down and let rotten idiots eat us all without a fight. "Look," I said. "I'm going to jump out and hold them off so you guys can—"

An armored hand grabbed my shoulder, pulling me higher into the shaking Waltz, and in seconds I was looking at Red in her Raptor-6 armor. "You've done enough for me and my people, Paladin," she said, holding me up in front of her with her hands under my arms like she was holding a toddler.

Then her blood red mask clinked down. "Now it's my turn," she said, her voice deeper and robotic.

She dropped me onto the back of my chair and punched

through the wall of the car like it was paper, pushing her hands out and making the hole big enough for her to exit. "Piper, Sam, and Beck, with me," then she leaped through the side of the Waltz, followed by Sam in his yellow overcoat and Piper in her white armor, red broadsword in hand.

"Wake her up, Jericho," Beck told me, dropping Blu beside me and climbing onto the opening, and I heard the first rounds of gunfire and shouts echo throughout the cavern. "Be back in a jiffy," she said, jumping into the fray below us.

"Blu," I said, pulling her to me. "Come on, baby, you need to wake up," I tried, patting her face.

Sloan, who had finally stopped crying, noticed me trying to rouse her and said, "You're not hitting her hard enough." She monkey-crawled across the back of the seats to get to me before climbing onto Blu's stomach. "I saw someone wake up one of his friends from a pistol to the head once."

Lacing her little fingers together, she bent them outward and gave them a crack, rolling her neck some and saying, "This shouldn't take long. Watch and learn."

Then she slugged poor, unconscious Blu's face as hard as she could, and I instantly saw a bruise on her perfect skin.

"Geez, kid," I said, shaking my head and reaching for her. "We're trying to wake her up, not keep her out."

"Just trust me," Sloan said, leaning out of my grasp and hauling off one more mega-slap to the other side of Blu's face.

I was about to try and grab her again when I saw Blu's eyes flutter slightly for a second. I glanced from her to Sloan, who was smirking at me with her arms crossed. "See?"

"Whatever," I told her. "Just do it again and get her awake."

After another hard slap and punch, Blu gasped and her eyes sprang open. "What's going on?" she asked before coughing and touching her face. Then she noticed the state of the Waltz and said, "Cranky, what happened?"

"Long story," I said. "Short version is we're being attacked by uglies and I can barely move, so get to your suit and help the others down below."

She looked a little disoriented, and I wasn't sure if it was from the initial rendering of unconsciousness or from Sloan's love taps. Either way, it took her a good thirty seconds before she stopped blinking or shaking her head.

"Right. Suit," she said, lurching onto her hands and knees. Her battle-armor had been dropped by Red before leaving the Waltz and was now clambered into a corner across from us, barely holding its position.

It took some doing, but Blu managed to make it to the red armor, hitting a few keys on her holotab and powering it up before it opened to receive her. "Stay inside," she said. "Get an assault rifle and find a corner. Kill anything that's not us."

And then there were two.

I rolled on the seat to my stomach and peered over the head rest to get a look at the battle below, willing my team to be winning. And, man, but were they not disappointing me. Actually, after almost thirty seconds of watching Red, Sam, and Blu bat gross looking humanoids aside while Piper cut them down and Beck circled above with her wings out, sniping anyone who tried to use a gun with her twin heavy pistols, I could see that the fight wasn't even fair.

"Looks like we're not going to be eaten today, kiddo," I said to Sloan, smiling while I watched. "These guys are weak."

When she didn't respond to my telling her that we weren't going to be torn to pieces and served charred with lemon, I glanced back at her and noticed she was looking above us. Frowning, I followed her gaze. When I didn't see anything I asked, "What's up?"

"They're on the car," she said, wide-eyed.

I was about to tell her that she must've been mistaken because, if crazy uglies would have been climbing up the side of the Waltz, it would be rocking from side to side. I didn't get a chance to tell her this because the Waltz started teetering suddenly and we heard a scraping sound coming from all around us.

My holotab lit up. "They're trying to get in!" Blu said. "Beck, stop them."

The car was really shaking by this time, and a loud metal-on-metal groan rang out when the Waltz started careening to the left, the spike tearing through the passenger side of the Waltz and sending Sloan and me flipping around like bugs in a mason jar. Then it fell, rolling end-over-end down the tall pile of destroyed vehicles before landing hard, broken glass raining onto me.

"Hello, friends," I heard and tried to crawl away, but whoever was talking grabbed my ankles. I kicked hard and was able to break free long enough to flip onto my back and face my attacker. It was the half-faced one and three others, and all of them had rifles or spears leveled at me. "How about you and I step outside so you can call off your running buddies, or I'll riddle you and the girl's faces with bullets."

"Ah, but that's the best part!" a big guy on half-face's right said, looking genuinely distraught over the idea that his friend might shoot up his favorite part of supper.

"Here's an idea," I said, trying to sound business-like and friendly while holding my hands up. "Why don't we all take a step back and talk about—"

The big one hauled me up by my feet and looked into my upside-down face with curiosity. Geez, but this guy was huge! Like, easily close to seven foot.

"I don't like the face," he finally decided. "Nose and ears are too small."

I happened to be looking into the face of a true, living monster complete with actual red eyes, pointed teeth, and bad breath. If I'd been attacked by this guy before the 1500s, I would have thought him a troll of sorts. Sloan screamed when half-face pulled her out of her hiding spot and dragged her out of the new hole in the Waltz, and the troll-guy followed him out with me in tow.

And I was terrified. Weeks ago, people were scared of me because I was the unstoppable force with all the power. Now the wheel had turned and I, Jericho Johnson, the once great and powerful super-human, was afraid because I, along with all my friends, was about to die.

The troll dropped me on the ground once we were in clear sight of the battle, and half-face went to work.

"Stop, you lot!" he screamed after he'd pulled me up from the ground to my knees and placed the cold barrel of his assault rifle to my head just behind my left ear. Sam was the first to see what was happening and let go of the one-armed man he was about to throw, holding his hands in the air just before getting tackled by four rotten men.

"Don't stop, idiots," I shouted when the rest noticed me. "Keep fighting."

One by one, my fellow comrades saw me and ceased their fighting, throwing guns and swords to the ground. "Out of the suits," half-face commanded and, again, my traveling companions obliged him.

"We don't negotiate with terrorists, guys," I tried again, but it was too late. After half a minute Red, Blu, Piper, and Sam were being herded toward me out of their suits, their hands bound behind their backs with what looked to be some kind of rusty wire.

Then I noticed Beck was missing, and I let my eyes flick above me for as long as I dared in case this was some kind of clever scheme that I wasn't aware of. When Blu was pushed down beside me, I tried to read her mind to get some information on Beck, but remembered, after a few failed attempts, that I was powerless now.

"Let's eat at least one now," a hideous woman lacking a nose and left ear proposed with a gleam in her milky eyes. "The little one. Joshua wouldn't miss that little morsel, I'll bet you."

"Let me talk to Joshua," I said suddenly, and all eyes turned to me.

I had a plan to spin some wild tale about an oncoming destruction in hopes the radiated humans would be dumb enough to believe it and keep us alive a little bit longer.

Except all I got was a sucker punch to the gut from half-face. "No one sees Joshua unless he wants to be seen, fleshy," he said before aiming a stock of his rifle at the woman who'd asked about eating Sloan. "And we can't eat any of them yet. Not until Joshua's seen them."

A man raised his hand in the middle of them and half-face frowned, something that didn't look correct without, you know, the other side of his face. "What is it then, Dax?"

"Begging your pardon, Griff, but if we don't bring food back to the hall, then I'm next. My number got drawn last week and tomorrow's my last day," the man said, and he didn't look too happy about the whole ordeal.

"Serves you right for not bringing grub back in over a month. You know the rules here, Daxy-boy. Feed or get fed on," Griff said. "New order from Joshua says anyone what gets a mind to sneak a snack before he gets an eyeful of newcomers gets the arena or gets cooked."

It was strange how impossible the situation seemed. Probably because any idea of pleading or striking a bargain was out the window when the fact that we were the next meal was considered.

I was still having trouble processing what was going on while I, along with my fellow brothers- and sisters-in-binds, were hauled to our feet by our laughing and howling captors then marched toward one of the openings in the cave wall, which I saw led into an old sewer tunnel.

Deformed cannibals.

Clearly, we had taken a wrong turn somewhere.

CHAPTER 44

The trip through the sewers of neo-Vancouver was, in a word, unpleasant. Although it didn't take but about ten minutes to reach the surface, being prodded and cussed the whole way, by people planning on killing and eating us, made it seem longer.

There wasn't much talking between us captives along the way because, well, there wasn't much to talk about, really. I did get a chance to ask Blu, after receiving a hard shove from behind and smashing into her, "Beck?"

She didn't have time to answer with words but merely shook her head quickly, which told me all I needed to know. Beck must've seen the hopelessness then jetted while she could, to step back and find another chance to save us.

I mean, I hoped she was coming back, anyway.

It *was* Beck we were talking about, here.

Vancouver looked about like the other cities left in the world, but without the snow.

And there were *lots* of rotten citizens bustling through the streets. Most of them saw us and pointed, either laughing, cursing, or licking their lips. By the time we'd reached two city blocks, there was a massive horde following the already forty creepers who'd captured us. The noise was unimaginably loud from the cheers and sneers we received when we finally came to a stop in front of a mammoth building that, shockingly, was still standing.

I say shocking because Vancouver was in pretty bad shape. Most buildings and even houses were in shambles, and the few that weren't collapsed in on themselves were overflowing with more and more cannibals. And the horribly gross people weren't just men and a few women but actually full-fledged families with kids, and I even saw one with a zombie dog.

Griff ordered his men to stay put while he and five others marched us through the opening of the building where there used to be a revolving door. At first glance, I figured this had once been a sort of mega-firm or bank, but I wasn't sure.

"How many people live here?" Blu mused to herself while we walked across the shattered marble floor of the lobby toward an elevator. Half-face stopped suddenly and hit her hard in the stomach with his rifle. "Shut it, pretty-hair," he growled.

Both Sam and I jumped at him, only to be yanked back by the big men behind us, flung to the floor, then kicked several times. "There ain't any heroes here, fleshy," Griff the half-face said.

I locked his gaze, ignoring the blood running into my left eye from the massive gash on my brow. "You're a dead man," I said, my voice strangely calm. "Mark my words, freak."

Laughing, Griff smirked his half smirk. "If I had a finger for every schmuck who told me that, I'd eat like a king the rest of my life."

"Which isn't far off," I said, getting to my knees.

He laughed that off, and then we were roughed up the long stairwell. "Elevator don't work, if you're wondering," Griff told us. "Plus, we don't want you heroes trying anything heroic in such close quarters."

"Just as well," Sloan said, wrinkling her nose. "You guys smell terrible."

"I'll cut your nose off first, runt," Griff growled at her. "Wouldn't want you to smell me when I flay your tiny legs and eat you while you're still alive."

That took the wind out of Sloan's sails as far as snarky comments were concerned, and silence accompanied us the rest of the way to the top floor of the tall building. Everyone was out of breath when we finally stepped into the hall, and our escorts got a real charge out of it. "Not used to moving without those suits, are you?" one of them cackled.

It was annoying, but more so because the people who looked like rotting corpses didn't look like they were out of breath at all after the sixty-story climb. Sloan had run out of juice about halfway up, and troll-guy had to carry her the rest of the way.

After a short hallway, we stopped at the double doors and Griff pushed an intercom on the desk sitting in a corner.

"Got some new fleshies for you, Joshua," he said.

After a short pause, the alleged Joshua responded, "How many?" the voice was normal compared to all the other residents of Vancouver I had the pleasure of meeting so far, and the accent was British sounding, making him sound seriously sophisticated.

"Six," Griff told him. "Got the soldier look you like. Not weak like the one guy yesterday."

"Bring them in."

We were bustled through the doors and into the massive office. It looked like the rest of the city inside, which was old, worn, and dusty, but the spacious area was furnished with old couches, chairs, and a desk in front of the large window. Sitting at the desk was who I was thinking was Joshua, the man in charge of this hellhole.

"Leave us," he said, standing and walking slowly around the desk. He was an older guy who was maybe in his late fifties, with a small, trimmed beard, and the clothes he was wearing almost looked like formal military attire.

Without question, the five men obeyed and exited the room, pulling the doors closed behind them. At first I was a little confused about their leaving one guy against five and a half in a room, until I saw the long-snouted revolver Joshua lifted off his desk.

Cocking the hammer back, he leaned against the front of his desk and leveled the powerful firearm at us. "I'm only going to ask this once," he said, sighing like the very words tasked him unto boredom. "And I've been in a foul mood of late so, please, do not think to try what little patience I have left."

"Are you Joshua?" Blu asked, and the floor at her feet exploded when the man fired his weapon inches from them.

"One question," Joshua said, once again cocking the pistol.

"Just ask," I said quickly, moving in front of Blu.

"Very well," he said, and once again he looked bored. Like he'd been doing this for years.

"Does the name Jericho Johnson mean anything to anyone standing before me?" After asking this, he looked at each of our faces until he frowned, noticing that everyone looked directly at me while I glared at the guy with the gun.

"Who's asking?" I said.

All boredom gone in a flash, Joshua took a few steps toward us, his mouth almost hanging open while he narrowed his eyes at me. "I've no time for games, so if you're him, finish this sentence: what is your theory on global warming and…?"

"…the mad cow disease," I finished.

Joshua lowered his weapon. "Jericho Johnson. You, sir, are quite the hard man to find."

"Well, we just dropped by for a pit stop," I said sarcastically. "So sorry to eat and run, but we've got places to go and people to kill, Joshua, so thanks for the hospitality but we were just leaving."

"I've got a few people that need killing, as well, my friend, but there isn't much I can do about them at the moment. You're the only one on my list within firing range, I'm afraid," he said. "Although, I've been given orders that you're not to be harmed, so it's your lucky day, Johnson." He pressed a button on his desk and added, "They're yours, Griff."

The doors opened again, and our guards entered. "Leave

the bald one," Joshua ordered. "Send the rest to the arena."

Griff looked a little disappointed, and he asked, "All at once, or do you want to save a few?"

Joshua had resumed his seat behind the desk and put the idea to serious thought, looking us up and down before saying, "Put colorful ones in first. The mob needs a little flare today, I'm sure. Save the big man and little girl for tomorrow."

I glanced at the "colorful ones," which was Red, Blu, and Piper, realizing that Piper's hair was so white that they looked like a living American flag in the order they happened to be standing in.

"Wait," I said when the guards started shoving them toward the door. "What do you want with me? These people are innocent of any reason you have to be hunting me."

Griff and his guards stopped at my courtroom outburst and glanced at their boss, who was spinning the chamber of his revolver nonchalantly and not even looking at us. After a pause he looked up and raised an eyebrow at his men. "Why are you still here?"

"Don't give up, Jerry," Sam shouted while being dragged from the room. "We'll get out of this scrape, mate."

I didn't know what to do and felt about as helpless as anyone could feel watching my friends get hauled to their deaths. Blu suddenly wrenched free of Griff, ran to me, and planted a kiss on my lips. Our hands were still tied behind our backs and everyone was watching, but I didn't care at that point. Griff pulled her from me.

"How dramatic," Joshua said dryly. "Pointless, too, I'd imagine. The games are a most loved and treasured ceremony in this city, and the populace doesn't like going without it for too long, I fear."

"Where are they taking them?"

Joshua stood after looking at me like I was an idiot. "I just told you. To the arena. It was a sort of stadium for some long dead sport, but now it's used for more practical entertainment. In short, I said pointless because over half of your friends will be dead within the hour, Jericho," he said, smiling and cocking his head to the side. "Joshua captured Jericho. That's a bit biblical, don't you think?"

He was standing next to his desk again, and I took a step toward him. "Don't get too excited, pal. The Joshua you're referring to had a little help, and something tells me you and the One who helped him aren't on the best of terms."

Joshua laughed at that. "No, I don't expect we are exactly acquainted," he turned, walking to the window with his hands in his pockets. "Look at it all," he said, shaking his head slightly. "The entire world gone in minutes and now, hundreds of years later, this is our normal. To kill anyone who gets in our way without remorse or ramifications and, for what, power? The right to say what happens to the few million people left on this planet?"

"What's with your clothes?" I asked, creeping toward the gun, still not sure what I'd do if I actually got it.

"I was once a high-ranking general of the Bears. Granted, it was strange to end up there because I'm about as Russian as you are. The Bears always were a close-knit lot, you see."

Keep talking, chump. I edged ever closer to the pistol on the desk.

"Who'd have thought?" I said.

"Of course, good things have a habit of not lasting long these days, and I was wrongly accused of treachery, stripped of my title, and left here to be eaten for my final punishment."

I was so close. What was I going to do with my hands tied behind my back again? Whatever. Maybe I could just get the gun away from him and go all primal rage. I was feeling a little better, too, which only meant I could move without feeling like I was about to die.

"That was ten years ago," Joshua said, sighing and taking in the view of destruction. "I was always good at inspiring people, Jericho, which is why I'm still alive. These people did nothing more than live in the wrong place at the wrong time and, like me, they are castoffs because of it."

When I was almost to the gun, he said, "It's not loaded, friend."

I blinked at his back before glancing down at the gun and realizing that the revolving chamber was void of any shells. So, his casual chamber spin a few moments ago wasn't as nonchalant as it appeared.

"Why were you after me?" I asked, stepping away from the desk.

"It's actually pretty open and shut," Joshua said, walking back to me. "An influential friend of mine let me know you might be heading this way soon and assured me he'd have my title reinstated should I nab you for him."

That made sense. More so if the mentioned influential friend was—

"Cross," I said.

Joshua smiled at that while sitting on one of the couches in the office. "Yes, the good doctor always has been one to hold his many apples in front of the neglected mules of this world."

"So, what, you call him, and he sends his goons to come get me?"

"That's how he made it sound," he said, lacing his fingers behind his head. "Though, he did mention that I might have trouble getting you into custody due to you being one of his super-human science projects," he frowned a little and took me in with a doubtful glance. "Not exactly his best work, I take it?"

"I'm actually taking the week off," I told him.

Joshua watched me for what seemed like a long time— probably because it was just weird to get stared at by some random evil dude—before he finally said, "Cross didn't tell me what you could do. Why don't you show me so I'll know what to look out for if you try anything?"

"Now, why would I do that?" I asked. "You're the villain in this scenario, so I don't think I'll be telling you anything, buddy."

Joshua chuckled knowingly. "That's what I thought. You can't do anything, can you?"

I don't know why I decided to be honest with the man about to kill my friends and sell me out, but I did. I guess if I would've been a real super-human, I wouldn't have been caught so easily or let my friends get sent to their deaths.

"No, I can't," I told him.

I suppose he wasn't thinking I was going to say that, because he frowned and said, "That's too bad because I wasn't going to give you to Cross in the first place."

"Wait—what?"

Joshua was thinking seriously hard, and I could almost see the wheels turning in his head. When he noticed me staring, he said, "Cross was the one who sent me here to die, but I let him know quick that I was alive and well, to rub it in his face. Now he thinks he can wave my stripes and rank in front of my nose and get me to do whatever he wants, but he is gravely mistaken."

"Listen," I said quickly, all business. "I was on my way to kill Cross. Let me go, and you'll be the first to know when I'm done."

Joshua thought about that before asking, "You're going to infiltrate Anchorage, break into a heavily guarded facility, get past advanced weapons and guards, then kill Cross without powers of any kind?"

It was a fair question, I thought. "Okay," I started. "I did have powers, crazy-good powers, too, but they stopped working almost as soon as we entered British Columbia. I don't know what happened, but I think maybe I can get them working again before I get there."

I hated telling all this to him, and I also hated admitting I was going to try and be a Paladin again. Don't get me wrong, because I was really missing lightning and super-strength right about then, but getting captured by cannibals aside, I was loving not being a Paladin. However, Joshua didn't need to know that.

CHAPTER 45

I was a little aggravated when Joshua ushered me into a working elevator for the ride down, and it must have showed on my face because he said, "This is my personal carriage, as it were. The citizens here never get tired, so stairs are nothing to them."

"How can anyone looking like these things not be at death's door?" I asked, glancing out the glass wall of the elevator at the ruined city. I also scanned the skyline of the buildings still standing, in hope that I might spy Beck about to do a sneak attack.

Beck.

I would've slapped my forehead if my hands wouldn't have been tied behind me. The sudden plan was rash and may or may not work, but I had to try something. I turned to face Joshua from my respective corner of the elevator, my hands hidden from view while I mentally turned on my holotab.

"Beck," I said, then coughed into my shoulder once, covering the slight beep my tab made while it dialed Beck and finishing with, "I mean, because they don't look like a million bucks to me, is all I'm saying.

"What they lose in charm and fair skin they more than make up for in brute strength and being impervious to any form of pain. In short, they are the perfect soldiers, and I mean to use them soon."

I heard a slight click in my head. "Jericho," Beck said, her voice in my head for only me to hear.

"How're you able to call me?" she asked.

"So, why are you taking us to an abandoned stadium to kill us, anyway?" I asked Joshua.

Beck didn't say anything for a few seconds then, after she caught on to what I was doing, she said, "What a clever boy you are."

Joshua shrugged. "It keeps the locals happy while also feeding the snow-cats. They haven't eaten in a few weeks, so the entertainment might be shortened."

I tried to recall names and landmarks in the city, trying desperately to give my accomplice the best possible coordinates to our location before it was too late. "I've been to BC Place Stadium before," I said conversationally. "It's about eight blocks from here to the east, isn't it?"

"More like ten blocks to the west," he said.

"Ten to the west," I repeated for Beck, nodding. "Forgive me. It's been a long time since I've been to this city."

"Yes, Cross told me you aren't exactly from around here," Joshua said, checking his own holotab. "Your friends will be there shortly. I'll tell Griff to hold off until we get there."

"Why?"

Joshua frowned and looked at me like I'd just asked what color the sky was. "Because I'm going to toss you in with them, of course," he said, shaking his head. "Honestly, Jericho, try and keep up with my plot, please."

Oh, what fun.

And, incidentally, a perfect time to let Beck know about his plot.

"Okay, let me see here," I said. "You hate Cross because he stabbed you in the back, so now that you have me, what you think is a prized possession of his, you're going to kill me and all my friends in an arena filled with—what was it?"

"Snow-cats."

"Right, snow-cats," I said, nodding. "And you're doing this just to rub it in Cross's face. That pretty much cover it?"

Joshua bobbed his head side to side. "Pretty much."

"How very heinous of him," Beck said in my head. "I know what building you're in. I'll head west to the stadium and see if I can get eyes on our people. If things get too out of hand before you get there, I'll have to intervene. Just try and not let your mouth get you shot."

"Well, thanks," I said, looking at Joshua even though the comment was directed at Beck. "Now I can cross getting eaten by feral mutant cats off my bucket list."

When we reached the bottom floor, we crossed the lobby and left the building, climbing into an armored car parked outside that rumbled to life and took us to the arena. BC Place was a nice stadium back in the day, and even though I was never a fan of sports, I was really hating the new use of the joint.

I frowned in thought. How could a football stadium be converted to a gladiator-style coliseum? I mean, wouldn't somebody be able to just, like, jump a small ledge or head down the stairs to get away?

These were comforting thoughts because maybe the radiation had fried everyone's brains here, so they might have been just too demented to realize the easy escapes I had in mind.

But when we rounded a corner and BC Place came into view, I knew my plans were for naught because the stadium seemed to be the only place the city-dwellers decided needed fixing up and fix it up they had. We're talking hurricane fences surrounding the entire thing with guarded checkpoints and the whole nine yards.

"You guys must get loads of visitors," I said dryly when we pulled the shaky armored car through the checkpoint and entered the parking lot of the stadium.

"Not as many as we'd like, I can assure you," Joshua said, peering out the small window next to him. "Though, these roadblocks you see aren't for escaped entertainers, but for the snow-cats. Dreadfully painful things to deal with if they're not contained properly."

"I'm here," Beck told me, and I tried not to sigh in relief. "Going to circle it once then try and find our team."

"Aren't you afraid someone might try an aerial assault on you guys while you're all stacked nice and neat in a football stadium?" I asked Joshua.

Our ride parked, and Joshua stood while one of his men opened the door for us. "Not many people are interested in this place," he said, stepping out onto the pavement with me being pulled out roughly behind him. "Although we do get the lone soldier-of-fortune every now and then, that flies above the city for a quick peek. Vancouver's auto-defense grid is still online throughout half the city, so they end up getting shot down before they get too far most of the time."

"Auto-defense grid, you say?" I said, too loudly, but I knew Beck hadn't heard what he'd just said because he was too far away. Think, Jericho, think. "I'll, uh, bet that's heck on the local birds around these parts."

I must've been trying too hard or something, because Joshua frowned at me from over his shoulder while we were escorted across the parking lot to the main stadium entrance. "Actually, yes," he said, stepping onto a broken escalator with me close behind. "We never figured out how to turn the grid off, so anything that flies overhead gets a blast from the arc guns stationed throughout the city."

"What do you know," I said, trying to get Beck's attention with emphasis on the know part. "Innocent birds shot down because no one in this entire city knows how to flip an accursed switch and turn off auto-defense grids. What a dump."

"I'm already back on the ground, idiot," Beck's voice buzzed in my head, annoying the utter crap out of me because I was actually worried about her, and that's why I was stretching my limits. "Good job, Jericho. Keep up that kind of good detective work and momma just might have to give you a gold star."

"How was I supposed—" I started to say, stopping myself and holding my breath because I just knew Joshua was about to turn around and find me out. When he didn't, I let the breath out and finished the climb up the steps. After reaching the top, the guards escorted us down a long hallway that had a great view of the arena because the glass wall was missing.

Gone was the fine green sod of the playing field that was replaced with hard dirt. I noticed the smashed cars littered throughout the field, making it look like an enormous paintball course and probably providing hiding spots, so the games of cat and mouse didn't end too quickly.

After one more flight of stairs, we entered the VIP lounge where, after I was ushered to the front of the room to the shattered window, I got my first good look at the filled seats of BC Place packed and jammed with the rotting, cheering populace of Vancouver.

Man, there was a lot of those ugly dudes.

I took my first initial scan of the place and said, "Where are they?" hoping I sounded like I was looking for my fellow comrades and not, in fact, talking to one right then.

"I'm under the field," Beck whispered. "There's five guards down here, and I think I just saw Sam and Sloan. Where are the girls?"

"So, why are you throwing the girls in the ring first?" I asked Joshua.

Joshua seated himself on the front row and laced his fingers behind his head while lifting one shoulder into a shrug. "The citizens haven't had games for weeks now, and they were simply flashier than the other two."

"That's going to throw a wrench in my plans," Beck said.

"Also," Joshua added, nodding to the guards, "don't forget that you will be joining them."

Looking back, I now know that I was too caught up in trying to help Beck save everyone to worry about myself. I also know that I was too busy, in general, to notice the large meat hook dangling from the equally large chain above my head that was attached to the larger cable anchored into the wall and trailing all the way down over the audience to the arena floor.

Kind of a hard thing to miss, I know.

But don't worry, because as soon as the four cackling guards lifted me off my feet and stabbed the huge, rusty hook into the back of my right shoulder, I got a good look at it tearing through my flesh on the front side before I was zipping down the cable while dangling over the now laughing cannibals.

I think I must've screamed about halfway there, because Beck tried to ask me something, and I couldn't hear her from either me or the crowd. When I reached the arena floor, my boots hit first and dragged until I was finally on my stomach, coughing in the dust.

"Welcome, all!" I heard the orator of the event shout into a megaphone, and the mob went berserk.

"Jericho!" I thought I heard someone call from nearby. I tried to get to my feet, and the pain hit again in full force and I collapsed.

This was bad.

There I was, sailing into an arena on a stupid man-sized fishhook to die with my friends and coughing in the radiated dirt in a pool of my own blood.

The fact that Joshua hadn't even bothered to untie my hands from behind my back let me know just how long he wanted this match to be.

"What's going on?" Beck shouted in my ear. I groaned and, miraculously, turned over onto my back.

"Well," I said weakly, my breathing becoming rattled in my chest, "the day is still young, but I think I'm about to die."

CHAPTER 46
Sybil

"He's dying," the robed woman said, opening her white eyes. "This was not supposed to happen, Stargazer."

The older Partisan looked frail, even in his translucent state. "Tis a barren and brutal road toward his Crusade, Sybil," he said, turning toward the opening in the great hall they were in. They had both been watching Jericho when he'd been threaded like bait on a hook and sent sailing into the arena. "Do not forget that this has happened before, child."

"The Crusade has happened before," Sybil corrected him sternly. "All roads leading to it are fraught with peril, as they always have been, but this—right now—has not happened before. What's different this time?" her blind eyes searched for something that normal eyes could not see.

"You have missed nothing, Sybil," Stargazer finally said before taking a shallow breath. It was meant to be a deep breath, but his energy was waning. Indeed, the fact that his being had not returned to the Cortex already after his death in Flagstaff had been a shock to him.

And also to his replacement.

"Will he listen to me?" Sybil asked him. "You have been Partisan to the First Paladin since the beginning. This will be the first timeline without you. And I have not been able to even contact him after Las Vegas—"

"You will do fine, Sybil," Stargazer smiled, feeling

himself slipping. "The Cortex calls me. Keep the Paladin on his course."

Sybil was still connected to Jericho's dimension after Stargazer melted into the air, watching the terrible scene of Jericho hitting the dust in the arena and crying out as his comrades attempted to get him to his feet and tend to his wound.

After hesitating, Sybil spoke to the empty air around her.

"He is not a Paladin yet. And, unless he stumbles upon a miracle, he is not ever going to be."

CHAPTER 47
Jericho

"Let the games begin!" the cry rang out and cheers followed. "Release the hunters!"

Metal grinded metal, when what I was guessing was some sort of large gate that I couldn't see began opening. Then I was surrounded by women on their knees.

"My God," Blu said when she saw my new piercing. "We have to get that out now." She barely touched the jagged point, and I gritted my teeth from the pain.

"Leave it," Red said, grabbing my feet. "Quickly, let's get him in a car."

I screamed when they lifted me and may or may not have blacked out for a second or two while they half dragged, half carried me to the nearest burned out car. "Stop," I shouted, and we collapsed into the dust with me leaning against the rusted vehicle.

"Jericho, we're about to have cats swarming us."

"Don't waste time on me, then," I told her. If I was already going to die, I wasn't going to take anybody with me.

"Pick him back up," Red commanded, but I laid my hand on hers, and she stopped long enough to look at me.

"I can't save the Rogues anymore, Red. You're better for them than I am. Please, just leave me."

We all heard the first roar/hiss issue from the other side of the death pit. "Go," I tried again, shifting slightly and biting back the blinding agony that accompanied the slight position change.

"No," Piper said, pulling a knife out of her boot and standing. "I'm not going to lose you again."

"Piper," I tried to shout, while she ran out of sight.

"Beck, where are you?" Blu shouted, turning on her tab.

"My, but you people are dramatic," we all heard Beck echo into our tabs. "I had to grab a few things from a dark, wet cave, so cut me some slack. Piper, Merry Christmas."

Then a white battle suit landed almost ten feet away from us. "I could only hold two, so I didn't get Blu's," Beck added, and Red's Raptor-6 landed close to where Piper was already getting into her armor. In seconds the bright white suit hissed shut, and Piper got to her feet while grabbing the hilt of her red great sword, demagnetizing it from her back plate.

Her facemask hadn't closed yet, and the pandemonium around us seemed to stop while we shared one last look at each other. "I'll be right back," she said.

Then she was gone.

"Give them Helheim, Pipe," I muttered, letting my head fall back into the car behind me and closing my eyes.

The audience had begun screaming foul play when the suits appeared, so I knew whatever we were going to do had to be done fast

Blu was still next to me, and she looked scared out of her mind. "Can't you get my suit?" she asked Beck.

"No can do," was the answer. "It took me forever to get those. Hold tight," Beck added. "I'm coming in."

In less than ten seconds, Beck landed close to us in a crouch, sending dust flying all around and making the already wild crowd gasp at her wings. "You two are on your own for now," Beck said to Piper and Red. "I'm going to get Blu and the invalid out of here."

"Where are they keeping the others?" Piper tabbed in.

"Just below the arena," Beck said, kneeling beside me and making a face at the hook in my shoulder. "There's a service exit on your right that's barricaded. Blast through it, make a left, and you can't miss them. They'll be the people in the big cage, should you have any doubts. Also, Piper?"

"What?" Piper grunted over the holotab, sounding like she was otherwise engaged and not in the mood for a chat.

"Archimedes is with them," Beck said.

Piper didn't respond immediately, and it could've had to do with her fighting off huge snow-cats. "I'm on it," she finally said.

"Look, I can take you both, but it's not going to be easy now because someone decided to go fishing," Beck told us while shaking her head at me before the ground exploded around us from bullet spray.

"Crocs!" Blu shouted, grabbing my good arm while she and Beck dragged me to the back end of the car. I rolled my head to the right and caught a glimpse of the cat fight going on.

Ha. Cat fight. Get it?

Piper was leaping and bounding better than any of the enormous things that resembled snow leopards, hacking away with her great sword while Red tried to hold a perimeter with every weapon she had. The first time I'd seen a Raptor-6 was with Chloe years ago, and I got a chance to pilot it. Mine wasn't weaponized, Chloe had explained, so I didn't get a chance to find out just how much of a punch they packed. The model had been designed for gun nuts, she'd also told me.

Red showed me just how powerful the older suits and their guns were. But as hard as she tried, there were just too many ghouls around us with guns.

"Okay, let's get awkward, shall we?" Beck muttered, pulling and smashing my aching body against hers. "Come on, Blu, time to make a Jericho sandwich."

"I hate you..." I wheezed out, but since my mouth was now in the general vicinity of her ear, she heard it and smiled.

Blu did as she was told, and she and Beck grabbed each other's arms with me in the middle. "Use that good arm if it still works," were the last words Beck said before she hauled us into the smoke-filled air and, just to make things even more uncomfortable, wrapping her legs around my waist for a better hold.

"Where are we going?" Blu screamed against the wind when she noticed we were heading to another part of the city and not away from it.

"To catch a new ride," Beck answered, and in less than half a minute we landed in front of what looked like a huge machine shop. The streets were empty due to everyone attending our celebratory execution.

"Stay put," Beck said, kicking through the tall double doors and entering the shop.

"Like we're going to go anywhere," I mumbled, my head being cradled in Blu's lap. I noticed she looked a little distraught, so I decided to lighten the mood by saying, "How's your day going? Because I have an iron hook stabbed through my chest."

"I don't understand," she said, her eyes on the blackened pavement while she shook her head slightly. "Your blood is a self-sustaining energy source that doesn't run out. Exposure to radiation can't be what's making it not work."

"We'll figure it out later," I lied. "Right now let Beck attempt to save us."

"Stop worrying," Beck said in my ear while crashing through the wall beside the very open doors in the large armored...something she'd hijacked.

"Was the door too easy?" Blu asked in annoyance, getting me to my feet and putting my good arm over her shoulders.

"Well, everyone else is being dramatic, so I thought I'd join in," Beck said, opening the side door and helping Blu get me inside. "Better strap him in somehow because it's about to get rough," she said, heading back to the driver's seat while I tried not to scream in agony when Blu cinched my seat's harness around me.

"I'm sorry," Blu said in tears. "I can't remove it until we're away from this place."

I think that's what she said, anyway. Hard to say because Beck floored it about that time, and the roar of the engine drowned out everything. "Get up top," she said to Blu through our tabs. "Use the gun when I say."

It wasn't easy because of all the hard turns and bumps Beck was throwing at her, but Blu was able to climb the short access ladder to the mounted turret. When she was finally seated in the dome, she asked. "What am I aiming for?"

Beck switched gears then, and my rolling head stuck to the back of my seat. "The side of the arena. It won't penetrate on the first shot, but it'll weaken it well enough for us to break through."

"Glad someone's feeling confident," a random voice said in all our ears.

"Archimedes," Beck said conversationally, like she'd just walked into him on a street corner. "Glad to see you weren't eaten."

"Aim for the south side entrance," Arc told her. "Piper and the woman Sam called Red came and freed us just now, and that'll give us a way out. It's only a small barricade, so it shouldn't be a problem."

"Almost there," Beck told him, putting the transport on two wheels in a wild turn. "Blu?"

"I see it," Blu confirmed, and I heard the whirring of the axis when she moved the gun slightly to the left. "Get down," she ordered to the people we were about to bust out, before firing off her shot.

We all heard the explosion through our holotabs, and Beck asked, "Geez, how close were you?"

After a few coughs, Arc answered. "Too close. Probably could've planned that better, not going to lie."

"What is he, American?" I mused to no one in particular. "I guess Mother Russia hasn't wiped us all out."

"Who's that?" Arc said to someone close to him.

"Long story," I heard Piper say before she cursed, and I

heard gunfire. "Anytime now, Beck."

"We're here," Beck said, slamming on the brakes, and I cried out in more pain because the stupid harness smashed against the stupid hook in my stupid shoulder.

This whole thing was just stupid.

Bullets pinged off the side of the transport, and Blu turned the cannon. "Here's a present, you bleeding crocs," she growled, firing a round over the heads of our crew and into the horde closing in on them.

Then the side door opened, and I rolled my head to the side to see the smiling face of Sam. "Bloody good shot, Blu," he said, clambering into the armored car. The others were close behind him while he frowned at me and said, "Say, Jerry?"

"Hmm?"

"You, uh, got a little something in your arm there, friend."

"What? Oh, this," I said, nodding once with my eyes closed. "Yeah, I saw it and couldn't live without it, so I just picked it up."

Sam smiled at that and was no doubt about to say something equally as witty, but never got the chance because two stray bullets found their way through the doorway and into the big man's back.

Sloan screamed when he crumbled to the floor, and before anyone had time to react, Red blocked the doorway in her large suit and shouted, "Go!"

Beck cursed and hit the gas hard, tearing us away from the firefight.

"We can't leave her," Blu pleaded with Beck while Piper pulled the door shut.

"You got a patient now, doc," Beck told her. "Red's in armor. She'll get out no problem."

Sam's face was already paling, and his breathing was more rapid. "Sam," I said, not really sure why I was addressing him while Piper, being the only one strong enough in her battle suit, turned him to his side, his face toward me so Blu could look at his wound.

He watched me for a few seconds, his blinking becoming slow and his eyelids heavy, and I knew my friend was dying.

Then he smiled at me. "Look at it this way, Jerry," he said weakly. "With me out of the way, the ladies might actually settle for you, mate."

"You're going to be fine, buddy," I told him. "I don't want a girl, anyway. Too much drama."

He chuckled and coughed, still smiling, his eyes closed. "They are that, my friend."

"Don't sleep, Sam," I said quickly, glancing at Blu while she sat back on her haunches and tried to wipe sweat off her forehead with her elbow because her hands were covered in Sam's blood. Then she looked at me and shook her head slightly, a tear slipping down her cheek.

I couldn't stand it. Unbuckling my harness, I went down to my knees in the rumbling car and laid a hand on the big man's chest. "Wake up, dude," I said, shaking him and wincing in pain from the movement. "I'm still alive, so you can't die yet, remember?"

His eyes barely flickered open. "Sorry... mate," he managed to get out, grasping at my hand on his chest. "Looks like... you'll be needing a... new friend."

His breathing stopped, his eyes unfocused and he was gone.

"No!" Sloan shouted, her small hands fretfully flying to her wild, unkempt hair, while she shook her head fast. "He can't die. Someone fix him!"

Blu's head had drooped, and her shoulders were shaking while she placed a bloodied hand on Sam's leg. Piper tried to console Sloan, but the little girl would have none of it and ducked around her, running to me and grabbing my bad arm. "You," she said quickly while I tried not to scream in agony. "You're the one who can save him. Shock him or something."

"My powers aren't working," I told her.

"Well, make them start working again."

"If I could do that, we wouldn't be in this mess."

Seeing that I was a lost cause, she dropped down on her knees and grabbed Sam's lifeless shoulder, shaking it violently. "Stop being dumb," she shouted. "It's just bullets, stupid."

No one had the energy to stop the girl, and after a minute Sloan crumbled on top of Sam's body and resumed her sobbing. The armored car stopped suddenly with a small lurch, and Beck climbed out of the driver's seat. "Blu, try and ping our location to your sister," Beck said, noticing the spectacle.

Blu exited the car to try and call Red, and Piper went with her, leaving Beck and me with Sloan. I was still on my knees next to Sam's body when I barely heard Sloan ask the wind, "Who's going to get me more chocolate now?"

And that did it for me.

With much effort, I got to my wobbly feet and lurched for the door.

"Where are you going?" Beck asked.

"Back to the city," I said, pulling the door open with my good arm. "I've had it with this damn quest."

"Why?" she asked, stepping toward me.

"You should ask everyone else risking their lives for me," I said, anger seeping to the surface. "I'm not worth anything at all anymore, Beck. Sam should've used me as a body shield. At least that way I could've actually accomplished something."

"Sam, along with the rest of us, knew the risks of this little road trip before we left." Beck said, matching my tone and crossing her arms. "But we all came with you anyway. And we all had our own reasons for going. We weren't just coming to keep you safe."

"I was a superhero then."

"That's not why—"

"Look at me," I said, meeting her gaze and feeling light-headed just from standing. "It's all gone, Beck. Everything."

"It's not like he jumped in front of the gunfire for you," Beck countered. "We were all running and getting shot at, if you didn't notice."

I shook my head and stepped out of the car onto the ground. "Just forget it," I said.

Vancouver was a long way off, and I knew that I wouldn't make it on foot. But I guess it didn't matter.

I was either going to die in the arena or die before I got there. "*Let's be friends until the day we die*," Sam had told me once. At least this way we were both going down on the same day.

I had walked only around fifty feet or so when something exploded with a blinding flash just in front of me, and I was thrown back into the black dirt.

"Jericho!" Piper shouted when she saw me getting blown back by the—what was it, anyway? Grenade? Mini-nuke? I'm guessing I hadn't walked far enough away to merit attention from Piper or Blu, who had both been trying to contact Red.

"What...?" I groaned, trying to roll on my side and failing. Piper, in her armor, ended up lifting me to my feet like a ragdoll before glancing at what had knocked me down. I was still a little dazed and couldn't exactly focus, but, strangely enough, what I thought I saw looked like—

"It's a person," Piper said, frowning. "Blu, get over here."

"Just get out of there," Blu was saying when she stopped beside us, sighing. "She's on the outskirts, but she's not out of the woods just yet."

"Who is that?" Piper asked her, pointing.

Blu saw the body and froze. "Where did that come from?"

"It just landed in front of me like an atom bomb," I grumbled, walking toward the body and trying not to stagger.

"The light," I mused to myself, sinking to my knees beside the man who was face down in the black dust. "I've seen that before." Then I noticed the shape of the guy. Geez, but he was messed up. Like, really, really messed up. His right leg was gone completely, and his left arm was bent the wrong way and there was large hole punched completely through his chest. "You still breathing, dude?" I asked, trying and failing to roll him onto his back. Blu got down next to me, and Piper, who seemed to be the muscle of our trio, squatted in her smaller battle-suit and turned the lifeless man over, exposing his face to us.

I don't know who I'd been expecting it to be, what with the semi-explosion of brilliance caused by the unbridled slash in time. I guess I had known from the get-go that it could only be one person.

And I was right.

Blu covered her mouth to contain a scream, and Piper even shrank back a few steps in shock while I was oddly calm about it. Well, I mean, about as calm as I could've been, given the circumstances.

It was me.

"Where am I?" I asked. Well, not me, but him. The other me. Gosh, this is going to be confusing, so I'm going to call the me from the future by his name.

"Where am I?" Jericho asked, and his eyes looked unfocused.

Blu removed her hands to say something, but I shook my head at her, grabbing Jericho's fluttering hand in mine and almost gasping when I saw that the remains of what could only be a torn-apart gauntlet of time was barely hanging on to his burnt forearm. "You're right here. When?"

"Three days," he said, coughing, and I saw blood in his mouth.

"Where?" I asked.

"Anchorage."

"Who?"

"Look, forget the stupid code," Jericho said as loud as he could, which wasn't much, and he gripped my hand, focusing his eyes on me for the first time. "Sam?"

"He died a few minutes ago," I said.

"God, no," Jericho muttered, closing his eyes for a second before saying, "Red's on her way back, but she won't make it. Tell Blu I'm sorry."

What?

Blu was on her feet in a second, queuing her holotab. "Red?" she asked quickly. "Please, get back. Now."

"Who else dies?" I asked angrily. "Why did you even—"

"It doesn't matter," Jericho said, looking at me one last time before his eyes rolled back into his head.

"No!" I shouted, grabbing his shoulder and shaking him hard. "Why did you come back here?"

When Jericho didn't respond, I tried Sloan's trick, slapping me hard in the face, which caused a small moan from him, and I think I heard a whisper.

"What?" I said, hunching over and putting my ear close to his mouth.

"Don't..." he was dying. I was dying. "Don't... fight it..."

And he was gone.

"I'm sorry, mates," Red suddenly chimed into all of our tabs. "There's too many of them."

Blu was crying now. "Red, you kill the crocs and get back here right now."

Jericho's grip vanished, and his hand slipped from mine. It was too much.

"If I don't stop them, then they'll be coming after you guys," Red said, and we heard gunfire. "Even if I made it back, it wouldn't matter."

Archimedes picked this time to climb out of the armored car, followed by Beck. "Why have we stopped?" he asked. "We can't stay here."

"We'll figure something else out," Blu pleaded with her sister, ignoring Arc. "Just come back."

"No," Red said. "I'm going to self-destruct my Raptor-6 and give you all a head start."

"Red, no—"

"Enough, Blu," she said. "And Jericho?"

I was still staring at my body in a state of shock, but I roused long enough to say, "Yeah?"

"Don't die, and take care of my little sister."

"Stop!" Blu shouted just as we heard the boom, and Red's tab was wrought with static. Blu shrieked and collapsed to the ground, her hands on her head while she screamed again.

Beck grabbed her, ignoring Blu's flailing, and told Piper, "We have to go."

Nodding, the Viking woman stepped closer to me and laid a hand on my shoulder. "Come on," she said.

"Thanks for nothing," I said to my future body, and I felt Piper's armored hands slip around me. "You showed up just in time to see your friends die again, genius. You're so stupid."

"You're not stupid, Jericho," Piper said, picking me up and walking to the armored car. "And I don't believe you're going to start acting that way in three days."

CHAPTER 48

We drove for almost a whole day and not a lot of interaction happened between anyone aboard the stolen armored tram. We did stop after a few hours to bury Sam in the radiated grounds of British Columbia, though. Sloan fought back tears most of the way through the small ceremony, but Blu, who hadn't actually stopped crying since we'd gotten back on the road, didn't.

I tucked Sam's Zune into my pocket while Beck, Piper, and Archimedes finished the grave. "Thanks for the tunes, Sam," I said. "I'll see you around."

We ended up silently standing around the fresh grave for a few minutes because no one really knew what to say until Sloan said, "He was a fat man. Like, really big and noisy."

Since last words weren't coming to anyone else, we all just headed back to the armored car which, if I hadn't explained before, wasn't exactly a car because it was massive. Like, about the size of a train engine with a lot more room. The inside was furnished like a mega RV or some kind with a few separate rooms in the back, bathroom and even a kitchen area. Most of these amenities, though, were hundreds of years old, probably, and definitely looked like it.

Blu also took advantage of the lull in the pandemonium to remove the hook from my shoulder blade and chest. I'm not going to go into great detail about how she did it or how I was feeling during surgery. Suffice it to say that it didn't take too long and hurt like Helheim. Blu stopped crying when she started working on me and was strong until she was wrapping my torso in some gauze she'd found in the car, then her tears came back and her hands began shaking.

"I'm sorry," she whispered, shaking her head as if to clear the sad thoughts from her mind.

I tried to comfort her the best I could, but she stood suddenly and walked to the back of the long-armored rig where Sloan was trying to sleep. That left me with Piper and her new man in the main cabin. Beck had already resumed driving after Blu had finished the most tedious parts of hook-removal. So there I was, naked from the waist up, with a half-done bandaging job, in front of my ex and her new boyfriend.

And I couldn't have cared less.

Death is an absolute thing. Watching Sam die had affected me more than the hook, but Red sacrificing herself to try and shake our pursuers was the worst part of recent events. Piper sat beside me and started on finishing Blu's wrapping while Archimedes sat across from us silently.

I had to hand it to the guy because he was a pretty patient sort. Had I been in his position, I most likely would've made a fool of myself by now. But he didn't, choosing instead to sit leaning back into the bench with his arms crossed. I didn't look at him much, but when I did, I couldn't read his face. That probably had to do with my not caring about the awkwardness anymore.

I winced when Piper cinched the last time, and I let out a small groan. "Blu would've done a better job," she said.

I shrugged and winced again before Archimedes surprised me by saying, "If we don't get the proper meds for him soon, he's going to be in bad shape."

"He has a name and can hear everything you're saying," I said, glancing at him. "I'm guessing you're the famous Archimedes I've heard so much about."

"Guilty," he said, smiling. "Sorry for not addressing you directly but, well, you look pretty bad off, to be honest."

Piper looked at him like he'd just told a kid that Santa Claus wasn't real, so I decided I'd clear the air a bit.

"I'm the guy who died and left Piper here."

Archimedes thought about that for a second before pointing out the elephant in the room. "Yet here you are. May I ask how?"

"It doesn't matter," Piper cut in, standing.

"I rather think it does, Pipe," Arc said, leaning forward and putting his elbows on his knees, lacing his fingers together. "The only reason our relationship existed was because he was dead."

I frowned. Geez, and I thought I was being forward. This guy really cut to the chase.

Piper didn't look like she was digging this particular topic and said, "Nothing's changed."

Arc smiled at that, even though his next words were, "Even if you don't go back to him, it still wouldn't matter. And it's fine, really."

"It's unfair," Piper countered. "You never talked about the person you lost, either."

"Because mine didn't die," he said, and Piper stopped talking. "It's not anything that you're thinking," he said. "It was my brother."

"But he's still alive," I said. "So how did you lose him?"

Arc looked at me with an odd sort of smile on his face that was, as I've said, terribly difficult to read. "It's complicated," he told me. "We only had each other to rely on growing up, but he decided to pursue a lifestyle I couldn't cope with. I haven't seen him since."

I frowned, narrowing my heavy eyes at him. "That's it?" When he nodded, I said, "Kind of lame, don't you think?"

"Jericho," Piper said, looking at me now like I'd confessed Santa's non-existence to a kid.

"No, he's right," Archimedes told her, still smiling and giving a small shrug. "Coming back from the dead is a lot more interesting than meaningless family disputes, as far as I'm concerned."

"But you always acted—I guess I always assumed—" Piper was trying to say.

"That I lost the love of my life like you did?" Arc asked her. "Loss is loss whenever it's someone you care about, Piper. I didn't want to pry about your reasons, so you never felt the need to pry into mine."

I couldn't help thinking how soap opera-like the whole thing was. I mean, what with someone you thought was dead showing up three years or six seasons later to throw a monkey-wrench in the fantastic relationship the other protagonists were only in because the first guy was supposedly dead.

Some root for the guy back from the dead because they didn't want him to die in the first place, while others root for the new guy who's been patiently getting all the attention for the last few years because people die all the time, and they believe people should move on.

I'm not sure which of those two categories you, my friend, fall into, and I'm not going to try and persuade you in either direction.

But, if I had to choose which one I'm in, I definitely would say that people do, indeed, die all the time. Though moving on isn't as hard as some might think. Whether Piper wanted me back or not, I'd made my choice.

"Don't worry, man," I said to Archimedes. "I didn't come back from the dead to win back anyone."

Call me hard, cruel, whatever you want, but Piper wasn't going to happen for me. Plus, I was going to be dead in a few days, anyway, but I wasn't about to mention that.

"Not to mention you're going to be dead in a few days if you don't do something about it," Arc said. Man, this guy was relentless. "What is your plan on that, exactly?"

"Jericho's not going to die," Beck called from the driver's seat. "Stop spreading gloom and doom, genius."

"Actually, it's a possibility at this point," I muttered dryly, touching my feverish forehead. Geez, I was tired.

"Unless you figure out what you came back to tell yourself," Piper ventured. "You wouldn't have just randomly showed up on your deathbed for no reason."

"I agree," Arc said, nodding. "Whatever he had to say to you must've been a way to not end up dying as he had."

I stood. "Look, it was nice meeting you, Arc, but I'm going to go lie down and sleep for the rest of my life."

"Sleep when you're dead," Beck said, glancing over her shoulder at me. "Don't worry, though, because you'll only have to wait two more days."

Piper didn't like that and jumped all over Beck about not helping, but I was already heading for the back of the rocking car to sleep. I just had to.

Blu and Sloan were in the left side compartment, so I took the right side, stepping into the semi-spacious room with a bed and small closet, pulling the sliding door shut behind me before sitting on the squeaking bed. For a few minutes I just sat there, willing meaningless thoughts to arise so I didn't have to live in the hell I was in now. My first and only thought I had before lapsing back into my situation was how odd it was that the armored car Beck had stolen was pretty clean for a rig owned by the undead.

The next thought was how Sam's face had looked before he died, and I ran my good hand over my peach fuzz buzz cut, dropping my head low and shaking it while squeezing my eyes shut. I just couldn't believe it. Sam and Red both dying because I wasn't able to do anything to stop it. I'd seen my fair share of death for a guy who, by all normal accounts, should be teaching history to college students and not, in fact, roaming the future in the year 2345 on a mad quest for revenge.

Revenge.

The word stood out in my mind, and I opened my eyes in the fading light of the small cabin.

Cross.

He was the one who had put the hit out on me in the first place and also gave me stupid powers that made everyone

I met fall in line behind me like I was some kind of god, following me to their deaths. He was the one to blame for this. For everything. All the lives lost so far I placed on his head.

Let's be friends until the day we die.

I closed my eyes again.

You've done enough for me, Paladin. Now it's my turn.

I gritted my teeth, digging my nails into my scalp.

Don't... fight it...

"Fight what?" I asked the air in a menacing whisper. "I needed to be able to fight hours ago. Now everyone is dead and there's nothing left to—"

Don't fight it, a female voice whispered in the dark.

I opened my eyes, glancing around the room. What little light spilling through the small porthole was all but gone now, and I was almost enveloped in darkness while I checked to see who was talking.

"What am I fighting?" I asked out loud. Then my head became fuzzy.

Sleep.

"What?" I slurred before falling back onto the bed.

I vaguely remember seeing a silhouette standing over me—literally because I almost felt feet on either side of my ribcage while the shrouded figure peered down at me.

I was going crazy, surely. I even tried to ask if I was but only got out, "Crazy?"

No, the shade said. *Sleep, Jericho.*

My eyes fluttered shut and I was out.

CHAPTER 49

Jericho.

I sat up straight, gasping for air. It was still dark in my room and also a bit gusty.

Like, really windy, actually. "What's the deal?" I asked in the general direction of my door. "Are you guys trying to freeze me to death?"

Stand up.

"What now?" I asked, frowning. Why was it so dark in here?

Get off the ground and onto your feet.

I then realized my hands were touching snow instead of sheets, and I gasped again, giving a start and wincing against the pain that I... that I didn't feel.

I instantly stood, touching my wounded shoulder, except it wasn't wounded anymore. The bandages were even gone, and I was back in my Paladin garb with my hood on.

"Awesome," I said. "My first actual dream in months and it's a good one. Nailed it."

Walk.

It was dark everywhere I looked, so I had no way of knowing where I was or anything about my surroundings. I had a good two-foot range of visibility, and I might've been freaking out if I hadn't been dreaming.

"Where am I going?" I asked, taking my first step in the crunching snow beneath me.

Forward.

Since it was my dream and it was looking to be a pretty lucid event, I decided that I didn't have to be serious about the mythical sounding female voice. "I know I'm going forward, genius. I want to know my destination."

The woman's voice remained silent at that, but I kept walking anyway, relishing the feeling of not having blinding pain with every step. I'm not sure how long I'd been walking when I started seeing mountainous landscape in the distance. Invigorated at the sight, I picked up the pace. I wasn't sure what I was looking at until I got closer. I thought it was a city at first, but when I finally stopped at the stone columned gate leading into it, I decided it wasn't a city at all but something else.

A big something else, too.

Go inside.

"Ah, you're back," I said, glancing skyward. "Just so you know, hearing voices is nothing to me. So who's the real victim, here?"

Enter the Citadel.

Shrugging, I walked between the off-white columns. Now that I looked at it, citadel was a good description of the towering structure. I stopped walking when I noticed that I had to cross a sort of rope-bridge to gain access to the joint.

Enter the Citadel, Jericho. The voice urged me.

"You enter it," I spat, glancing over the edge at the rushing river that was a sickeningly long way down. "I ain't about to cross this thing."

Are you afraid?

"No, I just don't want to die from a rickety rope-bridge, alright?" I said, annoyed that the voice sounded almost amused at my expense. "And, for the record, I've crossed bridges like this before, thank you very much, but none of them were thousands of years old."

It will not break.

"Prove it," I said smugly, not expecting anything.

Especially for someone to materialize three feet to my left and scare me half to death. "Who're you?" I asked the woman, stepping away quickly. She had arrived in a crouch, almost as if she were afraid she'd fall down if she appeared any other way.

Slowly, the black-garbed woman stood, her face turned toward the temple thing and her eyes closed so I couldn't make out much about her. I noticed her black cloak when she pulled on the hood of it and said, "Follow me if you're afraid."

Then she just strolled onto the ragged bridge in all its creaking glory without hesitation. "I said I wasn't afraid," I said to her back.

"Prove it," she said, using my own words against me.

After a few seconds of debate, I decided that it was, after all, a dream, and I would probably wake up before I hit the icy river.   "What's your name?" I asked when I made it to her side and we resumed our trek across the bridge.

"Sybil," she said.

"Prophetess," I said knowingly with a nod. "Figures I'd dream about destiny hokum when I finally get an actual dream."

"You are not dreaming, Jericho," Sybil said, and I chuckled and shook my head slightly.

"Whatever," I said. "What is this place, then, Sybil?"

"All of your questions will be answered inside," she said calmly.

"You won't tell me anything before I go in?"

"No."

"Not much of a sharer, are you," I told her, peering in wonder at the massive structure when we finally stepped off the rope-bridge which, might I point out, wasn't exactly as unsafe as I had originally thought. In front of us now was a long, frozen courtyard leading to a wide set of steps that went all the way to the large doors of the Citadel.

"Come," Sybil said to me.

I followed her without thinking, but we hadn't gone far when I stopped, frowning while I took in the ice sculptures all around the large courtyard.

"You've seen this before," Sybil said to me, her face still away from me. "When you met Stargazer."

"Yeah," I said, not really thinking about her knowing that because, like I said—

"You're not dreaming, Jericho," Sybil said again, this time with a little more power behind her voice, and she turned for the first time and I saw her face. She was pale, her face framed in red curls and her eyes looked strange. Too strange.

And I'd seen that before, as well.

"You're blind," I said simply.

"Like Stargazer, yes. All Partisans become blind sooner or later from the overexposure within the Citadel," she said, her face blank. "I still see, just not the way you do."

She walked slowly toward me, pulling her hood off and letting red hair spill out onto her shoulders. Watching her approach, I began feeling strange, and when the woman who looked to be around her early forties stopped in front of me and I took in her chiseled features and blank eyes, I knew, somehow or another, that I wasn't dreaming and that this was really happening. To me. Right then.

One side of Sybil's mouth lifted slightly into an almost smile and she said, "This is real, Jericho, and I've been waiting on you for a long time. Come with me into the Citadel, and I will teach you all you need to know."

I followed her when she turned around again, but I was still having trouble processing what was happening. "What did you say you were?"

"I am a Partisan," she answered.

"Partisan," I repeated. "Okay, what is it you do?"

"I help you."

"But how?"

"Every Paladin is assigned a Partisan at the beginning of his or her Crusade, to aid the Paladin in any way they can. Primarily we stay here in the Citadel and are your eyes and ears wherever you are," she said, turning her head slightly toward me. "Or *whenever* you are."

We made it to the steps, and Sybil stopped because she must have felt, I guess, that I wasn't following her anymore.

"What happens when I go in?" I asked, my mouth feeling dry.

"You will discover your destiny," Sybil said. "Your true purpose, Paladin, and not the many given to you by others. Now, come."

"No," I said quickly. I was scared for some reason, and I wasn't about to set foot in that place.

"You're a Paladin, Jericho," she said, her white eyes on me.

"I'm not," I told her, shaking my head. "All my powers are gone. Lost them a few days ago."

Sybil walked back to me and held up a hand close to my face. "May I?"

I wasn't sure what she was doing but figured it couldn't have been near as bad as going in the Citadel. "Knock yourself out."

She laid her icy hand on my cheek and closed her blind eyes. I didn't get a jolt of power or feel anything, really, and after a minute Sybil removed her hand from my face.

Then she slapped me hard.

"How could you be so selfish?" she asked violently, and I even shrank away from her for a second before realizing how stupid it was to be afraid of a blind woman.

"What are you talking about?" I asked angrily. "My powers stopped on their own in—"

"It was you," she said, her voice quiet again and her face aimed at the ground. "You were selfish, thinking only of yourself, and your entire being rejected the process."

"Here's a tip," I told her harshly. "Next time you pick a Paladin, why don't you grab a baby who's never had a life so you can train him up to not have feelings or emotional attachments like a damn Jedi and leave the grown folks alone."

"Partisans are chosen much like Paladins, but they have

no control over who the next Paladin will be," she said.

"What do you mean by the next one?" I couldn't help but ask.

Sybil shook her head. "I cannot tell you."

"Of course you can't," I muttered, sighing before saying, "Look, obviously whoever's in charge around here got the wrong guy this time around. So can you please just send me back now, or whatever?"

She was quiet for a short time, but she seemed to be trying to keep her mouth shut. I wasn't sure if she was trying to not berate me or not tell me something she shouldn't, being as how I wasn't a Paladin and all. She finally said, "Yes, you may go. Come here."

I walked to her and she lifted a hand again to my forehead, stopping before she touched me. "Is... is there anything else you want to know about yourself before you go?"

It was strange to hear her stammer some, because she was almost robotic in her fluid movements and speech. I told myself my final question was just to make Sybil feel better before I left, but really it was because I needed to know.

"Can I ever get my, uh, Paladin status reinstated?"

Sybil let out a breath that I hadn't realized she was holding, and I saw that this was what she had been hoping I would ask her.

"That is up to you, Jericho," she said, laying her hand on my forehead. "I can't make you do anything, nor can anyone else. Whether or not you become a Paladin again will be your decision alone."

"So, like, just get back and decide I'm going to be a Paladin again?" I asked.

"No," Sybil said, and I felt myself slipping away then. "Just remember that you're a Paladin with or without power, Jericho. Never forget that."

CHAPTER 50

I opened my eyes and flicked them around the cabin, not sure how long I'd been out. There was a small amount of light leaking through the porthole, and I could see some now. It stood to reason I'd been asleep for a while, but it felt like only a few minutes because I still felt groggy.

Then I noticed Blu was sleeping next to me, curled up a few inches away with her back facing toward the door. I thought about tabbing Beck but didn't want to wake Blu in case she'd only been asleep a few minutes, so I sat up slowly and swung my boots, which I hadn't taken off, to the rumbling floor. Obviously, we were still in route, but I didn't know how much ground we'd covered. I stood and exited the cabin, leaving Blu snoozing and not bothering to put on a shirt.

"He lives," Beck said with a smile when I entered the lounge area.

"How long was I out?" I asked, my voice breaking for some reason, because it felt like it hadn't been used in months.

Piper, who was sitting beside Beck with Sloan in her lap, said, "About ten hours. We're almost out of British Columbia."

"You're really pale," Sloan decided to tell me, wrinkling her nose at my appearance.

Beck laughed, but I noticed Piper's eyes running up and down my semi-cut frame slowly before she said, "I think pale works for you."

"Stop trying to rekindle crap, Pipe," Beck told her with a

slight shake of her head. "He just climbed out of bed with Blu, anyway."

"Yeah, how long has she been in there?" I asked, truly wanting to know. "I didn't hear her come in."

Piper and Beck looked at Sloan like she knew the answer, but the little girl hadn't heard any of our talking because she was still wrinkling her nose at my body. "Seriously, you need to get dressed because you're starting to freak me out."

"Fine," I said, sighing.

"Wait, let me look at your shoulder first," Piper said, sliding Sloan off her lap and standing. I sat on the bench across from Beck, who had her arms folded and a disapproving look on her face while Piper started unwrapping my shoulder.

I wasn't paying attention, really, and was too busy thinking about Sybil in my dream to notice Piper, but when she got the wrap off and gasped, I glanced at her.

"What?"

"It's gone," she said quietly, staring in shock before she smiled broadly. "The wound, Jericho. It's completely gone."

It was true. I ran my left hand over the now smooth skin where there was supposed to be a huge gash. There wasn't even dried blood anywhere. "You're full of surprises," Piper said, touching my shoulder and looking at me with a small smile.

I'd seen this look before from her. Why was she doing this? She was over me until Archimedes showed back up, and now she was subtly trying to... to... I'm not sure. But she was sure trying something.

Beck was all business now. "Sweet. What about the rest of your powers?"

"Not real sure," I said, looking at my hands. "I'm not hurting now, so maybe I can do everything."

"Arc, pull over," Beck commanded, and the armored rig instantly slowed.

"What for?" he buzzed over her holotab.

Beck didn't answer but opened the side door before we had come to a stop, and I was greeted by the full force of the frozen landscape and icy wind.

It was so cold. Not a good sign for me considering I used to be able to run shirtless through twenty-below weather.

After I'd gotten my clothes on and pulled my hood over my head, I followed Beck into the whiteness, walking a good forty feet from the car.

"Try some lightning," Beck said to me. "Make momma proud."

I clenched my fists and concentrated hard, my eyes closed as I tried to will voltage to the surface. After nothing happened for almost a minute, Beck sighed, "Well, we tried. At least you'll be useless and alive at the same time."

"What's the plan in the Yukon?" I asked, shoving my hands in my coat pockets and looking off into the distance.

Beck shrugged, putting her hands into her pockets, too. "There isn't much human activity in the Yukon. The main goal is to not be eaten by snow-cats. We should be fine in this rig, though."

"How is it on gas?"

"Doesn't run on it," she told me, shaking her head. "Like I'd steal something with half a tank to cross British Columbia and the Yukon."

We stood there staring into the rising sun for a minute before heading back to the car. The fresh air was good, and I can't explain how amazing it felt to, you know, not be wounded unto death and all.

"Just rest up," Beck told me before we entered the rig. "Take the quiet of the Yukon to try and summon your chi back. God knows we're going to need it soon."

I nodded and followed her inside so we could resume our journey.

Quiet, huh? I could go for some quiet time, actually, and I began to look forward to the Yukon. I knew it was a long stretch to Anchorage, and that made it better.

I also didn't know what I'd been thinking. Quiet time? You mean me, actually catch a break?

Rubbish.

The only quiet time I got was the next eighteen hours, and that's only because we stopped at the border of British Columbia to sleep.

I slept in the main cabin, saying the room was stuffy, but really just not wanting to be alone with Blu. No matter what she said, I was always going to see her sister's death as my fault. I couldn't fix it, but facing her throughout the day was bad enough. Alone in a room with her was too much.

"What are you thinking about?" I heard Beck ask from the other side of the dark cabin.

Blu and Sloan had taken one of the rooms, and Archimedes and Piper had taken the opposite one, which left me stuck in the main cabin with Beck. It wasn't that bad, really, because I'd been familiarizing myself with her for a while since she was the only person who understood half of what I was going through at times.

"Death," I said.

"It sucks, doesn't it?" she said. "You and I were lucky enough to come back, at least."

"If lucky is what you want to call it," I said. "Call me crazy, but I haven't exactly accomplished much since my resurrection."

I heard her sit up. "Cross wanted you to accomplish things for him. I think everything you do that's *not* for him is something great."

Beck was never serious. Be it in the face of danger, death and dismemberment or whether she was mad, sad, glad, or tired, she just wasn't serious about anything. So the few times when she actually was being on the level, I really listened.

But I still changed the subject. "Do you ever sleep, Beck?"

"For years, no, I didn't. It wasn't until a few months ago that I started the ghost walk thing."

What? I turned my head toward her. "You mean about the same time I woke up in Cross's lab?"

"I guess. What's that got to do with anything?"

An idea was forming. I could almost see the outcome.

"Good night, Beck," I said suddenly to her. "You're a good friend, but I'm beat so I'll see you in the morning."

Beck was a little thrown by my turning over and facing away from her, clamping my eyes shut and willing all my being in one direction as hard as I could.

Come on, Sybil. I thought. *We really need to have a chat.*

CHAPTER 51

Jericho took a breath, pausing the recording on his holotab and readying himself before starting into the most critical part of his story. Why was he even doing this? The thought had been evident from the start, and he had gone back and forth the past hour on whether or not he was actually accomplishing anything at all by telling his tale to... to...

That was the hardest part. When he thought about it, he knew *why* he was recording his story. But he never knew *who* he was recording it for. The first time he'd done it years ago was to keep a little of his sanity before possibly dying the next day. This time was different, and it almost felt like he was putting a message in a bottle.

His holotab lit up. "The council's ready for you, Commander Jericho."

Sighing, he stood and walked across his spacious suite in the massive facility located in the heart of Anchorage. "I told you not to call me that, Red," he said, annoyed.

The Australian girl chuckled at that. "It's your title now, Paladin. Best get used to it."

"How is Beck?" he asked, changing the subject while he stepped up to the glass wall of his suite, peering down at the snowy streets that were packed full of soldiers.

His soldiers.

"Still in surgery," Red informed him. "Blu's trying her best, but she's still not sure if it can be done."

Jericho closed his eyes, placing a hand on the cold glass. "Blu can do it. Just keep me posted."

"Will do, Commander. Red out."

Jericho didn't miss a beat, instantly selecting another contact from his tab.

"What's up, Jerry?"

"Thanks for not referring to me as Commander, Sam," Jericho said, truly meaning it.

"You got it, brother," Sam said, his face appearing on the thick glass in front of him and nodding knowingly the way he always did. "Titles dehumanize a man, if you ask me."

"How're my tanks?"

The big man shrugged, "Better than expected. Could really use Blu's expertise down here, though."

Jericho dropped his gaze. "She's still working on Beck."

"Still?" Sam asked, frowning. "Cranky, she's been at that a while."

Jericho merely nodded, and Sam said, "How goes the story-telling?"

Now Jericho shrugged. "My audience nodded off a few hours ago," he said, glancing back at the couch where Sloan was fast asleep.

Sam laughed at that before saying, "Tell the ankle-biter to take notes. She's going to be losing her mind one day, as well."

"Shut up," Jericho told him, smiling. "Just get my tanks ready, man."

"Yes sir, Commander," Sam said, winking at him. Just before he signed off, though, he became serious and said, "Listen, Jerry, you know you don't have to do this."

"Yes, I do," he answered simply.

The big Aussie nodded once, satisfied. "Right. Sorry, mate."

"No worries, man. Also, tell Archimedes to come up here when he gets a chance."

"No problem. Sam out."

Jericho headed back to the armchair he'd been sitting in. It was time to resume his story.

Only he passed the chair completely, heading to the main door. Maybe if he just went out for an hour or two and cleared his mind he could be back to finish before—

He stopped when his hand touched the doorknob, his head twitching slightly once while he listened.

"Sybil, I know, okay?" he said to the air. "I'm just frazzled and can't—" he was cut off and he listened some more. "Is this going to be a regular thing with you?" he finally asked. "What do *you* mean by 'what do you mean'? I mean you radioing in every time I make a move that's not part of the overall—"

Jericho stopped again, closing his eyes. "Yes, I know," he said. "I'll finish. Stop apologizing, because I know you're not sorry."

He sat back in the armchair and selected his tale on his holotab memory. He closed his eyes, sighed, and then went to press record.

"Your bedtime stories are humongous," Sloan said groggily from the couch opposite him, her eyes still closed. "Aren't you done yet?"

"No," he told her. "Not yet."

CHAPTER 52

Man, that's a lot of chapters. I apologize for the length, really. Believe it or not, this honestly is the most summed-up version I can tell at this point. I guess if I would've attempted this ten years from now when it was foggier, I probably would've forgotten a lot of the key points and been able to tell this thing in about fifteen minutes flat.

Anyway, please hang in there, whoever-you-are.

I hit the ground running when I landed in the snow, bolting blindly until I saw the citadel looming in the distance. "Sybil!" I shouted, glancing left and right into the sky like I might catch a glimpse of her somewhere. "We need to talk."

I know why you are here, her voice echoed. *You will not find my knowledge comforting.*

"Will you stop talking like a robot and show yourself?" I asked.

In a few seconds Sybil appeared in front of me, her hands clasped tightly in front of her while her blind eyes looked in my direction. "Yes?"

Since I hadn't come for chitchat, I delved right into my case. "Look, I know you think I'm a Paladin and all, but I'm not. I do know who is perfect, though," I said, smiling once before telling her—

"Beck is not chosen, Jericho," Sybil said simply.

Not going to lie, her cutting me off because she knew what I was going to say really ticked me off for some reason.

"Well, unchoose me, then," I said, agitated.

"That is not a real word," she informed me. "And I am sorry, but that is not how it works."

"Cut the crap, Sybil," I almost shouted. "Why don't you take a break long enough to tell me how it works, then?"

Her unfocused eyes never left me. "I tried to on your last visit here," she said, her voice sounding more edgy. "Since it would seem you have left your long-term memory functions in your reality, I must remind you that you declined most vehemently."

"Please tell me that was sarcasm."

The corners of her mouth twitched in that almost-smile thing. "It was."

"Look, can you explain to me why Beck won't work without giving me the entire rundown inside the Citadel?" I asked.

Sybil looked like she was thinking about that before she finally decided, "Beck is not a Paladin and, more importantly, she is not you. I will answer any question you have pertaining to Beck Sparks."

I took a deep breath, organizing my questions the best I could before I began.

"So Beck isn't a Paladin?"

"No," Sybil answered. "The way the world as a whole perceives Paladins is flawed, in the case that they only see power and nothing more. Beck is powerful; thus, you and your comrades believe she is like you for this, but she is nothing like you."

"How so?"

"I cannot tell you. The answer to that question pertains to you."

"She has Z-90 in her, just like me," I told her, not caring about her protocol. "She also has the same out-of-body experiences that I do."

For the first time since I'd met her, Sybil look confused. "What is Z-90?"

"You know, Z-90," I tried again. "The stuff that makes us Paladins."

Instead of a robotic answer, Sybil simply shook her head, almost looking sorry for me. "Flawed," she said. "You must come into the Citadel, Jericho. There is so much you do not know."

Now I was looking confused. "But Cross laid out the whole thing," I said, and Sybil took a step toward me suddenly.

"Socrates Cross?" she asked.

I frowned. "Uh, I never got his first name, actually."

"Confronting that man will start your Crusade. Are you not on your way to him now?"

"Yeah, but—"

"What about his younger brother, Archimedes Cross? Have you encountered him yet?"

I was shocked into silence. But when I finally regained words, I said, "I thought you could see everything that was going on with me since you were, like, my partner."

"Partisan."

"Whatever."

Sybil approached me. "I cannot at the moment. I had a good connection when you were in closer proximity with Stargazer and the Rogues or just Flagstaff, in general."

"Let me guess. Verizon?"

"What?"

"Never mind. What was the last thing you remember?"

Sybil reached up and put both of her hands on either side of my face, closing her eyes. "The last actual clear image I have," she said, "you were on your way to meet with Beck. I had bits and pieces of Vancouver, also."

I was stunned. "Whoa. That's way back there, Sybil."

"For some reason, the bond was strained when you met Beck, but it wasn't completely broken until you left Las Vegas, Nevada."

Vegas. The day I made a decision that I didn't want to be a Paladin. Oops. Sybil had picked that up last time I was here, actually, slapping me and calling me selfish.

"Why?" Sybil asked from out of nowhere. But I kind of knew what she was talking about.

"Can I level with you?" I asked.

"Certainly," she said, removing her hands slowly from my face.

I didn't have much to say except the truth. "Everything in my life that mattered is gone. I'm not even supposed to be here, Sybil. If I were this supposed chosen one, wouldn't I have been called to fix my time and not someone else's problem over three hundred years in the future?"

"Citadel. Now," Sybil said, and she sounded more human than I'd heard yet. "You know nothing, and that is dangerous."

I tried to pry more out of her for about five minutes, with no success. Finally, she said, "Why are you afraid to enter the Citadel?"

I sighed, walking away from her and putting my hands on my hips, clicking my tongue inside my cheek and glancing toward the huge ivory structure almost a mile away. I wanted to know what the heck was going on, really bad. Flying by the seat of your pants will only take you so far, I've learned.

"You said something about a crusade. Can you tell me about that?"

"Each Paladin is assigned a crusade," she said simply. "Crusades are assigned when time itself is in jeopardy."

"When did you say this crusade of mine will start again?" I asked, still looking at the Citadel.

"After you confront Socrates Cross," Sybil said.

"Why then and not now?"

"Things will be revealed that—" she stopped, catching herself.

I turned, smiling. "Ah, so you're really not a robot after all. I wish I would've known the last time I was here because I might have tried to seduce my answers out of you."

I was joking, of course, but Sybil didn't think it was very funny. Her cheeks burned and she faced the ground, her hands clasped tightly in front of her while she fidgeted her feet in the snow.

"Sybil, I was kidding—"

"I wasn't always like this," she said quietly while she lifted her face back up, and I hated myself. Of all the girls to mess with, a blind girl with an unfulfilled mission wasn't one of them. "I was a brilliant physicist during the first World War."

I was stunned. No, like, literally stunned with my mouth dropping open and everything. "How did you end up here?"

Sybil shrugged slightly and lifted one side of her mouth into a sad smile. "Dabbling too much in astronomy, probably." I didn't laugh because I wasn't sure if she was serious or not, and she continued, "I do not remember most of my life. Just bits and pieces. I do know that I was married, but I cannot remember his face nor his name."

I didn't say anything. Mainly because, well, I just didn't know what to say, but also because I know if I would've been stuck in one place for over four hundred years alone, I would've talked the first person I saw literally to death. But she didn't say anything else and just stood there, her hands still clasped together. I wasn't one for prying, but she did happen to know a lot about me, so I figured what the heck.

"Do you miss it?" I asked.

"What is to miss? I told you I do not remember my life before."

"What will happen to you when I finish my crusade?"

Sybil wasn't much of a shrugger. Just putting that out there. She looked like someone with all the answers, so when she was caught in the act of doing one of the most non-committal, no-answer gestures, it looked pretty odd. Shrugging, she said, "I am not entirely sure. It has been nearly four thousand years since the last Paladin was needed."

I stared at her in disbelief. "Come again?"

"What is it you are not understanding?"

"You're telling me that after four World Wars, countless genocidal acts, debauchery at every turn, and now is the time a

Paladin, who missed most of those, might I add, is needed?"

"You do not know what a Paladin is called to do, so I do not know how any of this could make sense to you."

I was quiet for a while after that, and I ended up staring at the Citadel again, mulling it all over in my head. "Do I have to go inside to get my powers back?" I finally asked.

"No," she answered.

"You said it was up to me," I said, looking back at her. "Can't you just give me a list or something that tells me how to go about getting them back, instead of giving me some crazy Zen junk to go off of?"

"I told you why your powers stopped on your last visit," Sybil said, and I thought she looked a little agitated about it still. "That is all I can tell you. You will just have to help yourself."

I scoffed in frustration, crossing my arms and shaking my head at that and was about to say something sarcastic until a thought struck me.

Help myself.

"Hey, Sybil, I got to run," I told her, walking quickly to her and grabbing her hands, placing them on my temples. "This has been very educating, though, so thanks."

Before I was gone, I saw Sybil smile an actual smile.

I sat up immediately in the dark cabin. "Beck, are you awake?"

When she didn't say anything, I said, "Look, if you're in super-sneak mode, get out of it because this is important."

"Fine," I heard her groan, rolling over and facing me. "What's up?"

"I think I know how to get my juice back."

Beck sighed and lay back on the bench. "Note to self, never take Jericho's level of importance seriously ever again."

"I think I know what me from the future came back to tell me," I told her, smiling.

"That you're going to die, I know," Beck said.

"No," I said. "He told me not to fight it."

Beck chuckled at that. "Well, yeah, did you see the shape future you was in, what with the loss of limbs and blood? I'd say, whatever you decide to fight a few days from now resulting in death should be avoided."

I was ecstatic. Everything made sense now.

Well, more sense than it had been making, anyway.

"I was talking about myself."

"Yes, you do that a lot."

"I meant me, from the future. I was talking about me."

I felt her signature frown in the darkness. "You were talking about fighting yourself?"

I thought about that, pulling one side of my mouth to the side and bobbing my head a little in an indecisive manner. "Yes and no. He was telling me not to fight the change. Like, the Paladin change."

Beck sat up again. "I'm not getting you at all right now."

So I explained it to her, talking for almost thirty minutes in the dark about everything I knew at that point. I started with the Blu incident, which Beck laughed at yet again, explaining how the ability to take over someone else's mind was frightening, to say the least, so I'd suppressed it in every way I could. I went on to Vegas then finished up with hijacking Beck's thoughts, leaving out everything pertaining to Sybil and the mysterious realm where the Citadel was located.

Once I was finished, I let out a breath, leaning back onto the bench and letting my head roll back a little. I felt good. Almost relaxed, for some reason, like the retelling of it all had, I don't know, taken something off my chest.

"Are you sure the taking-over-minds part wasn't what you were specifically talking about?" Beck asked, catching me off guard.

"What?"

It was light enough by this time, and I saw her shrug. "I mean, everything else about being a Paladin was kind of awesome, right?"

I wasn't sure where she was going with this. "Yeah, I

guess."

"So maybe future you was telling you not to fight just that part because that is what you're going to need most."

It made sense. Too much sense.

"Where'd that come from?" I asked.

She shrugged again. "I don't know. Just a thought, really. Maybe you should practice."

"I'll pass," I said, shaking my head. "If there was ever a part that was working fine it was—"

Don't fight it.

I stopped talking midsentence, Sybil's voice barely audible because it sounded far away.

You are going in the right direction, Paladin. Do not stop. Do not stop anything.

Not really sure if she could hear my thoughts or not, I aimed one back at her, stating that I didn't want to learn to control the minds of others or, worse, take over their bodies.

I am afraid you will not understand my description she said.

Then dumb it down, I thought.

Sybil was quiet for a few seconds. *It is all or nothing. Our connection is weak but restored because you are doing something right. You will need everything to complete your crusade.*

All or nothing, I thought, closing my eyes. *Then I'm in. Time to go big or go home.*

It was a moving moment in my mind. What with me taking a stand, and all that. Call it lame, if you like. All I know is that when I opened my eyes again, I was back, baby.

"Are you, like, thinking really hard, or something?" Beck asked.

"Something like that," I said quietly before standing. "Let's take a walk while everyone else is still asleep."

Beck swung her feet to the floor and pulled on a boot. "Sounds good, but Sloan has your long coat, so you'll have to swipe it somehow."

"No need," I told her, opening the side door and letting

the swirling morning snow smack me square on my bare chest and face. It felt awesome. "Wouldn't want to wake her."

Then I was off, dashing through the whiteness with nothing on but pants.

And I was loving it.

CHAPTER 53

"Hey, wait up," Beck tabbed in. "I want to see you running half-naked."

"Catch me, then," I told her, smiling while channeling the flow of energy into my legs. In moments they were overflowing with the brilliant volts of beautiful blue wonderment, melting the snow around me every time they sank into it.

I gave a loud, echoing whoop before I leaped into the air, soaring higher and higher before tucking myself into a ball, spinning all the way down and landing in the snow hard. I lay on my back almost a foot deep for a few minutes, relishing the power I could now feel flowing through me. I even made a snow angel just for kicks and was in the process of swiping a finger through the snow for the halo when Beck skidded to a halt beside me.

"Glad to see your artistic abilities are back," she said, curling a lip at my horrible snow angel. "Enough of that, though. Let's see that lightning, handsome."

I stood, looking down at my hands and curling them into fists, blue-white haze beginning to swirl around them while I let the power flow freely. "Check this out," I said, shooting the volts into each other and pushing them together, compressing it into the size of a baseball before rearing back and tossing it far away from us.

Beck's smile fell when it landed and didn't do anything.

"That's really something, Jericho."

Then I snapped my fingers and the miniature bomb went off, sending both of us flying backward from the force. "What did you do?" Beck said, scowling at me while dusting snow off her clothes.

"Sorry," I said, already back on my feet. "We were kind of close for that one, but you get the idea."

Beck stood and we walked up a small embankment, stopping at the top and watching the sun rise into the frigid morning sky. "This fixes everything," she finally said, and I looked at her.

"You're telling *me*," I said, shaking my head slightly and chuckling. "Don't know how we could've pulled off killing Cross without my powers, for real."

"You mean the powers he gave you."

It wasn't true, I knew that now. Everything Cross thought he'd achieved through his vast intellect had been planned for thousands of years, to hear Sybil tell it. I also couldn't help but think how strange it was that Stargazer hadn't been honest with me about the whole Paladin thing. I mean, wouldn't it have been easier to just tell me everything the first day he'd met me and skip the part where I'm ignorant of the truth for weeks before finding out?

Ah, well. I guess the guy had his reasons, being a Partisan or whatever. I'd ask Sybil about it later.

"Cross didn't do any of this," I told her, and she frowned at me. I wasn't sure how to explain it to her, since she was about as cynical as a person could be and still have all her limbs attached.

Hmm. Well, her limbs were fake because they'd been blown off years ago. Okay, I suppose she had some reason to be cynical.

"This is way bigger than Cross, the gauntlets, or any of it," I said. "I can't explain it all to you now, but I will after—"

"After we paint Anchorage red and take the world over?" Beck finished, smiling and cocking her head to the side slightly.

I smiled at that and nodded. "Sounds good. And thanks, by the way, for saving everyone's necks back in Vancouver."

Beck waved that off and extended her holowings, rolling her neck once. "Oh, you know, it was on my way," then she sprung into the air, kicking snow up all around me. "I'll catch you back at the car, Jericho."

I was about to sit down and finish watching the sunrise when Piper tabbed me. "Where are you?" She sounded worried.

"Got my mojo back earlier this morning," I said, selecting the spinning icon and making Piper's face tab in, floating above my forearm. "So Beck and I went to test everything out."

Piper's shocked face shifted to the left and another spinning icon appeared to the right of it. Frowning, I tapped it and Blu's face popped up beside Piper's.

"You got your powers back?"

"Yes, I did," I said, smiling. "Get your suit on and we'll build a snowman together."

"Or we could get back on the road," Blu said, and she looked tired for some reason. "If we don't die in the next few days, then I'll take you up on that snowman."

Before I could say that sounded good to me, I heard something behind me, and I glanced back. It had sounded like footsteps, but that didn't make sense considering the snow and heavy wind that would've masked almost any small noise like that.

Weak human.

My eyes widened. Who had I just heard speak? And who was calling me weak?

"Guys, I'm going to have to call you back," I said, logging out of the chat.

I will crush your bones.

Clearly whoever's thoughts I was picking up on wasn't the most upstanding of people. And his voice was really deep. I followed my footprints and ended up back at the top of the snow embankment, glancing left and right trying to get eyes on whoever was watching me.

"I don't know who you are, but if you come out now, I won't kill you," I said aloud.

No one jumped out of the snow or came out with their hands up, so to speak, but I did hear more thoughts.

Impossible, the deep voice said. *He cannot hear me.*

No, like, the voice was *insanely* deep. Like someone was doing a voice for a monster in a scary story they were telling.

"Actually, I can," I said, crossing my arms. "I'm not like normal people, pal."

He wears no clothes against the cold. His blood is strange and does not smell human.

Huh?

Whoa, hold on, he could smell my... blood? The strange way the guy spoke wasn't helping me exactly pinpoint whatever ethnic group he happened to be hailing from, but if I would've had a list of folks that could smell another person's blood from far away, it wouldn't have been very long at all.

Wait. What if it was the rotten people from Vancouver that had somehow followed us? I instantly lit up my hands. "Show yourself," I said. "And to think I was in a good mood this morning."

Something moved in my peripheral and I swung toward it, holding my hands up only to see nothing was there. Then I noticed the snow almost fifty feet away was shuddering slightly with movement, and I knew something was underneath the surface.

I kept my aim on the moving whiteness until it stopped. I don't really know what I was expecting. I mean, if someone or something was lurking beneath the surface of snow in negative twenty-degree weather, it couldn't have been just a regular guy out for a frigid stroll. So I guess you could say I was ready for something out of the ordinary to show itself.

Yeah, right.

The nose came out first, followed by a four-foot snout

with a long row of huge teeth adorning it. When the head had fully emerged, the wolf of the future shook his head once to rid any clinging snow to its dark skin, and its eyes found me. Lifting its lips, the thing let out a low growl.

I sidestepped slowly, keeping my hands aimed on the wolf, which by this time had pulled the rest of its massive body from the snow. It was a good twenty feet long and a lot taller than me, the thick ebony skin glinting in the white contrast all around it.

He is not human, the wolf thought, champing his mouth once in what looked like annoyance.

No, I'm not, I thought, and the wolf stood completely still, looking at me with a new interest.

I don't want to hurt you, I said to him, shutting off my hands. *You seem like an intelligent mammal, so why don't we shake hands and walk away?*

I grow tired of snow-cats. It has been a long time since I have tasted human flesh, he growled again and even barked. Well, it wasn't really a bark, per se, but more of a small roar.

"You said yourself that I'm not human, anyway," I told him. "Eat the next round of folks that pass through."

You are not human, but the ones who travel with you are.

Man, nothing got past that guy. "They're with me, wolf, and the kitchen's closed," I said, turning and walking away from him. "Go back to sleep, or whatever you were doing."

Looking back, I now know that turning my back on an ultra-wolf weighing almost two tons and rocking a crazy-feral taste for humans wasn't the smartest thing to do. It was probably because I had just been having an actual conversation with the beast that humanized him so much I wasn't afraid of him, maybe.

Anyway, bottom line is that when he rushed from behind and snapped his huge jaws on me, I was a little surprised. He'd attacked on my left side, so my head and right arm were hanging out of the side of his mouth when he crunched down and shook me hard.

It was scary, not going to lie. But after initial shock of the attack, I realized that it felt like I was being hugged by a sweaty person and not being chomped to death by a huge wolf.

I lit up my hands, my left jolting the crap out of him from inside his mouth while I clamped my right onto the beast's snout, turning the juice on.

The wolf whined in pain, shaking me harder and slamming his head into the snow again and again, trying to make me stop whatever I was doing. I was on almost full blast, so I was a little stunned that the wolf wasn't, you know, dying yet.

Just when the powerful animal gave one more shake before tossing me a hundred feet away, I remembered Beck telling me that these things could take a real beating.

Then I was airborne.

I screamed even though I wasn't in any kind of pain, and in my spinning and flipping, I caught sight of the wolf running below, his head looking up toward me and his ears perked up in expectation...

"You've got to be kidding me," I got out, before the wolf leaped into the air and caught me like a human Frisbee.

This time I felt a slight pain when one of the beast's many teeth punctured my right leg. I guess I wasn't as indestructible as I had thought, remembering that Red had been able to rip my arm clean off months ago.

It was time to end this little scuffle. Both my arms were free while my legs were inside the mouth being chewed on, so I had a few more things to try this time around. Grabbing the wolf's jaws, I pried hard, opening his mouth with some effort. Once my legs were free, I swiveled around and stood up, pushing the wolf's mouth open further and looking very cartoonish while holding it open. The wolf stopped thrashing around and just stood there, his head hanging low and his breathing rapid, and I was about to ask him if he'd had enough, when my accursed boots slipped on wet wolf tongue. I regained composure before I was swallowed, but just barely, and the beast and I resumed our standoff.

After about thirty seconds in I said, "You can't kill me."

False.

"It's true," I said, readjusting my footing again and peering down the throat in front of me. "Even if you swallowed me, I'd just tear my way out."

The wolf was silent, so I kept on. "We're kind of at a stand-still, here," I said. It wasn't that I was having a hard time holding his mouth open. But I was having a hard time trying to figure out how to get out without getting bitten again. "Look, if you're so set on killing me, how about you let me out so we can start over without you attacking from behind?"

Your words are meaningless and in too great a number.

Wow. I'd never been burned by an animal before. He'd just told me I was stupid and I talked too much in some ye old way of talking. I felt more pressure from his jaws and had to strain against them.

I do not fail in battle, non-human, nor do I engage in pointless talk in the middle of one. You will die by my fangs this day, non-human. Cease your struggle and give in to the inevitable.

I was about to say, "And *I* talk too much?" when I felt the first wave of heat come from the wolf's throat and hit me square in the face. At first I thought he was just breathing harder, but the next heat wave was pretty hot.

Really hot.

My eyes bugged when I saw the flickering light dance in the wolf's throat. The last thing I was thinking before the first fire funnel blasted into me was that I really wished I had been wearing a shirt.

I was shot out of his mouth like a smoking bullet, skidding on my back in the snow and melting it everywhere I touched. My foe wasted no time and jumped after me, his massive paws ready to crush me into the ground but colliding with the force field I'd thrown up instead, slipping off and slamming his head into it. I climbed to my knees about the same time the wolf did, and I took the few moments the beast was violently attacking the impenetrable bubble around me to take stock of my chest, which was horribly burned and hurt like Helheim.

The sizzling skin was starting to roll off my body, and there was nothing I could do but sit back on my knees and take deep breaths, my hands extended away from me like I was afraid for them to touch anything, while I tried not to gag on the smell of my own burning flesh.

My words are true. The wolf said to me, turning his head to the side so he could get and eyeful, noting my crisp condition. He didn't sound boastful at all but was merely stating that he had been right. And that, apparently, I was going to die by his fangs soon.

My head flew back, and I clamped my eyes shut, grabbing handfuls of snow, ready to smash them against me to try and stop the searing pain.

But the searing pain stopped on its own.

I opened my eyes and slowly dropped my gaze back to my chest, where my skin had already started to regenerate, the blackened muscles, sinews, and bones turning to a normal, healthy color. "Oh, crap. Oh, crap," I panted, not believing what I was seeing, while my body came back together, and in a matter of seconds, my chest was baby smooth.

The wolf had stopped growling and was watching the scene before him closely. I'm thinking he was shocked, but it's kind of hard to tell with wolves, you know. Especially huge ones with no fur that are trying to kill you.

"Well," I said, wonder evident on my face while I peered at my chest, touching the new skin, "that's a new one."

Impossible, the wolf said, and I could've sworn he shook his massive head slightly.

"Read 'em and weep," I said, getting to my shaky feet and hooking my thumbs at my regenerated chest. "Didn't see that coming, did you?"

The small victory felt big to me, since I'd been thinking I was about to actually die there for a few seconds, but I didn't have time to bask in the light of it because the wolf turned suddenly and loped away from me.

"Yeah, that's right, run, you wimp," I called after him, putting my hands on my hips. "Let me know the next time you want to get totally owned by—"

Then I realized the direction he was heading in at breakneck speed.

"Really?" I sighed, shutting down the force field and bolting after him. "Beck, come in."

She didn't answer. I flowed the juice into my legs and peeled out after the wolf, which was crazy-fast.

Faster than me.

So much for the glorious morning I was having. I hate the future. I tried to contact everyone back at the car with no luck.

"Un-freaking-believable," I said when Piper didn't answer her tab.

I always hated it when people never answered their phones. Mainly because, if you do have a smart phone, it's quite impossible to not see a text or at least a missed call.

So take that frustration and figure in holotabs—a device that literally is attached to your arm.

At. All. Times.

Yeah, I was a little upset no one was answering the phone, so I could tell them they were all about to die. No biggie, though, because I was gaining on the fowl creature with my acute swiftness and...

I couldn't even go close to the same speed as the black demon whose snow I was eating for breakfast, and I was going close to forty miles an hour, easy.

"Jericho," Blu chimed in. "Are you close to—?"

"Blu!" I shouted, glad but still annoyed that someone had finally glanced at, you know, their arm and decided to call me back. "Batten down the hatches, woman. There's a wolf heading your way."

"Wolf? Where?"

The armored car came into sight, and I noticed the wolf was a lot closer than I was. Thankfully, it looked like no one was outside frolicking, or something, and was safely tucked away inside.

A lone wolf can easily take out whole a squad of twenty armed and armored soldiers in a matter of minutes, Beck had told me before we left Flagstaff. *They can bite straight through just about anything, too, armored cars included.*

I wasn't fast enough, not by a long shot. The wolf would be tearing the car open in less than thirty seconds and I, with all my great powers, would arrive too late to save my friends. And even if I did save them, our only ride might be worthless after the attack.

You are a Paladin, Sybil's voice echoed in my mind.

"Nice time to finally weigh in, Sybil, but this guy's a lot stronger than I am," I said quickly, still running at top speed.

Physically, perhaps. But his mind is not.

"No way," I said, instantly knowing what she was suggesting. "What if—?"

You are almost out of time.

"I can't even touch him," I told her, watching the wolf close the last stretch to the car.

You do not have to, Jericho.

"How?" I asked frantically, not caring about anything but stopping the wolf when I saw him slow his speed for a collision with the car.

Sybil's next words were simple enough.

Super-sneak mode.

That was all the incentive I needed, switching to SS mode and letting my empty, speeding body crumple into the snow and slide and tumble while I closed my eyes and instantly appeared between the armored car and the wolf. I spread my arms wide as the monster phased through me, and then I was gone.

CHAPTER 54
Piper

"Get down!" Piper screamed, covering Sloan with her body while Arc and Blu huddled with her on the opposite side of the car awaiting the onslaught. Blu had gotten Jericho's warning too late, peering through the porthole and seeing the attacking wolf just moments before.

"Batten down the hatches," he'd told her, and they had all done the best they could, which wasn't much.

Piper closed her eyes, ready for the armored car to topple on its side, and when it didn't, she opened them again and glanced toward the porthole. Everyone in the cabin was silent, waiting for the oncoming attack. When nothing happened, Arc stood slowly and walked to the porthole, edging along the wall and leaning carefully to look outside.

"Well?" Blu asked in a whisper.

Archimedes shook his head and said, "It's just standing there."

"Why did it stop?" Sloan asked, removing her hands from her face and adding hopefully, "Maybe he's not hungry."

The wolf had put on a full stop just before attacking but was standing close, its huge body blocking most of the porthole that everyone was taking turns peering through.

"Where is he?" Piper asked, hitting her tab. "Jericho, come in."

The wolf moved then, causing her to give a start, and one

of its massive blue eyes came close to the round window and looked through it, flicking left and right before turning away from the armored car and walking back the way it had come.

When the beast was a good distance away, Archimedes' tab lit up and Beck said, "Where did this hellion come from?"

"We're not sure," he answered. "Jericho warned us just before it got to us, but it looks like it—I'm not sure. It's just leaving for some reason."

"It stopped," Beck said, and they could all hear the wind around her while she cut through the air above the wolf. "I'm trying to see what it's—oh, no," she gasped.

"What?" Piper asked.

"He's got Jericho," Beck said. "Watch out, he's heading back to your location."

Blu shoved everyone aside and took over the porthole viewpoint, watching the wolf that was loping back to them. When it was close, she saw Jericho's lifeless body in the wolf's mouth. Blu screamed and moved, thinking she could don her suit, but Arc grabbed her. "Wait," he said, glancing back toward to wolf, which was now right beside the car. "Something's not right, Blu. Why would he bring Jericho's body back when he could've eaten him in two bites?"

"What's it doing?" Beck asked in confusion. "It put Jericho on the ground."

Blu was in the middle of struggling with Arc when her holotab lit up with a message. She looked at it, and her brows furrowed. "Jericho?"

The message said:

Jericho: Would someone please get my body back inside? I can't open doors at the moment.

"What's wrong?" Piper asked her.

"I—I think he took over the wolf's body," she said, typing a message back.

Blu: Are you the wolf?

After a few seconds she got her answer.

Jericho: Took you long enough. Now, grab my body, tell Beck to chill out and follow me. I think I'm going to stay this way for a bit. At least the snow-cats will leave us alone.

Jericho's name turned dark, indicating he had logged off the holochat before Blu had the chance to ask how he was even able to message her in the first place, and the wolf, or Jericho, rather, turned his massive body and loped away.

"Jericho took over the wolf's body, and he's going to stay that way for a while," Blu said, all business now. "Arc, get his body and put it in one of the rooms. Beck, get back inside and take the wheel."

Beck seemed to be the only one beside Blu that wasn't completely floored by Jericho's latest commandeering, and after they had resumed their journey, with the enormous wolf now running in front of them, Arc said, "How is this even possible?"

But even though Beck and Blu had seen this before, that didn't mean they had an answer to that question.

"I've seen lots of wild stuff," Beck said, switching gears to keep up with the bounding creature. "Shouldn't even be alive as far as normal, everyday standards go. But Jericho?" she shook her head slightly. "He probably doesn't even know all he's capable of. God help anyone fighting against him when he finally does."

CHAPTER 55
Jericho

I ran for the next two days, stopping at night and curling up next to the armored car in wolf-mode. It was awesome, really, and some of the best sleep I'd had in months. It was a little disconcerting, though, that I could hear the wolf's thoughts about my using his body, and most of them weren't exactly nice. But, unlike stubborn humans, the wolf didn't talk non-stop and wasn't one to waste words on things he had no control over.

I messaged Blu every now and then via my, uh, mind, or something, and I wasn't sure how she was getting it, but it didn't matter, considering I could now hear her thoughts again and even had control over whether or not I chose to hear them. It was nice to be able to switch it off, let me tell you, but even after all the weeks of wishing I wouldn't pick up Blu's thoughts, I found myself listening to them more and more. Maybe it was because I'd gone so long without my powers that I wasn't as annoyed by old grievances concerning it, but there was a big possibility that I just wanted back inside her head.

My plan was to switch back to my normal body when we neared Anchorage, and my story was going to be that I just loved being a wolf, when in truth I really just wanted to avoid any drama inside the armored car. Even though most of them were now relaxed after I got my mojo back, there was still the uncomfortable static between Piper and I. Blu had been acting better since our make out session in Seattle, but then her sister gave her life to save us so, yeah, she wasn't herself by any means. Then there was Archimedes, the quiet guy who Piper had been with for a little over two years. He was hard to read, but at least he wasn't, I don't know, sarcastic or something.

Not to mention he was packing a big, game-changing secret.

How long will you require my body? the wolf asked me on the third night when I laid down. I hadn't been feeling as good that day and wasn't sure exactly why.

Just until we get closer to Anchorage, I told him.

I have not eaten in twenty-four days, non-human. When will you hunt?

So that's why I was feeling famished. Funny how missed-meal cramps feel different in enormous wolf bodies.

Hunt? Like, me go out, catch, kill, and eat something?

Does hunt mean anything else to you?

I was having a blast in wolf-mode but had doubts about killing a snow-cat and eating it.

Raw. With my huge mouth crunching on hair, bones...

If I let you go, what would you do? It was about time, I guess. We were about a day away from Anchorage, anyway.

I would hunt.

And you'd leave us alone?

You have proven that I cannot harm you nor your followers. I will hunt elsewhere.

That seemed good enough. But just before I severed the bond with the wolf's body, I had a thought.

Do you have a name? I asked.

No, was his reply. *I do not facilitate the need for names and titles. I am a wolf. If you must call me something, call me what I am.*

So, just Wolf, then.

Fitting.

He almost sounded sarcastic, something I never expected him to do. *How old are you?* I asked.

There are no more wolves like me, non-human. I remember the world before the snow and ice, when I was weak.

Since that would mean he was several hundred years old, I assumed by weak he meant when he was a normal wolf, if that was even possible. I was trying to get somewhere with him, though.

Okay, Wolf, here's the deal. You and I want the same things at the moment.

False, he said.

Hear me out, I told him quickly. *I'm about to enter a possibly hostile city and try to break into a fortified and for sure hostile mammoth lab/weapons facility filled with lots of people trying to kill me that I'll have to deal with.*

He didn't say anything, so I continued, hoping he was listening. *I can get in but my followers, as you called them, can't, and I won't be able to protect them.*

Get to your point, non-human.

I figure you and I could kick in the front door and deal with most of the opposition. That way my friends get in safely and you get to, uh, eat humans to your heart's content.

He was silent again. *What? You said you wanted to taste humans, right?*

Let me hunt now, and I will give you my answer upon my return.

Sigh. Oh, well. It was worth a shot. I knew he wasn't going to come back, and I didn't blame him. Wolf was hungry, and he'd just had his body hijacked for almost three days. Having Wolf's help would've rocked, considering he would've emerged with a full stomach and not a scratch on him. But I suppose he was sentient enough to decide his own fate.

Alright, Wolf, I said. *Have a good time hunting.*

Then I opened my eyes back in my body, instantly getting out of bed and heading for the main cabin. I peered through the porthole quickly, but Wolf had already vanished into the darkness. Blu, who'd been sharing the bed with me and Sloan, came into the main cabin. "What's wrong?"

I stood on the bench Beck had been sleeping on to get a better look out the round window, and I heard her grumble, "I'm going to kill you."

I sighed when I didn't see the wolf. "Just checking to see if Wolf really left or not."

"Wolf?" Beck asked, sitting up. "You let it go?"

"I let him go, yeah," I said. "He needed to eat a few snow-cats."

"Or get revenge on the slaving humans," Beck said, unconvinced.

"He won't," was all I said. "I'm going back to bed. Let's make our Anchorage plans in the morning."

Sleep came easy after I lay down on the opposite bench from Beck, who mumbled more obscenities about being woken up, before rolling over and facing away from me. I didn't visit Sybil that night, nor did I go into super-sneak mode, and for once, I awoke the next morning feeling refreshed and like I was finally getting the hang of my powers.

Then it was war council time.

"You can't attack Cross's facility for no reason," Archimedes threw out when we'd barely began. I knew why he felt that way but didn't want to bust him out about it. I had started out with the intention of killing Cross, getting my gauntlet back, and getting Piper home.

Now that I knew about Sybil and the whole Paladin destiny bit, the plans in my mind had changed slightly. Well, since I hadn't decided what I was going to do after sending Piper back, I guess you could say that I was adding to the plan.

"I have plenty of reasons," I said, crossing my arms. "First and foremost being he wanted to install a chip in my head and control me like a puppet. But he has my gauntlet, which I need. If he's level-headed enough to give it to me without a fight, then fine. If not, I won't lose any sleep over killing him for it."

"He also supplies weapons to warring factions," Piper added.

"Thus keeping everyone else caught in a never-ending

struggle for survival," Beck said. "Cross has to go."

Blu even weighed in. "This is also the man responsible for the trackers installed in most Rogues. Most of them lose limbs to keep their families safe."

"He's a scientist," Archimedes tried. "I agree with Jericho on this. Let me go in first and I'll talk to him."

Beck waved that off. "Yeah, like the almighty Cross is going to give the obsolete archeologist an audience."

If you only knew, I heard him think, and I glanced at him.

"I don't know," I said, my arms still crossed. "Old Arc here might be our best ticket in if we're trying to avoid a fight."

"We've been planning for a fight since the start," Beck said, looking at me like I'd just suggested we all be friends and sing kumbaya until judgment day. "He wanted to literally control you, and he could have if you hadn't found out about it. He's dangerous, Jericho. The world will be a much better place without him."

Archimedes looked like he wanted to say something else but stopped himself, dropping his gaze to the floor of the car.

"Beck's making all kinds of sense, Arc," I said to him. "If you're into saving tyrants, you're going to need better reasons than she's bringing to the table."

It was kind of harsh of me because of what I knew, but I gave him a chance. If he'd have just told everyone about Cross being his brother, then I wouldn't have had to bust him out in front of everyone.

"So, tell me," I began, leaning back in my chair and lacing my fingers behind my head, looking at him. "Is Cross the older brother or are you? He seems older to me."

Silence followed while my words sank in, and all eyes turned to Arc, who was looking quite shocked.

"I have no brother," he finally said.

You can lie to everyone in this car except me, I thought, aiming into his mind and giving him the scare I was hoping for, raising an eyebrow when he looked at me.

"Is this true?" Piper asked, and I could tell Arc was

heading for the doghouse after this council was over.

Archimedes could see that he wasn't lying his way out of this one. His head hung slightly, and he nodded.

All of us reacted differently.

Piper looked away, not knowing what to say. Blu took a step back, in case he tried anything rash. Sloan frowned, switching her gaze around the faces present and not getting anything going on at all. Before I dropped the bomb about the Cross brothers, though, I forgot how tight Arc had been with Beck before Piper had come along. I also forgot that Dr. Cross had been trying to get his hands on Beck Sparks for a while.

Random side note: I'm fast, like, ridiculously so, because there aren't many things out there that come close to my speed anymore.

Except Beck, of course. Who, needless to say, didn't take the treacherous news well and attacked Arc.

The most frightening part about me not being quick enough to stop her, though, was that I knew she would do what she did, and I thought I would've been ready to grab her.

But somehow, even in all my, uh, awareness, I guess, of the situation, Beck was somehow able to bypass my acute sense of, you know, things…

Forget it. Point is, Beck grabbed Arc and threw him like a ragdoll toward the back of the car, screaming obscenities before trying another charge. This time I grabbed her, slipping my hands under her arms before putting my hands on the back of her neck, prison-guard style.

"Easy, Beck," I said, struggling to keep a hold on her. "Let's try and talk about this like adults."

"*You* talk like an adult," she said dangerously. "I'm going to kill him."

"It's not like that, Beck," Archimedes gasped out from where he'd landed on the floor after slamming against the far wall. "I would never have betrayed you. I haven't seen my brother in ages."

"Then why go to Anchorage every year?" Piper cut in.

Blu, who seemed to be the only civil one left among us, walked to Archimedes and knelt to help him up. "It's a long story."

Beck scoffed at that. "Why is it that people automatically think that by saying a story is long they won't have to tell it?"

I released her when I felt she wasn't going to rip Arc's head off, but I stayed close to her just in case.

"There isn't much to tell," Archimedes said once he'd gotten to his feet.

"You just said it was a long story," Sloan said with a frown.

Beck smacked the little girl in the back of the head. "I just told you why people say that, genius."

Call us too preoccupied by the current situation to care, but no one said anything to Beck for her pointless reprimand of the six-year-old.

"My brother and I wanted to save the world, once upon a time," Arc started, walking back to us with a slight limp. "We parted ways years ago when we saw that our goal may have been the same, but our methods differed in every way possible."

"I've seen your brother's so-called *methods* firsthand, Arc," I said. "But you're an intelligent guy, so something tells me that moral grounds wasn't the deal-breaker for you."

Archimedes sat down at the table and leaned back, sighing with relief like he hadn't sat in months. Ramifications from Beck's love tap, no doubt.

"Socrates always had a clear vision of a new world. One that was free from war, starvation, poverty and, most importantly, ice. No, I didn't leave my brother's side because a few test subjects died inhumanely. I left because somewhere along the line in his quest, Socrates discovered true power and forgot who he was and what he was fighting for."

"I see," I said.

"No, I don't think you do," Archimedes said with a hint of sadness. "There was a time when my brother stood for the same things you do. But now he's become the very thing he set out to stop, yet he still says he's trying to make the world a better place."

"Hitler said the same thing," I told him, unconvinced.

"Cross's morals, or the lack thereof, mean nothing to me because at his lowest, he was probably leaps and bounds ahead of me on the morality scale," Beck said. "What I want to know is why you go to Anchorage every year if you're supposedly not speaking to your brother over petty issues."

"Beck, you know me—"

"No, I don't,"

"You never even asked why I was going. Like, ever," he said, leaning forward.

"You always said it was because of your work," Piper said, not sounding exactly sympathetic to her boyfriend.

Archimedes didn't say anything and kept his eyes on the holomap and layout of Anchorage. It looked to everyone else like he was guilty for not speaking, but I knew different because I was listening to his thoughts. I guess I could've tried touching him in super-sneak mode and getting his whole life on file, but I decided that it wasn't fair, considering he hadn't given me a lot of reasons to mistrust him.

The whole Piper thing aside, I could really see myself starting to actually like this guy. He was obsessed with history, liked blondes, and was American. Plenty of reasons to want to grab a coffee or play Halo with someone, as far as I'm concerned.

He wasn't a mole, though, that much was certain. And since he didn't seem like he was going to try to defend himself in any way, I decided to do it for him.

"It is for his work," I said, keeping my gaze on him for a second before glancing at Piper and Blu across the table. "He has a mole in Cross's lab that—" I stopped, listening for more information before I blinked and half-smiled, chuckling and shaking my head. "Ritu. Looks like you and Arc had the same contact, Beck."

Archimedes looked at me in mass confusion. "How are you doing this?"

Shrugging, I said, "Just listening in on your thoughts whenever I think I need to."

All eyes turned to me. Oh, yeah. I guess I hadn't exactly made that common knowledge yet. "Don't worry, guys," I said, holding my hands up. "I can control it now."

"When were you *not* controlling it?" Blu asked quickly.

Oops. "Uh... since our lab incident."

"So, you've been hearing my thoughts for weeks, and you never even thought to mention it?"

"How many of us have you been spying on?" Piper asked, and she looked ticked.

What had happened? Arc was just in the hot seat, but now I was somehow in it. "Okay, first off, I just learned how to actually eavesdrop on someone's mind a few days ago. Before then it was just Blu, and I haven't even heard hers since Vegas."

"Can you hear mine?" Beck asked, and all inquiring eyes glanced at her. I'd forgotten about touching her in SS mode.

I couldn't. I hadn't actually thought about it until then. "No," I said simply.

"Why not?"

I shook my head. "I'm not sure."

"See, people?" she said. "And they all said not being human wouldn't pay off."

I heard the wolf's thoughts. It had to be something else, but I wasn't about to mention it. Time to get Arc back in the crosshairs.

"So, what's up with Ritu?" I asked him, sitting at the table and making a point not to meet the gaze of anyone else. "She kind of helped me escape Cross's facility in Flagstaff."

Archimedes nodded and his expression was odd. "I was the one who gave the order. I'm glad she didn't get tossed out of window or anything."

"Hey, cut me some slack. I thought she was double-crossing Beck."

"There was no way possible for Ritu to keep in contact with Beck, and Socrates not know about it," he said. "He had to know about her exchanges and think he was in control of it."

Beck had her arms crossed and a disgusted look on her face. "Whose contact was she first?"

"Mine," Archimedes said, almost wincing. "She and I share the same goal of seeing Cross fail at his mission."

"News flash, pal," I broke in. "I'm his mission, and he kind of already succeeded at it."

He shook his head slightly. "Not anymore, you're not. The last time I contacted Ritu, before I got taken captive in Vancouver, she was headed for Anchorage via hovercraft. She told me that Cross had to start from scratch after you escaped, but he had basically gotten everything he needed from you prior to that. Whatever he was working on was big, and he was almost done."

I clicked my tongue inside my cheek in thought before saying, "I thought he wanted to control my mind or whatever."

"You sort of checked out before that step. Also, he wanted to find out if he could sway you without it. Mentally stationed subjects are great with motor skills and basic orders but must be assessed constantly to maintain the link, since the science behind such a project isn't exactly viable just yet."

"I thought you said this guy was an archeologist," I said to Beck.

"Aspiring," Archimedes said, and he got that strange smile on his face again. "Alas, there aren't many imprints for the trade these days, so I'm learning the old-fashioned way."

"Why free Jericho?" Blu asked.

"Ritu never gave me the details on my brother's test subject but said he was vital to his plans. So I told her to spring him."

"I sprung myself, thank you."

"Keep telling yourself that, pal," he said.

Chump.

"Attacks don't suit you. Go back to being the nice new

boyfriend, Arc."

"Ex," Piper said, leaving the table and heading for her battle-armor. "Finish planning our attack without me."

No one really knew what to say while she powered up her suit and exited the car.

"Way to go on fighting for her," Beck said.

"She'll come around," he said confidently. "I didn't lie to her about anything."

"Her coming around might be a little more anfractuous than you think," I said unconfidently.

"I've actually known her longer than you," he said, not sounding aggressive but just honest. "She'll come around, trust me."

"What do you do in Anchorage?" Beck asked.

Archimedes opened his mouth to speak, but I spoke first. "He runs a sort of underground uprising, if you will, that has been planning on—what?—overthrowing Cross, or something?"

The other Cross in front of me shook his head. "It's more complicated than that."

"What is his plan, exactly?"

"Socrates believes that sacrifice is the only way to fix the world. But what he simply labels as sacrifice, everyone else labels as genocide. Supplying weapons to warring factions was merely to keep them busy so he'd have time to finish his work." He looked uneasy and shifted in his seat before saying, "I'm not sure what he's planning, but whatever it is, it can't be good. I do know, however, that he can't be far from his goal being full term."

I studied him. "And why can't we kill this maniac, again?"

I've never had any siblings, nor did my adopted parents have any kids of their own, so I couldn't put myself in Arc's position.

But I sure as Helheim could read his mind, and it was a pretty conflicted affair.

"He's my brother," Archimedes finally said, closing his eyes and taking a deep breath. "Regardless of all the pain and suffering he's caused others; I don't want him dead."

"If we go in guns blazing, we can't guarantee anything," Beck said, unimpressed by Arc's brotherly love.

"That's why I want to go in first," he tried again, standing and hitting his holotab. A layout of the city of Anchorage appeared on the table and he said, "Socrates' facility takes up almost a quarter of the entire city. Getting a small team in without detection wouldn't be hard, but anything after that would be difficult. Most of his guards are synthetic and registered to the holocomputers on the third floor of the center building."

"We could go under," Blu said, hitting her own tab and shifting the map below.

Arc shook his head. "There isn't an entrance from below. We've been trying to find one for some time."

"So we kick down the front door," Beck said once again. "Jericho and I can't be stopped, so this entire meeting is basically moot."

This caused an argument between everyone around the table, and I looked at Cross's base. Geez, but it was a big place. Lots of places to house hidden guards, but also lots of places to hide. Beck was right about us kicking down the door, I knew. We were an unstoppable force when together and both of us running on all cylinders.

But then there was Archimedes not wanting his brother killed. Although I could understand that to a certain extent, I also couldn't promise anything. Cross wouldn't be one to just step down and allow himself to be taken into custody, that much I was certain, but I knew he couldn't do anything but what I said, once I actually made it to him. The real problem was all the guards we would be going through.

I sighed, rubbing my forehead. What we really needed was a diversion. Like a big, undeniably massive diversion.

I have finished hunting, non-human.

My eyes widened. "Everyone, shut up," I shouted at my companions, causing confused glances while I stood up quickly and cocked my head to the side to listen.

"How was it?" I said aloud, directing my thoughts to Wolf.

Snow-cats are snow-cats, Wolf growled. *I yearn for the taste of human blood.*

It was strange to hear an animal try and hint at something, and I smiled but didn't say anything. After a few seconds of silence, the wolf finally spoke.

You aforementioned a place I could have my fill of humans. When will this happen?

"Hold, please," I said, glancing at Arc. "How far are we from Anchorage?"

Archimedes blinked at me for a second before saying, "Uh, we'll be there tomorrow."

"Great, thanks," I said, nodding. "It'll happen tomorrow, Wolf. You in or out?"

Wolf growled again, but this time it sounded throaty and expectant.

I am.

"Awesome. Stay outside tonight, and we'll leave in the morning."

Tell your human compatriot in white armor she can return without my attacking.

Piper. I'd forgotten about her. "Hey, Pipe," I tabbed her.

"Jericho, your wolf is back," she answered. "Do your thing and make him leave so I can come back."

I walked to the hatch door and opened it, stepping outside into the crunching snow. Wolf was close by, his massive head turned and his left eye on me. He wasn't growling for once, and I took in the size of his frame while I crossed to him.

"He won't attack, Piper, you can head back," I said, stopping in front of him. "Lordy, you're big."

And you are small, he said, shifting to the left, crouching slightly and moving his head closer to me. *What is your name, non-human?*

"Jericho," I answered. "Welcome aboard, Wolf. I look forward to a long relationship between us."

As do I, Jericho. If at any time you need this body, it is yours to command so long as you honor our agreement.

I held up my hands when he lifted his lips and growled low. "Listen, man, if you stick with me, by the time I'm done with my quest, you're going to be so sick of humans you just might miss the snow-cats."

He snorted. Like, really actually snorted, shaking his big head once. *False.*

Piper gingerly walked up beside me then, and Wolf eyed her when she lifted her face mask and peered at the beast in wonder. After almost two minutes of stunned silence, she finally asked, "What is it?"

I reached up and laid a hand on the thick, pitch black skin of his snout and gave it a scratch before answering her.

"An undeniably massive diversion."

CHAPTER 56

I'd never been to Anchorage in the past. I guess because I never really had a desire to go. After seeing it in the future, though, I kind of wished I would've dropped by at least once. Vancouver had been different, but the little bit of knowledge I'd had from my previous visit had helped some.

The entire city was surrounded by a metal wall much like Seattle had been, but with a lot less security. Wolf had hung back about two miles from the gate, burrowing into the snow and basically telling me to call him when it was suppertime. Archimedes said he'd take us to a safe house within the city walls where we would wait until dark for our assault on Cross's facility.

Arc drove and flashed some sort of badge to one of the two guards posted beside the tall entrance, and we were in, navigating the semi-busy streets of Anchorage. I was in the passenger seat, taking it all in, when Archimedes suddenly said, "I don't know Piper better than you, Jericho."

I was a little taken aback, and I glanced behind us to make sure Piper and, well, anyone else was out of earshot. "You probably do, man."

He shook his head. "I don't. I'm sorry about everything that's happened between the two of you, but now that you're back, I think she feels conflicted—"

"Are we really going to talk about this right now?"

"—and that she's making a mistake with me."

"Because, you know, I'm not trying to take her from you."

"You want her to go back home," he said, giving me a side glance before hanging a right onto a wide alleyway.

"She was stranded here because of me," I told him, keeping my eyes forward. "I'm not going to tell her what to do, but I am going to give her the option."

"Do you love her?"

Of all the times he could've picked to have this conversation, now was definitely not it.

But, since he'd brought it up, and I hadn't talked about it to anyone else...

"It doesn't matter, Arc," I told him, shaking my head and looking out the passenger window. "Piper and I are never going to be the same. Heck, after we finally gave into feelings, we didn't even have a full day together before I got blown up three years ago, and while I was unconscious and under your brother's knife for almost two and a half of those, she was alive and with you. You do know her better than I do, but I have to give her a chance to go back home. That much I owe her, whether you understand or not."

Archimedes nodded before asking, "And if she wants to be with you?"

Dang it all to Helheim and back, but nothing ever got past this guy. And that was the part I didn't want to talk about.

Or was it? Every time I thought about what Piper did or didn't want, I always pushed it out of my mind because of Blu. I'd told her I'd get back to her on all her advances after we stopped Cross.

But now I wasn't so sure. Arc cut into my thoughts before I could dwell too much.

"We're here," he said, pulling our armored car into the parking lot of what looked like a warehouse of some kind. I frowned when I saw it bustling with life, because I expected the entrance to an underground secret society to be a little more incognito.

Arc must have seen my gaze because he chuckled and said, "It's underneath. The plant on top is our cover."

"How very *Schindler's List* of you," I said dryly.

"Wait here with everyone. I need to go inside beforehand to verify space, and to let my comrades know I'm here. Shouldn't be longer than ten minutes."

I stood after he left, and I headed to the back rooms, passing Beck, who was asleep on the bench. I went to open the door to the room Sloan and Blu were sleeping in, but hesitated. I turned around and knocked on Piper's door instead, telling her we'd arrived.

When she didn't answer, I had a quick vision of her sneaking out of her porthole window at night for some reason. I opened the door quickly, just in time to see her pull her black tank top on, her muscled back exposed for a second. I tried to drop my gaze only to realize she was in her underwear and then I had to avert my eyes. "S—sorry," I stammered.

"Glad to see you're good at kicking down doors," she said, turning to face me while pulling her long, white-blonde hair out of the shirt she'd just put on. "Your plan should work brilliantly tonight."

Piper didn't seem the least bit bothered by being half-naked in front of me so I tried to act as cavalier about the whole situation as she was—which wasn't easy.

"We need to talk," I told her, pulling the door shut.

"Whatever do we need to talk about?" she asked sarcastically, sitting on her bed. "Surely not us."

"Do you want to go home?" I asked suddenly, and she froze, her eyes locked on the floor.

"Why do you care?"

I wanted to cross the room, kneel in front of her and grab her hands in mine to show her how much I meant was I was about to say. But, as stated, she was just strutting about in a tank and panties and I didn't think it was the best idea. So I just spoke from my spot near the door. "I screwed up your whole life, and I want to fix it."

She was silent for a moment, her eyes fixed in front of her, before she finally said, "If you wouldn't have taken me with you on Svalbard, I would've died with Bjourn. You don't owe me anything."

"I could've taken you back. You knew your time was safe from Klaus's plan. Why didn't you even ask me about going back?"

Piper looked at me then. "You know why."

I smiled. "Yeah, but I just wanted to hear it."

"Jerk," she said, smiling and turning her head back from me.

I nodded before saying, "Archimedes is head over heels for you, Pipe."

"If he were, he wouldn't have lied to me,"

"He didn't lie he just didn't—"

"Cross has killed lots of Rebels, Jericho. He also tried to capture Beck on several occasions, and Arc was there the entire time."

"You heard him yourself. He didn't even have contact with Cross at the time and, since I, uh, you know, read his mind I know he wasn't lying. Even if he had come clean about everything, what difference would it have made?"

"Why are you so worried about it if you want me to go back to Svalbard?"

I shook my head slightly. "I never said I wanted you to. Just that I wanted you to have the option. Who knows, maybe Arc would go back with you."

Piper stood and crossed the room and I attempted (and sort of failed) to avert my eyes again as she took her white jumpsuit off the back of a chair and stepped into the legs. When she'd finished and zipped it up to her chin, I asked, "So Arc's completely off the table?"

Piper shrugged and headed for the door, which I opened and stepped out of. "That depends."

"On what?" I asked.

"Not sure. I'll let you know in an hour."

Archimedes came to get us fifteen minutes later, tapping on the hatch in his armored hand and telling us all to suit up and roll out. Arc didn't have a suit of battle-armor, and since we weren't exactly swimming in the things before we picked him up, he'd worn my mega-thermal long coat inside and came back out in a shiny black suit of armor with a transparent helmet with a wicked cool heads-up display crawling all over it, masking whoever was wearing it with all the information the pilot needed to operate the thing.

The walk to the warehouse was an interesting one because, although it wasn't a busy neighborhood, there were still folks tromping through the streets in armor and some jogging between buildings in layers upon layers of clothes. Sloan wore my coat while sitting on the right shoulder of Blu's Raptor-6. Piper and Archimedes brought up the rear, and Beck and I walked between all our suited friends. I drew more attention than anyone in my thin, dark gray jumpsuit because Beck at least had on her long coat with the hood, while I looked to be strolling quite leisurely in the frigid elements.

Archimedes took the lead, and we followed him into the massive double doors when they opened inward and a heat that could only come from a machine shop rolled out.

It was a pretty spacious joint, I noticed, peering up at the three stories of assembly lines, conveyor belts, and robotic arms piecing together all sorts of unrecognizable things. Blu looked like a kid in a candy store when she lifted the face of her helmet and glanced around in wonder.

"This plant primarily builds heavy duty motors for anything larger than an S-20 or a manned dreadnaught," Arc said, walking his suit down the only clear path toward the opposite end of the building. "I'll show you where we can store our suits then we'll get below."

"Who runs this place?" Blu asked him, her head still looking like it was on a swivel.

"Fellow by the name of Mit Kiser. He's a little old and on the cranky side, but he's manageable. Not to mention he's a large part of the underground movement—and not just because we live under his business."

After a short walk we reached a sort of weigh-in station or something, and all my comrades sporting suits hung a left and stowed their battle-armor in a handy sectioned-off area that resembled a small parking lot.

We climbed into an elevator that was a little farther down, and then we were sailing to the basement.

Or the center of the earth, maybe, because we seemed to descend for an alarmingly long time, and we weren't exactly going slowly, either. Again, my face gave me away to Archimedes, and he said, "It's not too much farther down. We have to be deep or else topside patrols could pick us up on their scanners."

I nodded but left the foreboding grimace on my face. I'm not one for underground stuff. Just FYI. I mean, the Rogue base was beneath the surface but not, like, *deep* beneath it and not at all a place to instantly trigger one's claustrophobia.

When the elevator finally reached bottom and the doors opened, Arc led us into the—well, I wasn't sure. The place where people conspired in the dark against the system, I guess. It was a lot smaller than the machine shop we'd just been through, and there wasn't as many guns and battle-suits as I was expecting.

"We're not a military operation, by no means," Archimedes said humbly, while his boots rang out on the grate below our feet. It looked like the area had been hollowed out and the grates dropped on the ice so people wouldn't slip and slide around. There were a few cabin-like structures made of metal thrown up on one side of the place and what looked like a makeshift (only, Arc informed me that it had been there quite a while) war room type area that covered the opposite side of the cavern.

All in all, I wasn't impressed.

"Let me guess," I mused, turning in a circle once when we'd stopped in the center on the cavern. "The massive army is just on the other side of the ice wall. Good call, Arc. Wouldn't want to clutter the place up with powerful weapons to defend yourself against the hordes of a mad scientist or anything."

Shrugging, he said, "Like I said, we're not a military op. Thanks to Ritu, though, we do have a detailed layout of the inside of Socrates' facility."

Beck, who had been relatively quiet for a while, asked, "Why wait for dark to attack?"

"It'll take a few hours to go over the layout, anyway," Archimedes said. "But also, attacking in broad daylight just doesn't make sense."

We all either nodded or grunted in agreement. Then we followed him through the meager camp to the tables littered with holocomputers.

Sloan suddenly grabbed my hand. "I don't like being underground."

"Me either," I told her. I had kind of forgotten about the six-year-old being with us and made a mental note to make sure she didn't accidentally come with us while the grownups were delivering swift justice on Cross.

I hope they don't die, I heard her think. *I really like Blu.*

Me, too, I thought, glancing in Blu's direction. She really was great. Dedicated, big-hearted, a genius, and beautiful. I still felt horrible about her sister's death, but since she hadn't laid blame on me, I was starting to feel myself being more drawn to her.

Romance, though, happened to be the furthest thing from my mind at the time because, if somehow our mission failed that night, I wasn't going to get the chance of cultivating a healthy relationship with, well, anyone.

There were five men working at the computers when we got there, and one of them, an older guy with a graying goatee, glanced up and shook his head before addressing Arc.

"You're late, boy," he said in heavily accented Russian.

"Everyone, I'd like you to meet Mit Kiser," Archimedes said, sweeping his hand to the frowning man who pushed himself from his holodesk and stood, looking at each of us with narrowed eyes.

"A pleasure, sir," Blu said, extending a hand to him.

"And who might this lot be, Arc?" Kiser asked, accepting Blu's hand. "More recruits for the good fight, I hope."

Archimedes shrugged slightly before saying, "More or less. This is Blu, Beck Sparks, Piper, the little one is Sloan, and this is Jericho Johnson."

"Well met, all," Kiser said with a nod in our direction. "Why are you here?"

"We're here to take care of your Cross problem," Beck said, folding her arms.

"Good," he said, smiling for the first time. "We only just obtained the layout of Cross's facility, but we have our best on it. Rest a while and give us time to form a plan of attack."

"We already have one," I said to him. "Just point us to the front door."

Kiser watched me closely with more narrowed eyes. "I take it you're not an average soldier, no?"

"No."

"Cross has changed out his garrison this past week in anticipation of your arrival, Jericho," he said, turning back to his holocomputer. "He now has a base filled to the brim with Synners and all of their uncanny weapons and arts. You were expecting this, no?"

Great. Of course, some of the only people that would keep us from busting in like a couple of superheroes would be guarding the place. "No, I wasn't. Guy's a bit paranoid, they tell me."

"They told you right," Kiser said, sitting back in his chair. "Archimedes is the only reason I haven't tried bombing his lab from the start—it probably wouldn't have worked, anyway. I don't know what you're planning on doing with him, but so long as his grip on this city is gone when the day is out, I will have no complaints about how you take out the garbage."

"How long on the layout?" Blu asked.

"Soon. Less than two hours, maybe," one of the other men on the holodeck told her.

"Rest," Kiser told us again. "God knows you are all going to need it."

The room Arc put us up in was nice, for being fathoms below the earth's surface, I mean, but none of us were able to even think about sleeping or lying down. It was spacious, though, and the furniture was comfortable.

"Bloody Synners," Blu said from next to me on a couch, shaking her head while fanning through her holotab.

"What kind of weapons do they carry, again?" I asked. "No one really explained it to me."

"Most advanced troops carry an electromagnetic pulse rifle or handgun these days. A simple design like that could stop a normal synthetic soldier but wouldn't even slow you down. A Syn's true weapon is a certain type of ammo they develop themselves that no one else supposedly knows how to make." My tab lit up when she sent me a video to watch. I selected the swirling icon, and footage of Synners in action appeared. They were dropping people who looked to be an uprising like flies.

"This was five years ago in a lab in New York. A scientist uploaded a virus into a group of synthetic officers, and they attacked. The Synners were called, and in less than ten minutes, the pieces of over two hundred S-Class synthetics were everywhere."

It was really something to watch. Whenever one of the Syns fired off a shot, they would hit about five of six robots from the aftershock.

"They keep their ammo formula a secret, more out of extortion than anything," Beck said, lounging across from us on a loveseat, her hands behind her head and her eyes fixed on the ceiling. "If anyone has a massive synthetic problem, then they can only call one place."

"I thought you guys said they were bounty hunters or something," I said, freezing the vid then pinching and zooming in over the battlefield in front of me to get a closer look at the white-armored mercenaries.

"They are, most of the time," Blu told me. "Gigs like the one they're doing for Cross are rare for them because they make more on the road in the wastes and badlands where they find most of their prey trying to evade society. They know the patterns and protocols of all types and subtypes of synthetics, so catching them isn't much of a problem. Cross must be paying them a massive amount of holos to stay here."

"What about their armor?" Piper asked from the table she was sitting at, her elbows on it and her fingers laced beneath her chin.

Blu pulled her mouth to one side while she tabbed information. "Looks to be pretty standard stuff. More of a uniform than battle-armor, really."

"Then they'll bleed like other men," Piper said.

"If Cross hired them, he knows we're coming; therefore, he's more ready for us than we are for him," Beck said, surprising me because odds had never been something she had particularly worried about much. "So, a surprise attack is what he'll be expecting, and he won't be looking for anyone to come ring his doorbell—which is what we need to do."

Blu closed her tab out and leaned forward, putting her elbows on her knees and staring hard at the floor. "If anyone tries that, they'll be cut to ribbons in seconds from gunfire."

With a sort of calmness, I was looking at the current move Cross had played. Because while everyone else was pulling their hair out over an army of Synners, I was thinking about my new point man, whom everyone seemed to have forgotten.

"I wouldn't say everyone would be cut to ribbons," I said, closing my eyes and sending out a mental message up through the ground and miles across the snowy landscape.

"Jericho, Synners are designed to kill people like you," Blu said.

My message was received, and a neural link established.

Is it time, Jericho? Wolf asked.

"Not me, Blu," I said, smiling. "But I know a guy."

CHAPTER 57

In about three minutes, I had briefed my teammates on my plan, and in about an hour, we were called to the war room.

"Cross's base, as you all know, is only three stories tall but honeycombs down almost ten stories below," Kiser said, activating his tab and switching the power point screen we were all watching. "Our only contact inside wasn't able to respond to any of our messages but was able to confirm that the Synners will only be on the top levels, due to Cross not wanting prying eyes in his labs. Cross knows there are no access points from below, so all his firepower will be trained on top," he finished, nodding to me. "You had a plan, you said?"

I stood and walked to the map of the first three stories, the entrance being the most prominent on the screen. Not many people were gathered for the briefing, and I realized that since not many were going, then not many needed to know the scoop. "The courtyard is where Cross most likely plans for all of us to die, so that's why I'm sending in an, uh, associate of mine first to get the attention of every last Synner in the place."

Archimedes let out a sigh of relief. "Thank you, Jericho. I'm glad you considered my—"

"Yeah, not you, Arc, sorry," I said, shaking my head. "I'm sending in Wolf."

"Boom," Beck said, nudging Arc, who was looking at me in confusion. "Didn't see that coming, did you?"

Kiser inquired who Wolf was, and in about two minutes

(man, I was really getting good at the how-we-first-met story about Wolf), I had fully informed Kiser, as well as everyone else present, of my wild plan.

"I know what one wolf is capable of, Jericho," Kiser said in an unconvinced tone. "How can you be sure he won't wreak havoc in the rest of the city?"

"He won't," I assured him. "He and I have an agreement of sorts."

"That's your plan?" Kiser asked, stroking his short goatee thoughtfully. "Just to drop an unstoppable wild animal into the mix to bide you time to get to the lower levels?"

I thought about it, making sure my plan wasn't more elaborate than that. "Yeah, that's pretty much it," I said.

"Half-cocked," Archimedes said.

"Dangerous," Blu said.

"Kind of crazy," Beck said, even though she was supposedly on my side with this.

"I love it," Kiser said, surprising everyone. "My only regret is that I won't be there to see it. My men and I will be able to offer support from right here once Blu gets in the lab and uploads our bypass measures. In theory, you won't get to a door we can't open for you."

"That'll for sure come in handy," I said, then turned back to my comrades and leaned against one of the desks, crossing my arms and surveying them. "I don't want to risk any more lives than I have to. Blu and Beck are necessary, but there's no reason for Piper or Archimedes to go."

"I have thousands of reasons to go," Arc said, standing. "The first of which being that if I, or Piper, for that matter, want to go, it's not your decision to make. We know the risks involved. Besides, Blu will need someone to cover her while she's activating Kiser's modification."

"I fought for years without you, Jericho," Piper decided to throw out in an unnecessarily bitter tone. "And no, you can't tell me what to do."

Then she stood and stomped off in a fume.

"Your girlfriend doesn't look very happy," Kiser said, still rubbing at his goatee. "Perhaps you should go after her."

"She's not my girlfriend," Archimedes and I said at the exact same damn time.

We ended up looking at each other after our fumble of synchronism, and silence followed for a few seconds before Sloan, who didn't really need to be there because she wouldn't be aiding anyone during our raid, said, "Awkward."

"Shut up," we both said at the same time again, before glancing at each other and saying, "Stop that," together.

"Like I said," Sloan said, wrinkling her nose at us, "awkward."

Beck cleared her throat exasperatedly. "Maybe we can get back to the very dangerous mission at hand."

"Whatever," I said. When had I started acting like the jealous ex competing against the new guy, anyway? I reached out with my mind and touched Piper's mind, while the rest of the gathering discussed what time we would ascend.

I know, I know, okay? But I had to see what she was thinking. Her thoughts were harsh at first and mostly aimed at me, while some were angry thoughts about Arc, but when they started changing, I left, muttering something about needing to lie down before the attack, shoving my hands in my long coat pockets and watching my boots on the grate while I walked.

By the time I made it back to the room, I knew everything I needed to know about Piper and how she was more conflicted than I was. I felt downright removed at times. Whereas her feelings on me were exposed like a nerve, hence her aggravated nature of late. All and all, she hadn't made up her mind about me.

Not that she was in turmoil about whether she was in love with me or not, but because she didn't know if she wanted to go back home when given the chance.

Or leave me, which would be a more accurate way of saying it.

I laid down on one of the couches, slipping my hands

behind my head while still listening to Piper's mind.

He told me not to go once before, she thought. *I would have died if I had gotten my way back then...*

See? Like I said before, turmoil. Then her thoughts turned way dark, and she began imagining what would have happened if she had gone and got herself killed like Chloe and I had.

Then her thoughts turned back to Archimedes, and I ended up turning the channel off after about ten seconds because, contrary to popular belief, I now knew that Piper was in love with someone other than me.

I guess I'd known it all along and just didn't want to take the time to actually stop long enough to think about it. I had great excuses like, you know, trying to not die during the road trip from hell and juggling my crazy powers and, sometimes, the lack thereof that resulted in two of my friends dying.

But, now that I had stopped long enough to think about it and see it pictured so plainly in Piper's mind, I felt sick to my stomach. I sat up and swung my boots to the floor, rubbing my hands together slowly and peering around the empty room.

Jericho, I heard her think. *I must see him.*

What?

Before I had time to think much, Piper walked into the room. "Hey," I said conversationally, standing. "I was just thinking about you."

She didn't say anything, crossing the room at a fast pace and putting her arms around my neck quickly. I was stunned, standing there like an idiot for about three seconds before I put my arms around her and returned the hug, feeling her shaking.

"It's alright, Pipe," I told her, putting a hand on the back of her head. "I don't want anything bad between us. Like, at all."

"I don't, either," she said, sniffing and rubbing at one of her eyes. "I was just so angry with you after you died."

"You would've died, too, if—"

"What of it?" Piper asked, pulling away but keeping her

hands on my shoulders and looking into my face.

"Why do you think I didn't want you to go in the first place?" I asked, matching her gaze.

"Do you honestly think that I travelled across the very fabrics of time, breaking every natural law ever put into place, just to stay behind while you ran off to your death?"

"Piper—"

She was really crying by that time. "Life without you wasn't life to me, Jericho. Can't you see that?"

"But you didn't die," I said, smiling and putting a hand on her cheek. "You've accomplished a heck of a lot more than I have, and you did it without, well, my awesome powers."

She smiled, shaking her head and looking away. I knew she would smile at that. "Besides, you got Arc now."

Piper nodded slowly, her eyes on the floor. "He's helped me a lot."

"He's a little too full of himself for my taste," I said casually, letting out a breath and putting my hands on my hips. "But, as luck would have it, I don't have to date him."

She laughed a little, but I could tell that my jokes weren't going to make her feel better. "Look," I said, sitting on the couch and pulling her down beside me. "I thought I was always going to be there for you, but I wasn't. Archimedes really loves you, and I wouldn't just say that to help get him out of the doghouse. I've listened to his mind, Piper," I told her, nodding reassuringly. "Dude's crazy about you."

She didn't say anything, so I finished my speech.

"You wouldn't have met him if you'd died with me," I said, and she nodded slowly, a tear rolling down her cheek before she laid her head on my shoulder. I wrapped an arm around her and sighed.

Peace. Finally, after weeks of Piper being at my throat and hating me for reasons I wasn't sure of, we'd finally worked things out.

"Of course, I'm a lot better looking than he is, but that's true in most cases."

I've never been happier to receive a hard elbow jab in the ribs.

"And, come on, I've got to be a better kisser. Have you seen that guy's lips? Be like making out with Alan Rickman."

Piper was smiling now, and the jokes, even though they were light-hearted, still somehow managed to make the sickish feeling reappear in my stomach. Piper thought for a moment before saying, "You two are pretty evenly matched, I'd say."

I acted aghast, but I suppose I had it coming. Then I asked, "Have you decided about Svalbard yet?"

The question didn't catch her off-guard like I thought it might, since it was so random, but her smile wavered and she said, "I'll let you know."

"I could always read your mind," I told her, touching my temples with two fingers and narrowing my eyes at her.

"I haven't decided yet," she said, standing. "You'll be the first to know when I do, though."

That seemed fair enough, I guess.

Then our tabs lit up.

"It'll be dark in twenty, people," Beck echoed to all her comrades. "Jericho?"

"Yeah?" I asked, falling in step behind Piper toward the door.

"Brain-message your new friend and tell him it's almost suppertime, then get to the elevator. Time to finish this thing once and for all. Oh, and don't forget that Cross has to fix me before we kill him."

"Uh, yeah, we're not going to kill him," Archimedes buzzed in.

"Ready?" I asked Piper, while we traversed the darkened hallway toward the main chamber.

I felt her hand grab mine. "I really like you, you know."

"I know," I said, squeezing her hand. "Don't worry, though, because I'm all super-human now, remember? What's the worst that can happen?"

PART III

Death

CHAPTER 58

Wolf, come in.

Insert pause.

Yes?

It's time to roll out, buddy. You ready for this?

Insert absolutely no pause whatsoever.

In fact, he actually started talking before I had finished telling him it was time.

Once I am inside the city, you shall take control of this body and guide me to my meal, yes?

I shall, I told him. *I need five minutes once you start chomping folks. Can you give me that?*

I shall give you ten.

Attaboy, Wolf. Tell me when you're inside.

I severed the neural link and looked around the jostling tram that Kiser was hauling us through Anchorage in. It was smaller than the armored car we'd rolled into town in, and Kiser had also informed us it had once been a transport for convicts, which explained the close and cramped seating.

"What kind of battle-armor will be at the other safe house?" Blu, who was sitting beside me, asked Arc, who was sitting opposite us.

"You can have your pick, but I would recommend the fully weaponized and outfitted Raptor-Z," he said, not really paying attention when Blu gripped my arm and bugged her greens eyes.

"Excited, much?" I asked.

"Are you kidding me?" she said, like I had just asked her what color her hair was. "The Raptor-Z is still a prototype and isn't due to hit the market for another year."

"Sorry. I must've missed that issue of Nerd Magazine," I said.

"I hate you."

"No, you don't."

"Specs?" Blu asked Arc, narrowing her eyes at me one last time before smiling and planting a kiss on my left shoulder.

"Massive, for starters. Almost seventeen feet tall. Quad upgrade on the armor, even though there's a duel force field generator on it."

"Duel?" I couldn't help but ask.

"I can shoot out, but nothing can shoot in," Blu informed me. "What else?"

"Well, it doesn't fly like a Dragonov and it's not near as maneuverable as a Raptor-6, but the R-Z was designed less for dodging and flying and more for death and destruction, which it pulls off perfectly, looking completely boss while doing it."

Blu grinned from ear to ear. "I'll take it."

"Will you be able to do Kiser's bypass in a suit that big?" Piper asked, her white-armored arms folded while she sat next to Archimedes in her Ghost suit, her enormous red broadsword leaning against the bench beside her.

"Anyone can relay the signal needed to patch me in," Kiser said, lighting up Blu's holotab. "The Raptor-Z needs to be deployed on this mission if we want to succeed, and something tells me the blue-haired girl is a better pilot than you, Arc."

"The shield will counter almost anything the Synners have, too," Blu said, her mind whirring while she chewed on her lip and started tapping away on her holotab. "Okay, here's my modified bit. Piper and I will stay up top with the wolf and give the Syns more than what they bargained for, while Arc, Beck, and Jericho get below. Arc will have the bypass module,

Beck will provide any cover he needs, and Jericho will be point man until breaking into the labs. After that it shouldn't be a problem reaching Cross."

"We have arrived at safe house seven," Kiser announced over our tabs. The hatch door hissed when it opened, and we all stood, exiting the prison tram and stepping into another shop, only this one was empty. The heavy iron doors slid shut behind the tram, and lights flickered on, revealing the large area.

"The Raptor-Z is just below us," Kiser said, stepping off the tram and walking past us. "Is everyone ready?"

It was strange to think that we were about to embark on a dangerous mission. I guess because the last time I'd done something like this, I'd stayed awake all night. This time it seemed rushed, like we were going to miss our window of opportunity if we didn't move fast, whether we were ready or not.

"How close are we to Cross?" I asked.

"Very," Arc answered, walking beside me. "There's just one building between us. Once your wolf breaks through the front gate, we'll slip in through the access door right next to the street. Ritu said she could disengage that lock and that lock alone, so that's where you, Beck, and I will enter. Blu can just blast off from the street and clear the wall in the R-Z."

"Mind if I get a lift?" Piper asked.

"Not at all," Blu told her with a smile.

Then I realized I was the only one who was actually stressing about the mission. What was the deal? I mean, I was the only real super-human on the assault team, and everyone else was acting shockingly cavalier about the whole thing.

Do not worry, Jericho, I heard Sybil's voice in my mind.

We really need to talk about the times you deem appropriate to show up with words of wisdom, Sybil.

The floor in front of us opened, and the Raptor-Z began rising on a wide lift, which I saw led down to a setup resembling the previous safe house we had just been in.

Confront Cross. Only after that will your Crusade begin.

Yeah, you told me that already.

Farewell, Paladin. I look forward to our next meeting.

Blu was almost running around the Raptor-Z like a child who just received a puppy for Christmas.

A huge, very powerful and deadly puppy.

It was the same signature red of the previous Raptor models I'd seen, but, as I've said, it was gigantic. Archimedes had already told us the height, but seventeen feet had sounded shorter in a sentence because I felt like a fetus next to it. Wide-barreled turrets adorned each wrist on the top and bottom, and there was a huge canon on the right shoulder.

"The grid is completely blank, so you can sync your holotab to it," Arc said to her. "Power it up when you're ready."

Blu keyed out a few commands on her tab, and in seconds the mammoth battle-armor lurched a little. The inside of the cockpit, which was completely visible through the twelve-inch thick ballistic glass that covered the pilot, lit up brightly, and the armor knelt closer to the ground, the front opening on top and on both sides to allow access.

Beck whistled. "That's a lot of machine, Blu. Can you handle it?"

Blu didn't answer, instead walking to the suit and turning around, stepping back into the thin, metal foot attachments which clamped around her feet. Reaching up, she slipped into the hand inserts and pulled herself into the cockpit. After the back base clamped around her, Arc said, "A cerebral lace is going to lay across your spine, giving you physical control over the suit, and you'll have almost full range of motion while being suspended in the cockpit."

Blu just nodded as the thick glass and metal sealed back shut and the suit stood up straight. I could see her clearly through the glass while she winced as something attached to her spine.

"You good?" I called to her, holding up a thumb in question.

I saw her move, and in perfect unison, the Raptor-Z took

a step toward us and placed its massive hands on metal hips. "I'm great," Blu said through my tab, and I could see her broad smile. "Cerebral lace was bloody cold, is all."

She looked at her hands, and it was quite awesome to see the R-Z mimic her actions. "Weapons?" she asked.

"It's all mentally activated from here on out," Arc said. "The targeting system is completely different from a Dragonov's, and you'll have more freedom with your weapons —which means if you suck at shooting in real life, you're guaranteed to suck at it in the Raptor-Z."

"Thanks for the tip," Blu said and held up her right arm, the massive guns coming to life and extending. "I think I'll manage, though."

I am outside the gates, Wolf told me. I was still confused how he was able to somehow mentally contact me, because I thought I was the administrator or something, but I wasn't caring too much, considering I really needed him to talk to me the next half hour.

"Wolf's ready," I told my team, slipping out of my hooded long coat and passing it to Archimedes. "Since you're not going to be wearing a suit, you might as well look fabulous."

He nodded, pulling on my duds. "Thanks, man."

Piper attached her red sword to the back or her armor and walked to the Raptor-Z, turning back to us. "You three need to get closer. What is in the next building?"

"Clothes factory," Kiser told her, heading for a stairwell beside the large elevator. "Get inside and make sure you stow Jericho out of sight while he's using the wolf."

Then we were off, walking toward an exit on the far left of the warehouse. "And, Jericho?"

I stopped and turned back when I heard Piper call. "Yeah?"

"Try not to die this time," she said.

"Yes, please don't," Blu chimed in on my tab.

I turned back and followed my point team. "I'll see what I can do."

I was kidding, of course. I had no intention of dying, but I had every intention of giving Cross his long overdue comeuppance.

CHAPTER 59

We quickly crossed the darkened street to the factory, sidestepping around the tromping suits and bundled people on their way home after a long day at work. Or something like that. I wasn't sure how easy it was to get a job these days, but something told me the economy between four thriving cities couldn't have been the best. I mean, what about population growth? Was it even cool to have kids anymore, or did they die young because of the cold?

Wow, that's severely off subject.

We stepped onto the sidewalk and entered the warm factory. It was a poorly lit area with a low hanging ceiling, and it was filled wall to wall with long rows of tables, which Arc led us down.

"This looks like a sweatshop," I mentioned, frowning while still taking it all in. "Do I need to come back here after we finish with Cross?"

"Do you have to say it like that?" Archimedes asked. "We're not killing him. And yeah, do whatever you want. The owner of this place is a real piece of work, but he does pay his workers, at least."

"Don't they have robots or something that have replaced men and women in about every physical task?"

Archimedes shook his head. "You've seen too many grams, my friend."

"What?"

"Grams," he repeated. "Holograms. Wait—what did the people of your time call them? Oh, yes, movies. You've seen too many movies."

We were embarking on a deadly mission, but I couldn't resist. "They still make movies?"

He nodded. "Yes. Though, they're all made in Australia."

Figures. Australian actors were taking over when I left 2012.

There were a few people left in the building, but the depressing men I saw looked to be janitors or something of the like. We made it to the other side of the wide workspace and Arc stopped, turning to me and saying, "This is as good a place as any."

Nodding, I got on the floor, lying on my back.

"Lazy," Beck said, shaking her head.

"Don't judge me. Besides, you guys would probably let me face plant if I went lifeless."

I closed my eyes and focused, feeling my being leaving my body, and in just a few seconds, I was in wolf mode.

Welcome, Jericho, Wolf told me. *Lead the way.*

Hold tight, Wolf, I thought to him. *You'll be back in control in a minute.*

Then I was running, kicking up snow behind me while my enormous paws dug deep and sped me toward the very flimsy iron gate blocking my path. The poor saps who'd been at the gatehouse when I'd entered the city hours ago were still on duty and saw me coming, pulling their assault rifles and firing. I didn't slow down, but instead picked up speed, gathering the fire burning within, opening my mouth wide and shooting searing flames into the gatehouse when I saw the guards abandon their post and dive out of it and into the snow, instantly incinerating the small shack before I dipped my massive head and plowed straight through the front gate.

Pandemonium ensued instantly, and panicking pedestrians fled in all directions, clearing the street in seconds and giving me a perfect shot down it.

I ran until there was a fork in the road, and I took a left before leaping into the air and landing hard on one of the nearest buildings, resuming my ferocious dash across the rooftops, clearing every section of street and sidewalk like it was nothing and continuing on. Cross's massive facility loomed in the distance.

You see it?

Yes, Wolf said eagerly. *How many humans?*

Loads. Just don't hurt my guys. They'll be inside, as well.

I remember their scent. I shan't touch them.

I was almost there, and I mentally tabbed Blu before I leapt from the last building, landing on the cement, crossing the final stretch, and jumping the tall fence surrounding the base. I landed hard and saw that word of a wolf sprinting across town must have spread because a long line of Synners were guarding the front entrance to the facility.

There they are, pal, I told him. *Lined up like a buffet.*

Beautiful, Wolf said, and I felt that, wherever his subconscious was residing, he was smiling.

I heard a loud blast to my right and turned just in time to see the Raptor-Z shooting through the air with fire coming out of its feet. Blu landed hard, and the ground literally shook before she fired off her first shot from the shoulder canon, hitting the second floor and causing panic everywhere before all Helheim broke loose.

I closed my eyes inside the wolf and opened them again in my own body, sitting up and accepting Beck's hand. "Time to go, people."

Then we busted out, sprinting the wide street to the access door inside. Archimedes got there first and tried to open it, but it was locked. "No," he shouted, slamming his fist into it. "Ritu said she'd have it—"

Beck shoved him out of the way and kicked the door completely off its hinges, ripping out the reinforced plating as well. "Stop whining," she told him and entered with us close behind.

"I had forgotten you two were, well, uh…"

"You're about to get a good reminder," Beck said, spotting two guards at the end of the hall. "Guards."

"I see them," I said, kicking in my overdrive and peeling toward them, clearing the seventy-foot gap in seconds, connecting my speeding hands to their chests and slamming them both hard on the metal floor. "Stay down, now," I said in a fatherly voice, giving their chests one last pat while they writhed and wheezed on the floor.

We traversed the rest of the hall, and Archimedes said, "Take the next right, and the first door on the left will enter the stairwell leading to the labs."

We hung a right, hit the first left door, and took two flights of stairs down before we met the locked down door to Cross's super-secret labs. Beck kicked the thick iron door hard, but it didn't budge.

"We're stuck at the lab entrance, Kiser," Arc tabbed quickly, and I heard shouting from somewhere above us, an explosion that shook the building then a loud roar.

"You are within range. Uploading bypass system."

We waited for almost ten seconds, with more battle sounds all around us like elevator music, before Kiser said, "Done." The heavy door hissed open, and we were running again through a very white environment that smelled of disinfectant.

"Cross will be only three more floors down," Kiser told us. "There will be synthetic resistance arriving on your floor in —" his signal broke off suddenly.

"Kiser, come in," Arc tried more than once, and we stopped running. "This isn't good. He was going to be our eyes and tell us about any upcoming obstacles."

After another failed attempt to establish contact, Archimedes said, "He knows we're in his lab. He's blocked our tabs somehow, and he's probably watching us right now."

"Running scared, now?" I called out into the lab, my voice echoing.

My response was an uncountable amount of turrets dropping from the ceiling all around us and firing instantly, giving me barely enough time to throw up a force field around all of us, hot lead hitting everywhere on the bubble at once. The sound was deafening, but after almost a minute of this, the turrets ceased firing. After the smoke cleared, a small ball-shaped object floated down from the ceiling and a hologram appeared in my line of sight, projecting around the sphere.

"Jericho," the green hologram of Cross said like he'd just bumped into an old colleague, something that always bugged me about him. "I see you're doing well."

"Cut the crap, Cross," I told him, still maintaining my shield while my comrades watched the turrets nervously. "You have something of mine. Give it back to me and I won't kill you."

Cross had his hands in his pockets when he walked slowly toward me, the spinning sphere hovering in place around the hologram's midsection. "Your gauntlet, right? Tell me, what do you plan on doing with it once I return it to you?"

"That's none of your concern."

Cross got close enough to us and stopped walking, frowning and pulling his head slightly to the left for a better view. "Arc?" he said unbelievingly. "Is that you?"

Archimedes turned and faced his brother. "It is. I must say that you're doing well for yourself, Socrates."

"You didn't make it easy with a dramatic departure such as yours but, yes, I manage," Cross said, nodding slightly. "It is good to see you again, little brother, really, it is, but now you're not only here but you're also assaulting my humble lab—"

"You're insane," Arc said suddenly, cutting his brother off. "I know what you've done, what you're planning on doing, and I've come to stop you."

"Nice job," I said to Arc, smiling at him before turning back to Cross. "He and I both seem to share a sort of disdain for you, it seems."

"You haven't the foggiest idea what I plan to do, Arc,

or you wouldn't have come here, I can assure you of that," Cross said, sighing. "Anyway, it was good to see you again, Archimedes. I'm sorry you had to die by my hand, but you did attack me first." Then, oddly enough, he addressed Beck. "And how are you this fine evening, Miss Sparks?"

"And then there were idiots," Beck said sarcastically. "I'm super. How're you?"

"Decent," he told her. "I'd feel better if code CS-3400-58-FG89V was still in order, but you know how it is. Well, I'd best be off," he turned to leave but stopped short, holding up a finger and slightly turning back to us. "Oh, yes, and Beck? Be a dear and kill Archimedes for me. He hurts my head."

I laughed out loud. "Man, you're a piece of work," I said, shaking my head. "You really think that Beck is going to—"

Beck attacked Arc.

Right there in the middle of the force field we were all three sharing, Beck punched Archimedes hard in the side of his head and he fell. She bent quickly and would've smashed his unconscious head into the metal floor had I not spun around and intervened, prying Beck's hands away from his head just in time. "Beck, what're you doing?"

She paused, her head clicking to the side and she said, "Obstacle encountered that is not primary directive. Confirm new structure pattern?"

I stared at her in disbelief. The voice wasn't even hers. It sounded robotic and... and...

I still had a hold of her hands when I swung my head back toward Cross just in time to see him smile and say, "Confirm."

CHAPTER 60

I was still shocked about what was happening, and Beck grabbed my head with lightning speed and planted her knee square into my face, sending me flying into the force field hard before she was kicking and punching me like a madwoman. "Beck, stop!" I shouted, guarding my face and hunching against her blows.

"She can't hear you, Jericho," Cross told me, walking closer to the spectacle, his hands still in his pockets. "When Atrium asked me to rebuild her years ago, he and I agreed to install a failsafe should Beck ever begin to experience massive side effects from her spinal grafting. Her brain was at a terrible risk, you see."

I was being pummeled and kicked the whole time he was talking. "You're sick," was all I got out. Even with all my super-strength, I just wasn't built to withstand getting beat up by someone equally matched. But I couldn't fight her. Not Beck.

"If I had a holo for every person that's told me that," he said, chuckling and shaking his head at the thought. "It'd help repair some of the damages from your little entrance, for starters."

"Beck, come on, it's me," I said, lashing out and grabbing both her wrists again. "Get a grip!"

She stared at me, but the thing in front of me wasn't Beck anymore. Her eyes were dead when they looked at me. She jumped, kicking both feet into my stomach, and I doubled over.

"Tab Blu," I shouted, but Cross tsked me.

"Holotabs are offline, remember? It's just you, Beck, my brother, and a room full of auto-locked turrets waiting for anyone to exit your bubble."

I didn't know what to do, and Beck stopped beating at me long enough to turn back to Arc's unconscious body. "Retargeting primary directive," she chortled out in a synthetic voice.

No. I didn't want to hurt her, but Beck killing Arc wasn't happening. "Try it," I said, flying into her and head-butting the living heck out of her as hard as I could before shooting off a few punches.

Cross was right, though, this wouldn't work forever. I needed help. This was it. The moment I was worried about for days. I could leave the force field and have a good chance of surviving, but Archimedes would definitely die.

Then I thought of something when I wrapped my arms around Beck, squeezing tight and holding her the best I could. Closing my eyes, I sent off a neural message.

And, no, not to Wolf.

Blu, I thought. *Please tell me you can hear this.*

She didn't answer, and Beck got out of my hold, elbowing my ribs and throwing her head back into my face hard before resuming her barrage.

But then I heard it.

Jericho? Was that you?

It's kind of hard to mentally talk to someone whilst getting your butt handed to you. Just saying. I don't know how I managed it, but I did.

We're stuck on the first floor of the labs. Beck's attacking us now, and Arc is in danger. There's turrets, and I'm pinned. I blocked a wild haymaker and punched her in the stomach hard before spinning and driving a fist into her back. *I don't know what I need, but I need something.*

She was quiet for a few seconds, no doubt hashing out things in her mind first before she answered.

Heads up.

Then the room shook hard and things began falling over. I lost my footing and, thankfully, so did Beck. Then the lights suddenly went out, and we were enveloped in complete darkness.

Then I went to work, shutting off the shield and kicking Beck across the room before grabbing Archimedes and dashing toward the door.

"Status?" I heard Cross bark while he listened to a report. "Get the lights on, or you're all dead men," he finally said, sighing. "One of your compatriots flew a Raptor-Z into the substructures of the top floors. Now half of them have collapsed."

"Cool," I called back to him, closing the iron door after I tossed Arc out of it and jabbing an electrified fist into the door controls, ripping all the important guts out of it so no one could follow me.

Send Piper to get Arc. He's outside the lab door. Thanks, Blu.
She's on her way. What about you?

I gathered bolts into my fists. *I'll be fine.*

Then the power came back online and so did the turrets. I flung a lightning bomb toward each side, and the effects weren't disappointing. After a few more tosses, all the turrets were non-functional.

But then I saw Beck still standing in my way, with Cross's unimpressed hologram standing behind her.

"Last chance, Cross," I said menacingly, walking toward them. "Give me my gauntlet and let Beck go, or I'll kill you."

For the first time since I'd seen him again, Cross looked aggravated. "Ever the gallant knight, aren't we? You were useful in Flagstaff, and if I hadn't been able to study you for so long, I wouldn't have finished what I set out to."

His hands weren't in his pockets anymore, so I'm guessing I had finally got him on edge. "You were just another pawn, Jericho. The only problem with you is that you're still alive. Now, stop meddling and die like a good test subject."

He was almost shouting now, but he got a rein on his volume, rubbing a hand on his forehead. "Kill him," he almost muttered with a slight shake of his head. "Just kill him."

Beck sprang into action, but so did I, crossing the gap between us and jumping into the air when she did, colliding with her and landing hard on the floor. She kicked onto her feet and tried to stomp my head, but I rolled away, pushing off with my hands and spinning back into the air and onto my feet.

We circled each other slowly. "I said let her go," I told Cross.

"And I said no. Stop being a child."

I know what you're thinking.

Why not just shoot her with your ever-so-helpful-and-handy lightning, Jericho? She's almost completely synthetic so that'd *have* to mess her up!

These were the thoughts I was battling because I knew what would stop her cold, but I also didn't know what effect that would have on her if I hit her with a bolt. I didn't want to kill her or jack up her body beyond repair.

But things were spiraling out of control fast.

"Beck, please try and listen to me," I tried, but Cross laughed at that.

"You're basically talking to a tree right now."

Beck attacked again, and this time I wasn't ready and got a hurricane kick to the side of my head, sending me slamming into a row of desks to my left. I was dazed out of my mind when she mounted my chest and started pin-wheeling my face with heavy punches.

"This is almost sad, really," I heard Cross say, and I reached my hands up and grabbed the hood of Beck's long coat, pulling hard and sending her flying off me. I rolled to my feet and made a mad dash for the opposite door that I was hoping led to another stairwell. If Cross wanted to keep control of my friend, then I'd break every bone in his body until he let her go.

But Beck caught up with me, landing on my shoulders from above me and flipping backwards, pulling me down with her and wrapping her legs tight around my throat. I couldn't breathe, and I was shocked that I could be choked. Somehow, after experiencing everything I could do, I just figured not needing oxygen went hand in hand with being super-human.

Boy, was I wrong.

Cross appeared in front of me whilst Beck was still tightening her grip, and my eyes fluttered against the pressure. "Pathetic," he said, seeming truly sorry for me. "I used to think you were going to be my perfect design, and yet here you are, being killing by an older, outdated model."

I tried to glare at him, but I could feel blackness creeping around my vision. I knew that if I wanted to get past and away from Beck, I was going to have to use a different tactic.

A more deadly tactic. I had been holding back, but I couldn't any longer. There was just too much at stake now.

I reached up and grabbed Beck's right arm with both hands. *I'm sorry,* I thought, before pulling with all my strength and instantly hearing straining gears and metal before ripping her arm completely off. Fluid and wires hit me in the face, and Beck loosened her grip on my neck just enough for me to slip out and kick onto my feet, spinning and slamming my heel into the side of the kneeling woman's head, sending her flying.

I walked to where she was having trouble getting up, and I grabbed her, pulling her up hard and kneeing her in the stomach three times before sending her crashing through more glass tables and desks.

Once again, I was there when she tried to get to her feet, and I dragged her up, elbowing her hard in the head on the way and looking into her face. She still looked like a dead robot, but she also looked dazed.

"I'm sorry, Beck," I said simply, driving my boot into her left knee and breaking it backward, metal jutting out of the synthetic skin. I shoved her back hard, and she landed in an unmoving heap.

I was breathing hard, and I watched her body. She seemed to still be functioning but didn't look like she was going to be attacking again anytime soon. I turned around and walked toward the hologram Cross was hiding in, and I was about to tell him he would be dead in a few minutes, when Beck grabbed me from behind.

What? How did she—?

She wrapped her only arm around my neck, and out of instinct I reached behind my head and grabbed hers in my hands with every intention of trying to pull her over my shoulder.

But I fired off two bolts into her head.

She instantly went limp and crumpled to the floor. "Beck," I said, not believing what I'd just done, dropping to the floor next to her.

"Oh, God," I mumbled, touching her face and looking into her eyes. Or eye, rather, because her left one had ruptured and exploded from aftershock. I hadn't meant to do it. It... just happened.

"Well, that was unexpected," I heard Cross say from behind me.

Cross.

This was his fault. I gritted my teeth and dropped my head low, squeezing Beck's lifeless shoulder once before standing. "You know what's funny?" I said, still looking at her body. "I was willing to look the other way on just about everything you've ever done, if you would've only just given me my gauntlet."

I turned back to face him, the rage building inside. "This is the third time you've taken someone from me, and I'm going to kill you for it."

"If you keep going, you will die," he said, sliding his hands back into his pockets. "But it should be fun to watch, I suppose."

I lifted a hand. "I'm coming," I said, shooting a jolt into the sphere and shutting down the hologram. I took one last look in Beck's direction and took a deep breath.

"I'm sorry," I said again. "This one's for you."

Then I lit up my entire body, white energy shooting in all directions. I looked at my hands. Archimedes had said Cross was three stories down. That seemed like a good place to start.

I pulled both my hands into the air and turned on all the juice I had, melting a few glass tables close by, and I slammed both fists into the floor, the metal buckling under the first blow and exploding on the second. I didn't fall through but kicked the hole wider before aiming both barrels into the hole and firing into the next floor down, heating the metal.

After about ten lightning seconds, I dove headfirst into the hole, my blue/white frame breaking through the second floor. I fired off everything I had into the last floor, shouting when I hit with both fists and puncturing through, flipping once and landing in a crouch on Cross's floor.

I stood and glanced around the room. It was smaller than the three I'd just jumped through and resembled Cross's office in Flagstaff.

Speaking of Cross, the man was sitting at his desk, watching me. He didn't look surprised at all to see me, but I wasn't caring about his thoughts at the moment, only about how his spine would look in my hand.

"Jericho—" he tried to say in his pleasant voice.

"Don't," I said harshly, holding up a hand and walking toward him at first but stopping dead in my tracks when I noticed the person standing next to Cross's desk.

Cross followed my gaze and said, "Oh, don't mind him. He's a little off right now because he's about to kill himself."

I blinked, my white-hot anger replaced by mass confusion. "How?"

It was me standing beside Cross, my hands tucked obediently behind my back, and my face staring blankly in front of me.

"It wasn't that hard, really," Cross said, leaning back in his chair. "After I obtained a miniscule amount of element zero a few months ago, I was able to get a nice, neat version of you without all the patchwork. The transfusion was done in less than a day; whereas, it took me almost a year on you. I confess that knowing your biological makeup in and out helped speed everything along quite nicely, and now, here he is. He's you without all the flaws. The perfect soldier."

I instantly fired off both hands at Cross, but the other me threw up an awfully familiar force field.

"How very eager of you," Cross said, unimpressed. He stood and walked around to where the other Jericho was standing. "The first thing I did to this Jericho was completely wipe out his brain and start from scratch. Now, he can't even blink without my command. His entire brain is basically dormant, so he won't question any order he receives."

"What's your game?" I asked, sidestepping slowly. "Surely one super-soldier isn't all you wanted."

"It's not," he said modestly. "But it's a start. He isn't the only one I made but I can't recreate the materials needed. If I had more EZ for the gauntlet, I could literally make an infinite number of troops such as these, but I only have enough for a one-way trip at the moment. Which brings me to this."

He reached into his desk just then and produced the gauntlet, passing it to the other Jericho who walked toward me with it. "I have no intention of taking over the world of the past. As I see it, the earth is in its prime. That's why I'm giving you a chance to return back to your life. 2012, wasn't it?"

Evil Jericho stopped in front of me and held out the gauntlet for me to take.

"You were once a billionaire who lived without a care in the world. Now you're on the run in a place you don't belong, trying to save a world you have no ties to whatsoever."

Don't listen to him, Sybil said suddenly, and my eyes flicked from the gauntlet to the dead-eyed thing holding it. *You're a Paladin, Jericho. Chance and happenstance did not bring you here.*

Then I saw it all. Everything laid out in my mind in rapid succession.

I had done this before.

I had made it to this office, squared off against evil me, had my arm and leg removed in the fight and my chest ripped open. I didn't regenerate that time because I wasn't a Paladin and had made a quick choice to use my last breath as wisely as I could.

By using the one-way trip on the gauntlet to land a few days prior to my doom and warn my past self, with only a few vague yet extremely important words:

Don't fight it.

Not just the changes involved with being a Paladin, but everything that went along with it.

"Chicago is sounding really good right about now," I confessed. "But, you see, I'm kind of on a crusade, so I'm sure you'll understand why I can't accept your offer. Also, you might want to move."

Then I kicked the Helheim out of evil Jericho, sending him flying back over the marble floor and through Cross's desk, which he'd barely managed to evade.

I had finally heeded the warning, and now I was ready for anything.

"I haven't danced with myself in a while," I said, walking toward where Cross and evil me were trying to get to their feet. "This should be fun."

CHAPTER 61

"Attack," Cross shouted, crawling away from his crushed desk while his puppet flew into action. I blocked a left hook only to get hit by his right. I growled and grabbed his jumpsuit, wailing punch after punch into his face. He didn't even try to block anything, and after I'd got done, my hand ached and evil me didn't even have a small bruise or blemish.

Then he took his turn, head-butting me and making me see stars. He grabbed my shoulder, and then I was sailing through the air across the office, crashing into the far wall and landing in a heap on the floor.

I was tired and fading fast. The faceoff with Beck had left me a little wasted, and my moves were sluggish compared to the other Jericho, who was beside me before I had time to get up. He kicked me in the stomach, sending me into and through the wall I'd just bounced off of.

I groaned from the floor of the next lounge room, and then he was on my chest, punching me in the face. I lit up my entire body, roaring at him and lighting him up, flowing all the juice I had into him.

But he didn't stop. Nothing was working. He just kept raining blow after blow.

He stopped punching when Cross commanded it, standing quickly and stepping over me. I lay on the floor with a bloodied face and an eye that had already swelled shut. My chest rattled when I took even a small breath.

"So, how's Chicago sounding, now?" Cross asked, leaning against one of the couches that hadn't been broken in our bout. "I'm actually recording this, as this is the other Jericho's first fight. Have to log data, you understand."

I rolled onto my stomach and almost passed out from pain. Something was wrong with my torso, for real. And why wasn't I healing like I had when my chest got burned off in the Yukon? With much effort, I gathered my extremities under myself and somehow managed to get to my feet and, after a few staggers, faced my foe again.

Unless I pulled something out of a hat, I was going to die. I held up my hands and shot a bolt between them, building the swirling ball.

"You can't hurt him with that attack," Cross said, unimpressed. "You can't be hurt by it yourself, so why do you think it will work?"

By this time, I had finished compressing my bomb into my favorite ping-pong ball size. "I know it won't work," I said with as much strength as I could muster. "It's not for him, genius."

Then I threw it hard in Cross's direction, but evil me was way fast, leaping to the right and catching it like an outfielder.

I watched him menacingly while he held it. "Fascinating," Cross said, his inner scientist getting the better of him, and he walked closer to the glowing sphere.

I snapped my fingers, and my lightning bomb deployed, exploding in the other Jericho's hand and blasting him back. I was sent skidding back, too, but I'd also been bracing myself so I was able to stay on my feet. I heard Cross cry out and saw him writhing on the floor on the opposite side of the room in a small pool of blood.

Using the last of my reserves, I bolted across the static-filled suite, sliding on my knees the last bit into Cross, grabbing his collar, and raising back a fist. "Call him off," I shouted. "Now!"

He wasn't going to die, that much was evident, but I

could tell he wasn't used to battle wounds. "Sure," he said, coughing, his once fine hair missing on one side of his head, some of his skin blackened, and his ears bleeding. "Kill him."

I realized too late that my scare tactic wasn't going to work, but before I could break one of his arms to show I meant business, my raised hand was grabbed and I was hauled off of Cross, my legs kicking and sliding on the marble floor.

"Just kill him," Cross said weakly, rolling on his side and attempting to get up. "No more games."

I was spun around, and evil me delivered the most powerful blow he'd issued yet, right to my face. All sounds vanished, and I saw complete white for a second before he hit me again. The room, sound, and pain all came rushing back.

I'm going to die.

There wasn't anything I could do but take the beating, my precious blood splattering with each super punch, and I was beginning to recede in and out of consciousness.

So, let's take stock of my mission thus far.

Arc may have died, I had to kill Beck, and I was getting the life literally beat out of me by a brain-dead clone of myself.

Then I was lying on the ground with the sun shining bright above me.

And Sybil was standing next to me. "Jericho, you can't die."

I wasn't in any pain while in the peaceful place, but before I could tell her that I didn't have control over whether I lived or died anymore, she vanished and I was back in Cross's office receiving more punches.

Then evil me stopped and I saw his dead eyes examining me. I didn't know why until his right hand moved slowly above me into the perfect position he needed.

"Finish it," I heard Cross say, and without hesitation the other Jericho gave his final punch, his lightning-engulfed hand going straight through my chest and smashing into the marble floor below me. I gasped, blood instantly filling the back of my throat.

I tried, Sybil, I thought, my eyes closing. All I wanted was to go back to the sunny place, and I used my last brain function to will Sybil to welcome me there quickly.

"Don't fight it," I barely heard Cross say, his voice sounding miles away.

You heard him, Sybil said.

Then I was standing next to the other Jericho, his right hand covered in my blood and my body lying in front of us. I was in super-sneak mode, and I panicked. "Please tell me I'm not a ghost now," I said frantically. I'd been next to my body before, but never without a chance to go back inside.

"Sybil, tell me what to do," I shouted. "You're the one with the answers to every—"

I felt cold in my legs and glanced down just in time to see my feet vanish.

"No!" I crouched, grabbing at where my feet used to be, just as my knees began disappearing.

I always thought that I'd die heroically. You know, like pushing a mother and her five kids out of the way of a speeding bus or by saving an elderly couple from a burning building. So, I guess you could say that I wasn't taking my actual death well. I'd been beat to a pulp without even the slightest chance of winning, before getting my heart punched through, leaving my body, and then slowly disappearing one limb at a time.

"Good job," I heard Cross tell his puppet, who was standing still and looking at my body. My legs were completely gone when I heard him scoff and say, "Like you actually can hear me."

That sounded about right. Cross ridiculing his perfect project just because he'd made his mind completely dormant, or whatever. I slumped to the ground next to my body, my hands vanishing now.

"This really blows," I whispered to myself, closing my eyes. I was dead and the other me didn't even know it because Cross had—

I opened my eyes. My shoulders were gone now, and I

looked at evil me.

His mind was blank.

Dormant.

You see now, Sybil said. *Don't fight it, Paladin.*

My eyes were the last part to of me to go, and I closed them, pushing my being into the husk in front of me.

Then everything went white.

CHAPTER 62

Cross

Dr. Cross sighed with relief after the brawl. The original Jericho hadn't stood a chance, yet somehow still managed to wreck his entire suite and burn his face and hair before dying.

Things would be different now.

Jericho Johnson had been necessary when he'd first discovered him, but now, after perfecting his soldier, he could finally start his true work.

Finally.

Nothing could stop the original Jericho, with all his flaws and spare parts. Now he had a better version. A complete version. One that listened to his every word and heeded without question or remorse.

Speaking of which. "Take the body to the eighth floor," he said to the new Jericho. "We need to remove all of the Z-90 from him for the stockpile. And clean yourself up before you come back."

He crouched to rummage through what was left of his desk but realized that he must not have heard him well because new Jericho was still standing in the same spot.

Dr. Cross stood and walked to him, ready to repeat his command, but his creation sank to his knees suddenly.

Cross cursed, rushing to his side and laying a hand on his shoulder. Had something happened to him during the battle? Was his new loyal subject not as indestructible as he'd originally thought?

Asking if something was wrong would be a waste of time, he knew, so he held up his holotab and scanned the hunching man. No, not a man. He had to keep reminding himself of that.

He checked the brain first because, even though there wouldn't be any activity, he still needed the brain to control the clone's motor skills, among other things.

Then the clone shook violently and vomited white bile onto the marble floor, making Cross give a start and step away from him.

"No, no, no..." Cross said, dropping to his knees and keeping his tab steadily scanning new Jericho's vitals. Had he missed something? No, he couldn't have.

It's not me, he thought, shaking his head. *Something else must be wrong.*

He froze when his creation laughed.

No. It wasn't supposed to speak or think—let alone laugh. What had he missed in his flawless data?

The new Jericho leaned back on his knees and let his head roll back, his eyes closing as he took an enormously deep breath. He held it in, then let it out, his eyes popping open and a smile spreading across his face. "Whew! Thought that was it for a minute, there. Man, Blu is going to freak when I tell her about this."

Cross stood, backing away slowly. His scanner was showing brain activity off the chart—but that wasn't what Cross was having trouble believing. He'd seen these neural patterns before.

For almost three years.

"No," he said aloud, lowering his arms. "This isn't possible."

"Yeah, well, lots of stuff nowadays isn't," Jericho got to his feet, rolling his neck and looking at his new, perfect hands. "Talk about daylight and dark."

Then he turned, facing him.

Cross bolted for the side door, but Jericho somehow

appeared in front of him, grabbing his collar, hauling him into the air, and slamming him into the wall. "I should kill you," he said between his teeth, glaring into Cross's frightened face.

Then his eyes wavered, and he looked away. "But now that I can, I don't want to."

Cross gasped when he let him go, and he slid down the wall, sitting in a slump, his head feeling light.

"This feels so right," Jericho said, looking at his hands again and giving them a flex. "I know everything I'm capable of," then he glanced down at Cross. "I'm leaving, now. I have a mission to attend to that's eons bigger than you, so I suggest you stay out of my way from now on." He held out his hand. "Gauntlet, please."

This was his chance. "It's just there, by my desk."

When Jericho turned and headed for the broken desk, Cross pulled the pearl gauntlet from his lab coat and slipped it on, punching in dates for two days prior. He wouldn't be coming back, but he would know everything that was coming and could plan accordingly. Then he noticed the screen was fuzzy and realized that Jericho's lightning explosion might have damaged it.

Jericho was squatted down looking for the gauntlet and asked, "You sure it's over here?"

"Yes, keep looking. It was on my desk," he said, sweat rolling in his eye, and he took the chance of lightly tapping the screen. It blinked once and said something about confirming a previous destination just when Jericho stood, his hands on his hips. "I can't find it."

Panicking, Cross hit enter and felt his body beginning to slip away. He didn't know if he had enough element zero to get back and didn't even know where he was going, but anywhere was better than here.

Jericho turned around too late, and the last Cross saw of him he was rushing toward him.

Everything was black until he materialized on his hands and knees, his hands full of dirt.

Bloody dirt.

He got to his feet and saw that the pool of blood was coming from beneath a fallen man close by. He was big, Cross noticed, and had a long red beard that was braided into two neat rows. Then he heard the sound of a battle and saw a burning town not two hundred yards away.

"Farewell, Piper," the man gasped out. "And take care of Jericho."

He noticed the arrows stabbed in the man's back about the same time that one struck him in the chest, knocking him off his feet.

It started raining then, and he watched the darkening sky above him while he faded away.

The last words he heard before dying were, "I got him! I got Bjourn the Berserker!"

CHAPTER 63

"You've got to be kidding me," I shouted when the last of Cross vanished with my gauntlet, and I kicked the wall hard, my foot crashing through it. Geez, but I was a lot stronger now.

I wasn't sure where Cross has traveled to, but wherever it was, I hoped he got what was coming to him.

Everything I could do before was heightened a thousand-fold, and I knew it automatically. "Blu, you there?" I asked, sending the message mentally.

Jericho, what happened? she thought back to me. *Piper got Arc and Beck out, but we didn't know what happened to you. The battle is over, and the Synners retreated from the city.*

"Awesome," I told her. "How's Beck?"

Not good. I can't even think about trying to fix her without more of your blood. And I mean a lot of it.

"No kidding?" I asked, glancing at my old body that was just lying there without a purpose. "I got enough for you. Can you do it?"

Where is it coming from?

"Long and, well, kind of a gross story," I said, picking my old corpse up and slinging it over my shoulder. "I'll tell you when I get up top."

I whistled all the way across the trashed suite and pressed the elevator button.

Well done, Paladin.

"Sybil," I said happily. "How're things?"

Your Crusade has just begun. You must enter the—

"Yeah, yeah, the citadel, I know," I said, stepping into the elevator when the door opened and selecting three floors above me.

You are completely Paladin physically, but you still do not understand your purpose or all of your abilities, Sybil said.

"Give me a little while, Syb," I told her. "I'll meet you later tonight, I promise."

I met up with Blu, Piper, a limping Arc, and a gorged Wolf topside, walking out onto the decimated battleground whilst carrying my old body over my shoulder.

Needless to say, it took me a bit to explain everything to my comrades, but we did it on the way across Anchorage to, get this, another swanky place Cross owned. Or used to own. Now, Archimedes was running things, he told me.

Wolf bid me farewell and left the city, saying that he wouldn't be far should I ever need him again, which I had a feeling he wouldn't have to wait long on.

The lab within the building was enormous, and Blu instantly went to work on Beck with my old body in tow by Piper.

"My brother had built an army here without anyone's knowledge," Arc told me when the two of us were in the fast elevator to the top floor. "I haven't had a chance to go over his data completely, but if what I did see is correct, I think he designed living, breathing troops that can receive orders and messages mentally."

"Cross never did anything halfway," I told him, leaning against the thick glass of the elevator and looking out over the flickering city below us. "How much do you want to bet he wanted to control their minds?"

"That can't be it or else he would've just used synthetics."

"He knew synthetics had limits, and he was also aware of humanity's place in the food chain," I said, and we made it to the top floor, walking into the large office. "Look over whatever you need to and let me know what you find."

Archimedes nodded but frowned, probably not used to me giving orders.

I could also hear his thoughts, so I knew that's what he was thinking. "I'll explain everything to you later, Arc," I said to him, sitting in one of the armchairs. "Got to hand it to your brother, though, he sure knew how to design a sweet office."

Arc nodded, pulling up his brother's computer and transferring data to his tab. "I'm going to get a few more scientists to help me. What are you going to do?"

I looked at my right arm thoughtfully. "Can I record messages on my holotab?"

Arc frowned, not sure why I asked that. "Yes. Why?"

Shrugging, I said, "Just curious. Might use it for a few minutes later."

A few minutes. Yeah, right.

After Archimedes left, I laid my head back in the chair, instantly closing my eyes and reopening them next to my Partisan.

"Welcome back, Paladin," Sybil said. "I am glad to see you."

I had emerged in front of the infamous Citadel, and Sybil had been there to meet me in her black cloak. "You, too, Sybil," I told her, looking at the tall cathedral-looking structure.

"Are you still nervous?" she asked politely.

I shrugged, then because I remembered she was blind, I said, "Sort of. How long will I be in there before I know why I'm here?"

"Not long. Think of it as an imprint. You will enter, and your Crusade will be inlaid into your very being. In seconds you will know everything you have to do and everything you can do."

"Hmm," I mused, taking a deep breath. "And then I, like, leave, or what?"

Sybil seemed to not have any information on that, but she said, "Your Crusade will start. The rest will be up to you.

With me aiding you in any way I can, of course."

I nodded, closing my eyes for a few seconds. When I opened them, I started up the steps. "Alright, Syb, let's get this over with."

We climbed the long flight of steps and made it to the tall door. "After you, Paladin," Sybil said, waving her hand, and the door opened inward.

It was unbelievably bright inside, and I had to shield my eyes against the brilliance. I took a step before stopping short and asking nervously, "And you're sure I'm the one who's supposed to be doing this?"

Sybil reached and took my hand in hers. "You are. Shall we go in together?"

I hesitated, glancing back down the flight of stairs once before finally nodding. "Together."

Then we walked into the light and the massive doors shut behind us.

There was no going back now.

EPILOGUE

"I'm scared," Sloan told Sam while she huddled against him in the damp cell the rotten guards of Vancouver had thrown them in.

"Don't you worry, ankle-biter," Sam told her, giving the little girl a pat. "Jerry may be out of commission, but Beck wasn't caught, and that sheila can really make a stink when she wants to."

"Shut up in there," one of the hideous guards barked at them, kicking the rusted cell door and brandishing his rifle. "We're already missing the games because Joshua is making us watch you two, so keep your fleshy mouths shut or I'll bite them off."

"Try it, ugly," Sam said, glaring at him.

The man pulled his rifle up and aimed it at them through the bars. "What say I tell the boss that you broke free and tried to run? Shooting might've been the only way I could stop you."

Sam's mouth was dry, and he tried to swallow.

"Not 'im, Gat," the other guard, who was a lot bigger than Gat, said to him. "Do the lil'un an' save the big'un for the arena. 'E'd make for o' fine match, 'e would."

Sam instantly put the little girl behind him and held up his hands. "I meant no trouble, mate. Leave the girl be."

"Too, late," Gat said, his long tongue darting out of his mouth and licking at his left eye, which was red and drying out. "Move, or so help me, I'll shoot the both of you."

Sam shook his head, lowering his hands. "Do what you like, mate, but I ain't budging."

Gat cackled at that. "A real hero, he is, isn't he?" he laughed to his brother-in-rotten-arms. "So be it, fat man."

When he cocked his rifle, Sam moved his hands behind him and found where Sloan was cowering and whimpering. "Close your eyes, ankle-biter," he told her, squeezing his own eyes shut and turning his face away. "It'll be over quick."

Gat laughed before gasping so loud that Sam opened his eyes and glanced at him. The rotting man's already dead eyes were bugged out, and his mouth was hanging open.

Sam frowned at him, noticing he was shaking slightly. Then he saw that the bigger guard was doing the same thing.

"What's all this, then?" he asked, moving closer and peering at the quivering guards.

Then he heard whistling and approaching footsteps. "Cranky," he muttered. It had to be more guards. "These two bloody break, and they replace them in seconds."

But when the whistler came into view, Sam gasped. "Jerry, over here," he whispered fiercely because he looked like he was just going to walk past their cell without noticing them.

"Sam," Jericho said, smiling broadly and taking a large bite out of a red apple he had in his hand. "It's so good to see you, friend," he said through a mouthful.

Sam was a little confused at Jericho's leisure pace but said, "You, too, mate."

Jericho walked right up to the guards, and they parted for him. "I mean, really, it feels like we've been apart for weeks, man," he said, grabbing the heavy gate with his free hand and ripping it off its hinges easily.

"You got your powers back?" Sloan asked, allowing Sam to pick her up. "That's good. Now none of us have to die, huh?"

Jericho stared at the little girl strangely and smiled broadly, looking genuinely happy for the first time since Sam could remember and clapping the big Aussie on the shoulder,

"That's right, kiddo. None of have to die today."

"What's wrong with them?" Sam asked, hooking his thumb at the paralyzed guards.

"I have them, as well as the rest of the city, in a sort of stasis at the moment. Now, come on, I'm really going to need you in a few weeks."

Sam fell in step behind Jericho, who was still humming and chomping on his apple, and he asked, "What's in a few weeks?"

Jericho finished his apple and tossed the core. "War," he said. "Or stopping one, rather."

Sam was incredulous. "*You're* going to stop the war?"

"I prefer *we're* going to stop one, but that's cool, too, I guess."

Sam didn't know what else to say. He thought about asking how, but instead asked, "Why?"

"Why what?"

"Why're you bloody going to try and stop an unstoppable war, Jerry? And why do you need me? I can't even —" he dropped his head low, ashamed for some reason.

Jericho stopped walking and turned to him, putting a hand on his shoulder and looking him square in the face. "I need you because we're friends until the day we die, remember?"

Sam nodded, "I do, mate."

"Great. Now, let's go."

They resumed walking side by side up the long tunnel. "So, why're you going to try again? You didn't ever say," Sam said, glancing sideways at him, and even Sloan looked at him from her perch on his shoulders.

"Because," Jericho said, looking at them and smiling, "I'm not done yet."

End of Book Two of The Phoenix Cycle

Made in the USA
Monee, IL
01 March 2023

28983960R00243